Dreamboat

Novels by Judith Gould

Sins
Love-Makers
Dazzle
Never Too Rich
Texas Born
Forever
Too Damn Rich
Second Love
Till the End of Time
Rhapsody
Time to Say Good-Bye
A Moment in Time
The Best is Yet to Come
The Greek Villa
The Parisian Affair

JUDITH GOULD

Dreamboat

TIME WARNER
BOOKS

TIME WARNER BOOKS

First published in the United States of America
in October 2005 by New American Library
First published in Great Britain in December 2005
by Time Warner Books

A CIP catalogue record for this book
is available from the British Library.

ISBN 0 316 72712 1

Printed and bound in Great Britain by
Mackays of Chatham plc, Chatham, Kent

Time Warner Books
An imprint of
Time Warner Book Group UK
Brettenham House
Lancaster Place
London WC2E 7EN

www.twbg.co.uk

This novel is dedicated to Christine Flouton, whose help, encouragement, loyalty, generosity of spirit, and sense of humor have gotten me through some rough patches with a smile.

Now is the season of sailing; for already the chattering swallow is come and the pleasant west wind; the meadows flower, and the sea tossed up with waves and rough blasts has sunk to silence. Weigh thine anchors and unloose thy hawsers, O mariner, and sail with all thy canvas set . . .

—Leonidas of Tarentum, fl. 274 B.C.
Greek Mythology, J.W. Mackail, ed. (1906), sec. 6, no. 26

Journeys end in lovers meeting,
Every wise man's son doth know.

—William Shakespeare, *Twelfth-Night,* II, iii, 46

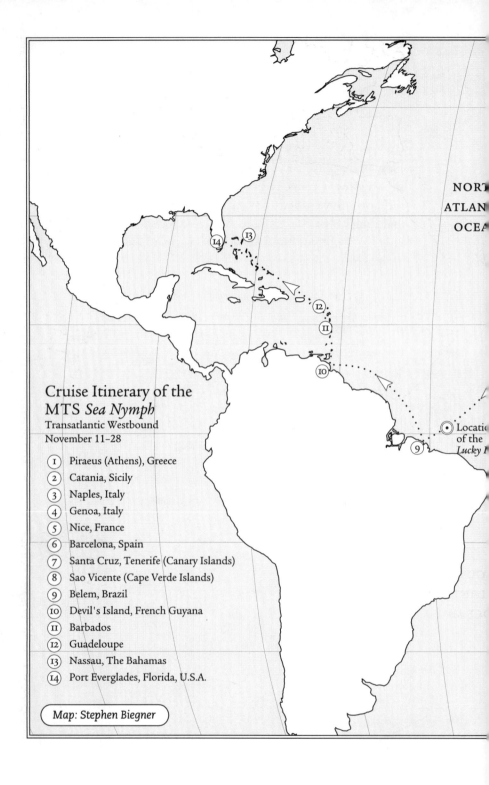

NOR[T]
ATLAN[TIC]
OCEA[N]

Cruise Itinerary of the MTS *Sea Nymph*

Transatlantic Westbound
November 11–28

1. Piraeus (Athens), Greece
2. Catania, Sicily
3. Naples, Italy
4. Genoa, Italy
5. Nice, France
6. Barcelona, Spain
7. Santa Cruz, Tenerife (Canary Islands)
8. Sao Vicente (Cape Verde Islands)
9. Belem, Brazil
10. Devil's Island, French Guyana
11. Barbados
12. Guadeloupe
13. Nassau, The Bahamas
14. Port Everglades, Florida, U.S.A.

Map: Stephen Biegner

Locati[on]
of the
Lucky [

9

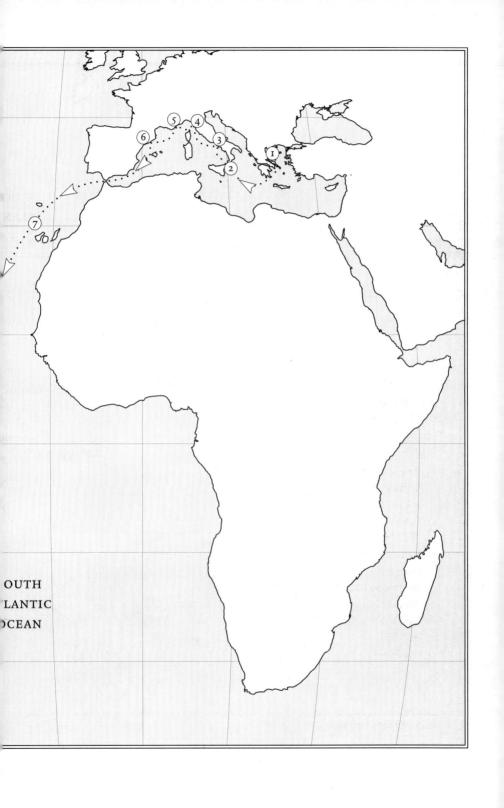

Prologue

Georgios Vilos sat behind the large mahogany George II desk in the office on the top floor of his Eaton Place mansion in London's fashionable Belgravia. Outside, the trees had shed all but a few of their leaves, dry, brown stragglers that held on to denuded branches, rattling in the wind. The chill drizzle of a late autumn rain beat a steady tattoo against the mansion's windowpanes. Within the sumptuous confines of his home office, Georgios Vilos was oblivious to the inclement English weather. While the lower floors of his vast mansion—one of the few in the neighborhood not yet broken up into smaller apartments—were abuzz with the endless activity required to maintain the residence in its opulent state, his office was a sanctuary. There, Georgios Vilos often withdrew to contemplate the future of his empire, to plan and strategize, and sometimes to do as he was doing today: study the latest figures given to him by his accounting division.

The report from Adonis Papadrakis, his CFO, confirmed what he already knew to be true. Vilos Shipping, Ltd., the small company he had inherited from his father and expanded into an international empire worth billions of dollars, was sinking, like a torpedoed ship, under a load of staggering debt. Now, two of his chief rivals, Panos Simitis and Spiros Farmakis, who like himself were Greeks of middling origin who had built enormous empires, were making inroads on the Vilos empire.

Georgios Vilos closed the file, which was stamped CONFIDENTIAL in bloodred letters on its cover, and sat back in his mahogany and gilt Thomas Hope-designed chair. He ran his thick fingers through his silver hair, exhaled a sigh, and took off his gold-rimmed eyeglasses, placing them atop the report. His heavy-lidded eyes, often remarked on as mischievous and full of merriment, or, alternately, calculating and intense, came to rest on one of the two silver-framed photographs that decorated his desk. Fiona, his elegant British-Greek wife, stared out at him from one of them. Her strawberry-blond hair was swept back into a loose chignon, a few errant wisps of hair carefully arranged to better frame her beautiful face with its high, prominent cheekbones, mesmerizing blue eyes, and long, narrow nose. Her skin, so perfect as to be almost translucent, was as radiant as it was flawless. On her ears were diamond earrings, with nine-carat D-color pendants dangling from clusters of seven smaller stones. A matching choker encircled her long swan neck. The jewelry had been made by the legendary old Russian firm Alexandre Reza, located in Paris since after the revolution, and Georgios vividly remembered the day he had successfully bid on them at Sotheby's in Geneva. When the hammer fell and the diamonds were his, Fiona had turned to him in the salesroom and, in front of the roomful of assembled bidders, kissed and hugged him excitedly.

Georgios emitted another sigh, his gaze still fixed on the photograph. It had been taken several years after the auction, and the smile on Fiona's lips was forced. Their marriage at that point had become a battleground upon which they waged perpetual war against each other. It had begun with his liaisons with other women, trifling flings of no consequence as far as he was concerned. But Fiona didn't see his behavior in that light, and had reacted in kind, taking a series of lovers whom she flaunted in the most disgraceful manner. They had eventually come to a kind of truce and remained married, but in name only. The wounds they had inflicted on each other in the past had never quite healed, and though they occupied the same sumptuous homes and sometimes went out together, traveled together, and entertained as a couple, they lived separate lives. Fiona was civil, as was he, but he knew that it was only the money that held them together. He also knew that Fiona wouldn't hesitate to leave him in search of greener pastures if his empire crumbled.

He abruptly pushed his chair back and rose to his feet, walking over to one of the windows, where he looked out at the dreary London day. His tall, big-boned frame practically filled the window. *It's the Germans,* he thought angrily. *Those goddamned German bankers.* He loathed them. No matter how much of their money they loaned him to build new ships, he would never feel comfortable with them. Now the money was spent, the loans were soon due, and the banks were not willing to change the original terms of the deal. There would be no extensions, no reprieves, no negotiations, no further credit extended. Vilos Shipping, Ltd. would have to give the banks the two hundred and fifty million dollars they were due or his ships would be impounded. It was as simple as that.

My beautiful ships, he thought sadly. *The most beautiful ships afloat. And the reason for all of my problems.* At a time when other cruise lines were building bigger and bigger vessels carrying three thousand passengers plus another two thousand in crew, Georgios Vilos had chosen to go in the opposite direction. Deciding to add to his aging fleet, he had built two small, elegant ships that carried a mere eight hundred passengers in pampered luxury. These ships weren't merely small and luxurious, however; they were also the fastest ships ever built, capable of maintaining a speed of twenty-eight knots for long periods of time, even on trans-Atlantic voyages. The *Queen Elizabeth II* could go that fast, but the ship would shudder to pieces if it tried to maintain such a speed. His ships could cross the Atlantic and make the trek to Hawaii in two days—a feat that took most ships five. He was proud of the *Sea Nymph* and the *Sea Sprite,* but the cost overruns had been ruinous. Materials and labor costs had skyrocketed during the long process of building the beautiful vessels. Before they were anywhere near completion, he'd had to start seeking the funds to finish them, then more funds to launch them. The pride and joy of his fleet, they had proven to be his downfall.

He had sought credit elsewhere to pay off the note, but had come up empty-handed. Virtually no one would extend him credit in his current financial predicament. In fact, more than a few financial institutions had seemed to take great pleasure in refusing the great Georgios Vilos. Like a computer virus, word of his dire straits had quickly spread. He endured more than a few cold shoulders and outright taunts, even among the large, tight-knit community of enormously rich Greek families who had their principal homes in London and conducted their financial enterprises from there. *Bastards*, he thought. *They love nothing more than to see one of their own suffer, to see one of their fellow countrymen fall from the heights of glory.*

He turned from the depressing sight out the window and went to the Regency library table that served as a bar. From the large silver tray he picked up the bottle of ouzo and poured a generous portion into an antique St. Louis crystal glass. From the silver ice bucket he took several cubes, dumped them in the glass, then swirled the drink around, watching as the ouzo became cloudy. He might have come a long way from the village he'd grown up in outside of the port of Piraeus, where his father's small business had its offices, but he felt that his heart and soul were still Greek to the core. He took a big sip of the anise-flavored drink, then went back to his desk and sat down on the Thomas Hope chair, a chair that he'd always thought suited a man of his influence, wealth, and power. He set the drink down, then drummed his manicured fingernails on the desktop for a mere instant.

Well, I won't give the sons of bitches the pleasure, he thought, smiling tightly. *No, indeed. They've got a surprise coming to them. Georgios Vilos is not beaten yet.*

He took another swallow of the ouzo and shook with a brief chuckle. *They think the old man has had it, but I'll show them what this old man can do.* He set the glass down on the desk, and his gaze fell on the other silver-framed photograph that sat next to the one of Fiona. Makelos, his only child and heir. Georgios's features suddenly took on an aspect that was a mixture of pride and puzzlement. Makelos—Mark, as he had anglicized his name—was one of the most handsome young men he had ever seen, and that, he knew, was not simply a proud father's opinion. Makelos made heads turn walking down the street, and all eyes turned to him when he entered a room. The girls were crazy about him, and he had his pick among the international set with whom he socialized. His black hair and dark eyes, his chiseled features and hard, muscular body, and his graceful yet manly movements were riveting. He was an excellent sailor, as any man of Greek descent should be, Georgios thought, and he had done well enough on the rugby field. Now, he was a worthy adversary on the polo field and tennis courts. He was also intelligent and had done well at the expensive private schools where he'd been sent, and then had performed tolerably well at Oxford.

Georgios picked up the ouzo, swirled it around in the glass again, then took another sip, his gaze still focused on his son. Makelos—Mark! Would he ever become accustomed to the name?—was also, he knew, spoiled and arrogant. He was used to getting his way, and God help anyone who tried to stop him. There had been a problem or two with the girls over the years—nothing serious, he thought—and Georgios attributed them to his son's inborn, high-octane testosterone, nothing more. Perhaps time would temper his interest in women and the endless round of parties that seemed

4

to occupy the young man. For a long time Georgios hadn't worried about his son's perpetual dalliances, remembering his own wild youth. But there had come a time, he reminded himself, when that stage of his life had simmered down as his work had taken over, then consuming him, as he built Vilos Shipping, Ltd. into the international company that it had become. It was time that Makelos did something useful to help the company. His son owed him, he thought, and it was time he paid his debt.

His gaze swept around the magnificent office in which he sat, taking in its mahogany-paneled walls, the immense fireplace with its Adam mantel, the perfectly faded silk Tabriz on the floor, the antiques that glowed with rich patinas, and the Impressionist paintings that graced the walls. There were even a few Greek antiquities of impeccable provenance. No power on earth would force him to give all this up.

With that thought, he picked up the telephone and dialed his personal assistant. She picked up on the second ring. "Georgios Vilos's line," she said in her clipped British voice.

"Rosemary," he said, "check to see when my appointment is with the bankers in Athens."

"The appointment is at four p.m. on Thursday. That's Athens time, Mr. Vilos," she retorted. "They called to confirm this morning."

"Good," he replied. "Call the pilot to get ready for takeoff and tell Mrs. Vilos that we'll be flying to Athens today."

"Yes, sir," Rosemary said. "Will I be going with you, sir?"

"Yes."

"Are there any files that I should bring with me?" she asked.

"I think I have all the files we need here," he answered.

"I'll make the calls and get ready right away, sir," she said.

"Good-bye," Vilos said, hanging up the receiver without waiting for a reply. He sat staring at the telephone, lost in thought. He found the idea of this meeting with the Lampaki brothers repugnant, but he had no other options left. There was a chance they would give him a loan to meet his obligations with the German banks, but they would charge an astronomically usurious interest rate. Simply repaying them would require a vast and potentially crippling cutback in day-to-day operations, above and beyond the trimming he'd already done. If it saved his empire, however, the costs, no matter how high, would be worth it. Should the Lampakis turn him down, he would have to use a backup plan, one that eliminated dealing with the banks altogether.

He picked up one of his cell phones—the one with his most private number—and dialed the number he'd memorized months before. He waited impatiently through three rings. On the fourth ring, his call was answered.

"Yes?"

"Can you talk?" Georgios Vilos asked.

"For a moment."

"Is the package I ordered ready?"

"Yes."

"Very good."

"When and where do you want it delivered?"

"At my office in Piraeus, Greece, on the date we discussed."

"What time?"

"Noon."

"The second payment must be in my account the day before."

"That's not a problem, I assure you," Vilos replied.

"Then I will see you in Piraeus."

"You must—" Georgios Vilos began, but there was no one on the line. Azad had hung up.

He flipped the cell phone shut, sat back in his chair, and took a deep breath. He disliked dealing with this revolting man even more than dealing with the Lampaki brothers, but as with them, he had no choice. The munitions dealer was by necessity secretive—and exorbitantly expensive—but he was also needlessly arrogant, Vilos thought. It was as if he could see the smirk on the man's face the few times he'd spoken to him by phone. He could hear the condescension in his voice, as if he thought he was dealing with a helpless juvenile.

Georgios Vilos sighed. He had to tolerate the munitions dealer until his problems were resolved. Where else could he get the plastic explosives he might need on short notice? It took time to penetrate the veils of secrecy that surrounded underground munitions dealers like this one, and he didn't have that luxury. If Lampaki didn't give him the loan, he needed to be prepared.

Georgios Vilos took the last sip of ouzo in the glass, setting it down on the desk when he was finished. If the Lampakis turned him down, he would use the munitions dealer's plastic explosives to blow up the *Sea Nymph*. Then the insurance companies would have to fork over the money to pay off the bank loans. He hated to see the ship destroyed—

blown to smithereens, with hundreds of innocent passengers aboard—but if that's what it took to save Vilos Shipping, Ltd. from certain ruin, then that's what he had to do.

Picking up his cell phone again, he pressed the speed-dial code for Mark, hoping that he could reach his son. *Yes,* he thought again, *it's time for Mark to help me out. To pay me back for providing him with a life of unbridled luxury.*

Chapter One

Crissy Fitzgerald ran her fingers through Beatrice Bloom's long, bleach-streaked tresses. As nice as Beatrice could be and as generous as her tips were, Crissy was in no mood to spend the next two hours dying Beatrice's gray roots and adding new highlights. Beatrice, a regular customer, hadn't been to the salon for the last couple of months, and today her hair would require extra work. Crissy restrained from sighing aloud, however, and forced a smile to her lips. Holding a hank of hair, she looked up into the mirror and saw that Beatrice was watching her closely.

As if she could read Crissy's mind, Beatrice said, "You've got a real job on your hands this time, sweetheart. It's been a long time since I've been in."

Crissy nodded. "It sure has, Beatrice," she replied amiably, "but don't worry. We'll get you fixed up."

"I was in Europe," Beatrice said, "and I didn't have my hair done the whole time I was gone. I don't trust just anybody, so I decided to wait till I got home to see you."

"Oh, that's so sweet," Crissy said, dropping the hank of hair and picking up a brush. She began brushing the woman's hair in long strokes, examining it as she did. "But I'm sure there're lots of great hairdressers in Europe. Where did you go?"

"Here and there," Beatrice said, crossing her age-spotted hands in her lap. Crissy noticed, as she had many times before, the beautiful rings that the woman always wore. Large diamonds set in yellow gold. A huge aquamarine surrounded by diamonds. "London for a week, then Paris and Venice."

"It sounds so fabulous," Crissy said. She had been saving up for a trip herself, she just didn't know where to go.

"Well, I can't get enough," Beatrice replied.

"Do you want to go with the same colors today?" Crissy asked. "We did two the last time."

Beatrice nodded. "Yes," she said. "I love the lighter and darker streaks the way you do them." She laughed genially. "They help hide some of the gray when my roots begin to show, too."

Crissy smiled. "I think you always look great, Beatrice," she said, meaning it. "I'm going to go mix your color, and I'll be back in just a minute. Do you want a magazine?"

Beatrice glanced at the stack on the counter. "I'll take the *Vogue*," she said.

Crissy handed it to her. "Be right back."

Beatrice nodded and began flipping through the pages of the magazine.

Crissy went to the back of the shop and opened the door to the supply room, closing it behind her when she went inside. It was a relatively quiet refuge from the noisy shop. Today the pop music on the radio and the chattering of the hairdressers, manicurists, and customers were grating on her nerves. She took a sip of the coffee she'd left in the room some time ago. It was cold and tasted terrible, but she drank it nevertheless. *Anything to jump-start my motor today*, she thought. She pulled on plastic gloves to protect her hands from the dye, then chose the appropriate color for Beatrice's roots, a medium chestnut brown. She put some into a plastic container, then put in the developer and began stirring the mixture thoroughly, taking longer than necessary. Usually cheerful and energetic, Crissy felt tired and grumpy today. *What's wrong with me?* she wondered idly, even though she knew the answer to the question. She was bored with her job and bored with her life outside work. *I'm just bored, period*, she thought.

Nothing exciting ever happens to me, she thought. *Nothing. I'm in a dead-end job, and I don't know what to do about that. I don't have a boyfriend or any prospects. I never go anywhere interesting, like Beatrice, or do anything particularly interesting either. I'm always listening to other people talk about the excitement in their lives, and I don't have anything happening in mine.*

She gave the mixture one last stir with the brush, then went back to Beatrice, who was engrossed in the pages of *Vogue*. "Here we are," she said, setting the container down on the counter.

Beatrice closed the magazine and left it in her lap while Crissy began gently pulling up hanks of her hair and generously brushing in the dye along her roots, repeatedly dipping the brush in the plastic container to replenish the dye.

"You don't seem so happy today," Beatrice said in a quiet voice. Her head was angled downward, her chin almost resting on her chest, while Crissy went to work on the back of her head.

"Oh . . . I'm okay," Crissy said, surprised that the older woman had picked up on her gloomy mood.

"No, you're not," Beatrice said. "I may be old, but I'm not stupid. You're unhappy about something."

Crissy laughed lightly. "You're too shrewd, Beatrice," she said.

"And you are young and beautiful and have your whole life ahead of you," Beatrice retorted. "You shouldn't let things trouble you so."

Crissy felt flattered by what Beatrice had said, but she didn't really believe the words. "You're so nice to say that," she replied.

"And I mean it," Beatrice said. "What's bothering you, sweetheart? Boyfriend trouble?"

Crissy shook her head and laughed again. "No. I don't have a boyfriend," she replied.

"Aha!" Beatrice exclaimed. "So, that's it. No boyfriend."

"Not really," Crissy said. Then she added, "Well, maybe that's part of it. I'm just . . . I don't know. I feel sort of tired, you know?"

"Crissy, sweetheart," Beatrice said. "You'll have a new man in your life in no time, I'm sure. You're too beautiful not to. You must have men after you all the time."

Crissy shook her head. "I wish," she said, sighing. "But I don't." It was true, too, Crissy thought. She didn't have men after her. Not like most of her friends. And she never had. Growing up in Albany, she'd always felt left out and different, in part because she was Asian American. She'd had girlfriends, but the boys had often teased her, calling her "slant eye," "chink," "China doll," or "Tokyo Rose." More recently, she'd heard men refer to her as "sushi." She'd laughed, telling her friends that the growing popularity of Japanese food had provided a whole new vocabulary of slurs, but in truth she had been crushed.

"I find that hard to believe," Beatrice said, abruptly raising her head and looking at Crissy in the mirror.

"Well, it's true, Beatrice," Crissy said. "I really don't."

"Oh, sweetheart, I didn't mean to upset you," Beatrice said. "I-"

"You didn't," Crissy broke in. "I'm sorry, Beatrice. I guess I'm just tired today."

Beatrice shrugged. "No offense taken."

They fell silent for a little while, and Beatrice turned back to her *Vogue*. "There are so many things in here that you'd look darling in," Beatrice said at last, tapping a clear-lacquered fingernail against the magazine.

Crissy laughed. "Sure, Beatrice. Like I make enough money to buy anything in that magazine."

Beatrice smiled. "They make great knockoffs nowadays."

"Don't I know it," Crissy said. "I get a lot of ideas from there, then go shopping at discount stores."

"You always look great," Beatrice said.

"Thank you, Beatrice. You're still very attractive, too," Crissy said honestly, "and you're certainly young in spirit."

"Thank you," Beatrice said. "I think that's part of what attracted Sidney to me. We may have been in our sixties when we met, but we were both still interested in life and what's going on in the world."

"You didn't meet him until you were in your sixties?" Crissy said. "I didn't realize that. I knew he was your second husband, but I didn't know you'd married that recently."

"I met him about a year after Harry died," Beatrice replied. "I missed Harry, of course, and I was lonely. I have some good friends, you know, but it's not the same without a husband. So, I set out to find one."

"You did?" Crissy asked, somewhat astonished with Beatrice's straightforward honesty. "What did you do?"

Beatrice laughed. "I went on a cruise," she said. "A very long cruise."

"No," Crissy said with a laugh.

"Oh, yes," Beatrice said. "I knew it would mostly be older people because it was a three-month-long trip. Most younger people can't get that kind of time off if they work, so it was mostly retirees." She laughed. "Also, it was very expensive, so I knew that the price would eliminate a lot of younger people. Usually only older people have the kind of money it cost."

"You're so smart," Crissy said. "I would've never thought of that."

"But it wasn't just about the money," Beatrice said. "It was about *widowers*. She slapped the *Vogue* with a liver-spotted hand. "When you get together a boatload of old people, there're bound to be some widowers aboard, even if they're outnumbered by widows. And, sure enough, that's how I met Sidney."

She and Crissy both laughed. "I don't believe it," Crissy said.

Beatrice shrugged. "It's called putting two and two together, sweetheart. The funny thing is, Sid was on the cruise for the same reason I was. Grace, his wife, had died a little over a year before, and he was lonely like I was. So . . . bingo! We hit it lucky, and we've been happy ever since."

"That's so wonderful, Beatrice," Crissy said.

"And you could do the same thing," Beatrice said. "Maybe you can't take a three-month cruise, but you could take a shorter one. Besides, sweetheart," she went on, "you need to see some of the world. Something besides Albany, New York. And see it while you're young and can still get around."

"I'd love to do something like that, Beatrice," she said. "I've always dreamed of traveling."

Crissy proceeded to add the highlights. After the bleach mixture had done its work and Crissy shampooed it out, she began trimming Beatrice's hair, taking pains to do a good job, studying her work both close up and in the mirror's reflection. When she was finished, she massaged a light setting liquid into her hair, then blew it dry. "Okay, Beatrice," she said, "how do you like it?"

Beatrice looked at her reflection straight on, moved her head to one side, then the other, and finally gazed into the hand mirror that Crissy held up so that she could see the back. "I love it, sweetheart," she said. "You always do a terrific job."

"Thank you, Beatrice," Crissy said.

"And you're the best colorist between here and New York City," Beatrice added. "Everybody says so."

Crissy laughed. "There's not much competition, is there?" She helped Beatrice out of the protective smock she was wearing and shook it out.

"Don't belittle yourself," Beatrice said, looking at her with an arched eyebrow. "Good colorists are hard to come by, and you know it."

Crissy nodded. "You're right," she said. She scribbled out a payment slip for Beatrice, then handed it to her. "Pay Rosy up front as usual."

Beatrice gazed at the slip, then picked up the black alligator handbag she'd placed on the Formica shelf running along Crissy's workstation. She rummaged in the handbag, finally pulling out a wallet. Crissy discreetly turned away while Beatrice got her tip out.

13

"Listen to me," Beatrice said in a low voice, holding out her gnarled hand. "Take this and tuck it away someplace safe. I want you to use it as a down payment on that trip you've wanted to take."

"Oh, Beatrice," she replied, palming the money without looking at it. "You're so sweet." She slipped the folded bill into the pocket of her smock.

At the front of the salon, Beatrice exchanged pleasantries with Rosy while she paid her bill, then slipped into the dark mink coat Crissy held open for her. "Thank you," she said. "I'll see you soon, and remember what I said." She winked, then left the salon.

Crissy watched her cross the parking lot to her big silver Mercedes, then turned to Rosy. "Who do I have scheduled next?"

Rosy looked at her over the top of the glasses that rested near the tip of her nose. "Connie Parker. She called and said she was on her way, so you've got a couple of minutes. Why don't you make yourself useful and make some fresh coffee for us?" She stared up at Crissy belligerently.

"Sure, Rosy."

She didn't ask why Rosy hadn't done it herself, since she'd long finished with her last manicure and had sat slurping coffee for the last twenty minutes or so, gossiping with waiting customers and beauticians while she flipped through *People* magazine. Instead, Crissy went to the back of the shop where the coffeemaker was and started a fresh pot. Then she went back to the storeroom and closed the door behind her.

She reached in the pocket of her smock and felt the crisp, folded bill that Beatrice had given her. She took it out and looked at it. Crissy could hardly believe her eyes. Beatrice had given her a hundred-dollar tip. For a moment Crissy was stunned. Then she took her pocketbook from the shelf and put the money in her wallet. Sitting down, she wondered at Beatrice's generosity. What was it the older woman had said? Something about using the tip as a down payment for a trip? She already had built up a sizable nest egg, and this would add to it nicely.

The door abruptly opened, and Rosy stuck her head in the room. "Why don't you turn on your fucking cellie?" she groused. "Jenny's on the phone, but I'm going to tell her to hang up and call your cell number."

"I'm sorry, Rosy," Crissy said, restraining herself from lashing out at the ill-tempered woman. "I'll turn it on right now."

Rosy eyed her malevolently, then slammed the door shut.

Crissy shot the bird at the closed door, then took out her cell phone and switched it on. She knew that Rosy was an extremely unhappy woman, obese, unattractive, and resentful, but her nastiness was hard to take. Crissy didn't have much choice—not if she wanted to continue working at the shop. Rosy was the manager, and Tony Ferraro, the owner, trusted her completely.

Her cell phone rang, and Crissy answered it. "Hi, Jenny," she said.

Jenny laughed. "That bitch told you to turn on your cell phone, didn't she?"

"Oh, yes," Crissy replied. "In fact, she told me to turn on my 'fucking' cell phone."

"That's just one of the things that makes her so attractive," Jenny said. "Her lovely way with words."

"She's really getting hard to take," Crissy said.

"Don't let the bitch get you down," Jenny said. "She's just jealous."

"I don't know why she's jealous of me," Crissy replied. "She's got a boyfriend, and she's got Tony eating out of her hand. She runs this place like she's some kind of queen and we're all her servants."

"Oh, you're feeling blue today, aren't you?" Jenny ventured. "Come off it, Crissy. You know why that ugly bitch is jealous. You're pretty and nice and popular. None of which she'll ever be."

Crissy sighed. "I guess."

"Listen," Jenny said. "Why don't we go out tonight? There's a hot new club on Central Ave. that's got a great DJ. Nine One One it's called, and I'm dying to try it out."

"I . . . I don't know," Crissy prevaricated. "I'm trying to save my money, and—"

"Oh, come on, Crissy," Jenny said quickly. "I'll treat. I just got my alimony check from Pete the Prick."

Crissy laughed. "Can't wait to spend it, huh?" Maybe she should go out tonight, Crissy ruminated. Yes, she decided, that's what she ought to do. She and Jenny always had a good time together.

"I'll swing by your place about eight, eight-thirty. How's that?" Jenny said.

"What's this place like?" Crissy asked.

"Really cool, I hear," Jenny said. "Fancy enough that a lot of the guys who work at the Capitol go there, expensive enough to keep the rednecks out."

"You mean the parking lot won't be full of pickup trucks with gun racks?"

"That's exactly what I mean," Jenny said, laughing. "Come on, say yes, and I'll pick you up."

"Okay," Crissy said. "What are you going to wear?"

"Something sexy," Jenny said.

"Tell me something I didn't already know," Crissy said. "I meant, like casual or what?"

"Probably slacks and a cute top," Jenny said. "Maybe this new glittery number I've got that shows a lot of boob."

"You're shameless," Crissy said.

The door to the storage room swung open, hitting the wall with a loud bang. Rosy stood in the door frame, her body occupying it entirely, with a highly unattractive scowl on her face. Crissy, her mood considerably improved by talking to Jenny, almost laughed aloud. Rosy looked as if smoke would pour out of her nostrils at any minute.

"Your next customer is here, if you care," Rosy snapped.

"I'll be right there," Crissy said sweetly.

Rosy didn't budge, nor did the expression on her face change.

"I have a customer," Crissy said into the cell phone, "so I've got to run. I'll see you tonight." She pressed the call end button, flipped shut the phone, and rose to her feet. Yes, that's what she should do. She decided she would really make an effort tonight, get dressed up and made up, and try to put a little extra zing in her step. Who knew? Maybe she would meet the man of her dreams at Nine One One.

Chapter Two

Dark had already descended when Crissy parked her little blue Neon on the street and got out with her big carryall. Friends often joked that she ought to leave the keys in the car's ignition to make it easy to steal. They could laugh all they wanted, Crissy thought as she locked it, but she loved her used, banged-up wreck of a car. It was hers, and it was paid for. She looked over toward Washington Park as she walked down the block to the old house where she rented a studio apartment. Most of the people she knew lived on the outskirts of Albany in modern apartment complexes with swimming pools and saunas, but she loved being in the center of town. She enjoyed the little park with its large old trees and ponds, and liked to ride her bicycle there in good weather.

She reached the old gray house where she lived, and after unlocking the front door, she checked her mailbox in the entry hall. Nothing but junk. Advertising fliers and catalogs she would never order anything from. She pitched everything in the wastebasket provided by Birdie, her ancient landlady, then went to her door, just to the left.

Her apartment had originally been the dining room of the once-grand house, which had long since been broken up into apartments, and it retained a semblance of its former glory with heavy moldings and ornate plasterwork on the ceiling. At the far end of the room, a kitchenette stretched along one wall and a door led into the small bathroom. The apartment was painted eggshell white, and on the scratched parquet floors were rugs that had once been a dusty rose shade. Like the house itself, the furniture was old and worn—flea market finds—but was serviceable and comfortable. Crissy treasured the apartment, down-at-the-heels as it was, because it offered a refuge. She had tired of sharing with friends, discovering that as well as she got along with them, they were often irresponsible, messy, and noisy. Even though it had been a strain on her budget, she had managed to hang onto this place by herself. Now, with a growing following, her tips alone took care of the rent.

Crissy went to the one closet in the apartment and began rummaging through her clothes, trying to decide what to wear tonight. It was really a no-brainer, she decided, since she didn't have that many things to choose from. At least not the kind of clothes she wanted to be seen in tonight. She took a long-sleeved T-shirt out, slipped it off its hanger, and laid it on the bed. It was made out of a glittery black stretch fabric that looked a lot more expensive than it was. It was clingy as well, emphasizing her ample breasts and slim waistline. Going back to the closet, she wondered whether to wear trousers or a miniskirt. *What would a powerful man who worked at the Capitol like?* she wondered, then laughed aloud at the thought. She finally decided on a pair of sleek black trousers that fit her to perfection, then she quickly showered and blow-dried her hair.

She took great pains putting on fresh makeup: eyeliner, mascara, shadow, lipstick, and blusher. She dabbed her favorite perfume, *Femme,* under her ears. She loved its scent, and had to be careful not to use too much. Looking into the mirror over the sink, she examined her face and hair closely and decided that she looked good. Sexy, but not hookerish. The club would be dimly lit, so she was wearing a bit more makeup than usual to compensate. Her black hair, cut in a deceptively simple A line, shone with vitality, and her dark eyes sparkled. The eyeliner and shadow she'd used slightly accentuated their Asian slant. Cat's eyes, her father had called them, and while they were an indication of her mixed lineage—a liability, some would think—she thought they were one of her best assets.

In the bedroom/living room, she put on a lacy black bra and slipped into black, high-heeled mules that were stylish but comfortable and easy to take off if she danced a lot. Finally, she went to her chest of drawers and took out the small box that held her black satin belt. It had a rhinestone-studded buckle in the shape of a Maltese cross, and it was one of her favorite articles of clothing. She put it on, then retraced her steps to the bathroom, where she checked herself out in the full-length mirror on the back of the bathroom door, turning this way and that. She adjusted her top, tucking it in just so, then switched off the bathroom light and closed the door. Almost done, she thought.

From the chest of drawers, she took out the box that held her small black satin evening clutch, and removed it from the layers of white tissue paper she'd wrapped around it. Like the belt, it was a favorite, and she took care great of them both. She put in her wallet and car keys. Although Jenny had said she would pick her up, Crissy was certain that she would be asked to drive, and she didn't mind. She was nearly always the designated driver nowadays, since she could have no more than a glass of wine. Like so many Asians or part-Asians, she had Asian alcohol syndrome, and couldn't drink much without getting drunk, sick, or both. From her closet, she took the fluffy black fake-fur jacket that she wore for dressy occasions in the winter. Friends often joked with her about it—what kind of animal is that?—but Crissy didn't mind. She didn't like the cheap furs she could afford, like rabbit, and though she loved the look of more expensive mink and sable, their price was out of her reach. Besides, beautiful as fur could be, she could never rid her mind of the gruesome images of slaughtered animals that she'd seen at animal rights protests.

She remembered when she was a child her father, a Vietnam vet, had somehow struggled to buy her mother, Lily, a fur coat. It had been an inexpensive one, but her father, who was on disability and drank most of the time, had been very proud of the cheap fur. Later, after Lily had built a successful spa, she'd divorced Crissy's father and thrown out the fur coat. She promptly bought herself an enormously expensive mink.

Crissy cringed thinking about her parents. She'd worked very hard to escape their household, and while not always happy in her work, she was more than happy to have left her alcoholic father and mean-spirited, bitter mother to their own unpleasant lives.

There was a tap-tap-tap on the door, and Crissy went to answer it. "Is that you, Jen?" she asked.

"The one and only."

Crissy opened the door, and Jenny gave her a hug and kissed her cheek. "Oh, you look so great, Cris!"

"Thank you," Crissy said, eyeing Jenny's outfit as her friend flung off her big fox coat. "And you look . . . well . . . you look out of this world!" she said, helplessly laughing at the mixture of flowers, animal prints, and leather that her friend was wearing.

Jenny twirled on long, thin legs, and her hair swung luxuriantly around her shoulders. "Yeah, I know it's way out there," she said, "but I couldn't help myself."

"Where on earth did you get it?" Crissy asked, her gaze still on Jenny's outrageously eye-catching ensemble. The blouse, with its plunging neckline, was a leopard print, while ruffles around the sleeves and neck were a flowered pattern. The skirt was very short and consisted of many layers of ruffles, each layer in a different print—ocelot, tiger, zebra, and more flowers. It was cut in different lengths, the back longer than the front, and worn over leather pants that appeared to have been painted in leopard spots. Only leopards, Crissy reflected, weren't metallic gold and silver and bronze.

"New York," Jenny said, twirling again. "As in City. Went down last week and spent two days shopping, shopping, shopping." She finally stood still. "I got everything at Roberto Cavalli. Is it the cat's meow or what?"

Crissy laughed again. "It's definitely 'or what,' " she said.

"Well, *I* think it's gorgeous," Jenny said defensively, her dark eyes flashing, "and I don't care what anybody else thinks. I know that the guys are going to go crazy for it."

Crissy nodded. "You're probably right about that," she agreed. "If they're into the rich hooker look."

Jenny's eyebrows rose in surprise. "You . . . you prude," she said. "You're just jealous. Believe me, there are very few hookers who could afford this. It cost thousands of dollars."

"Thousands . . . of . . . dollars?" Crissy echoed, hardly believing her ears but knowing that Jenny was telling her the truth.

"Hey," Jenny said. "This little number is about a thousand yards of the best silk chiffon and hand-painted leather. That doesn't come cheap, you know."

"I'm sure it doesn't," Crissy said.

"Anyway, you ready to go?" Jenny asked.

Crissy nodded. "If you are," she said.

"I'm hot to trot," Jenny said with a laugh.

They both put on their coats and left the apartment. "What if I drive?" Crissy asked. "You can leave your car here."

"I don't know," Jenny said. "It doesn't look good arriving in that beat-up old thing of yours, but the guys'll cream over my Jaguar convertible."

"Who's going to see?" Crissy asked reasonably. "The guys are going to be inside. Besides, if I drive, you can drink all you want to. You know I can't drink much."

"That settles it," Jenny said, throwing her head back and laughing. "You're driving."

Club Nine One One was located in a nondescript building on Central Avenue, and when they pulled up into the parking lot, Crissy was disappointed. "It sure doesn't look so great, Jen."

"Wait till we're inside," Jenny replied. "Tom Gentry told me it's fabulous, and he knows what he's talking about."

"Well, then, it's bound to be great," Crissy said. Tom was one of the multitude of eligible men Jenny had attracted since her divorce from Peter Schwartz, her philandering ex-husband, and she supposed Tom would know. He was a hotshot lawyer by day and a club-crawler by night, often arriving with a small entourage of friends. His clique could make or break a club by its mere presence, as if its being there gave the place a kind of seal of approval that no amount of promotion could provide. Club owners were very generous with complimentary drinks for Tom and friends, hoping to earn their gratitude and approval, because they knew that a plethora of scene-makers and trendsetters would follow in his wake if he kept coming back.

Crissy found a parking spot and maneuvered her Neon into the space. She and Jenny click-clacked to the entry on their heels, filled with anticipation. A small crowd of twenty or so people waited for entry at the door, but when the doorman spied Jenny, he waved her and Crissy toward him.

"Hey, beautiful," he said to Jenny, pulling the big black door open for them. He nodded to Crissy, and she smiled.

"Hiya, Tony," Jenny said. "How much is it tonight?"

"Forget it," he said.

"Wow," Jenny replied. "Thanks."

"Anything for you," he said, winking lewdly.

Jenny laughed, and they entered the dark hallway. "Who's he?" Crissy asked.

"Tony?" Jenny laughed. "I don't really know much about him, but everybody knows him. He's one of those big bruisers they hire to work the door at places. I think he probably sells drugs on the side."

"Oh, one-stop shopping," Crissy said. "Drinks inside, drugs at the door."

"Nothing serious," Jenny said, looking at her. "You know. Just ecstacy, coke, stuff like that."

"Oh," Crissy replied. *Nothing serious!* she thought, but she didn't say anything. She didn't want to get into a discussion about drugs with Jenny right now.

The walls on both sides of the hallway were lined with mirror panels that reflected the tiny diffuse pink spots in the black ceiling above. Huge art deco sconces gave off very low-wattage light. They checked their coats and walked to the end of the hallway, where they entered a huge room with a large dance floor. Surrounding it was a carpeted area on which banquettes and tables and chairs were arranged against a four-foot wall. Over the wall Crissy could see another area containing three separate bars and more arrangements of built-in banquettes and tables and chairs. Columns rose from the low wall to the ceiling, and the bars were built in the art deco style, with lots of mirror, glass, steel, and black metal. Overhead lights washed the entire club in a kaleidoscope of constantly changing colors, and the music, a great dance mix, was cranked up loud.

Most of the tables near the dance floor appeared to be taken, and there was a large crowd dancing. The crowd varied in age, Crissy noticed, anywhere from twentysomethings to well over fifties. "Where do you want to go?" she asked.

"Just follow me," Jenny said. She took Crissy's hand and led the way through the throng of dancers. Crissy noticed that heads turned when they saw Jenny coming their way. When they reached the nearest bar, Jenny turned to Crissy. "What's your poison?" she asked.

"A glass of white wine," Crissy said.

"Oh, for God's sake." Jenny groaned dramatically. "Live a little. Have something good for a change."

"I'm driving, remember?" Crissy said. "Besides, you know I can't drink much."

"Oh, all right," Jenny said. She turned back to the bar and ordered for them. When the bartender had their drinks ready—a Cosmopolitan for Jenny and white wine for Crissy—Jenny opened her purse to take out money. Before she could give it to the bartender, a handsome man grabbed her hand.

"Let me take care of that, Jenny," he said.

"Oh, Tom," she cooed. "You don't have to do that."

"But I want to," he said, pulling a crisp twenty-dollar bill from a money clip and slapping it down on the bar.

"Oh, this is my friend, Crissy," she said. "Crissy, this is Tom Gentry."

"Hi," Crissy said, extending a hand.

"Oh, there's Jimmy Golden," Jenny cried. "I'll be back in a minute." She rushed off without a backward glance, intent on seeing her friend.

Tom Gentry took Crissy's hand in his and pressed it gently. "Nice to meet you," he said, looking into her eyes. He was in his mid- to late thirties, tall with dark blond hair, and his eyes were such a startling, intense blue that Crissy wondered if he wore tinted contact lenses.

"It's nice to meet you, too," she said, surprised that he hadn't relinquished his hold on her hand. His gaze, she noticed, quickly swept her up and down, assessing her, she felt, as if to determine whether or not she was worthy of his attention. She didn't feel offended, just a bit curious. She wouldn't have imagined that Tom Gentry would greet her in anything more than a perfunctory way. He was, after all, a very important man about town, a social and professional titan who had his pick of the local women.

Apparently, she passed inspection. "Would you like to dance, Crissy?" he asked.

"Sure," she replied. She set her wineglass on the bar, and he took her hand and led her out onto the dance floor.

The music segued into a slow number, and smiling, Tom took her into his arms, leading her gracefully about the dance floor. He was a very good dancer, she thought, and a gentleman, too. He didn't try to squeeze her against him, groping her, trying to cop a feel, as so many men would do. Occasionally he would look down into her eyes and smile, an almost sleepy look in his gaze, but friendly and sexy in a nonthreatening way. When the music segued into the next number, a fast one, he held onto her hand but led her off the dance floor.

"Let me get you a drink," he offered.

"You already did," Crissy said with a laugh. "I left it at the bar."

"In that case, I'll get myself one," he said, "and we can have a drink together. Is that okay with you?"

"Sure," Crissy said.

"Do you see yours?" he asked when they reached the bar.

"Here it is," Crissy said, picking up her glass of wine.

He ordered an Oban on the rocks, then turned to her. "So you and Jenny are good friends, I take it?"

She nodded. "We met at the university," she said, "and we've been friends ever since."

"She's some girl," he said, smiling. "About as wild as they come."

"She's pretty out there," Crissy agreed, "but she's always been a really good friend to me."

"I bet," he said. "The loyal type, but I wouldn't want to be her enemy. She raked Peter over the coals when she got a divorce. Managed to get herself a nice big settlement and alimony." The bartender brought his drink, and he took a small sip.

"Peter was playing around on her," Crissy said in Jenny's defense, "and everybody knew about it."

"Yes, Peter was pretty stupid getting caught with his pants down. Jenny had better sense. She played it real cool." He looked at her and smiled. "No way was she dumb enough to get herself caught."

"Do you mean—" She looked at him questioningly.

He nodded. "You didn't know?" He smiled again. "Jenny was getting it on with at least two guys I know."

"I don't believe you," Crissy replied incredulously.

"Ask her," he said. "She acted like a devoted little housefrau until the divorce was over and she'd gotten her hands on his money, then she really let loose, doing whatever—whoever—she wanted to."

Crissy was disturbed by what he said. She had been Jenny's confidante during the divorce proceedings. She'd listened to her tales of woe, held her hand, and wiped away her tears. She found it hard to believe that Jenny wouldn't have told her the truth, that she herself was playing around on Peter. She really didn't know what to believe, but she didn't know why Tom Gentry would lie to her. What did he have to gain by it?

"I . . . I really don't like talking about her this way," Crissy finally said. "Behind her back. Whatever Jenny might or might not have done is in the past, and she's not here to speak for herself."

Tom looked at her, studying her face for a moment. "You're the loyal type, too, aren't you?"

"I think so," Crissy said. "If someone is my friend, then I stick by her." She looked up at him. "And I expect the same thing from my friends."

Tom abruptly reached over and took one of her hands in his. "You're a serious . . . and beautiful . . . young lady," he said, looking with intensity into her eyes, "and I like that. It's a winning combination."

Crissy was somewhat startled by his remark and his sudden, more intimate proximity. She liked the way his hand felt, however, and liked what he had said.

"Thank you, Tom," she said. Then she laughed nervously. "If you mean that."

He looked offended momentarily and let go of her hand. "Of course I meant it," he said. "I don't know what you might have heard about me, if you've heard anything at all, but I think you'll discover that I don't waste my time on women that I don't find interesting . . . and I find you very interesting."

Once again Crissy was jolted by his words, and she was temporarily at a loss as to how to respond. "You . . . you're not at all what I expected," she replied, looking down into her wineglass, then back up at him.

"Why don't we go sit down and continue this conversation in a quiet corner," Tom said with a smile. "Is that okay with you?"

Crissy hesitated, then nodded. "Yes," she said. "Why not?"

"Let me get you another glass of wine first."

She shook her head. "No, thanks," she said, "but I will have some water."

"Fizzy or still? Lemon or lime?"

Crissy smiled. "Fizzy, with lemon."

He ordered her water and paid for it. Handing it to her, he said, "Take my arm, we'll find a spot."

Crissy took his arm and followed his lead through the throng of people crowding off the dance floor toward the bar. Several people greeted Tom and gave her the once-over, she noticed, but he didn't stop to introduce her to anyone. They were probably wondering who the stranger was that Tom Gentry had deigned to include in his court tonight, she thought, and she couldn't help but feel a little privileged by his attention and excited by the interest that it generated in others. She recognized a few of the faces, but she didn't know any of the people. The crowd appeared to be more upscale and mature than those that frequented the clubs she usually went to with friends.

They reached a distant corner where no one was around, and Tom indicated the banquette with a hand. "How's this?" he asked. "Okay?"

"Fine," Crissy replied. "You don't want to join your friends?"

"Not now," he said. "Besides, here I think we can actually talk to each other without shouting." They put their drinks down on the black glass and chrome table, and he let her sit down and scoot across the banquette's leather-upholstered seat, making room for him. He sat close to her, but left enough room to turn sideways to face her with one leg up on the seat.

"It's actually fairly quiet here," Crissy said, feeling somewhat unnerved by such close proximity without other people around. She certainly wasn't afraid of him. No, it wasn't that at all—he'd been a perfect
gentleman, hadn't he?—but his interest in her was a little unsettling and
aroused her curiosity. Perhaps, too, she reflected, it was the confident,
masculine, well-bred air that surrounded him, as well as his charm and
handsomeness. *Oh, hell,* she finally admitted to herself, *he's all that and
just plain sexy.*

"I guess I seem a little aggressive," he said, as if he could read her
mind, "and I don't want to scare you off. But I didn't want to pass up the
chance to get to know you a little better." After taking a sip of his drink,
he added, "Why don't you tell me about yourself?"

"What do you want to know?" she asked with a laugh.

"Everything," he replied, looking into her eyes. Then he laughed, too.
"Well . . . everything that you'd like to tell me."

"Oh . . . well . . . I wouldn't even know where to start," Crissy said.

"Then I'll ask you twenty questions," he said. "How's that?"

"Okay," she said with a nod. "At least, I guess it's okay." She laughed
again.

"I promise I won't ask anything too . . . personal," he replied, smiling.
"Are you from here?"

Crissy nodded. "I was born and raised here. In a little house in
Guilderland." She looked at him questioningly. "And you?"

"Yes," he said.

"Where?" she asked.

"Loudonville."

Naturally, she thought. *He would be from the most exclusive part of
town.* "That's nice," she said. "There're so many beautiful houses there."

"Did you go to school here?"

"Oh, yes. I went to Central. You?"

"I went away to school," he said. "To Deerfield."

"A boarding school?" she asked.

He nodded. "And your parents were from here?"

"My dad was from Castleton," she said. "A little town south of here
on the Hudson." She didn't add that he was a hopeless alcoholic who only
came by to beg money off her.

"I know where it is," he said. "A pretty little place."

"Well, maybe parts of it are pretty," she said with a laugh, "but a lot of it definitely is not what you'd call pretty."

"And your mother?"

"She's from Vietnam, and now she owns a spa here in Albany," Crissy replied, hoping that he didn't ask her anything else about Lily, her difficult, complex mother.

"Aha," Tom said. "So he met her during the Vietnam war." He swirled the ice around in his drink. "Excuse me, I mean 'conflict.' "

Crissie nodded. "Right. They met, fell in love, and got married."

"That's explains why you're so beautiful," he said. "You're part Asian."

She felt the blood rush to her face, and knew that she was blushing. "Yes, and I bet your parents are both from old Albany families."

"No, actually," he replied. "My mother is from an old Saratoga family." He smiled. "My dad's from here, though. An old Albany family, as you say. But that's enough about me. I'm boring, and my family's boring. I want to know about you." He paused and took another sip of his drink. "So you met Jenny at SUNY. What did you study there?"

"Liberal arts," she replied, "and I was thinking about majoring in art history before I dropped out."

"Oh, so you didn't finish," he said. "Why not?"

"My family quit supporting me," Crissy said, "and I started working full-time so I could get a place of my own. You know, away from home. Then Karen, this friend of mine, was getting her beautician's license and talked me into going there, too. So I did. It was affordable and didn't take too long, and I saw that I could make a lot more money than working for minimum wage in department stores and places like that."

He nodded. "So you're a hairdresser?"

"Yes," Crissy said. "A hairdresser, more or less by accident."

"Do you think you'll go back to school?"

"I don't know," Crissy said. "I'd like to, but I think I want to see some of the world first." She didn't mind his questions, but she was beginning to feel as if she was getting the third degree. Was this part of a background check, to see if she was worthy of his attention? she wondered.

"Sounds reasonable," he said. "Do you like what you do?"

Crissy laughed.

"What?" he asked, smiling. "What's so funny?"

"Oh, nothing," she said. "You just ask a lot of questions."

"I told you that I'm interested in you," he said. "It's just my way of finding out about you."

"I know," she said. "It's . . . it's just that . . . well, you seem so serious, and you're asking a lot all at once." She paused thoughtfully then said, "I guess most of the men I've known haven't really been all that interested in me. At least they haven't asked these kind of questions right off the bat. They've mostly just been interested in . . . well . . ."

"Getting in your pants," he supplied.

Crissy nodded.

"I can't blame them," he said, looking into her eyes. He took one of her hands in his. "Like I said, you're beautiful, but you're also intelligent."

The touch of his hand seemed intimate for some reason. Crissy suddenly felt her pulse begin to race, and her body seemed to awaken to desires she hadn't felt in a long time. She could hardly believe this was happening, and she wondered if he was experiencing a similar reaction, if he was aroused by her. She only had to wait a moment for the answer.

"Would you like to leave?" he asked. "I know you haven't been here long, but I think we could have a much better time talking someplace else. Someplace with privacy, where we could really get to know each other." He held her gaze unflinchingly.

She nodded without a second thought, as if it was the most natural thing in the world.

"Good," he said in a whisper, still holding her hand in his. He stared at her silently, then said, "Why don't we get our coats?"

"Okay," she replied.

They got to their feet, and he took her hand again, leading her toward the front of the club. "I've got to let Jenny know that I'm leaving," Crissy said. "I drove, so I've got to make sure she's got a ride home."

"Of course," he said. He turned toward the dance floor, his gaze searching for Jenny's long mane of streaked hair. "I see her," he said. He looked at Crissy, grinning. "She's dancing with Jim Golden. Let's go tell them."

He led the way onto the dance floor, weaving around couples, until they reached Jenny and Jim. They were gyrating madly in time to the music, oblivious to Crissy and Tom until he touched Jenny's shoulder. She jerked and looked around. "You leaving?" she cried above the thunderous music.

"Is it okay?" Crissy asked, raising her voice to be heard. "Can you get a ride?"

Jenny laughed and nodded. "Jim?" She poked her dancing partner in the back, and he turned around, his eyes closed, his body still moving to the music.

Tom clapped a hand on his shoulder, and Jim opened his eyes. He smiled widely, but kept moving. "Hey, what's happening?" he asked.

"Do you mind giving me a lift home?" Jenny asked him.

"Are you kidding?" he said. "Of course I'll take you home." He moved against her, still dancing, running his hands up and down her sides, pressing his pelvis against hers.

"See you later," Jenny said with a laugh. "Have fun."

Crissy blew her a kiss, and she and Tom wove their way back through the throng of dancers to the front of the club. At the coat check, he helped her into her fuzzy fake fur, then put on his overcoat. Outside, they said good night to the doorman, then walked hand in hand toward the parking lot.

"You can come to my place," he said, "but it's a disaster area. I'm having it painted, so everything's covered up with drop cloths and the smell is not exactly conducive to good conversation."

"We can go to mine, if you want to," Crissy said. "It's nothing fancy, but it'll do."

"That's great," he replied. "Where is it?"

"In a house on Washington Park," she said.

"What if I follow you there?"

"Okay. I've got a little blue Neon, and it's . . . over there." She pointed with a finger.

"I'll put you in your car, then you can wait at the exit for me," he said.

They reached her car, and Crissy unlocked it. He held the door open for her, then leaned in. "See you in a few minutes," he said. "I'll be right behind you."

Crissy nodded. "I won't drive fast."

He turned and walked off, and Crissy started the Neon and drove to the exit, where she waited for him. Through the rearview mirror, she saw a shiny British racing-green Jaguar convertible pull up behind her. She recognized Tom's face before he honked the horn.

29

She found a space on the block where she lived. As she got out of the car and locked it, Tom rolled down his window and called to her, "I'll find a place to park and be right back."

Crissy waited on the sidewalk in the chill wind, but she didn't really notice the cold. She hadn't been this excited about seeing a man in a very long time. When she saw him coming up the sidewalk toward her, she felt her pulse race once again. *I can't believe this,* she thought. *I feel like I'm living in a dream.*

"Hi," he said, sidling up next to her and taking her hand.

"Hi," she replied.

"This is it?" he said, looking toward the old, once beautiful mansion.

"This is it," she said, echoing his words.

They walked up the steps to the front porch and went inside.

"This used to be quite a house," he said, looking around the hall and up the ornate staircase.

"A long time ago," Crissy said, "but I like living here. It's quiet, and it's on the park. And it's my own."

She had left a table lamp and the radio switched on, as she always did. Soft music filled the apartment, and the light, she thought, was just right. "I'll hang up your coat," she said, turning to Tom.

He took it off and handed it to her, his gaze sweeping the single large room in which she lived. "This is nice," he called to her as she hung up his coat. "Very homey."

"Thanks," she said. "You want something to drink? I have some Johnnie Walker scotch."

"That'd be great," he said. "Just a little bit on ice."

"Oh," Crissy said, looking at him. "I didn't even think. You want me to hang up your jacket?" He was wearing a very expensive-looking suit and tie.

"That's okay," he said. "I'll just put it on a chair, Crissy." He took it off and tossed it over the back of a chair, still looking around the apartment as he loosened his tie. He took it off and tossed it on the jacket. "This was probably the dining room," he said.

"It was," Crissy said, coming back from the kitchen counter. She handed him his scotch.

"Thanks," he said. "What're you having?"

"I think I'll have a glass of wine, now that I'm home," she said. "Be right back. Have a seat. Make yourself comfortable."

Tom sat down on the love seat and took a sip of his drink. When she returned, he looked up at her and smiled. "Cheers," he said, lifting his glass.

"Cheers to you, too," Crissy said.

"I like your place a lot. It's comfortable and not too girlie, if you know what I mean."

Crissy laughed. "I know exactly what you mean. I have girlfriends who live in pink rooms full of stuffed animals and lacy everything."

He laughed. "Makes me cringe," he said, "but this looks like a grown-up lives here."

"Thanks," she said, sitting down on the love seat. She had positioned herself in the corner rather than next to him, but there was very little space between them, since the love seat was so small. She realized that his jacket had concealed a powerful-looking chest and well-developed arms. Wondering if that moment of intimacy she'd felt in the club could be re-captured, she took a sip of her wine. She knew that having more wine was risky—she might get tipsy or worse—but she decided to throw caution to the wind for a change. Tom Gentry excited her, and he was worth the risk.

He took a sip of his drink and set the glass on the little coffee table, then took her free hand in his. "Where were we?" he asked with a smile.

Crissy laughed. "I think we had reached my job. Whether or not I like what I do."

"Do you?"

"I'm . . . bored with it," Crissy said frankly. "Tired of giving ladies highlights and color and being their shrink."

"I bet you're a good listener," he said. "That's why they tell you their problems."

Crissy shrugged. "I suppose," she said. "A lot of them are very nice people, and I like them. Some of them aren't, of course. But it doesn't re-ally matter. I need to be doing something else, but I'm not sure what that is yet."

Tom nodded as if he understood. "You said you want to see some of the world."

"Yes," Crissy said. "I want to get out of Albany and see what's out there."

"I can't blame you for that," he replied. "This is a small town. I'd hate it if I didn't get away a lot."

"Where do you go?" she asked.

"Here, there, and everywhere," he said. "I go to Europe at least once a year, and sometimes I take a trip to someplace new. Safari in Kenya. The Great Barrier Reef in Australia. That kind of thing. On weekends I go up to the Adirondacks to a place I have up there. Sometimes I go riding down near Old Chatham with the hunt club. I board a horse down there."

"You *are* busy," Crissy said. "It sounds so exciting."

"Uh-huh," he said. "It can be pretty exciting, and I keep very busy." He pressed her hand gently and gazed into her eyes. "But it feels really good to be here relaxing with you right now."

"It . . . I feel good, too," she responded, setting her wineglass down.

He slid an arm around her shoulder and ran his fingers through her hair.

She could feel his breath on her neck and could smell the distinctly masculine aroma that he exuded. It was provocative and erotic, and once again she suddenly felt as if her body had awakened to long-dormant desires.

"I want to make love to you," he said softly. "You excite me, and nobody's done that for a long, long time. Not really. Not like you."

Crissy felt herself melt. She didn't know another word to more accurately describe what she was feeling, and she wanted him more than ever. It was as if her mind and body had wants and needs over which she had no control, so powerful was the feeling. She couldn't say no; it was unthinkable.

He leaned closer, and his lips brushed against her ear, then slowly, almost reverentially he brushed her neck with those sensuous lips, barely touching her skin. Her breath caught in her throat. He brushed his lips across her cheek, still barely touching her, then across her lips as if in a whisper of a kiss. A barely audible groan escaped his lips, and he took her into his arms, pressing her against him gently but firmly, his desire for her mounting. She felt a shiver rush through her body, charging her with an electric longing that she hadn't known existed until this moment. She encircled him with her arms, drawing him closer to her, lusting for the touch of his body against her own, her mind closing out the rest of the world. His lips were pressed to hers, and his tongue slowly parted them, tenderly at first, then delving farther, exploring, in an eager desire to know her and please her, to possess her.

32

Crissy felt herself let go completely, intent only on the pleasure that she was capable of giving him, fearlessly daring to expose herself to this man as she had no other. When he suddenly withdrew from her, releasing his gentle hold of her and pulling back, she gasped almost as if bitten, but she opened her eyes and saw that he was gazing upon her with an expression that was at once carnal lust and pure joy.

"Let's get undressed," he whispered, expelling a long breath. He ran a finger down the side of her face. "Then let's get in bed." His face was flushed with pleasure.

She nodded, and he rose to his feet, extending a hand for her. She took it, and he pulled her up beside him.

She kicked off her mules and started to take off her glittery top, but he took her hands in his. "Let me," he said, and she stood still as he slowly slid it up to her neck, then over her head, sliding the sleeves off her arms at the same time. He laid it on the loveseat, then his eyes swept over her before coming to rest on her lacy black bra. He unhooked it, then slipped it off her. She heard his sharp intake of breath and could see a new intensity in his eyes as he focused on her pert, ample breasts with their small, rosy nipples. He reached out with a finger and barely brushed against first one nipple, then the other, back and forth, until Crissy moaned with pleasure. With both hands he cupped her breasts and held them, stroked them, feathering her nipples lightly before leaning over and licking them tenderly.

Taking his hands away, he turned his attention to her slacks. He unfastened the button and unzipped them, but didn't let them fall to the floor. He went down on his knees and slipped the slacks down over her thighs, on down to her ankles, then waited as she lifted first one foot then the other, freeing her from the garment. He looked up into her eyes, then pressed his face against her stomach, swirling his tongue around her navel. As he did so, he slipped her panties down, down, down, and removed them as he had the slacks. Looking up at her again, he held her gaze for an instant before pressing his mouth against the black mound between her thighs. He placed his hands on her ass, pulling her firmly against his face, and moaned as he began to lick her there.

Crissy felt his tongue enter her, and for a moment she thought she would collapse on top of him. So exquisite was the sensation that she had to restrain herself from crying out. Her body began to tremble, and she could feel the wetness on her thighs as she began to approach an orgasm.

He abruptly stopped, however, and swiftly rose to his feet. He kissed her, then rapidly removed his shirt and undershirt, undid his belt, and stepped out of his loafers. Kissing her as he unbuttoned his trousers, he then unzipped them, and let them fall to the floor. He stepped out of them and put out a hand for her to take, leading her over to the bed. At its edge, he took her into his arms and kissed her, running his arms up and down her back, and gently kneaded her round ass. Crissy could feel his hard cock against her, and she pressed him closer to her, in awe of his arousal and his intense desire for her.

He drew back. "Lie down," he whispered.

Crissy did so, lying on her back, looking up at him. His body was perfection to her eyes, with a lean, well-defined musculature. His shoulders were broad and powerful and his arms were well developed. A long, slender waist was accentuated with ropey, horizontal abs that seemed to pulse with his every movement. His manhood sprang erect from a dark blond nest. It throbbed with life, and she could hardly wait to feel its length and breadth within her.

Tom eased himself onto the bed and got on his hands and knees above her, looking down into her eyes. He smiled, then leaned down and kissed her. Crissy put her arms up around his shoulders to pull him against her, but he had other ideas. His lips moved to her neck, his tongue flicking at her in feathery licks, then moved on down to her breasts, where he laved each one, licking her erect nipples. Crissy squirmed with delight and moaned, anxious for him to enter her, but he wasn't ready yet. His tongue trailed from her breasts down to her navel, circled around it several times, then flicked its way to her dark mound. Repositioning himself, he placed his hands on her breasts, stroking them, thrumming her nipples delicately, a prelude, she discovered, to his tongue entering her most private place. She cried out and spread her legs wide, swept up to new heights of ecstasy as he fed on her juices, licking in a furor, delving deeper and deeper.

"Tom," she gasped. "Tom . . . I'm . . . you're . . . oh . . . oh . . . " She writhed from side to side, certain that she was going to be overcome by an orgasm at any moment, but he stopped, knowing that he had brought her to the edge. Rising up on his knees, he stared down at her before lowering himself atop her. Crissy threw her arms around his shoulders, relishing the feel of his powerful masculinity against her soft and yielding flesh.

He entered her slowly, watching her face as he did so, taking pleasure from the gasps of delight that escaped her lips. When he was entirely inside her, he stopped momentarily, and she savored him there, engulfing her with his manhood before he began to slowly move, in and out, in and out, until they were moving together in a rhythmic dance that gained speed as their desire mounted. Crissy cried out as wave after wave of exquisite contractions engulfed her in ecstacy. Tom, driven to new heights of passion by her orgasm, could control himself no longer. In a final plunge, he entered her to the hilt of his cock, his body tensing, before he emitted a lusty cry and burst forth inside her, his body trembling as his juices gushed in a torrent of lust.

He lay atop her then, his arms hugging her to him tightly. They were silent as they caught their breath, but he planted kisses on her lips and cheeks, her nose and eyes. He rolled to his side, holding her to him, careful to stay inside her. His hands slowly began to stroke her, tenderly, and when he could speak, he whispered, "That was wonderful, Crissy. *You* are wonderful." He sighed with contentment and hugged her again, possessively, unwilling to let her go, she thought.

"I . . . I've never felt anything like this before," Crissy said. "It's never been this . . . good . . . this . . . exciting." She meant what she said. Although she'd had boyfriends in the past and had made love with a couple of them, the lovemaking hadn't been satisfying, let alone passionate. For a long time, she had avoided sex because her earlier experiences had been terrible.

He kissed her sweetly and hugged her closer.

As she lay in his arms, Crissy reveled in the golden afterglow of their lovemaking. She had never felt as sated, as fulfilled, as she did now.

Tom propped his head up, resting it on the palm of his hand, and stared at her face. His expression was difficult for Crissy to read, but she saw what she thought was a mixture of happiness and some degree of curiosity, as if perhaps he was wondering who she was and where she came from, beyond what he already knew.

"What are you thinking about?" she finally asked him, when he continued to openly study her.

"What an exceptionally beautiful, sensitive, and sexy lady you are," he replied, smiling.

She laughed. "Think so, huh?"

He nodded. "I know so," he said. "You're . . . different somehow. Special. And I like that. I like it a lot."

"What do you mean?" she asked, intrigued by what he'd said. "How am I different? And special?" She wondered if it was merely because she was part Asian, but she didn't think that was what he had meant. That had hardly entered the conversation tonight, and it didn't seem of any particular importance to him.

He shrugged. "I'm not really sure," he confessed, "but part of it is that you're so unlike a lot of the women I go out with and work around. You haven't asked me what I do for a living, for one thing. You know, sniffing around like most women, trying to see how much I've got to offer in the money department. You haven't tried to impress me either. Dropping names of local bigwigs you know or have met. That sort of thing. That's really rare."

Crissy laughed softly. "Maybe that's because I don't know any."

"Oh, everybody's met *somebody*, if you know what I mean. You know, like they've been to a cocktail party where the governor was. Or the senate majority leader. Or some visiting celebrity."

Crissy laughed again. "Maybe I should've told you who my rich clients are." She paused. "What a joke that would be." She looked at him. "I'm afraid I would disappoint you in that category. I'm just a simple person trying to make a living, and I guess I'm not particularly drawn to the powers that be in Albany."

"You mean that politicians and lobbyists and their wives don't fascinate you to death?" he said with a laugh.

"I've met quite a few of them, the wives I mean, but they aren't usually my most interesting customers. Sometimes, but not often. I guess I'm attracted to people who are a little bit . . . different."

"Am I different?" he asked.

"You're certainly different from most of the men I've gone out with," she said.

"How?"

"You seem more . . . caring. More . . . sensitive." She looked at him. "And you're a real gentleman. A dying breed, I think."

"Do you think I'm good-looking?" he asked.

"Of course you are," she said. "You know that. You're extremely handsome."

"And am I sexy to you?"

She laughed. "Very, very sexy."

He leaned close and kissed her. "I'm glad you think so," he said softly.

He began stroking her back lightly and running his hands over her rounded buttocks, kissing her all the while. Crissy brushed a hand down his powerful arm, then up to his shoulder and down his back, amazed anew by his hard, defined musculature. She mewled when she felt his flaccid penis begin to grow within her, and clung to him tightly. He began making love to her again, even more slowly this time, and they reveled in every moment of their time together, every movement of their bodies as they explored. And afterward, she was left with a sense of completeness.

They talked into the wee hours, cuddled and giggled, periodically raided the refrigerator, and grew to know the geography of each other's bodies. When dawn's first light began to seep through the windows, he knew about the little mole on her thigh, and she could describe the scar near his knee, where he'd had a torn ligament repaired. Their bodies spent, their minds still dazzled but exhausted, they finally slept, entwined together on the bed, their scents mingling in a perfume of carnal bliss.

Sometime around ten o'clock, Crissy awoke and saw him quietly dressing. She didn't stir but watched him in silence. When he was nearly finished, she sat up in bed. He turned to her and put a finger to his mouth, shushing her before she could speak. He leaned down and kissed her chastely on the forehead, then silently slipped a card in her hand. He straightened up and made a pillow of his hands, laying his head against it. Then, without a word, he turned and left, quietly closing the door behind him.

Crissy looked down at the card. It was made of a heavy cream vellum and was expensively engraved, not embossed. THOMAS H. GENTRY III, AT-TORNEY AT LAW, it said, then gave his office address, telephone and fax numbers, and email address. Crissy pressed the thick card to her lips, kissing it. She could detect his scent on it, and held it there against her lips for a long time, loath to relinquish this, the only physical reminder of himself he'd left behind.

She could hardly wait until he called, to hear that deep, sonorous voice of his. Maybe she would even hear from him later today, after he'd had some sleep. If not today, then he would call tomorrow, she was certain. She looked down at the card again. If for some reason he didn't have time or couldn't get to a phone this weekend—she remembered that he was having his house painted—she would call the business number on the card on Monday morning. Then she wondered if that was a wise move. She'd met him in a club after all. What if he was just playing her? What if he'd just wanted to get his rocks off and that was that? She doubted that many people found true love in a club. She would have to wait and see, but she had really enjoyed tonight. Monday now seemed an aeon away, as if time itself had been altered by the transformation in her life last night. She finally drifted off to sleep again, the card still in her hand, and slept deeply, peacefully, and full of hope for the future, even as she had doubts about his intentions.

Chapter Three

"I've never seen you shoot out of a place as fast as you did last night," Jenny said with a laugh. "How was it?"

"Heaven," Crissy said, brushing hair out of her eyes. The telephone's persistent ring had woken her, but she still wasn't fully alert. "That's the only word for it, Jen. Absolute *heaven.*"

"Ooooooh," Jenny squealed. "I'm so glad, Cris. He's got to be the hottest man in town, and I mean that."

"Do you really think so?" Crissy said. She got out of bed and went to the bathroom, where she got her bathrobe. Slipping into it, she went to the kitchenette. She had to have some coffee.

"Oh, please," Jenny said. "Everybody knows that. He's drop-dead handsome, built like a god, and rich as the devil. And he knows everybody who's anybody."

"Well, I don't know about all the rest," Crissy said, "but I know he's good-looking and he has a great bod. I mean, I knew that he was a big shot on the social scene and all but—"

"Cris, hon," Jenny said, "you don't know the half of it. Everybody, and I mean *everybody,* is after him." She paused, and Crissy could hear her taking a puff of a cigarette. "So tell me," she went on, "it was really that good? He's a real stud, huh?"

"Jen!" Crissy laughed. "You've got a one-track mind." She ground the coffee beans and poured them into the filter, then switched on the pot.

"You bet I do," Jenny replied. "Now tell me: What was it like? What's 'heaven'? Jenny needs to know."

"Oh, well . . . " Crissy began. "It's . . . it's hard to describe, but we talked a lot. He wanted to know all about me. It was like he was really interested, you know? And he was a real gentleman. He didn't come on too strong like some kind of Neanderthal. He took it slow and easy, and . . . Oh, Jenny, it was the best night of my life, I swear."

"Oooooh!" Jenny squealed again. "I'm so happy. He must be some fuck. Has he got a big dick?"

"Jen!" Crissy cried. She couldn't help but laugh. "That's none of your business. Besides, this was much more than that. I mean, it wasn't just the sex. It was . . . everything. Everything I had only imagined before, except I never imagined anything could be this great."

"Jeez," Jenny said, "it sounds like you've been bitten by the love bug."

"Well, I can't wait till he calls," Crissy replied.

There was an ominous pause, then she said, "So he's going to call you? This wasn't just a one-night stand?"

"Oh, no," Crissy said quickly. "It wasn't like that at all."

"Je-*sus,*" Jenny exclaimed. "I always heard he was a love 'em and leave 'em type. Nobody's ever been able to pin him down, you know?"

Crissy felt mild alarm bells go off in her mind, but she ignored them, remembering the blissful night she'd had. "I don't know if I pinned him down," she said, "but I think last night was definitely the start of something . . . maybe something big."

"You're serious, aren't you?" Jenny said.

"Yes," Crissy replied. "I couldn't be more serious." The coffee was finally done, and she poured a mugful, then stirred in some skim milk and a packet of Sweet'N Low. "How was your night?" she asked. "Did you and Jim Golden do anything?"

"Oh, yeah," Jenny said dismissively. "Old reliable, that's Jim. You can count on him for a five-minute fuck."

"Jen!" Crissy laughed, almost sputtering coffee. "I don't believe you said that."

"Jim's idea of foreplay is to tell you you're hot, grope your tits, squeeze your ass, then hammer away at you like there's no tomorrow. You can practically set your watch by him. Five minutes max. A big grunt when he shoots. Then he rolls off, puts his clothes on, and leaves."

"Oh, my God," Crissy said. "Sounds like high school."

"That's the way most of them are," Jenny said. "They never develop beyond that stage. You should know that."

"I guess you're right, but I haven't had as much experience as you have," Crissy said with a laugh.

"Not many women have," Jenny said, shrieking laughter again. "And I intend to have a lot more. In the meantime, I've got to go take a long soak in the Jacuzzi and then slowly start getting ready for tonight."

"Already?" Crissy said. Looking at her alarm clock, she could hardly believe it was after three o'clock in the afternoon.

"You know how long it takes me to get ready."

"Who you going out with?"

"I've got a date with David Klein."

"Who's he?"

"He's this really cute guy I met last night," Jenny said, "and he asked me out to dinner tonight."

"I don't think I've ever met him," Crissy said.

"He's new in town. Some kind of lobbyist," Jenny said, "but he's not as old and dull as most of them."

"Well, have a good time," Crissy said.

"What are you doing tonight?"

"Nothing," Crissy replied. "I've got appointments back to back all day tomorrow, so I'm going to try to go to bed early. I told Rosy I thought I was coming down with something, then called today's appointments and changed them so I wouldn't have to go in. But I'm glad I did: I'd be a zombie if I'd had to go in to work today."

"Yeah, but it was worth it, right?"

"You bet it was," Crissy said. "Now I just can't wait till the next time."

"Ooooh, I think I smell love in the air," Jenny said. "Anyway, I'd better run. I'll talk to you tomorrow."

"Have fun tonight," Crissy said.

"Hon, I always have fun," Jenny replied. "Even if it's five-minute Jimmy." She laughed. "And I just know you're going to have more fun with Tom."

"I can hardly wait," Crissy said.

"I bet you won't have to wait long."

"I hope not," Crissy replied. "Anyway, I'll see you later."

Crissy pushed the OFF button on the remote and took a sip of her coffee. She suddenly realized that she meant what she'd said to Jenny: She

41

hoped she didn't have to wait long to see Tom again. She wished that he was here right now, curled up on the bed next to her. Just the thought of his body and his gentle touch stirred something deep down inside her, and she felt the heat of desire course through her body. *Oh, my God,* she thought. *He can't call soon enough.*

Tuesday at ten o'clock Crissy arrived at the shop and barely acknowledged the greetings and waves from her co-workers and customers. Despair enveloped her in a cloud of such pain, she felt like a wounded animal. She had waited for the ring of the telephone on Saturday, but no one had called. Sunday, after work, she'd checked her machine, but there wasn't a message from him. She told herself that Tom had gone someplace for the rest of the weekend, remembering that he was having his place painted. Then, Sunday night—in the wee hours of Monday morning, actually—she'd awakened and realized that, astonishingly, he didn't have her telephone numbers, not at home or work or her cell. She hadn't given them to him, nor had she told him the name of the beauty salon where she worked. *He probably doesn't even remember my last name,* she'd thought. She had clutched the bedcovers to her breasts and laughed aloud, relieved that there was a simple explanation for his silence since he'd left her apartment Saturday morning.

Monday morning, as soon as nine o'clock rolled around, she'd called his office. She held her breath as the telephone rang, and had to force herself to speak when a secretary said, "Good morning, Gentry and Gentry."

"Hi, I'd like to speak to Mr. Gentry, please," Crissy said.

"Mr. Gentry the second or third?" came the reply.

"Oh," Crissy said with a nervous laugh. "Tom Gentry the third."

"Whom may I say is calling?"

He's there! she thought excitedly. "Crissy . . . Crissy Fitzgerald," she said. "He'll know who it is."

"Just a moment, please."

Crissy held onto the phone as if it were a lifeline. She could feel her heart racing anxiously and could hardly wait for the sound of his voice.

She heard a click, then, "Mr. Gentry's in a meeting."

Crissy's heart sank. She couldn't help but wonder if he was actually in a meeting or if he was avoiding her. "I . . . I . . . could I leave my number, please?" she stuttered.

"Certainly," the secretary replied.

Crissy gave the woman all of her numbers, cell, home, and shop, and told her the name of the beauty salon after repeating her own name twice. "Thank you very much," she finally said.

"You're welcome," the secretary said and hung up.

She had already dressed for work and was ready to leave, but she'd sat by the telephone waiting for him to call back until, finally, she had to rush to get to the beauty salon on time. She'd made certain her cell phone was turned on, and anxiously waited at work for a return call. When her cell rang—twice—she'd almost dropped it in her excitement to answer his call, but it had been Jenny the first time and her mother the second. She'd quickly gotten them off the line and promised to talk to them later in the evening. As five o'clock approached, Tom still hadn't called, and she couldn't stop herself from trying his office again, even though she thought it was bad form to seem so anxious to speak to him. The same woman had answered the phone and, after putting her on hold, had given her the same response: Mr. Gentry was in a meeting.

Disheartened, Crissy had rushed home from work and waited. And waited. To no avail. The telephone did not ring. This morning she had re-peated Monday's routine, and had received the same response yet again: Mr. Gentry was in a meeting. Mr. Gentry, it seemed, was always in a meet-ing. At this point she told herself that there was no doubt whatsoever but that Tom Gentry was deliberately avoiding her. He'd had her numbers all day Monday, Monday night, and Tuesday morning, but he hadn't called or taken her calls. She finally admitted to herself what she'd known all along: If he really wanted to talk to her, he would have called.

This morning, on her way to work, Crissy had begun to weep, quietly at first, tears filling her eyes and spilling down her cheeks. She'd driven only a few blocks before she began wailing uncontrollably, tears blinding her to the extent that she had to pull the car over until she got a grip on herself. She'd felt like a fool before, but nothing compared to this. She'd been certain that the exciting connection she'd felt with Tom was mutual, but now there was no question that he hadn't shared the feeling. Tom Gentry's gentlemanly act, she decided, his tenderness and gentleness, and his apparent interest in her had all been part of an elaborate scheme to get her into bed. That and nothing more.

She worked quietly, merely going through the motions, forcing herself to respond to her customers and co-workers in as cheerful a manner as she could muster, but it was all she could do to keep in check the flood of tears

43

that continuously threatened to burst forth. The mere thought of his touch, of his kiss, of his powerful body sent her spiraling down into an abyss of lonely despair.

As she showered off the detritus of the day, Beatrice's words came back to her. Maybe Beatrice was right, she thought. Maybe just the thing she needed to get Tom Gentry out of her mind was to get out of Albany. At least for awhile. She could see about one of the long cruises that Beatrice had told her about. *I've got enough money,* she thought. *I've been saving for something like this for a long time. Yes,* she decided, *I'll get away from Albany and try to forget all about the rotten Mr. Tom Gentry.*

By the time she was finished showering, she resolved that she would go to a travel agent this week and begin to explore the possibilities available to her. The sooner the better, she thought. She dried off and put on a bathrobe, tying it at the waist, then dried her hair. When she was finished in the bathroom, she flipped off the light and started for the bed.

There was a knock on her door, and Crissy stood frozen, staring at it for a moment. No one ever came by without calling first, and she wondered who it could be. She went toward the door and called out in a low voice, "Who is it?"

"You are at the top of my shit list," a female voice said from the other side of the closed door, "and I mean that."

Crissy couldn't help but smile, then laughed as she opened the door. "Jenny," she cried, throwing her arms around her. "I'm so glad to see you."

Jenny hesitated before returning her hug and kissing her cheek. "I shouldn't even be speaking to you," she said.

"I know," Crissy said. "I've behaved very badly."

"Deplorably," she said. "Well, aren't you going to ask me in, or are we going to stand out here in the hallway?"

"Oh, come in," Crissy said, backing into the apartment. "It's so wonderful to see you, to hear your voice at the door. You don't know."

"You've heard my voice for days on your machine at home and on your cell phone voice mail," Jenny replied huffily, "but you didn't bother to return my calls, did you?"

"Jenny, you have every reason to be mad at me," Crissy said, sitting down on the couch beside her, "but . . . but I've been in a real funk. I mean the worst, and I didn't want to . . . Well, I just didn't feel like talking about it." Unbidden, tears suddenly sprang into her eyes.

Jenny put an arm around her shoulders and pulled her close. "Tell me about it," she said in a concerned voice. "What's happened?"

Crissy told her about Tom Gentry, and her feelings of acute shame and embarrassment after not hearing from him, how humiliated the experience had left her.

"Oh, you poor baby," Jenny said.

Crissy shook her head as if to clear it of cobwebs. "Tom. Whew . . . He swept me off my feet." She looked at Jenny with a puzzled expression. "I don't think I've ever fallen so hard. It was worse than a teenage crush. I feel like such a fool."

"He's a real smooth operator."

"I've never met anyone quite like him before," Crissy said. "He was so convincing. He worked me like a . . . well, like a master puppeteer. And I was his stupid puppet."

"My Lambchop," Jenny said, grinning.

Crissy punched her playfully. "You make me feel so much better."

Crissy fell silent, wanting to wipe every thought of Tom out of her mind. A cruise would do that. She'd forget all about him if she left town for a good long while.

"What are you thinking about?" Jenny asked.

"I've been thinking about taking a trip."

"That's a great idea. I need to take one myself."

"I've been saving all of my tips, and I'm going to a travel agent tomorrow at lunchtime to see what I can find out."

"That's so great," Jenny said.

"This customer of mine, Beatrice Bloom, has been encouraging me, just like you have. Anyway, Beatrice says I ought to take a big European trip. Maybe a long cruise." She paused and looked at Jenny. "She says that a lot of the people are older, of course, but that there are always some interesting younger people, too. I'm not sure about it, but—"

"Listen," Jenny said, grabbing her shoulders in her hands and looking her in the eye, "I'm going with you tomorrow to the travel agent. Okay? Because I want to make sure that you choose something that'll really be fun. What do you say?"

"I'd love that, Jenny," Crissy said. "I don't know much about what there is out there, you know?"

Jenny's dark eyes sparkled. "Oh, I do," she said. "I have a question for you, though. Are you going to go by yourself?"

"I don't know," Crissy replied. "I haven't even thought about it. Besides, who do I know that could go?"

"You know who could go," Jenny said, "and might be a lot of fun to have along?"

"Who?"

"The answer is staring you right in the face."

She shook her head. "Who? You?"

"Yes, me. I'm bored, and I'm tired of having nothing but time on my hands."

"That would be perfect," Crissy exclaimed. "Oh, I'm so excited. I'm just so thrilled that you showed up at my doorstep tonight. I feel like . . . like a new person."

"You're the same wonderful person you always were, Crissy," Jenny said solemnly. "Hopefully, you'll start living out some of those dreams of yours real soon." She winked. "I have a few dreams of my own."

The next day at lunchtime, Jenny picked Crissy up. When she got in Jenny's Jaguar convertible, she was carrying her shoulder bag, in which she'd placed her check book and an envelope of cash.

"They do have banks nowadays, Cris, or didn't you know that?" she said.

"You know I do," Crissy said. "But this is all tip money that I'd rather not show up as income. You know what I mean?"

"Smart girl," Jenny allowed. "Hiding it from the government, aren't you? Hard to do that with alimony."

"Everybody does," Crissy said. "Waiters, hairdressers, people like us, but I do declare some of it or else it would look odd. A hairdresser who never gets tips?"

"I don't think they'll come looking for a small fry like you," Jenny said.

"You never know," Crissy said.

They reached the travel agency and gave the young man the deposit for the trans-Atlantic cruise that Crissy and Jenny had decided on. "I've been studying up on this ship," the agent said, "and did you know it's the fastest passenger ship on the seas? Other ships can reach its speed, like the *Queen Elizabeth II* and the new *Queen Mary II*, but they can't maintain it. They'd vibrate all to pieces. But this little wonder is like a Jet Ski. Wish I was going myself."

46

Jenny gave Crissy a look, and Crissy knew what she was thinking. *I would jump ship if somebody as nerdy as you are was onboard.* She nudged Jenny with her elbow.

"Maybe you ought to try to book the same cruise then," Crissy told him. She noticed that his name tag said MELVIN, and thought that the name suited him somehow.

"Naw," the young man replied, "no way I could ever get a month off work at this point. Only been working here a year."

"Oh, well, maybe later on," Crissy said optimistically. "I hope you get to someday, Melvin."

He nodded. "So do I, but I don't think it's in the cards for me."

"Get yourself a new deck," Crissy said in a kindly voice.

Jenny laughed.

"It should be so easy," the young man said. He paused and looked at them. "Well, you're all set, ladies. Make sure your passports are in order and that you've got the visas required for Brazil. All the pertinent information you need is in the folders I gave you. Oh, and don't forget the yellow fever vaccinations."

"Yellow fever vaccinations?" Crissy said.

"You'll need those for Brazil," he said. "Anyway, you can get them from the county health department. The telephone number and that info is also enclosed in your packet."

"Thanks a lot, Melvin." Crissy rose to her feet. "It was nice to meet you."

"You, too," he said, getting up.

"Yeah, a real pleasure," Jenny said, her voice sardonic. She pushed herself up out of her chair. "Let's vamoose, Cris," she said. "This place is airless, and I'm about to suffocate."

"Bye." Crissy waved to Melvin as they went out the door. From behind his desk, Melvin returned her wave with a big smile.

"Oh, Jesus," Jenny said once they were outside the store. "I don't know how you could keep from laughing out loud at that jerk. He's so . . . pathetic."

"Oh, he's all right, Jen," she replied. "He's just different, you know. And probably sad and lonely."

"Yeah," Jenny said, "and probably some kind of fucking serial killer to boot."

"You're crazy," Crissy said with a helpless laugh.

Jenny grinned. "He does look like the type, you know? Weird outcast boy from next door. Probably watches the neighborhood girls with binoculars from behind his bedroom blinds. With one hand in his pants."

"Oh, hush!" Crissy cried. "I'm sure he's not like that at all." She laughed despite herself, then added: "You're so mean."

"I'm just honest," Jenny said. "I call a loser a loser, and that guy is a first-class loser." She paused and giggled. "And probably a psycho, too, because people like me have made fun of him all his life." Her laughter reverberated throughout the end of the mall where they were walking, and shoppers turned to stare.

Crissy rolled her eyes. "You're going to get us chased out of here," she said mirthfully.

"We're on our way out anyway," Jenny retorted. "Why don't I take you to lunch? What do you say?"

"Oh, I don't know," Crissy said. She didn't like taking advantage of Jenny's generosity too often, even though her friend could well afford it. Crissy liked to pull her share, and she didn't want Jenny to come to think of her as a mooch.

"Oh, come on," Jenny said. "I want to go to Provence for lunch. That place over in Stuyvesant Plaza. And I don't want to go by myself." She grabbed Crissy's arm. "Come on," she cajoled. "I hardly ever get to see you with your work schedule."

"Okay," Crissy finally agreed, "as long as we don't talk about Tom Gentry."

"I promise not to bring him up," Jenny swore.

"Good," Crissy said. "But then I really do have to get back to work and then home. I've got a lot to do."

"Like what?" Jenny asked as she pushed open the door to the parking lot.

"After work things like laundry and cleaning the apartment. Glamorous things like that," Crissy said.

"Good. I'll spare you of all that for awhile," Jenny said.

"Sometimes I don't mind it," Crissy said. "It's almost like therapy or something. Peaceful and soothing, you know?"

"That's because you're not getting laid enough," Jenny quipped.

"Jen." Crissy turned to look at her. "You think the whole world revolves around sex."

"It does, sweetheart," Jenny replied. "Believe me, it does."

After lunch Jenny pulled over in front of the beauty salon and braked the Jaguar with a lurch. "Ta-ta," Jenny said, throwing her hand up in a wave. "Talk to you later."

"Bye." Crissy waved as Jenny roared off, then turned and walked into the shop. Despite not discussing it during lunch, she still couldn't stop thinking of the night Tom had seduced her. She had thought he was so special.

I'm sick of being taken advantage of, she told herself. *I'm sick of being unhappy, of allowing other people to make me feel that way. And it's going to stop now.*

But no more tears, she thought. *It's time for action.*

Chapter Four

Georgios Vilos folded the *International Herald Tribune* and placed it to one side of the big mahogany desk. He received the paper with the English edition of *Kathimerini,* the Athenian newspaper, tucked inside. He was pleased to see that the *Sea Nymph*'s imminent departure from the port of Piraeus was duly noted and that not only was his name and the company's cited but that the ship's superb design, subtle luxury, and exceptional speed were mentioned. What an irony, he thought, that the crowning glory of his empire was one of the principal causes of its near collapse.

He swiveled around in his chair and looked out the floor-to-ceiling windows that overlooked the harbor in Piraeus. He and Fiona, along with Rosemary, his assistant, had flown down on the Gulfstream V. Now, in the near distance he could see the *Sea Nymph* docked at the recently cleaned-up piers that surrounded the harbor. She was a truly beautiful ship, he thought, sleek and modern, yet built along classical lines. He loathed the huge new ships that resembled floating buses, nor did he have a taste for the ugly, egg-shaped aerodynamic designs that so many shipbuilders had a penchant for lately.

Turning back to his desk, he eyed a small pile of paperwork with a malevolent glance. He was in no mood to attend to details at the moment. He felt a sense of unease that made him irritable. The meeting with the Lampaki brothers was coming up, and he'd still not been able to get hold of his son. He'd been trying to reach Mark all day, trying his office number and his cell phone, but to no avail. When he'd tried Fiona in Zákinthos, where she was overseeing the closing up of their Greek island house for the winter, she'd professed to know nothing of Mark's where-abouts.

"I doubt that he's anywhere in Greece," she'd said, "or I would have heard about it from one of my friends here. Besides, if Mark is anywhere in Greece, whether it's Kolonaki or on one of the islands, it would be re-ported in the press."

Her reference to the exclusive neighborhood in central Athens, Kolon-aki, brought a snort of derision from Georgios. Mark was sure to find rich layabouts like himself there.

"Why would he be here in November anyway?" Fiona had asked. "Nobody in his right mind will be here until after Easter, when it starts warming up."

"I thought it was a possibility," Georgios told her. "I haven't been able to reach him anywhere, and he's not responding to voice mail I leave on his cell phone."

Fiona scoffed. "What's new? You badger him to death. If I were Mark, I wouldn't answer my voice mail, either." She paused. "Why don't you try leaving him alone, Georgios? Have you ever considered that? Maybe then he would come to you."

Georgios Vilos wanted to slam his telephone shut, but he thought bet-ter of it. Fiona had her own malicious ways of retaliating for his every lit-tle slight, and she didn't hesitate to use them. "Maybe you're right," he said at last. "When will you be back?"

"I'm not sure," she said. "I'm thinking of going to Barbados with Dolly for some sun. I'll let you know."

"Okay," he said. "Talk to you later."

He flipped the cell phone shut, and sat staring glumly at the wall. "Bitch," he spat. His office door abruptly opened, and Georgios looked up with surprise. Rosemary always knocked before entering, but it wasn't his secretary.

"Hello, Dad," Mark said, stepping casually into the office, one hand in a trouser pocket, his strong, athletic body filling the door frame.

"I've been trying to reach you," Georgios said angrily, glaring at his tall, lean son, helplessly impressed as he always was by his son's darkly handsome appearance after not seeing him for awhile. "So your mother was wrong. You're here in Greece after all. I've left messages everywhere, and you didn't bother answering them."

Mark looked at him arrogantly. "I've been busy," he said.

51

"Doing what?" Georgios snapped. "I haven't been able to get you at your office here or in London."

Mark sat down in one of the leather chairs that faced his father's desk, crossing one long leg over the other, an expensive loafer-shod foot dangling just over a knee. He didn't respond immediately, taking pleasure in his father's anger and curiosity. *Let the old tyrant simmer,* he thought. He inspected his fingernails in a gesture that he knew would fuel his father's anger even further. Finally, he cleared his throat and gazed at Georgios with his dark brown eyes.

"Well?" his father said, leaning forward in his chair.

"If you must know, I've been busy with Marina," Mark said, stretching his long, muscular arms, then placing them on the chair's armrests. He flashed a brief smile that exposed perfect white teeth.

Georgios slowly sat back in his chair and sighed. "Women," he said. "At your age, you ought to be thinking about settling down."

"That's why I was seeing Marina," Mark retorted with an edge of sarcasm. "You wanted me to pursue her. You thought she was such a great match. You're the one who said she had everything going for her. Looks. Money. Family. You're the one—"

"All right," Georgios conceded. "Enough. Enough." It was true, he thought. He had urged Mark to see Marina Kavala. She was Constantine Kavala's only heir, and he was one of the richest men in Greece. "So what happened?" he asked.

"I just broke up with her," Mark said matter-of-factly. "It took some doing because she didn't want to end it."

"She's upset?"

"She'll get over it," Mark replied in an equally neutral voice.

"I hope you haven't done anything to upset her family," Georgios said. "We don't need—"

"Look," Mark said heatedly. "Marina Kavala's been putting out since she was thirteen. Half the men I know have had her. So if her family's upset, then they're crazy. This isn't anything that hasn't happened before."

"Okay, okay. Forget it," Georgios said, backing down. The conversation was not going in the direction he wanted it to, and he didn't want to antagonize his son now. He needed him too much. "I want you to do me a favor," he said, looking at Mark.

"I'm leaving for the States," Mark said truculently. "You know that. The *Sea Nymph* is getting ready to leave, and I'm going to be on it."

Georgios nodded. "I know that. In fact, it has to do with the *Sea Nymph*. You know that the German banks won't extend my loans."

"You can get the money somewhere else," Mark said. "You always do."

Georgios slowly shook his head. "I've been everywhere," he replied. "I'm even going to the Lampaki brothers."

"That's ridiculous," Mark snapped. "I don't believe you."

Georgios Vilos bent his head down, then looked back up and stared silently at his son with mournful eyes. Pain was etched into his features, and he looked close to tears. Mark didn't believe he'd ever seen his father appear this sad before. An air of defeat had replaced Georgios Vilos's normal warrior spirit, he thought.

"We're about to lose everything, son," Georgios finally muttered in a small voice. "Everything we've got. Vilos Shipping, Ltd. is on the brink of bankruptcy. If the Lampaki brothers don't come through, then"—he shrugged—"I don't know what will happen."

Mark returned his gaze, then looked away, embarrassed for his father. He knew that his father would never ask the notorious Lampaki brothers for anything unless he was truly in dire straits. He also knew that his father's admission of the extent of the dire straits the company was in took a monumental effort on his part.

"I need your help," Georgio said, his voice still barely above a whisper. "I need you to do something for me."

Mark looked back at his father. He swallowed, then cleared his throat. "I don't see what I can possibly do," he replied.

"You can help save the company," Georgios said, "if you do me a small favor."

Mark drew his chair nearer the desk to better hear his father's soft murmurs.

"What?" he asked.

Georgios motioned him closer with a hand, and Mark got out of the chair and leaned over the desk toward his father, looking at the old man with a curious expression. "We must keep this between ourselves," Georgios whispered. "No one, not another living soul, can know about this."

Mark nodded slightly.

His father motioned him still closer, then began whispering in his ear.

As Mark listened, he stiffened and started to protest, but he heard his father out and vowed to do his bidding.

Chapter Five

The flight to Athens, where they would board the ship, was long—
nearly ten hours—but she and Jenny laughed that they had managed to sleep and eat their way to Greece, for after dinner was
served by the flight attendants, they both fell into deep, refreshing sleep.
After breakfast, they immediately slept again. When the jet set down at
Eleftherios Venizelos Airport, they were still in a fog, half-awake but excited. Retrieving their luggage, they quickly got a taxi and set off for the
small hotel in the Plaka where they had reservations. After mere minutes
of washing faces, brushing teeth, applying fresh makeup, and changing
clothes, they set off for the Acropolis to see the Parthenon, guided by the
hotel manager's instructions.

The Plaka, with its multitude of restaurants and gift shops built on
marble lanes, delighted them. They were surprised to find the district busy
in the cool Athens weather, and they heard a dozen different languages.
After climbing the steep steps to the Parthenon and seeing the remarkable
testament to the architectural genius of the ancient Greeks, they toured
the small but exquisite museum. Outside, they walked the perimeter of the
Acropolis in awe of the cream-colored city spread out at their feet,
climbed the surrounding mountains, and ventured all the way to the sea
in Piraeus, where they would board the ship tomorrow. After being told
that Athens was dirty, congested, and generally unpleasant, Crissy was
surprised that she liked the cosmopolitan city. Perhaps today was rare, but
the air was clear and the sea sparkled in the distance.

After descending the mountain through the olive trees, they made their
way back to the Plaka, where they ate in an outdoor café, enjoying the

cool but sunny weather and the handsome, flirtatious waiter. Gales of laughter erupted, attracting the stares of nearby diners, when Jenny discovered "fresh cock" on the menu.

"I hope this is a sign of things to come," she said.

Helplessly amused, Crissy only shook her head.

Back at the small hotel, they discovered they were exhausted and napped, awakening more than two hours later. Crissy was disoriented at first in the dim light, but quickly remembered where she was. She tiptoed to the bathroom, where she showered and got ready to go out again. Jenny soon awakened and followed suit, while Crissy waited downstairs in the lounge, fascinated by the news on Greek TV. She could hardly follow any of it, but there was no mistaking the content of certain stories, since they were accompanied by video clips. She was shocked by the gruesome carnage of a car accident, something that would never be shown on American television. The hotel manager, Constantine, joined her, explaining some of the stories, most of them concerning the strikes, rallies, protests, or other gatherings that erupted on an almost daily basis in Athens.

Jenny appeared and sat down with them. Constantine glanced appreciatively at her expensive and revealing outfit, with its plunging neckline and miniskirt.

"Where are you young ladies going now?" he asked.

"I don't have a clue," Crissy replied. "Can you recommend a place for dinner?"

"It's very early for dinner here," Constantine said, glancing at his watch, "but you might enjoy the nightly parade in Kolonaki. A lot of wealthy Athenians live there or go there to see and be seen at the cafés, and you could have a coffee or drinks, then eat later. I think you would both enjoy it. It's a nightly ritual here, and if you're interested in meeting young men, the area will be thronged with them."

"Oh, sounds like just my kind of place, Cris," Jenny said.

Constantine and Crissy laughed. "The hormone level there is pretty high," he said.

After getting directions from Constantine, Crissy and Jenny walked to the exclusive neighborhood of Kolonaki. Unlike in the Plaka, there were no tourist shops, nor did there appear to be any foreigners like themselves. They passed shops with familiar merchandise that might have been sold on Manhattan's Madison or Fifth avenues: Gucci, Prada, Burberry,

DKNY. What made the elegant neighborhood distinctively different from Manhattan, however, were the dozens of sidewalk cafés that lined many of the blocks, one running into another and all of them crowded.

They found an empty table at one of the cafés and took a seat. After they ordered coffee and mineral water from a beautiful, harried young woman, they took in the incredible sights around them. Under umbrellas or canopies, people of all ages flocked around the tables, but Crissy noticed that as animated as their conversations appeared to be, few of them failed to take note of new arrivals or passersby, everyone checking out everyone else—male and female alike. Even the elderly participated, she saw, but most of the energy—and the air practically crackled with electricity—came from the hordes of young men and women who were dressed and groomed with great care specifically to be noticed here. They table-hopped, constantly consulted with friends on cell phones, drank copious amounts of coffee, mineral water, beer, or liquor, and openly flirted.

"I've never seen anything like this in my life," she said to Jenny.

"It's like one huge singles bar," Jenny replied, "only they let in old people and children, too."

Crissy laughed. "I think that's really nice."

"Yeah, it's okay," Jenny agreed. "I just can't believe all the outrageous flirting right out in the open in front of the old folks and kids."

"Well, the old folks made the young ones, Jen," Crissy said, "and I'm sure some of them are still probably doing it."

"In the age of Viagra," Jenny replied, "you can bet your life on it. Probably half the old geezers sitting around with their coffees are nursing big hard-ons under the tables."

"I should've known you would turn this into something like that," Crissy said.

"Like what?" Jenny asked. "I'm just being realistic, honey. I tell it—" She abruptly quit talking, her eyes trailing an attractive man who'd passed close by their table and kept turning back to stare.

Crissy smiled. "I think you've caught somebody's attention."

Jenny drew her gaze in with a smirk. "Look again," she said. "He's not looking at me. He's looking at you."

Crissy felt herself blush slightly. She wanted to see if what Jenny said was true, but she was too embarrassed to look.

Jenny studied her for a moment, then reached over and put a hand on

Crissy's. "For God's sake, Cris, give the guy the eye," she practically growled. "He's a real hottie. I mean drop-dead hunk."

Crissy reddened again, but she finally turned her head slightly to look, and her gaze was met by a very handsome man. Thirty to thirty-five, she thought. Meticulously groomed and dressed. Tall and well-built. Jet-black hair swept back away from his face. Olive-complected. Perfect white teeth on display because he was smiling at her. She felt a frisson of excitement when she realized that, indeed, his open and genial smile was directed toward her.

"Smile back, stupid," Jenny said in a whisper, kicking Crissy under the table.

But Crissy paid no attention to her, for she had already returned his smile and was watching, mesmerized, as he approached their table. "Oh, God," she said, turning to Jenny. "Now what?"

"Relax," Jenny said. "Remember, we may be in Greece, but he's a man. A horny man. On the make."

He reached their table and looked down at Crissy, his dark eyes full of mischief, then glanced at Jenny. "My name is Adonis," he said, putting out a hand for Crissy to shake. She took the proffered hand, thrilled at the warmth it transmitted.

"Get out of here," Jenny said. "That can't really be your name."

He looked at her with a serious expression. "Yes," he replied. "It is. In fact, you will find that in Greece it is not an uncommon name."

"It's a wonderful name," Crissy said.

"Thank you," he replied. "May I ask yours?"

"Crissy Fitzgerald," she said.

"It's a pleasure to meet you. Is this your first time in Athens?"

"Yes," Crissy said. "We're going on a cruise that leaves from here."

"And I'm Jen," Jenny interrupted, holding her hand out for a shake.

Adonis took her hand in his and shook it gently. "It's a pleasure to meet you, too," he said. He turned his attention back to Crissy. "I hope you will be spending some time with us in Athens."

"I wish we could," Crissy said, "but we are leaving tomorrow from Piraeus."

He nodded. "A pity. I would have loved to show you our city." He paused, then added, "But perhaps I can take you both to dinner. What do you say?"

"Why not?" Jenny said before Crissy had a chance to respond.

"Wonderful," he said. "Don't you agree, Crissy?" he asked, studying her face closely.

"I . . . I guess so," she said, unsure that it was a wise idea.

"You don't seem certain," he said with a smile.

"Well, we did just meet," she said.

"I have lots of friends here tonight, and if you like, I can get them to vouch for me." He smiled again. "They will all tell you the same thing: That I am very dependable, a man of honor, in fact, and that you will come to no harm with me."

Jenny laughed. "Plants, I bet," she offered. "All of them, working in cahoots with you. You're really a serial killer."

Crissy looked at her with astonishment. "Jen—" she began.

Jenny flapped a hand. "Just kidding," she said. "Jeez, don't you recognize a joke?"

"Do you mind if I join you?" Adonis asked. "That way we can get to know each other better, and perhaps that will put your mind at ease."

"Sure," Crissy said, without looking at Jenny for confirmation.

He pulled out one of the white canvas director's chairs and sat down. "I see you have coffees and mineral water. Would you like something to eat? Or would you like to go elsewhere for a drink?"

"You said the magic word," Jenny said. "I could sure use a drink."

They chatted for awhile at the table, the conversation centering around Greece in general and Athens in particular, their jobs—he was a lawyer—and the States.

"I've been to New York several times," he said, "and to Miami a couple of times. I love them both. The energy."

Finally, Adonis signaled the waitress and paid their bill, and they rose from the table. "We can eat here in the neighborhood if you like," he said, "or we can take my car to someplace more adventurous. Do you like Italian food? French? Greek?"

"I'll try anything," Crissy said. "Whatever you think."

"Ditto," Jenny said, "as long as it's not too spooky."

"Spooky?" he said, looking at her without comprehension.

"You know. Weird. Like octopus or bugs or something."

He laughed. "I don't think that will be a problem," he said. "Shall we go?"

He held his arms out, one for each of them to take. "My car is nearby, and we'll go to the restaurant in it. It's not far."

A few blocks away, they reached the car, a black Mercedes sports model with a convertible top, and set off for the restaurant. His driving, like that of most Athenians, was fast and reckless, with little regard for lights or pedestrians. Crissy held her breath, and in the backseat, Jenny laughed. Soon he slowed down and began looking for a parking place. When one didn't materialize after a few minutes, he adroitly maneuvered the car up onto the sidewalk at a corner.

"You surely can't park here?" Crissy said.

He smiled. "I am, aren't I?"

"But won't you be towed or something?"

He shrugged. "Noooo. This is Athens."

They got out of the car, and Adonis led them up the sidewalk. "This is called Psirri," he said. "It is a very old Athens neighborhood that has become something like New York City's Tribeca. There are lots of old houses and what used to be old warehouses and offices, but everything is being converted to cafés and galleries and shops. Also, living lofts, like you have in New York."

"I see what you mean," Jenny said. "It reminds me of Tribeca or SoHo."

"But it has a long way to go," Adonis said.

Up the block, he led them into a restaurant. Inside a derelict-looking building was the epitome of ultramodern minimalist decor, with a long, shallow pool running down its center. Greeted by a very chic young woman, they were immediately seated and placed drinks orders while they perused the menus.

"It's still early for dinner," he said. "It's only nine o'clock. Around eleven or twelve o'clock, it will be packed."

"How in the world do people get to work?" Crissy asked.

"We don't sleep much." He grinned. "Actually, a lot of us still have siestas like the Spanish after lunch, then reopen our offices or businesses in the late afternoon and stay open late. It depends on the business, of course, but a lot of Athenians live that way."

"I think I could deal with that," Jenny said.

The waitress brought their drinks, and Adonis ordered for them all. "I hope you don't mind," he said.

"Not at all," Crissy said, not having a clue what the menu offered, since it was in Greek.

"This is old-fashioned Greek cooking with a very modern twist," Adonis said when their food arrived, "but it is very good, I think."

59

He asked them questions about the trip they were going to be taking, and they talked about Greek food while they ate. Crissy thought it was one of the best meals she'd ever had. An artfully arranged Greek salad of feta, Santorini tomatoes, cucumber, onion, and peppers was followed by a delicious grilled sole. It was accompanied by a tatziki-topped bread that melted in her mouth. For dessert, they each had a thin slice of honeyed chocolate-walnut cake with homemade pistachio ice cream. They washed it down with an excellent Santorini wine.

"Now," Adonis said as he signed the credit card slip for the waitress, "would you like to go to a dance club?"

"We have to get up early to get to the ship," Crissy said, "and I—"

"Oh, come on," Jenny broke in, "what's a few hours of missed sleep? We've got nearly a month to relax on the ship."

Adonis looked at Crissy to see her response.

"I'd love to," she said, "but I'm really exhausted." She was suddenly aware of her body's demand for recuperating sleep, and while she enjoyed Adonis' company and appreciated his interest in her, she didn't feel that there was a special chemistry between them, not the kind that would carry her through a night of dancing with a big day on the horizon.

"Crissy!" Jenny cried. "Think about it. This is the only night we have in Athens, and you may never come back again."

"Oh, I don't think that's remotely possible," Adonis said. "I definitely think she'll be back."

"Well . . . I don't know. . . ." Crissy hesitated.

"We certainly don't want to go unless you do," Adonis said, "but I think you would enjoy it. Most visitors never get to see a place like this."

She saw that he was serious, and she hated to disappoint either Adonis or Jenny. Finally she nodded. "Okay," she said, "but let's not stay too late."

After a nerve-racking race through city streets, they arrived at a dance club overlooking the Saronic Gulf. It was a multilevel, expensively decorated place with a crowd of twenty- to fifty-somethings that looked exceedingly attractive and well-heeled, danced wildly, and drank a lot. Adonis was greeted by many of the crowd, and he introduced Crissy and Jenny to everyone. Crissy was surprised to discover that nearly everyone spoke excellent English. They drank champagne and danced for a long time. Crissy, however, enjoyed breaks on the balconies that overlooked the sea. Although it was dark, the lights of tankers, ships, and various-size yachts winked at her from the distance, and the salty tang in the air was refreshing after the smoke and noise of the club.

"Are you enjoying yourself?" Adonis asked.

"Oh, yes," she said. "It was awfully nice of you to ask us out. I really appreciate it."

"It's been my pleasure," he replied, "and I'm glad you've liked it." He edged closer to her and put an arm across her shoulders. "I wish you weren't leaving tomorrow."

Crissy was slightly unnerved by his proximity, and she didn't know how to respond. "I . . . well . . . we have to," she finally said. "We've been planning this for a long time."

He gently hugged her with his arm. "I know," he said, "but it's too bad. I think we could have a very good time together."

Crissy could swear that her heart was beating faster. She wasn't prepared for his attraction to her, and wasn't sure what to make of it. "I've recently had a bad . . . experience," she said. She thought that she might as well level with him. "And I'm not sure I'm ready for . . . for seeing anyone."

"I'm sorry," Adonis said. "For you and for me."

"I guess I have a problem with trust," she said with a sigh.

"Perhaps I can overcome that."

She shook her head. "I'm the only person who can do that," Crissy said. "You've been wonderful, Adonis, but I just can't handle anything . . . anybody . . . right now."

"I won't push it."

"Thank you," she said. "I think we'd better get going soon."

"Okay," he replied. "That is, if I can find your friend. She seems to have danced with every man in the club tonight."

They both laughed. "That's Jenny," Crissy said. "She'll probably leave a trail of broken hearts."

He looked at her with a serious expression. "It is you who will leave a broken heart," he said, "and it is you who is the more beautiful and beguiling."

Crissy felt that frisson of excitement that she'd experienced when she'd first exchanged glances with him. She didn't know whether to believe him or not, but she couldn't deny that she loved hearing what he said. "I don't know about that," she said lightly, "but Jenny's the one who always gets the men, not me."

"Then American men are stupid."

"Maybe, but this American has got to get some sleep."

Finding Jenny did not pose a problem, for she was in the middle of the dance floor with a circle gathered around her, clapping and shouting as she and her partner performed an obscene bump and grind with each other. Her heels, held aloft on a finger by their sling-backs, were twirling in the air, and she was alternately thrusting her pelvis, then her breasts at him as he met her with thrusts of his own.

Adonis smiled, and Crissy laughed. "See what I mean?" she said.

"She's a little wild, isn't she?" he replied.

"Still man-crazy at thirty," Crissy said.

"I don't know," he said. "I don't think she really likes men much. She seems contemptuous of men to me."

Crissy eyed him curiously. That was an astute observation. "I hadn't thought about that."

The dance came to an end, and the crowd applauded wildly. Jenny and her partner hugged and kissed. Adonis took Crissy's hand and led her through the dispersing observers to Jenny.

"Brava," Adonis said. "You've put on a great show, but now it's time to leave."

"Already?" Jenny cried. "It seems like we just got here." She bent down and slipped her heels back on, then straightened up.

Her dance partner put an arm around her shoulders. "I can take her home," he said. "I'm Mike, by the way."

Adonis and Crissy nodded. "Hi," Adonis said, introducing Crissy and himself. "The ladies are leaving on a ship in a few hours, so I think we'd better get going."

Jenny looked at Crissy, who mouthed "please." "I guess you're right," she said, then turned to Mike. "It's been a blast," she said, "but I really better run."

"Ah, no," he said. "I can take you back." He looked at his watch. "It's only four. Stay another hour or two, then we'll go."

"Sorry," Jenny said, making a little wave with a hand. "Got to run." She gave him a kiss on the cheek. "But I loved meeting you and had a great time."

They went to the club entrance with Mike on their heels, trying to persuade Jenny to stay, but she was emphatic. After speeding back to the hotel, Adonis walked them to the door. Jenny went in after thanking Adonis and winking at Crissy.

"I'll be right there," Crissy said. She thanked Adonis. "You've been really wonderful," she said, "and I appreciate it so much."

"Here," he said, "take this." He handed her an engraved business card. "It has all of my numbers on it. Please call me anytime."

Crissy took a card out of her wallet and handed it to him. "Likewise," she said, "but I won't be there for a month."

He took the card and tucked it in his trousers, then put his arms around her and hugged her to him. "I've loved meeting you," he said. "You're one of the most beautiful women I've ever met." His lips brushed her hair.

"Thank you, Adonis," she said nervously, "but I'd really better get in."

Reluctantly, he released her and opened the hotel door for her. She went inside, then waved good-bye.

Adonis stood watching her as she walked the short distance across the lobby. When she reached the corner, she waved again. He blew a kiss to her but didn't move.

When Crissy reached the room, Jenny had already slipped into a nightie and under the covers. "We didn't bring an alarm clock," she said.

"I told the desk that we needed a wake-up call before we left," Crissy replied. "At nine o'clock."

"Oh, jeez," Jenny groaned, covering her head with the blanket.

Crissy got ready for bed quickly. After she turned out the light, she lay in bed, her mind whirling with the events of the day. *It's only been a few hours into the trip,* she thought, *and it seems as if magic has already happened. I met a man who called me beautiful. Beguiling. Others stared at me with obvious admiration.*

I hope, she thought sleepily, *tonight is a harbinger of things to come.*

Chapter Six

When they arrived in Piraeus, the taxi let them out in front of a vast ship terminal. Jenny had almost fallen asleep in the cab, but Crissy was so excited by the prospect of boarding the ship that she was wide awake. The terminal was lackluster, but once they had gone through security, she caught her first glimpse of the ship. Although she'd seen pictures of it, they hadn't prepared her for the reality of the *Sea Nymph*.

"Oh, Jenny," she said enthusiastically, "it looks so much like a yacht."

Jenny looked at her with a dull expression. "Well, Cris. That's what it is. A ship."

"I know, but what I mean is, it doesn't look like one of those buses they're building with umpteen decks. It looks like a giant yacht."

"I guess so," Jenny said. Crissy could tell that she was hung over, exhausted, and really didn't care what the ship looked like.

They were early, and only a handful of passengers were boarding. After getting their pictures taken at one of the security checkpoints, they were given key cards to their room. As they walked down the hall, Crissy glanced about, taking in the beautiful wood paneling and the soft palette of colors used in the upholstery and carpeting. The furnishings were very tasteful, she thought, and surprisingly nothing seemed to be plastic or fiberglass. They reached the elevators and took one to the next deck. They went down a corridor, noticing that all the rooms were named. When they found theirs, Crissy saw that it was Mykonos, an island in the Cyclades she'd read about. She swiped the card, and they went in.

"Oh, my God, it's really nice," Jenny said.

"It's beautiful," Crissy said. They stood in a small entry with a large closet on one side and the bathroom on the other. Immediately in front of them was a small sitting area with a built-in couch, chairs, and a table. On it was a basket of fruit and a bottle of wine. Straight ahead was a large picture window. There were twin beds with built-in bedside cabinets, many built-in drawers, and a mini-fridge. A long desk area against one long mirrored wall held a television set. As in the public areas they'd seen, the color scheme was predominantly sea green and blue, and there was beautiful wood paneling. Crissy gravitated to the window and looked out at the view of the harbor.

Jenny plopped down on one of the beds and curled up. "Oh, this feels so good," she said.

Crissy turned to her. "Do you want to look around the ship?" she asked.

"Are you kidding me?" Jenny replied. "I want to be right where I am for awhile." She rose on her elbows. "But first I'm going to check out the minibar, see what's to drink."

"How can you have anything to drink now?" Crissy asked.

"It's the best cure for a hangover," Jenny replied with a laugh.

Crissy smiled. "Maybe you're right," she said. She opened the mini-fridge and looked in. "There's a split of champagne, white wine, sodas, mineral water, juice."

"Champagne," Jenny said. "Let's celebrate. Just the two of us."

Crissy took the champagne out and started to open it. There was a knock at the door, and she looked at Jenny questioningly and then went to open it. A porter had their luggage, which he deposited in the entryway. "Thanks so much," Crissy said, handing him a tip that she had readied in advance.

When he was gone, she opened the champagne. The cork flew off and bounced against the mirrored wall before falling to the floor. They both laughed merrily. She poured two glasses of the bubbly and handed one to Jenny. "To new beginnings," she said.

"New beginnings," Jenny echoed, swallowing a large gulp. "Oh, I think I feel better already." She took another sip. "Did you get a look at some of the hotties in uniform?" she asked.

Crissy blurted laughter. "I did, but I didn't know you'd seen anything. You looked half-asleep."

Jenny shook her head slowly. "I may've looked that way, but let me tell you, I saw some real hunks."

"I should've known," Crissy said. She began glancing through the packet of materials that were on the desk.

"Do you miss your boyfriend from last night?" Jenny asked.

"Hmmm," Crissy replied, "I . . . don't know. It seems so unreal now. Almost like it never happened."

"Well, honey," Jenny said, "it happened. Believe me. And he's missing you. I can tell you that for sure."

"Do you really think so?"

Jenny nodded. "Are you crazy? I know so. He really had the hots for you."

Crissy shrugged. "It was great, and I have to tell you that I loved being . . . noticed. But I think he was just . . . maybe . . . a little—"

"Horny," Jenny said. "He was horny, Cris. For you."

"If you say so," Crissy said. "Whatever it was, it was nice for a change. Anyway, you want to check out the ship with me? This is a small ship, but it has everything: A spa, gym, theater, disco, pool, library, casino, everything. I think I'll take a stroll around and see what it's like."

"Yeah," Jenny said, seemingly revived by the champagne. "We can check out some of those uniforms, too."

"That too," Crissy said, taking the last sip of her champagne.

The door to their cabin suddenly opened, and a young woman burst in, saw them, and smiled widely. "Hi, welcome. I'm sorry to bother you. My name is Iskra, and I'll be your steward." Her voice was heavily accented. "I didn't realize you'd boarded, and was just going to check and see that everything here is ready."

"I think it is," Jenny said.

"We're leaving anyway," Crissy said, getting up and retrieving her shoulder bag. Jenny pushed herself up off the bed and slipped into her shoes, then got her bag.

"Have a nice time," Iskra said from the bathroom, which she was stocking with soap and shampoo.

"Thanks," Crissy said, "we'll see you later." She took a map of the ship out of a folder on the desk before leaving the cabin.

In the hallway, she looked at the map. "This is going to take some getting used to," she said, "until I get my bearings."

"Oh, let's just follow our noses," Jenny said, already walking toward the elevator and stairwell.

Crissy followed her, still taking in the map. "We're on Deck Four," she said. "The Venus Deck."

"I like the sound of that," Jenny said, pushing an elevator button.

"Why don't we take the stairs?" Crissy said.

"Oh, okay," Jenny said with the slightest grumble.

On Deck Five, they saw another large reception area with an information desk, a shore excursion desk, and, after passing through corridors with staterooms, a large formal dining room with a view out to sea on three sides. They greeted a number of boarding passengers and crew who were hurriedly readying the ship for departure. From the dining room, they discovered another stairwell, this one much bigger than the one near their stateroom.

"Oh, look," Crissy said, pointing. Up and down the stairwell's length, huge glass panels were etched with poetry, on one side in Greek, on the other in English. "Isn't that beautiful?"

"Neat," Jenny said.

They climbed to Deck Six and passed through a piano bar and card room, then peeked in the library. Aside from the small selection of books in various languages, they discovered a letter-size newspaper of four pages spread out on a table. There were copies in English, French, German, and Dutch. Crissy picked up the English one, and glancing at it saw that it offered news highlights. There were several computers with Internet capability, and they saw that you had to purchase a card to use them.

"Want to email somebody?" Jenny asked.

"No," Crissy said. "I can't think who it would be."

"Me either," Jenny said.

Back out in the main passageway, they eyed the windows in the three small duty-free shops. The largest one sold liquor, cosmetics, tobacco, candies, and a small selection of jewelry. The two smaller ones offered souvenirs of the ship, bathing suits, sun hats, scarves, and a selection of formal wear. A small casino was farther down the passage.

"Oh, this looks like fun," Jenny said, seeing the gaming tables and slot machines. "They've got a lot of the latest slots."

A young man smiled when he saw them. "Hello. We won't be ready until we're at sea, but I hope you'll come back." He spoke with a British accent.

"Oh, I'm sure we will," Jenny said.

"Good," he replied. "I look forward to it."

On they walked, past a smoking room that looked as if it were a room in a men's club, then they reached the large theater, the Hercules Lounge. It was decorated in a vibrant red—walls, plush seats, carpeting—and had a small stage and dance floor. "This is one of those 'see Broadway stars of tomorrow' places," Jenny said.

"You never know," Crissy said.

Walking forward, they finally reached a huge dining room situated near the bow of the ship. It was cafeteria-style, less formal than the other one, but looked out to sea on three sides also. They went through sliding glass doors out onto the deck, where they saw other passengers congregating. A large open-air bar was serving drinks, coffee, and soda, and tables were set up in the sunshine.

At the bar Jenny ordered a glass of white wine, and Crissy decided to have a Coke Lite, as she discovered Diet Coke was called in Athens and on the ship.

They took their drinks to a table and sat down in the sun. It was a cool day and slightly windy, but the sun shone brightly. "I love the smell of the sea," Crissy said, "don't you?"

"What? Fish? Salt? It stinks to me," Jenny replied.

Crissy laughed. "I guess you're right, and I romanticize it. But I really do love the way it smells. It's . . . bracing."

"Oh, my God," Jenny replied. "Don't look now, but catch a gander of that stud coming down the stairs to your left."

Crissy spotted him out of the corner of her eye. He was indeed extraordinarily handsome, in his thirties, tall and well-built, with black hair, dark eyes, sensuous lips, and an aquiline nose. He wore a navy blazer, tan trousers, deck shoes, and a predominantly red scarf tied about his neck. He carried himself with a regal, superior air, she thought, and he didn't seem to notice them. He was, she decided, the best-looking man she'd ever seen.

"Oh, I think I'm going to drool," Jenny said.

"Well, he certainly doesn't seem to feel the same way," Crissy replied.

"I wonder who he is?" Jenny said. "He's not in uniform, so he must be a passenger."

He strolled to the bar and placed an order, then turned their way. Crissy averted her gaze, but Jenny kept her baby blues focused on him. When she kicked Crissy under the table, Crissy looked at her. "What?" she asked.

Jenny was smiling widely, but not at her. Crissy looked in the direction of Jenny's gaze and saw that the young man was smiling at her. When the barman brought his order—a coffee—he walked directly to their table. "Mind if I join you?" he asked.

"Oh, no," Jenny replied. "Have a seat."

"Thank you," he said. "I'm Mark." He had the merest hint of an accent that Crissy found alluring.

Crissy and Jenny introduced themselves.

"How do you like the ship?" he asked.

"It's wonderful," Crissy offered.

"Yes," Jenny agreed, "and gets better all the time." She looked at him flirtatiously.

Mark smiled. "I'm glad you like it. There are very few Americans aboard. It's mostly a crowd of Dutch, Germans, and French, with a few Brits, Canadians, and Italians."

"I wonder why?" Crissy said.

He shrugged. "Who knows? Maybe because the trip begins in Athens. Maybe because Americans are leery of foreign travel. I don't really know, but we won't pick up most passengers until we arrive in Nice. There will only be a little more than a hundred of us until then."

"On this whole ship?" Jenny asked.

He nodded.

"How strange," Crissy said.

"Not really," he said. "It shaves a week off the travel time, so it's less expensive and time-consuming. Plus, it's easier for a lot of the older people to get to Nice than Athens."

"I don't know how some of them get across the street," Jenny said unkindly.

He laughed. "I know what you mean. There will be wheelchairs and canes, and if we have rough seas, lots of bruises and cuts."

"You seem to know a lot about the trip," Jenny said. "How's that?"

He shrugged again. "I have my ways."

"Oh, come on," Jenny said, but they were interrupted by another, equally handsome man in a snowy white uniform with black and gold epaulets, various medals, and a small name tag above one breast pocket that read CAPT. DEMETRIOS PAPADAPOLIS.

"Pardon me for breaking in," he said with a smile, "but I wanted to welcome you aboard the *Sea Nymph*. I hope you will have a pleasant journey."

Crissy and Jenny thanked him, but Mark nodded, then stared straight ahead, avoiding the captain's gaze.

"If you need anything," Captain Papadapolis added, "let me or one of the officers know. I'll be off, but hope I get to see you again."

"Thanks," Crissy said. She watched him enter the dining room through a sliding glass door. Turning her attention back to the table, she said, "Isn't he charming?"

"Yes," Jenny said. "A real smoothie."

Mark ignored them, still staring out toward the harbor. "I must go," he said abruptly, getting to his feet. "Perhaps we will meet again."

"Leaving?" Jenny said. "Already? But—"

He looked down at Crissy. "It was a pleasure."

Crissy was momentarily nonplussed. What an oddball, she thought, but an extraordinarily sexy oddball. "Yes," she said, "it was. I hope we see you later."

He walked back to the stairs and went up them without a backward glance, his posture rigidly straight.

"What a snotty bastard," Jenny said with a malevolent expression.

"He sure was mysterious," Crissy commented.

"Let's see what's up there on the next deck where he went," Jenny said.

Crissy looked at her map. "That's the Dionysus Deck," she said. "Deck Seven. And according to this there's the pool and pool bar and pizzeria, the spa and beauty salon, gym, and a disco. Plus, the biggest suites."

"Ohhh," Jenny said, "let's go."

After touring Deck Seven, they stood at the deck railing, looking below to the outdoor area where they'd had their drinks. More and more people were gathering there, nearly filling up tables that overlooked the docks and Piraeus. Turning around, Crissy looked up at the enormous funnel that contained the ship's smokestacks. It was truly an awesome ship, she thought. She turned back to Jenny. "I've got my digital camera," she said. "Let me get some pictures of you."

"Okay," Jenny readily agreed. She loved having her picture taken no matter the occasion.

"See those decks that run along below the funnels?" Crissy said. "Let's start over there."

They went past the pool and bar, through heavy doors, and out onto a long side deck above which the funnel rose into the air with majestic grace. Metal stairs led up to a walkway around the bottom of it.

"Why don't you go up the stairs," Crissy said, "and I'll get you from down here. Maybe I can get the shipping line's logo in." It was a highly stylized blue trident that stood out on the snowy white funnel.

Jenny climbed the metal steps and stopped when she reached the top. Peering down at Crissy, she waved wildly. Crissy snapped several pictures, then called up to her, "Why don't you change positions? Look out to sea or something."

Jenny was game, and posed with a hand over her brow, looking out at the harbor as if she were searching for something on the horizon. Crissy snapped a couple of pictures, then began backing up on the deck to take some from another angle. She didn't see the person who'd come out onto the deck and was directly in her path.

"Ah! So sorry," a man said.

Crissy straightened up instantly. "No, it's my fault," she said. "I'm so sorry."

A uniformed ship's officer smiled. "I saw you," he said, "but then I looked up at your friend and didn't realize you were moving."

Jenny saw them talking from her perch on the stairs and quickly descended. "Hi," she said to the young man.

He tipped his cap. "Hello. I apologize for interrupting your photo session," he said. "I nearly knocked your friend here down."

"I'm Jenny," she said.

"And I'm Crissy."

"I'm Manolo," he said. "It's nice to meet you."

"Are you a ship officer?" Jenny inquired.

"Yes," he said.

"You must love working on the *Sea Nymph*," Crissy said. "It's such a beautiful ship."

"Yes, it is," he agreed. "It's also the fastest ship in the world."

"You're kidding," Jenny said. "It's so small compared to most of them nowadays."

"Yes, we're only 25,000 tons and 590 feet long, but fast. We cruise at 28 knots. The *Queen Elizabeth II* and a few others can go that fast, but they can't maintain that speed like we can. That's why we can get between ports and back and forth across the Atlantic so fast."

"How many passengers are there?" Crissy asked.

"The ship has a capacity of 836, if all the doubles are occupied with two people. Plus there are 360 crew. So, you see, we are minuscule compared to most ships being built today."

"That's one of the things I like about it," Crissy said.

"It's a lot more intimate, isn't it?" Jenny said, smiling at Manolo.

"Oh, yes," he said. Then he added, his eyes on Jenny, "Much more intimate."

"It was nice to meet you," Crissy said, seeing that the two of them had made a connection and deciding to let them pursue it without her hampering them. "It looks like the pool bar is open now, and I think I'll go get some water." She looked at Jenny. "I'll meet you there or see you in the cabin later."

Jenny sketched a little wave in the air. "Bye," she said.

Crissy went through the heavy doors back to the pool area. Through its windows, she could see Jenny and Manolo talking. She got a mineral water from the bar, then returned to the railing and looked down at the deck below. The crowd was dressed casually, but she spied one of the most extraordinary-looking women she'd ever seen coming through the sliding doors that led onto the deck. It was her hair that first caught her eye. It was a wild but carefully contrived silver mass that seemed to have been teased straight up, though as she focused she saw that it was not precisely straight up, there was the slightest curl in the obviously dyed silver. Her makeup created a virtual Kabuki mask. Drawn arched brows, heavy mascara lines above and below her eyes, the one beneath in a straight line that made no pretense of following the natural curve of her eye. *Is she trying to look like Cleopatra?* Crissy asked herself. Heavy purple shadowed her eyes, and bloodred lipstick slashed across her lips. Her powder or blush was the palest ivory and the contrast was shocking. When Crissy finally tore her gaze away from the woman's exotic hair and makeup, she looked at her clothes. She smiled helplessly at the sight. A glittery top with silvery sequins was worn over a knee-length skirt of glittery silver palettes. Her high heels were sandals of gold and silver, and she carried an enormous handbag of gold leather. Her walk across the deck was almost a mince of very short steps, her head held high, the slightest smile always on her lips. She was of an indeterminate age, surely past forty but not yet sixty.

Crissy saw her nod to several people as she made her way to a table where a fortyish couple seemed to await her arrival. They rose, and the three exchanged kisses in the continental manner, brushing both cheeks, then sat. The younger woman was dressed in a laser-cut white pantsuit, and she was striking, nearly beautiful, with her hair pulled back into a chignon into which she had stuck chopsticks. Her husband—or the man accompanying her—was handsome at first glance, with a dark trimmed mustache and small goatee. As Crissy looked closer, she could see that he was well put together, as was his wife, but there was something almost feral about him that the neat trimming didn't conceal.

She turned back to where she'd left Jenny with Manolo, but they had disappeared. She couldn't help but smile. Jenny, she thought, *would* find someone within the first hour on the ship—before they had even set sail. Turning her attention back to the deck below, she decided to descend the staircase and mingle. She headed for the silver-haired woman and the younger couple.

As she had on the upper deck, she stared out at the harbor and sipped her water before glancing about at her fellow passengers chatting around the crowded tables. The woman with the chopsticks in her hair smiled at Crissy. "Would you like to join us?" she asked in accented English. "We have one of the few vacant chairs."

"Oh, thank you," Crissy said, "but I wouldn't want to impose."

"It's no imposition," the woman's husband said. He stood and drew back the empty chair for Crissy.

"How nice of you," Crissy said as she sat down. "I've been on my feet for a long time after being up nearly all night."

"My name is Mina," the woman said, extending a hand. Crissy took it in hers, and they shook. "This is Monika Graf." She indicated the silver-haired woman, and the woman nodded from across the table, her smile unchanged. "And this is Rudolph, my husband." He took Crissy's hand in his, brought his lips toward it, and made as if to kiss it.

"I'm Crissy Fitzgerald," she said to the table.

"Ah, you are American," Mina said.

"Yes," Crissy said with a nod.

"Where are you from in America?" Monika Graf asked in good but accented English.

"New York," Crissy said, hoping they wouldn't question her further. She would like for them to think that she was from the city, rather than the provincial, unknown upstate area that she actually called home.

"Oh," Monika Graf said, her eyes bright with interest. "New York City?"

Crissy couldn't lie. "No," she replied. "I'm from Albany, the capital of New York. It's about three hours north."

Monika Graf's eyes immediately dulled, and she looked away. Up close, Crissy could see that the woman wasn't as old as she'd first thought. She could see the dark roots that were beginning to appear beneath her silver Medusa do, and the perfect skin that lay beneath the heavily applied makeup. Her hands, a telltale indicator of age, were visible, but just barely because of the number of bangle bracelets and rings with big jewels she wore. She was probably in her mid-forties, not more than fifty.

"Where are you from?" Crissy asked.

"We're from Austria," Mina replied. "From Graz." She tinkled laughter. "Where your movie star Arnold Schwarzenegger is from."

"I'm from Vienna," Monika Graf said, turning her attention back to Crissy. It was almost as if she wanted to make certain that Crissy was aware that she wasn't from a provincial backwater but from the operetta set of Vienna, the glorious former seat of the Hapsburgs and the Holy Roman Empire.

"All of you speak such good English," Crissy said.

"We take English from the time we start school," Rudolph replied.

"Yes," Monika Graf added. "It's not like in America where hardly anyone seems to speak a second or third language. Most of us speak a bit of several. I speak seven languages quite adequately."

"Seven," Crissy said, impressed.

"You have to remember that we live in close proximity to the people who speak those languages," Mina said diplomatically. "The Germans, the French, the Italians, and so on."

"That does make a difference," Crissy said.

"Yes," Mina said. She turned her attention to her husband. "Rudy, darling, I'd best get back to the cabin. I have to take a bath and a nap, I'm afraid." She looked at Crissy. "We were up all night dancing," she said, "at this completely wild place in Athens. So we haven't had any sleep, and I want to be fresh for dinner and dancing tonight."

"It was very nice to meet you," Crissy said, "and I hope to see you again."

"I'm sure we will," Rudy said, getting to his feet. "Surely at the disco tonight."

Crissy smiled. "I'll be there."

They left, and Crissy looked across the table at Monika Graf. The woman's perpetual smile was in place, but she focused on Crissy as she had not before. "They are a lovely couple, aren't they?"

"Yes," Crissy said. "They seem to be."

"It's too bad they have that terrible guttural accent like your Mr. Schwarzenegger. So provincial."

"I didn't know," Crissy said.

"Oh, yes," Monika Graf said, warming to the subject. "It's quite embarrassing, really. Certainly in Austria." Her beautiful violet eyes twinkled with mischief. "I adore them, of course, but we can't help but laugh about it, you know."

"We have accents we laugh about in America, too," Crissy replied.

The woman nodded vigorously. "Oh, I know," she said. "I've been to the States many times. New York, Los Angeles, Las Vegas, Miami. So I know a little of your country—the more glamorous places, anyway."

"Yes," Crissy said. "I guess they would be the more glamorous." She noticed that the woman was sipping a glass of champagne and supposed that together with her hair, makeup, and clothes, glamour was one of her principal interests.

"Have you been on a cruise before?"

"Only once," Crissy said, "but it was nothing like this. I just went on a weeklong cruise from New York to the Caribbean."

Monika Graf nodded. "On one of those big new boats?"

"Yes," Crissy said.

"I love those," she replied. "So much more glamorous than this boat. So *big* and shiny, with enormous casinos and lots of shops."

Crissy didn't want to tell her that she much preferred this ship. "The trip wasn't very interesting, though," she said. "We hardly saw the islands, really. We had such short trips ashore. It seemed most people were there to drink on the ship."

Monika Graf laughed, exposing teeth that were too white. "I know what you mean," she said. Her expression became serious. "Are you traveling alone?"

"No," Crissy said. "A friend of mine, Jenny, came with me."

Monika nodded. "I see," she said. "That's nice." She paused, then looked at Crissy. "What sort of work do you do in America?"

"I'm a hair colorist," Crissy said. "I also cut and set, but mostly I color."

Monika nodded. "How interesting."

"And you?" Crissy asked. "Do you do some sort of work?"

Monika nodded. "I am a novelist," she said.

"Oh, how exciting," Crissy said with genuine enthusiasm. "What kind of books do you write?"

"Romance," she said. She smiled more widely than before, and her eyes twinkled. "Love, love, love," she said.

"That's wonderful," Crissy said. "I've never met a romance novelist before." As a matter of fact, she thought, she'd never met anybody who wrote anything.

"It's wonderful work," Monika said, "to write of love. It is the best sort of thing to write about, don't you agree?"

"I have no idea," Crissy said, "but it sounds very exciting."

"Have you been in love?" Monika asked. "Or married?"

"I . . . I've been infatuated," Crissy said honestly, "but I don't think I've ever really been in love. And I've never been married."

"A beautiful girl like you?" Monika looked at her with surprise. "I'm shocked. I should have thought you'd been married at least once and had many lovers."

"Well, I've had boyfriends," Crissy admitted, "but none of them were really . . . serious or satisfying." She looked at Monika questioningly. "Are you married?"

Monika tinkled laughter. "Twice. Both disasters," she replied merrily.

"Did you have children?"

Monika shook her head. "No, thank heaven," she said. "Neither man would've been a good father, and I'm devoted to my work. Children require a great deal of care, and I probably wouldn't make a very good mother."

"I would like to be a mother someday, I think," Crissy said thoughtfully.

Monika reached a bejeweled hand across the table and patted her. "We must see about that," she said with a smile and slightly arched brow.

Crissy laughed. "I don't know. . . ."

"Oh, I do," Monika said. "There are some very interesting men aboard." She paused, then added, "Single, too, if that matters."

Crissy laughed again. "It does."

"You must stick with me," Monika said with a wink. "I can steer you in the right direction."

Crissy was momentarily nonplussed. "I . . . well . . . thank you," she said. "But I don't really think you can force these things."

"You can help them along," Monika said. "Oh, yes. You can definitely help them along. I'll show you." She lightly tapped her breast with a hand, her rings flashing in the light.

Crissy smiled and shrugged. "It's kind of you to offer, but—"

"But nothing," Monika said. "I will be your guide in the world of romance. Perhaps we can begin tonight. You and your friend can join us at table for the second dinner sitting at eight-thirty. The first sitting at six-thirty is far too early for a ship, don't you think? With the late-night activity, which is the most interesting thing aboard a ship"—she paused and laughed her tinkly laugh again—"one wants a few winks in the afternoon and plenty of time to prepare for the evening's festivities, don't you agree?"

"It's probably a good plan," Crissy said.

"The early sitting is for the geriatrics who collapse into bed by nine, I think." Monika put a hand across her smiling mouth as if to keep such thoughts from escaping her lips again.

Crissy smiled. "Maybe you're right," she said.

"So tonight," Monika went on, "tell the maître d' that you want to be seated with Frau Graf's party. We'll be looking for you. There'll be Mina and Rudy and Doctor Von Meckling. He's an older man but quite distinguished. I think you and your friend will enjoy the company."

"Thank you," Crissy said. "I'll ask Jenny about it when I see her. I don't know if she's made any plans or not."

"Unpacking, I suppose," Monika said.

"Actually, I think she's met one of the ship's officers," Crissy said, "and they went off somewhere together."

Monika's eyebrows arched. "Already?"

Crissy nodded.

"Fast worker," Monika said, laughing. "I must meet this one."

Crissy laughed, too. "I guess I should start unpacking, now that you mention it."

"Yes, my dear," Monika said. "I must do the same." She sipped the last of the champagne in her glass and rose to her feet. "I will see you at dinner, I hope." She nodded in a formal fashion.

"Yes," Crissy said. "I look forward to it."

Monika turned, and with the long straps of her huge gold handbag clutched in one hand, she walked in her tiny steps toward the sliding glass doors, the handbag nearly scraping the floor. Crissy watched until she was gone, then looked at her watch. She saw that they would be leaving port soon. Maybe she would have enough time to unpack and get back out on deck beforehand. She wanted to take some pictures of Piraeus as they left.

She went back through the big dining room and down one flight of stairs to Deck Four, where she found her cabin effortlessly. She swiped her card and went in. Jenny was sprawled naked on the bed, and quickly pulled a sheet up over her breasts.

"Oh!" she cried. "I thought you would stay out on deck till we left."

"I decided to unpack first, if I have time, and get my camera." She added, "Are you going to nap?"

"Uh, well, I don't know," Jenny said. She nodded toward the closed bathroom door and in a whisper said, "Manolo's in there, getting ready to leave."

Crissy tried to stifle a laugh. "You *are* shameless," she whispered back.

"And he is a stud," Jenny replied.

The bathroom door opened, and Manolo stepped out, adjusting his cap. He saw Crissy and stopped in his tracks. "Why, hello," he said. "I walked Jenny back to her cabin. I hope I haven't imposed on you in any way."

Crissy shook her head. "No, of course not," she said. "You're welcome anytime."

He looked at Jenny. "I'd better run," he said. "I hope I see you again."

"Oh, yes," Jenny replied. "I do, too."

"We'll soon set sail," he said, "so if you want to see Piraeus and Athens from the sea, you'd better get above decks."

"Thanks," Jenny said. "I might stay right here and savor it through the window."

When he was gone, Jenny looked over at Crissy, who had begun to open her luggage. "You would not believe this," Jenny said.

Crissy stopped and glanced at her. "Oh, yes, I do," she said with a laugh. "Was it fun?"

"Oh, it was heaven," Jenny said, "even if it was a little fast. You know, they're really not supposed to mingle with the passengers. Well, not like this, anyway. But he said he couldn't help himself." She paused and adjusted the sheet across her breasts. "Neither could I."

Crissy began taking clothing from one of her suitcases and hanging it in the closet. "Trust you," she said. "We haven't even set sail, and you've already found a real hottie."

"God, he is, too," Jenny gushed. "What've you been up to?"

"Talking to these fascinating people out on deck," she said. "They would like for us to join them for dinner. The second sitting at eight-thirty."

"Who are they?"

Crissy told her what she'd learned about Monika, Mina, and Rudy. "What do you think?"

"Fine with me," Jenny said. "If I don't like them, I can always change tables." She had a dreamy expression on her face. "I wish I could eat with Manolo."

"Maybe you'll spot somebody at dinner," Crissy said, placing folded items on the closet's shelves. "Maybe there'll be some good-looking single man alone."

The ship's horn blasted, and afterward there was an announcement in three languages that visitors must leave the ship as departure was imminent. Jenny yawned and closed her eyes.

"Don't you want to be out on deck when we leave?" Crissy asked.

"Oh, I don't care," Jenny said. "I think I'll take a nap." She smiled conspiratorially at Crissy. "Postcoital bliss and all that."

"Whatever," Crissy replied. "I'll see you in awhile."

Crissy left the cabin and went back up the stairs toward the top deck. When she reached the Deck Seven landing, she saw two sailors emerge from an elevator, carrying a large, handsome steamer trunk, one at each end. Its top and front were emblazoned with a large V in the middle of what appeared to be a heraldic crest of some kind.

Following the sailors out of the elevator was Mark, the handsome young man she and Jenny had talked with earlier. He didn't see her, as he was engrossed in conversation with the sailors. She watched as he pointed down a hallway, directing the sailors, she supposed, then saw them turn the corner and head that way. Trailing behind them, Crissy saw them stop at the door to a suite. She knew that these suites on the top deck were the most expensive aboard the ship.

Turning in the opposite direction, she walked toward the pool deck, fascinated by what she had just seen. Mark must be extremely rich, she thought.

She reached the railing, which was already crowded with passengers who'd stationed themselves there for the departure, but as she watched the harbor of Piraeus disappear, she couldn't shake the image of Mark and the sailors with the trunk from her mind. How extraordinary it was, she thought, to be able to travel in such a fashion. Surely, there were very few people who could afford to go anywhere with a steamer trunk nowadays, and to think this one belonged to a handsome young man. How odd that it hadn't already been brought aboard, she thought. She wondered why they'd waited until the last minute. Perhaps he got some kind of special treatment other passengers didn't get. Still, it seemed curious.

Chapter Seven

Georgios Vilos picked up his cell phone and pressed in the number that he had memorized so that it would never be found written down anywhere. The number could be found in his cell phone records, should it ever come to that, but he wasn't going to invite trouble by having it in an address book or lying about on his desk.

The man answered on the third ring. "Yes?"

"Is my package in place?" Vilos asked.

"Of course," came the arrogant reply.

"Did you oversee this yourself?"

"That is none of your business."

Georgios Vilos wanted to shout obscenities at the impertinent bastard, but he didn't dare offend him until he was absolutely certain that his plan was in motion. "I see," he finally replied in a neutral voice. "But you are confident that the package is where it should be?"

"Yes. Do you think I am a fool?"

"No. No. Certainly not," Vilos said hastily. "But these things can go awry, can't they?"

"Not when you're dealing with me."

"Anyone can make a mistake," Georgios Vilos said before thinking.

There was the sound of a click as the man hung up.

Georgios Vilos pressed the END button on the cell phone, flipped it shut, and hung his head in his hands. *God, how I hate him!* he thought miserably. *I wish I could hang him up by his balls!* He slammed the cell phone down on his desk. *But I have no choice. None.*

He leaned back in his chair and looked out the window but didn't see anything beyond the glass, lost in thought. He was taking a huge risk, he realized, but it was the best way to go about the business. Hiding the explosives in Mark's steamer trunks was the easiest and most efficient way to get them aboard the ship. The customs officials wouldn't dare check his son's luggage. He would be greeted by everyone at the ship terminal like a crown prince and waved through by security as if he were a conquering hero. The buzz of metal detectors would be ignored, should anything set them off. No one in his family ever had to submit to searches, let alone remove change, belts, or shoes. Certainly not in Piraeus, and the port of Piraeus was all that mattered. If the explosives were used, then there would be nothing to discover later on. There would be no ship.

Georgios Vilos heaved a sigh. He certainly didn't want to endanger Mark in any way, but Mark would have plenty of opportunities to abandon ship, so that wasn't a problem. There were several ports of call before the vessel crossed the Atlantic to Brazil. Georgios shifted in his desk chair uncomfortably. He hoped it wouldn't come to that. The despicable Lampaki brothers could prevent his resorting to such a terrible course of action, and he could only hope that they would come up with the money to save the company.

Meanwhile, he thought with some degree of satisfaction, if what Azad said was true, then the explosives were on the ship, safely secured in Mark's trunk, and Mark himself was not in harm's way. It was a brilliant plan, he decided. No one would ever imagine or believe that Mark Vilos would hold the destruction of his own father's prize ship in his luxurious suite.

By the time Crissy and Jenny reached the dining room, a line had formed. The maître d', aided by a few stewards, was adept at seating passengers, and they were swept into the elegant dining room and quickly seated with Monika Graf, Rudy, Mina, and the doctor.

Rudy rose to his feet, and the older doctor more or less propelled himself into a semistanding position as the women were seated.

"It's so nice of you to join us," Monika said enthusiastically. "Let me introduce everyone. You must be . . . Jenny, is it?"

"Yes," Jenny said, unabashedly staring at the older woman's hair, makeup, and glittery clothing as if she were an exotic animal she'd never seen before.

After the introductions, the wine steward appeared and took their drink orders. Jenny and Crissy decided to get a bottle of white wine, which they were told would have their cabin number on it for the next meal if they didn't finish it tonight. As they perused menus, they chatted about their afternoon—everyone, it seemed, napped—and talked about the ship.

"I'm very disappointed," Monika said. "It's not at all glamorous."

"My dear," Dr. Von Meckling said, his eyeglasses reflecting the light, "it was very tastefully built and decorated, and its size is ideal. Not so many people and thankfully no children. We are very fortunate." He spoke in an authoritative voice that suited his distinguished appearance. Carefully dressed in an immaculate dark suit, he had short white hair, a neatly trimmed mustache, and a pristine white handkerchief in his breast pocket and a small red rose on his lapel.

"That's true," Monika said, flapping a bejeweled hand in the air.

"I love it," Mina added. "It's *intime* and, like the doctor said, very tastefully decorated."

"It's also very fast," Rudy added. "The fastest in the world, I'm told."

After placing their orders, they discussed tomorrow's stop. "Have you been to Sicily before?" the doctor asked Jenny, who was seated next to him.

Jenny shook her head. "No," she said. "I've been to Europe a couple of times, but not Sicily."

"Are you going on one of the excursions?" Mina asked Crissy.

"Yes," she said, "I'm going to Taormina. I read a little bit about it and decided to do that instead of going to Mt. Etna."

"Oh, spare me Etna," Monika said. "That terrible sulfurous stench. Besides, you can't shop, and in Taormina there are gorgeous shops."

"I wouldn't miss Etna for the world," said the doctor. "Been there before, but can't wait to see it again. Not good for heart patients—the altitude, you know—or asthmatics, what with the smoke and all, but I must go." He looked at Jenny again. "You, my dear?"

"Mt. Etna," she said. "It's hot." She smiled lasciviously. "Besides, I figured, what the hell? There'll be lots of opportunities to shop, and Crissy wanted to see Taormina, so we can exchange notes."

Salads and starters arrived, and everyone ate with relish. The entrées followed, and everyone seemed pleased with the food. When dessert arrived, Crissy was surprised to see that the Europeans all had the cheese platter, while she and Jenny opted for a delicious rum-soaked cake and ice cream.

It was agreed that everyone would meet in the Hercules Lounge on Deck Six for the nightly show at ten-thirty, after going their separate ways after dinner.

Crissy and Jenny excused themselves and left the dining room, not failing to notice the many glances from still-seated diners that followed them. In the hall outside they saw a door leading to the deck. "I'm going to have a smoke out on deck," Jenny said.

"I'll come with you." It was windy on the deck, despite its being protected by bulkheads and lifeboats hanging on davits, and dark, with only the light from small mounted wall lamps and spilling from windows in doors or the occasional lit-up office or stateroom. They stood at the railing looking out at the darkness. In the distance they could see what must be another cruise ship, its lights appearing in the black emptiness as if it were some sort of chimera. Leaning over the railing and looking down at the water, they quickly backed away, both laughing at the spray that covered them in a fine mist, even though they were five decks above the sea. Only a few other passengers strolled by or stopped at the railing, mostly couples, many of them having an after-dinner cigarette or cigar.

"This is a good place for a smooch," Jenny said. "Especially in one of the dark corners."

"Or you could climb into one of the lifeboats," Crissy joked.

"Now that's an idea," Jenny said.

"Are you going to see Manolo tonight?" Crissy asked.

"Maybe," she said. "He'll probably be in the disco around midnight, and if he is, we'll sneak off someplace."

"Sounds like fun," Crissy replied.

"Hmmm," Jenny replied, "it's fun, all right."

They went back inside and made their way to the Hercules Lounge, where the show would be. Just inside the double doors, Mina and Rudy were waiting to one side.

"Hallo," Mina said. "We got great seats with tables if we want to order cocktails." She had changed into a fiery red gown with a skirt of several rows of ruffles, reminiscent of a flamenco dancer, and wore a glittering necklace, earrings, and bracelets, whether real or rhinestone, Crissy and Jenny couldn't tell.

"How nice of you," Crissy said, "and I love your dress. It's beautiful."

"Thank you," Mina replied.

They followed the couple to red plush seats nearby, where Monika and the doctor were engaged in conversation. Monika nodded, and the old doctor half rose from his seat to greet them. After they were gathered around the small table, Rudy proposed ordering a bottle of champagne.

"Oh, you're my kind of guy," Jenny said.

"And mine," Mina said, putting an arm around him possessively.

Rudy summoned a waiter and ordered the champagne.

Dr. Von Meckling turned his attention to Jenny as he had at dinner. He seemed entranced by her, and his interest was not lost on the other members of the party. Jenny fell into polite conversation with him, while Crissy chatted with everyone else. The champagne arrived, and the waiter poured six glasses. When he had gone, Rudy proposed a toast. "To an exciting and romantic journey," he said, holding his glass aloft.

Everyone clinked glasses and sipped champagne as the house lights began to dim. The show was about to begin. The orchestra struck up a tune, and a tall young man, a handsome African-American, came out onto the small stage. The audience began applauding politely. "Ladies and gentlemen," he began in English, "welcome to the *Sea Nymph*." He proceeded to tell a number of jokes, ranging from funny to pathetic, but his efforts were greeted with wild applause. Finally, he announced: "Tonight's show is called 'Eastern Delights.' "

The three members of the orchestra segued into an exotic Middle Eastern-sounding number, and a dance routine began that featured women costumed as belly dancers and men dressed as sheiks. At the end of the routine, the leading lady was carried offstage in the arms of her sheik pursuer.

Monika whispered to Crissy, "Absolute nonsense, isn't it?"

Crissy nodded with a smile. "They're all pretty good, though, aren't they?"

Monika arched one of her drawn brows. "Well, if you're trapped on a ship at sea. . . ." she replied, then placed a hand over her mouth as she laughed.

The show was brief, no more than thirty minutes or so, then the orchestra played dance music. Many couples took to the small dance floor. Dr. Von Meckling turned to Jenny. "A dance, my dear?"

"Oh, wonderful," she replied, smiling mischievously at Crissy.

She and Dr. Von Meckling rose, and he escorted her down to the dance floor, where Rudy and Mina joined them. "There will be more available men in the disco," Monika said to Crissy.

"Really?" she replied.

Monika nodded. "Oh, yes," she said. "A lot of the older couples will be in bed, and the younger people turn up. You wait and see. Also some of the ship's officers." She grabbed Crissy's arm. "Drop-dead handsome, some of them. Only you don't want to become involved with any of them."

"Why?" she asked.

"Most of them have someone at home, despite what they say," Monika replied. "And besides, they don't offer particularly good prospects, if you know what I mean."

"I don't," Crissy said, looking at her in puzzlement.

"Money, darling," Monika said, emphatically tapping a long red-lacquered fingernail on the table. The ring on her finger caught the light and glittered magnificently. "They don't make much. If you fall for a sea-man, it must be the captain of the ship. He's the only one worth pursuing."

"So much for romance," Crissy said with a laugh.

Monika smiled. "One must be practical as well," she said. "It's very difficult to sustain love when one is hungry or one hasn't the money to pay the telephone bill."

"I can see your point," Crissy agreed, although she was beginning to see Monika in a different light. She wasn't quite the romantic Crissy had at first assumed.

The dancing was brief, and everyone agreed to go to the disco.

"I want to go change clothes first," Jenny said. She looked at Crissy. "You want to come with me?"

"Sure," she said. They got to their feet. "We'll see you in the disco," Crissy said to the table in general.

"You better be there," Rudy said. "I want to dance with you. Mina can't dance every single dance with me."

"I'll be there," Crissy said, winking.

On the way to their cabin, Jenny told her how Dr. Von Meckling had felt her up on the dance floor. "I swear," she said, her voice full of laugh-ter, "he is one horny old toad. I thought I'd tease him, but *he* started it. I kept grabbing his hands, but I couldn't keep the old coot off me."

In their cabin, Jenny changed into a cleavage-revealing, floor-length leopard-print gown with slits up both legs. "I can even flash a little panty in this if I feel like it," she said merrily. "I'll show that old doctor a thing or two."

Crissy laughed. "How many animal-print dresses do you own?"

"Lost count." Jenny glanced curiously at Crissy. "Aren't you going to change?"

Crissy shrugged. "I don't think so," she said. "It's not a formal night."

"Yeah, but you've got sexier things than that," Jenny said. She went to the closet and swung the doors open, then began rifling through the clothes hanging there. "Look," she said, holding out cream hip-hugging trousers and a matching cream top with a plunging neckline. "This would look great on the dance floor. The pants show off your butt and flare out at the bottom, and the top shows some tit."

Crissy was hesitant at first, but finally she took the hanger from Jenny.

After they were dressed, they took the stairs to Deck Seven. Entering the disco was like suddenly being transported to another time and place. It was darkly lit, except for the small bar area, and in intimate plush booths along the entrance area, they saw a few couples having drinks and exchanging kisses. There were about seventy-five tables surrounding the small dance floor in a U. Monika waved from across the room.

"As if we could've missed her," Jenny quipped. "With that hair and makeup and her sequined dress and shoes, she'd light up the darkest hole in hell."

They wove their way through the tables and chairs and across the room to where the foursome sat. A bottle of champagne was already open. "We got two extra glasses," Rudy announced.

"Oh, thank you," Crissy said. "That was so thoughtful."

"Yes," Jenny said, "just the thing to prime the pump."

They sat down and Rudy poured, then they all lifted their glasses and clinked them as they had at the show. "This could get to be habit-forming," Jenny said.

Mina laughed. "Rudy adores champagne," she said. "Always we have it. At home, out at dinners, on trips. Always it is the occasion for champagne."

Crissy's gaze shifted to the bar, where she saw an elegant older woman in an expensive-looking evening gown drinking and smoking while in conversation with two middle-aged men.

On one side of her sat a very handsome man, apparently alone, who seemed absorbed in the music, tapping time with one shoe on the bar stool. He had short light-blond hair and wore a navy blazer with a white handkerchief in the breast pocket, cream trousers, and white buckskin shoes. He appeared to be so muscular that the jacket could barely contain his body. When he passed near her on his way to ask a single lady at a table to dance, she could see that he had penetrating gray eyes. Crissy didn't know what to make of him, and didn't know what it was that intrigued her about him. But he did intrigue her, she thought. She would love to know his life story.

Rudy and Mina danced to a fast number, and they attracted everyone's attention. Mina's dress stole the show, its ruffled skirt flying in every direction as Rudy virtually performed acrobatics with her on the dance floor. Afterward, he asked Crissy to dance, and she took his proffered hand and joined him for a slow dance, then a fast one, on the small floor.

The crowd grew in size as it got later, and some of the ship's officers and a few of the young women who worked aboard in the duty-free shops or elsewhere took tables together. Crissy was sitting alone, enjoying the spectacle on the dance floor, when the tall, muscular stranger who sat alone at the bar approached her.

"Would you honor me with a dance?" he asked in a polite and formal manner. He had the slightest accent, but she couldn't place it.

"Yes," she said, feeling a flutter in her chest. "I would like that." She took his hand and let him lead her to the floor. A slow number was playing, and he led her around the floor expertly. When the music changed to a fast piece, he looked at her questioningly. "Okay?" he asked.

She nodded. He took her hand and proceeded to twirl her around the floor, leading her through wild, nonstop paces, occasionally taking her in his arms and dipping her first one way, then another, then twirling and whirling her again, until Crissy was practically dizzy but having a wonderful time. He made her look better on the dance floor than she actually was, she thought. When the number was over, she told him she wanted to go back to her table for a drink.

"Why don't you have a drink with me at the bar?" he asked.

Why not? she thought. "Okay," Crissy said. He escorted her to the bar, where she sat on a stool next to the one he'd occupied all evening.

"What would you like?" he asked.

"Water," Crissy said. "I've already had my limit of alcohol, I'm afraid."

He didn't try to dissuade her. "Sparkling or still?"

"Sparkling," she replied.

He ordered her water, and a scotch and water for himself, then turned to her. "I am Valentin Petrov," he said, nodding formally and extending his hand. "And you?"

"I'm Crissy Fitzgerald," she said.

"It's a pleasure to meet you," he said, nodding to her again. The waiter brought their drinks, and he handed Crissy hers.

"It's nice to meet you, too," Crissy said. "And thanks for the water." She took a big drink, then another.

"Is this your first cruise?" he asked, lighting up a cigarette.

"I've been on one before," she said, "but it was a week's trip from New York to the Caribbean. Nothing like this."

"I see," he replied. "Do you not drink?"

"I do, but I have to stop after one."

"I see," he said. "It's a matter of discipline."

Then he smiled, and the short blond hair, intense gray eyes, and muscular body seemed less daunting, a little more human. "Most people have the same problem, do they not?"

Crissy shrugged. "I don't know about most people, but I know about me." She drank more water, almost finishing off the glass.

"Where are you from in the States?" he asked.

"New York," she said.

"The city?"

She shook her head. "No. I live in Albany. It's upstate. The capital of New York."

"And a sewer, from what I'm told," he replied.

Crissy didn't know what to say. While she wasn't particularly fond of her hometown, she didn't appreciate its being denigrated by a total stranger. "Well . . . " she began.

He looked at her again and smiled slightly. "I am playing," he said. "Don't take offense."

She returned his smile, but was somewhat perplexed by his form of play. "Where are you from?" she asked.

"Sofia," he said. "In Bulgaria. Part of the former Soviet Bloc."

"Oh, how interesting," she replied. "I don't think I've ever met anyone from there."

"No?" he said. "Not surprising. Not many of us ever leave. Not until recently, anyway. The Russians made it impossible, and now that we can leave, there is no money to get out." He took a long drag off his cigarette. "If there is a worse stink-hole in the world than Albany, it is Bulgaria."

"So I guess we're equal," she said with a laugh.

He frowned. "I don't know about that," he said. "You seem soft and tender, gentle and kind. Me? I come from the KGB's old recruiting ground. The Bulgarians are supposed to make the best assassins."

"You're joking," she said.

"No," he said. "I am quite serious." He stubbed his cigarette out and drank the remainder of his scotch and water. "Would you like to dance again?"

"Sure," Crissy said.

On the dance floor, he held her close to him during the slow dance, but didn't try to get fresh. When the dance was over, she told him that she should return to her table.

"Of course," he said, and he led her there. "It was a pleasure to meet you." He nodded formally again.

Crissy started to introduce him to Monika but Valentin had already returned to the bar. She sat down next to Monika.

"Tell me about him," Monika whispered at once. She now had an ornate fan, painted with courtly scenes highlighted with gilt, that she waved before her face from time to time in rapid little motions.

"He's from Bulgaria," Crissy said, "and his name is Valentin Petrov."

Monika nodded. "I see," she said. She held the fan in front of her face, then turned to Crissy. "I don't think he's remotely appropriate, darling."

"Well, I didn't have anything serious in mind, Monika," Crissy replied. "I just said yes when he asked me to dance."

"I would advise you to stay away from any of the Eastern Europeans," Monika said.

"Why?" Crissy asked.

"My darling," Monika said, as if addressing an imbecile, "they are a crude, uncivilized people, deprived for so long of practically everything—oxygen, even, if you see their air—that it will be years before they recover, if ever. Obviously, your young man is more clever than most, managing to get out, take a cruise even. But they're an untrustworthy lot. Gangsters, a lot of them. Ruthless, too."

"He's not my young man," Crissy said with a laugh. She could only laugh at Monika's take on Valentin, trying to pigeonhole him as a thug. What an imagination the woman had. What would he be doing on the ship if he were a gangster?

"Some of the ship's employees are Bulgarian, of course," Monika said.

90

"There are Russians, Romanians, what-have-you, but most of them are in servile positions, Crissy. That's all they know how to do. You'll discover that for yourself as the cruise goes on."

"I'm sure you're right," Crissy said, unwilling to argue with the woman, although her instincts rebelled against such harsh generalizations. "But you don't have to worry, Monika. I only danced with the guy."

"Oh, I know," Monika said, waving the fan, "but one thing does lead to another, doesn't it?"

Crissy could only laugh again. "Believe me, dancing with Valentin will not lead to anything."

"Good," she said. "Oh, look at the doctor and your friend. Dancing madly." She chortled, then positioned her fan to hide her mouth again. "I think Doctor Von Meckling is quite fond of your friend," she said conspiratorially.

"Well," Crissy said, "Jenny certainly does attract a lot of men. I don't know if she would really be interested in a man his age, but . . ."

"Age means nothing when it comes to matters of the heart," Monika said. "Or the pocketbook."

Crissy smiled. "Jenny is well fixed for money," she said. "She gets a lot of alimony from her ex-husband."

"Indeed?" Monika digested this news in silence for a moment. "A very clever girl," she said. "More so than one would think by looking at her."

"What do you mean by that?" Crissy said, prepared to defend Jenny.

"I'm simply surprised she has some brains to go with the sex appeal," Monika said. "Don't fret, darling. I'm not denigrating your friend, but she is rather obvious about trying to attract men. Nothing subtle about her."

Rudy and Mina returned to the table, their faces flushed. "You and Rudy are the stars of the dance floor," Crissy said. "You dance everything awfully well."

"We took lessons," Rudy said. "Many lessons. We love to dance."

All heads turned as Captain Papadapolis entered the room with two other officers. The man certainly had presence, Crissy thought, but it was one of the men with him who caught her eye and held it. Like many of the Greeks, he had raven-black hair, an olive complexion, and dark eyes, but he was taller than the others. He also seemed rather reserved. While the captain stopped and spoke to everyone in his path as they made their way to a table, the man who had drawn her attention stood a slight distance away. After they were seated, a waitress immediately appeared to take their orders. Then the captain and one of the officers popped back on their feet again, asking women seated close to them to dance. But Crissy's tall, dark stranger remained behind at the table, glancing about the room with apparent boredom, then sipped from a glass of white wine when it was brought. Perhaps it was his reserve, his difference from the others, that attracted her.

Her attention was quickly diverted, however, when Mina leaned close and said, "He's a fantastic dancer, isn't he?"

"Who?" she asked.

Mina laughed. "The captain, of course. He's an absolutely fabulous dancer, the most correct and graceful dancer in the room."

Crissy watched the captain on the dance floor, as nearly everyone in the disco had, and saw that what Mina said was true. He led the woman about the dance floor as if he were a professional dancer. His bearing and uniform enhanced his image considerably, she thought, but he possessed an innate grace and considerable training.

"I could watch him all night," Monika said with enthusiasm.

"Yes, he's good," Rudy agreed. "Come on, we must get on the floor and show him what we can do." He and Mina got up, and off they went, leaving Crissy with the doctor, who'd returned to the table, and Monika.

Mina and Rudy put everything they had into the dance, and when a Spanish flamenco air came next, they put on a show that drew a crowd of observers and enormous applause when it ended. Afterward, the captain asked Rudy's permission to dance with Mina, and they set the floor on fire during the next number. Nearly everyone was on the dance floor now, enjoying proximity to the ship's handsome captain and his beautiful dance partner.

Crissy watched silently, and noticed that Valentin was dancing with a middle-aged woman she'd seen sitting with another woman nearby earlier. Oddly, she felt possessive of him when she saw the woman enjoying herself, laughing at something Valentin had said into her ear. She wondered if he was telling her the same things he'd told her. But she brushed the thought aside when she saw that Jenny was now dancing with Manolo, her handsome young officer. Their arms were wrapped about each other, and they were practically making out on the dance floor. They brought a smile to her face, and she wondered if she would see Jenny again tonight.

Her question was soon answered when the dance ended and Jenny came to the table. "I'm getting my purse," she said, "and joining a friend. I'll see you later. 'Night." She leaned down to Crissy and brushed her cheek with a kiss. "I won't be in tonight, so don't worry about me."

Crissy nodded and watched her sashay happily toward the exit. Obviously, Manolo had gone on ahead, so they wouldn't be seen leaving together.

The doctor, his hooded eyes alert, watched her as well. He turned to Monika then and said, "The young waste so much of their youth, don't they? Chasing after the impossible . . . or the undesirable."

Monika nodded in agreement. "Yes, but you must remember what your own youth was like, Doctor."

"You're right, of course," he said. He turned his attention to Crissy. "Young lady, are you enjoying yourself?"

"Yes, Doctor," she replied. "I've been having a wonderful time, thank you. What about yourself?"

"Oh, I always do," he said with a wink.

He didn't look more than seventy, and from what Jenny said, he certainly hadn't lost interest in women. She turned her attention to the dance floor again, and saw Valentin dancing with yet another woman, this one also middle-aged. She was overweight and not particularly attractive, but she was having a very good time apparently, laughing at Valentin's chatter. She saw the captain returning to his table and followed him with her eyes. The tall, aloof officer she'd seen come in with him was still sitting at the table, sipping wine and looking bored. She hadn't seen him dance or talk with anyone, and found herself wondering once again about what sort of man he was. He was so good-looking but obviously wasn't enjoying himself, and she found that curious. Suddenly she realized that he was staring at her, and she quickly averted her gaze, hoping she hadn't made a fool of herself by studying him so intently.

Across the room, she saw that Mark, the handsome young man staying in the expensive suite, had just entered. He caught sight of her and immediately headed in her direction. Crissy shifted nervously in her chair. He was very handsome and had about him an aura of money, but what made her feel slightly uncomfortable was his sexiness. She had little time to reflect on her feelings, however, because he was standing at her side.

"Would you like to dance?" Mark asked, the hint of a smile on his lips.

"Yes," Crissy replied, her mind whirling. *Could this handsome, obviously rich man possibly be interested in me?* she wondered.

Mark led her to the dance floor and held her close as they moved in time to the slow tune. "Are you enjoying the ship?" he asked, his dark eyes gazing down at her.

"I love it," Crissy said. "It's really wonderful."

"It is a great ship," he replied in agreement, "and there are some interesting passengers."

"Yes," Crissy said, thinking that he must surely be one of the most fascinating men aboard.

"Like you," Mark added.

"Oh?" Crissy said, blushing. "I'm . . . I'm just an ordinary person from New York." She couldn't help but feel flattered by his remark, although she knew he had no reason to think she was interesting.

"You certainly don't look ordinary," he said.

She blurted a nervous laugh. "I'll take that as a compliment."

"You should," Mark said with a nod. "You're beautiful, but you also seem . . . accessible. Not stuck on yourself." *And you're certainly accessible to me,* he thought, *and anything I want from you. Aren't all women?*

"Thank you," Crissy murmured, not knowing what else to say. His sudden interest in her was disconcerting, perhaps because it was unexpected. Meeting Adonis in Athens had been a wonderful experience, but Mark, she thought, was in another league altogether. She imagined that with his looks, combined with his apparent money, he could have anyone he desired. What's more, she thought, his body felt strong and warm next to hers, as if he gave off a lusty animal heat that excited desire in her.

"I saw men delivering a huge trunk to your cabin," Crissy said, making conversation.

"Oh?" he replied. "So you've been spying on me?"

"No," she said with a laugh. "I happened to be in the hallway, and saw them follow you with it. I didn't know people traveled that way anymore. Not nowadays. It's so huge I couldn't imagine what you have in it. It's really grand, isn't it?"

"I wouldn't know," he said shortly. "I simply know that I am sometimes away for a long time and have to take clothes for many occasions."

"I didn't mean to be nosy," she said. "I just thought . . . Well, I never saw anyone traveling with a trunk before."

And in the circles you travel in, I doubt that you ever will, Mark

94

thought. He drew her closer and led her around the floor very slowly until the music ended. Then, still holding her, ignoring the musicians' segue into a fast tune, he gazed down into her eyes again. "Would you like to come to my stateroom for awhile?" he asked.

She could tell by the confidence in his eyes that he knew she would say yes. Didn't they all, knowing who he was?

But she wouldn't, not tonight. She was unnerved by her own attraction to him and didn't feel ready to act on it.

"I'd better not," she said. "Maybe . . . maybe another time."

Mark let her go and drew back, standing rather stiffly but with a small smile on his lips. "Maybe," he echoed. He put a hand on her back and led her toward the table.

Crissy felt that she had offended him. He had probably seldom been refused, if ever.

"I'll see you later," Mark said, pulling her chair out for her. "Thank you for the dance."

"I enjoyed it," Crissy said, but Mark was already turning to leave, ignoring her and the rest of the people at the table.

She sat down and took a deep breath.

Monika's eyes glittered from across the table. She looked at Crissy with obvious curiosity. "I don't believe it!" she began.

"What?"

"I leave for a few minutes and return to find you dancing with *him*," Monika said. "Tell me. How was it?"

"Fine," Crissy said. "He's so good-looking, isn't he? And he's a good dancer."

"My darling," Monika said, "of course he's good-looking and a good dancer to boot. Anyone with eyes can see that. That's not what I'm asking. Was there a connection? Will you see him again?"

"He asked me to go back to his stateroom with him," Crissy said.

"And you didn't go?" Monika asked, her eyes suddenly huge with surprise. "Do you know who he is?"

"No," Crissy said, "but I gather he's rich. I know he's in one of the most expensive suites. And he's exceptionally . . . appealing."

Monika let a hand fall to the table, her immense rings making a loud thunk detectable even above the loud, fast music. "My darling, he's not in one of the most expensive suites," she corrected her. "He's in the *owner's* suite. That ravishingly handsome young man is Mark Vilos. His family owns the shipping line."

"Oh," Crissy said, remembering the large Vs emblazoned on the steamer trunk. "I didn't know."

"Crissy, darling, he's the most desirable catch on the ship," Monika said.

Chapter Eight

The next morning Crissy went up to Deck Six for the cafeteria-style breakfast, and when she returned to the cabin, she found Jenny just getting out of the shower. "Oh, you scared me half to death," Jenny cried.

"Sorry, I didn't mean to," Crissy said, then smiled. "I bet you had a good time last night."

Jenny threw her arms in the air, then around Crissy's shoulders. "Honey, it was the best. He's the most fantastic lover ever."

"Ooooh, I see," Crissy said with a giggle. "Where did you go? Isn't there some rule about crew not sleeping with passengers?"

"I don't know if it's really a rule," Jenny said, releasing her hold on Crissy, "but he likes to be cautious. First we went to his office and closed the curtains. We had a couple of drinks there and made out on a little sofa sort of like this one." She pointed to the sofa in their living/dining area. "That went on forever, till I thought I was going to go crazy if we didn't get down to business. Anyway, he finally told me to wait there a minute while he checked to see if things were cool in his part of the crew quarters. He came flying back and practically carried me to his cabin. Then the real fun started, and I mean *fun*. All night long."

"All night?" Crissy said.

"Well, almost," Jenny allowed. "We did catch a few winks. The only hitch came this morning when I was sneaking out. Manolo looked and didn't see anybody, but this fat little bitch who's a manicurist in the spa is on the same hallway and came out just when I did. She saw me and marched down the hall and started asking me questions. 'What're you doing in the crew quarters?' Real nasty. Manolo stuck his head out the door and whispered to her, then told me to get moving. I did, believe me." She smiled at Jenny. "So here I am. Fucked again!"

Crissy put her hand over her mouth when she laughed. "You're too much, Jen."

"He's almost too much, honey. You should see!"

"No, no! I don't want to hear about it," Crissy said, laughing. "Anyway, are you about ready to leave? The shore excursions leave in about thirty minutes, but I want to go up on deck and take some pictures when we dock in Catania."

They took the stairs to Deck Seven, where a crowd had already gathered for the same reason they had. The ship was very close to Catania now, and Crissy and Jenny were both excited. They could see mountains in the distance, but they weren't certain that one of them was the volcano. The sky loomed low and gray, and rain threatened.

As they neared the city, they could see parks with palm trees and wildly baroque church facades that were almost black. Many of the buildings were built in the neoclassic manner with pediments and columns. The big ship entered the port, and they could see tour buses lined up waiting to take them away.

As they disembarked, the steward inserted Crissy's card in a slot, and her image appeared on a video monitor.

"That's amazing," she said.

"It's scary, if you ask me," Jenny said. "Talk about Big Brother."

Down the dock, they said their good-byes. "Don't get swallowed up by that volcano," Crissy joked.

"Don't worry," Jenny replied. "I've got too much to look forward to when we get back."

Crissy spotted Monika's silver hair a few feet away and went in that direction.

"Crissy, my darling," she called. "Rudy and Mina are already on the bus. They are saving us seats. We want to make certain that our little American friend is well taken care of."

They boarded and saw Mina and Rudy midway back, waving to them. Within minutes, after a head count, they were off to Taormina. They wound through the narrow streets of Catania, and Crissy found herself amazed with the baroque architecture. It was surely the most fanciful in the world.

"The black you see," Monika pointed out, "is not just grime. They are built of volcanic rock, you see."

"That's fascinating," Crissy said. "I'm glad you know these things."

"Now you do, too," Monika said with obvious pleasure.

Outside the city, they passed many housing developments. Most of them were built after World War II as part of the plan to rebuild Europe after the destruction of the war. The bus began climbing a mountain toward Taormina, and the road was treacherous, twisting and turning at the very edge of cliffs. Beautiful villas dotted the landscape all about. Looking up, she saw Taormina in the distance, and it was stunningly beautiful, appearing to hang suspended from the mountain. The bus soon pulled into a parking lot from where they would walk, the town being largely pedestrian.

When they reached the town, Crissy suddenly stopped and laughed.

"What is it, darling?" Monika asked breathlessly, as the climb had been arduous for her.

"The first store you see is Prada," Crissy replied. "Jenny will be really upset that she missed it."

Nearby was a lovely square dominated by an ancient tree of huge proportions, and to one side was a small sidewalk café. Shops chock-full of beautifully painted Majolica tiles, pots, and vases sprinkled both sides of the pedestrian lane, but there were also expensive-looking boutiques. Window boxes were colorfully planted with geraniums and vines. Just beyond an exclusive-looking cliffside hotel they passed under an enormous arch and entered the ancient theater that had helped put Taormina on the tourist map long ago. Crissy was awed by the first sight.

"It's still used for performances," Monika said.

Crissy nodded, then looked beyond the theater toward the gray skies. For a moment the clouds parted and the sun shone through. She could glimpse the top of Mt. Etna in the distance.

"Look!" she cried to Monika. "That's Mt. Etna, isn't it?"

The older woman followed Crissy's gaze. "Yes, darling," she said.

Almost before she had finished her sentence, the top of the volcano disappeared from view, covered by clouds again. Crissy's foursome soon left the other ship passengers behind and wandered back down to the town's main street with its beautiful and expensive shops. Even more fascinating to Crissy were the occasional glimpses she caught between buildings. To her right, narrow stone steps led up to restaurants, hotels, and shops on higher levels, and on her left, steep steps led down to other establishments.

"People must walk themselves to death here," she said.

"That is the curse of such a beautiful site," Monika said. "It's practically straight up and down, but it's well worth it."

They came to a large piazza with two imposing ancient churches. On one side of the piazza was a low wall, and they went to it. Looking straight out, the sea, sparkling even with the cloud cover, stretched into the distance as far as the eye could see. Wandering back to the small square near the entrance to the town, they sat at the sidewalk café and ordered espressos. Shopkeepers were stopping by for coffee or drinks, and Crissy noticed how well dressed and groomed they were. She also observed how men often walked arm in arm, chatting away. "You would never see that in America," she pointed out to Monika.

Monika tinkled laughter. "No, my darling," she said. "This is absolutely normal here. There is no fear of men touching or kissing here as in your country, but these men are probably more obsessed with machismo than Americans are. Obsessed with *bella figura*. Always looking their best. Bodies, clothes, the works. Image is everything."

"How odd," Crissy said. "Where I come from, those men we saw would be laughed at. Everybody would think they're gay."

"One of those little cultural differences, darling," Monika said. "See the pair over there? Near the newsstand?"

"Yes," Crissy said.

"Laugh at them or insult their masculinity, and you might end up thrown off the cliff."

Members of their group were straggling into the square, where they had been told to meet to return to the bus. Soon the vehicle set off back down the mountain, the twisting road no less hair-raising than it had been coming up. After going through the security checkpoint with their key cards, they boarded the ship. She and Monika went their separate ways, promising to see each other at dinner. In the cabin, Crissy found herself alone because Jenny had not yet returned from Mt. Etna or she was off somewhere else on the ship. She undressed and spread out on the bed, thinking that she would get up in a minute to shower and change for dinner, but she fell asleep almost at once.

*   *   *

Georgios Vilos' black Mercedes limousine pulled away from the curb in front of the Lampaki brothers' lighted building in central Athens, but he didn't give the bank's venerable marble facade a backward glance. Rosemary, his personal assistant, stared straight ahead, as did he, her teeth clenched in nervousness. She knew that her employer needed comfort—kind words, caring pats, anything—but she also realized that he would turn on her like a wild animal cornered by predators if she so much as mentioned what had happened in the boardroom at Lampaki.

A uniformed guard had met them at the lobby door and escorted them to the fourth-floor boardroom. They were ushered into the large, sedate mahogany-paneled room with its brass chandelier and gloomy portraits of long-dead bankers—an imitation of an English bank—and faced a long, wide conference table around which sat the four brothers and two assistants, both women. They were all of middle age or older, the men wearing dark pin-striped suits and conservative ties, their carefully cut hair gray or graying, the women in dark suits that deemphasized their sexuality, their hair almost identical in small, brown-tinted curls.

The men rose to greet Georgios Vilos and Rosemary, and after introductions, they took the seats proffered. Water was poured into crystal glasses from a silver pitcher, and they were asked if they wanted coffee.

"Not for me," Georgios replied. "Rosemary?"

She shook her head. "No, thank you."

Several minutes of small talk followed—long, interminable minutes to Georgios Vilos—concerning the cool weather and other such innocuous subjects. Finally, Niko, the eldest of the brothers at the table, opened a folder in front of him, then placed his hands on it ceremoniously. He looked down the table at Georgios Vilos with clear blue eyes from behind wire-rimmed spectacles. "Mr. Vilos," he began, clearing his throat, "we've reviewed your application and of course have studied your financial statement with great care."

Georgios Vilos nodded. "As I would assume," he replied. "As you can see, it is no secret that Vilos Shipping, Ltd. is in dire financial straits, but we have considerable assets and a very good international reputation." He paused and scanned the faces at the table. "We've been in business all of my life and my father's before me, and we've grown steadily over the years to arrive at this point. Unfortunately, we've overextended ourselves in the present economy, but I've already taken drastic measures—and will take many more—to reduce our expenditures and get us back on a solid financial footing."

"Be that as it may," Niko Lampaki began, "we here at Lampaki, after careful consideration of your application, find that we cannot lend you the requested monies to repay the German banks to whom you are indebted. Regrettable, I know, but we see no choice."

Georgios Vilos digested Niko Lampaki's words, trying to keep his facial expression as neutral as possible. His stomach roiled and lurched, however, and his mind began to race in a dozen different directions at once. Buying time before speaking, he picked up the crystal glass in front of him and took a long drink of water. Setting the glass back down, he looked directly at Lampaki.

"I was under the impression, Mr. Lampaki," he said, "that you were perhaps willing to cover these loans for me at a very high rate of interest. As you know, I have considerable collateral. My ships, my tankers, the office buildings . . ."

"We here at Lampaki don't take the same view of the situation, Mr. Vilos," Niko Lampaki went on.

The words drifted over Georgios Vilos barely heard, as if they were dust motes in the air. He soon listened as the other brothers, one barely distinguishable from the other, repeated what in essence Niko Lampaki had already said, driving home the awful truth. They were not under any circumstances—no matter the interest rate—going to make him the loan.

After their endless discourse, much of it a litany of Vilos' financial woes that he knew better than anyone, Georgios finally took a deep breath and gazed about the table again, making eye contact with everyone there. "I understand what you have to say," he said in a clear voice, "and I know that what you say is true." He took a sip of water. "But I am begging you. Put whatever price you deem necessary, whatever conditions you desire, on this loan, and offer it to me." Looking at each one in turn again, he added: "I have never begged anyone for anything, but I am begging you now."

The room was silent, and Georgios Vilos could sense their embarrassment for him; perhaps, too, their pleasure in being able to deny him the wherewithal to save his company. Even though they were a notoriously usurious group, these were low-profile bankers, and rich men all, and they conducted their lives behind closed doors in a luxurious privacy that the outside world was seldom permitted to view. Georgios Vilos—in their eyes, at least—was a high-profile, high-living profligate whose family peo-

102

pled the fashionable magazines and press, their palatial homes and expensive exploits endlessly featured for all the world to see. He was of another caste that they found vaguely distasteful—*nouveau riche,* but worst of all, careless. He knew it was useless to pursue these men and their money any further.

Rising to his feet, quickly followed by Rosemary, who snapped her briefcase shut, Georgios Vilos looked around the conference table one last time. "Thank you," he said. "We'll be going now."

He turned and walked toward the tall mahogany door that led out of the boardroom. Rosemary nodded politely at those still seated around the table, then hurried to catch up with him.

The guard who had escorted them upstairs dashed to catch up with Georgios and Rosemary as they headed toward the bank of elevators. Georgios turned to the guard. "We can find our way back down."

"I'm following instructions," the guard said.

Georgios started to protest but thought better of it. Let the man do his job, he thought. On the lobby floor, he exited the building with his head held high, and allowed his driver to hold the limousine's door open for him and Rosemary. When he sank down into its redolent leather upholstery, he fixed his gaze straight ahead, ignoring Rosemary, who sat beside him. He knew that she was restraining herself from saying or doing something solicitous of his fraught emotions, but he was in no mood to reassure her that he would be fine.

When the driver moved out into traffic, Georgios told him to take them directly to his house, then he turned to Rosemary. "He'll drop you off afterward, if you don't mind."

"Not at all, sir," she replied.

Georgios faced straight ahead again, stony-faced and silent. He tried to clear his mind of the meeting. The vultures, he thought, would love nothing more than feeding upon the carrion of his company, but he wasn't about to give them that opportunity. He would give no one that chance. He would have to put his other plan into action. He had no choice.

When they arrived at the Vilos mansion in Kifissia, Georgios didn't wait for the driver to come around and open his door. He exited the car with a curt nod to Rosemary and strode to the house, tapping in the security code to open a rear door. Going straight to his study and slamming the door shut behind him, he sat down at his desk, flipped open his cell phone, and pressed in a number.

The phone was answered on the third ring. "Yes."

"Is the package in place?"

"Yes."

"You're absolutely certain about that?"

"I can assure you that I saw it taken aboard."

"But was it placed where I ordered?"

"Of course."

"You saw this with your own eyes?"

"Yes."

Georgios Vilos swiped the sweat from his forehead with his free hand and cupped the cell phone closer to his lips. "I want you to make certain it is still there."

"That's unnecessary. I—"

"Just *do* it," he snapped, "and report back to me immediately." He suddenly didn't trust the word of Azad alone. After his failure with the Lampaki brothers, the world was a darker, more treacherous place. Azad's word was not enough. Now he would have to rely on his man aboard the *Sea Nymph.*

Georgios Vilos pressed the END button and closed the cell phone. He would wait here until the call was returned. Pulling a linen handkerchief from his trouser pocket, he wiped his sweat-soaked hand dry, then dabbed his face. *This fucking Athenian humidity,* he thought, knowing that the weather in Athens had nothing to do with the perspiration that continued to bead on his face.

She awoke with a start. The cabin was dark, and she was momentarily confused and uneasy. Sitting up, she turned on a light and looked at her watch. It was nearly eight o'clock. When she rose from the bed, she abruptly felt sick to her stomach and light-headed. She was also aware of the ship's movement as she hadn't been before, despite its smooth passage through the water, and she felt a queasiness, as if her body was out of sync with the rhythm of sea and vessel. Her forehead beaded with perspiration. She fetched a cold bottle of water from the minibar and drank several gulps, but rather than soothing her queasy stomach, it made her feel worse. Oh, no, she thought. This wasn't seasickness, surely. Didn't that happen when there were rough seas, in storms and such? The wonderful day suddenly seemed to lose its magic, and her spirits sagged. She knew it was because she didn't feel well, but knowing still didn't help.

She picked up the ship's daily schedule to find out where the hospital was located. When she went in, there was no one in the small reception area, but a nurse-receptionist appeared almost instantly.

"What can I do for you?" she asked in heavily accented English. Her badly bleached hair was pulled back into a small chignon, but brassy orange tendrils escaped both it and the small, pristine hat pinned to her head. She wore black-rimmed glasses that magnified her eyes, and she looked unfriendly and stern, not a source of comfort.

"I'm feeling sick to my stomach," Crissy said. "I don't know if it's seasickness or what. I was sweaty, and I just don't feel . . . right."

"Right?" the nurse repeated, looking at her as if she were an idiot.

"I-I don't know how to explain it," Crissy said, "but I feel sick." The nurse was beginning to make her angry.

"Please fill this out," the nurse said, handing her a form on a clipboard and a pen.

Crissy sat down and quickly did as she was told, then handed everything back to the nurse, who scanned it with her enormous-looking eyes.

From behind the paneled partition that separated the reception area from the rest of the hospital, an elderly woman emerged, a young man holding her arm reassuringly. He saw Crissy and nodded with a smile as he escorted the woman to the exit. They exchanged a few words in a foreign language—was it Italian? Crissy wondered—before he turned to her and the nurse.

"What seems to be the problem, Voula?"

"She doesn't feel 'right,' " the nurse said with a hint of derision.

Crissy suddenly realized that she'd seen the doctor before. She felt herself blush, embarrassed by seeing him in such close proximity after last night. He was the handsome young man who'd shown up in the disco with the captain's party around midnight; the one who hadn't danced but had remained at the table alone. The one she'd stared at until she realized he was staring at her.

"You don't feel 'right'?"

There was that word again, making her feel as if she was a six-year-old, unable to explain her symptoms. "I have an upset stomach," she replied nervously, "and I feel the ship moving. In a different way. I—"

"Come with me," he said, indicating the door leading through the partition. "We'll get you feeling right again." He smiled, and Crissy felt relieved. He wasn't making fun of her. At least she didn't think he was.

105

Crissy went through the doorway into a corridor, and he led her into an examination room. "Sit down there," he said, pointing toward the examination table.

Crissy did as she was told.

"I'm Dr. Santo," he said, "and I'm here to make you better."

He spoke almost without any accent, she noticed.

"Now," he said, "tell me when this started and describe how you feel as best you can."

His dark eyes never left hers as he listened to her, except when he looked down to scribble notes. Crissy was unnerved by his steady gaze, but told herself that he was a doctor, after all.

Finally, he said, "You have the symptoms of seasickness, but you also may have caught a virus of some sort. You were on a long flight, which can cause problems, and you've been keeping late hours and getting very little sleep."

He smiled that wonderful smile again, and Crissy wasn't certain that he was admonishing her. It seemed more that he was enjoying her tale of neglecting her body's need for rest.

"Plus you've been eating some things your system isn't used to, so it's hard to say without a lot of tests exactly what the problem is," he went on. "What I suggest is a round of antibiotics to take care of any bug you might have picked up, and I'm going to give you scopolamine patches for seasickness. You'll put one behind your ear every day until your trip is over. If you aren't seasick, they won't harm you, and they'll diminish the effects of seasickness if you should get it later on."

"Okay," Crissy said. "I really appreciate this. I can't believe it. The trip has barely begun, and I get sick."

"We'll make you feel better very quickly," he said, "so you'll be able to enjoy the rest of it. I suggest that you start the medication tonight and that you eat lightly. Also, eat food you are accustomed to."

Crissy nodded. "I don't know if I can eat at all."

"Even if it's some yogurt, you should eat something," he said. "Now wait here while I get your medicine. It will just take a minute."

"Okay." She watched him leave the room. He was so handsome, she thought, and he had a wonderful, reassuring smile. He also seemed efficient and no-nonsense in his approach, but he did seem to draw an invisible line between himself and his patients—at least her. She remembered his aloofness last night and wondered if this was connected to his professionalism or if it was a character trait.

He came back into the room holding a small bottle of pills and a little box. "This is the antibiotic," he said, handing her the bottle, "and these are the scopolamine patches. Let me show you how to use the patches." He took the box from her, opened it, and shook out a small sheet of patches enclosed in plastic bubbles. He tore off one of the patches and peeled off the plastic bubble, then held the patch on a finger. "Pull your hair back," he said, "and I'll put it in place."

"Does it matter which side?" she asked.

"No," he said, grinning.

Crissy pulled the hair back over her right ear, and he pressed the stick-on patch firmly in place, rubbing it several times to make certain it was secure.

"There," he said. "All done. You'll take that off tomorrow night and put on another one. And start with two of the antibiotics right away," he said. "As soon as you get back to your cabin." Then he looked thoughtful for a moment, and said, "Let me get you a glass of water. You can begin now."

He took a paper cup from a dispenser and poured bottled water into it. Taking the antibiotics from her, he shook out two and handed them to her. "Here you are."

Crissy did as she was told. She was surprised by his attentiveness. He didn't have to start her on the round of medicine, did he? He seemed to be going if not out of his way, then beyond that invisible line she had felt he'd drawn.

He checked his watch. "If you go to the dining room now," he said, "you can still join your friends there and have something to eat. If nothing on the menu appeals to you, tell them you want some yogurt or soup. You can tell them that I told you to do that."

"Okay," Crissy said, "and thanks again. I think I feel better already because you've been so . . . great."

He smiled. "That's what I'm here for."

She slid off the examination table and went to the door. "It was very nice meeting you."

He nodded. "Feel better."

Crissy went back into the reception area, and Voula looked up at her. "I hope you're 'right' now," she said, her creepily magnified eyes focused on Crissy with amusement.

"Thanks," Crissy said, choosing to ignore the woman's condescending attitude. She opened the door and left, slowly climbing the stairs to Deck Five, where she knew dinner was already being served.

After filling Monika's group in on her bout of seasickness and eating a yogurt, Crissy left the dining room, still feeling sick. When she reached her cabin, Jenny was not in, but she wasn't surprised. She was certain that Jenny and Manolo had managed to sneak off somewhere on the ship together. They were probably entwined in each other's arms at this moment, she thought as she undressed for bed.

The beds had been turned down, chocolates in place, and the ship's schedule for the next day had been delivered. Crissy put the chocolate in her bedside cabinet drawer and picked up the schedule and excursion brochure before spreading out on the bed. Tomorrow they would be docking in Naples. She had been very excited by the prospect of seeing nearby Pompeii, and she hoped she would feel well enough for the excursion. When she was finished, she retrieved the book she'd brought from the bedside cabinet and began reading.

She had been engrossed in the novel for about a half hour when she heard a knock at the door. It's probably the maid, she thought, here to restock the minibar or something. Calling "Just a second," as she got out of bed, she grabbed the kimono she'd brought and put it on over her T-shirt. When she opened the door, she was surprised by the sight that greeted her eyes.

"Hi," Dr. Santo said, taking his cap off. "I was passing by and thought I would see how you are doing."

Crissy held the door open and simply stared for a moment, then was jarred into action when he smiled and said, "Have I come at a bad time? If it's inconvenient, I can—"

"No-no," Crissy stammered, opening the door wide. "I'm sorry. Please come in. I was just . . . just—"

"Surprised to see that it was me?" the doctor said, stepping into the small hall. He smiled, and his dark eyes seemed to light up the dimly lit entryway.

"Well, yes," Crissy admitted. She felt herself blush, a reaction that irritated her. *Why do I react this way?* she wondered. *Like I'm some kind of schoolgirl or something.* She retreated and went to the small sofa, nervously knotting the tie around the kimono.

"I wanted to check up on you," he said. "Are you feeling any better?"

"I think so," Crissy replied. "Maybe a little bit." From her position on the couch, he seemed to tower over her and dominate the cabin, making it look as if it could hardly contain his strapping body. He was over six feet tall with broad shoulders, and he was long-waisted and long-legged. He appeared to be in his early thirties and in peak physical condition, with black hair and olive skin. She hadn't realized that he was such a tall and imposing man when she was in the hospital, perhaps because she was so distracted by the queasiness she felt.

"I still feel 'off,' if you know what I mean, but it's no worse and maybe a little better."

"Very good," he said. "Do you feel feverish at all?"

Crissy shook her head. "No," she replied. "I . . . Why don't you sit down? I am so rude. Here"—she indicated one of the chairs that faced her—"please take one of these."

"Thanks." He sat down and crossed one leg over the other so that one ankle rested on his knee. "Are you going to have an early night?"

Crissy nodded. "I came straight back here from dinner," she said. "My dining companions were off to the show, but I thought I'd try to get a good night's sleep."

"You're not going to be sneaking off to the disco later?" he asked.

"No," Crissy said. "I'm not the greatest dancer around anyway."

"I'm not either," he said seriously. "I guess it's because I was always in school, always studying. I didn't have time for dancing or drinking—you know, the normal stuff other people did. So even now I feel like a fish out of water when I'm in social situations like that." He looked at her, those sensuous lips set in a half smile.

Crissy found it difficult to believe that this man, obviously so good-looking, well-educated, and intelligent, could ever have felt that way. He was, she thought, a superb specimen. He was the sort of man who could walk into a room and draw everyone's attention simply by being there, as if he possessed an aura that held people in thrall. Now she understood his aloof behavior in the disco, while the captain and other officers socialized with passengers. It was not a part of the world that he was comfortable with yet.

"But you seem to have such a way with patients," she said. Then she smiled. "Certainly from my perspective."

"I'm trained as a doctor," he said, "and the doctor-patient relationship seems to come naturally to me. I guess it's harder for me to deal with people when they aren't patients. On a more personal level, if you know what I mean."

Crissy nodded. "I know what you mean," she said. "It's like in my work. I'm a hair colorist, and some of my customers tell me their secrets, really intimate things. But outside the shop, I'm not their friend. Some of them wouldn't even give me the time of day outside the shop."

"Oooh," he said, "I don't believe that. You're so amiable, so easy to talk to. Why would they be that way?"

"I'm a colorist, for one thing," she said, "so I'm not on their social level, you know?"

"But that's ridiculous," he replied. "You're beautiful and smart. Besides," he added, "America doesn't have a class system, does it?"

"Oh, please," she said. "You don't believe that any more than I do. It may not be as rigid as in some places, but America definitely has a class system."

He smiled mischievously. "Of course," he said. "I know that. My mother is American. She grew up in Main Line Philadelphia and Palm Beach. And my father grew up in a Florentine palazzo, but he went to school in England. Eton and Oxford."

A rich family, Crissy thought. "I see," she said. "That explains your perfect English."

He paused, then asked, "You are from New York, right?"

"Yes," Crissy said. "Upstate New York. Albany."

"I love New York City," he said. "So much energy and so sophisticated."

"I do, too," she replied, "but where I live is very different. It's not so big, and it's certainly not as sophisticated."

"But you seem pretty sophisticated to me."

Crissy laughed. "Don't put me on."

"I'm not," he protested. "Really." He gazed at her for a moment, then said, "I'm Luca, by the way." He put out a hand for her to shake.

"I'm Crissy," she replied, "but you knew that."

"Yes, but I didn't want to be too forward and call you that."

"And I certainly wouldn't have called you anything but Dr. Santo," she said with a laugh.

"Please call me Luca," he said.

"It's a pleasure to meet you, Luca," she replied.

"And it's very much a pleasure for me to meet you, Crissy," he said. "I hope I can see you again."

"I-I do, too," Crissy said. Then before she could think, she added, "I would like that very much."

"Wonderful," he said. "I'd better get going now. I have to meet Captain Papadapolis for the nightly appearance at the disco."

"Oh, so you're going partying," she said.

"I wish you were going to be there," he said. "Maybe then I would dance. With you."

Crissy felt herself blush again. "I would like that, too," she said. "Or just sitting and talking."

He got to his feet, and Crissy rose from the couch to show him out. At the door, he turned to her. "Take care of yourself," he said. "Have a good night's sleep."

She nodded. "I will."

He opened the door. "Good night."

" 'Night."

He went down the corridor, and she closed the door behind him. *Oh, my God,* she thought. *I don't believe it. He's so smart and handsome and gentlemanly and sexy. Yes, that, too. And he said that I'm beautiful!*

She felt like pinching herself to make certain that she wasn't dreaming. He had called her beautiful and smart, even sophisticated. She got back into bed and turned out the light. *I hope I see him again soon,* she thought. *He had to have meant what he said, didn't he?* Even after Mark had called her beautiful, she still didn't know what to make of the compliments. Mark, she felt, might have been playing with her. And he hadn't mentioned smart or sophisticated. Luca seemed utterly sincere. Her mind returned to that fateful night when she had met Tom Gentry, and the ensuing heartache she had endured because she had been convinced that they'd had something very special between them. She didn't believe that Luca Santo was capable of such deception, but she really didn't know enough about him to make a decision like that. What she did know was that she wouldn't give herself to him until she was convinced of his honesty and integrity. She'd have to stifle this physical yearning that she hadn't felt in a long time. *Yes,* she told herself, *you're not jumping into bed like Jenny. You're not like that.*

She was still trying to convince herself when she finally fell asleep.

The man looked up and down the corridor. There was no one in sight. He quickly slid the key card down the groove, then shoved down on the door handle. The door opened silently and smoothly on its well-oiled hinges. Once inside, he quietly closed the door behind him and stood in the entrance hall, his ears alert for any sign of habitation. He knew that Mark wasn't in the stateroom, but it was possible that a steward or some other ship employee had come in to perform some service.

When he didn't hear anything, he ventured into the large sitting room, scanning the room with a sweep of his eyes. His gaze fell at once on the steamer trunk, emblazoned with the large Vs. Placed against the wall, it was too big to be stored in one of the stateroom's closets. As many as there were in this luxurious suite, none of them would accommodate its size.

Approaching the trunk, he removed a key ring from his right-hand trouser pocket and found the oddly shaped brass key that fit the trunk's single lock. He inserted the key and opened the lid. An assortment of old quilts were piled in the trunk. Quickly and efficiently, he removed the quilts, neatly placing them on the floor, until he saw what he was looking for.

Near the bottom of the trunk, cushioned by a layer of quilts, the cache of plastic explosives, Semtex, lay inert and innocent, wrapped in plastic shopping bags from Hondos Center in Athens. He replaced the quilts he'd taken out and closed the lid atop it, then locked the trunk. Turning, he crept through the stateroom to the door. Opening it a mere hair, he looked out. A lone elderly woman was coming down the corridor. He closed the door, but kept his hand on the handle. When he heard her pass, he waited a moment, then opened the door once again and looked both ways. All clear. He slipped out of the stateroom, letting the door close behind him. It would automatically lock.

Feeling the cell phone in his pocket, he took it out. He would go out on deck to make the call where there was no one about. He could assure Georgios Vilos that the explosives were in place.

Chapter Nine

When she awoke, Crissy felt much better, if not fully recovered. Jenny still hadn't come in, but she wasn't concerned. She took her time showering, then carefully put on makeup and got dressed. Her appetite had returned—she felt starved, in fact—so she went straight to the cafeteria-style dining room, the Sky Garden, on Deck Six. There were already a number of passengers about, most of them elderly. She got in line and filled her tray with scrambled eggs, bacon, yogurt, fruit, and mini croissants, then took a cup of coffee with sugar and cream. It was a huge breakfast for her, but she felt that she really needed it after eating so little the night before.

There were plenty of empty tables on the deck outside, so she took her tray to one and sat down. The sky was clear today, and the sea was calm. There was no land visible, but different seabirds looped in the air about the ship. She was sipping the rich aromatic coffee when a tall, skinny orange-haired woman passed her table at a fast pace, followed by a few elderly men and women, struggling to keep up with her. As Crissy watched, the line of power walkers trudged up a flight of stairs behind the woman, who stood walking in place at the top of the stairs, urging them on. She was obviously the German fitness expert who led the morning walk mentioned in the daily schedule and also held various fitness classes throughout the day.

"Well, well," came a voice from behind her. "Eating alone?"

Crissy turned her head and saw Mark coming down the stairs. As before when she had met him, he was flawlessly dressed in a navy blazer, an ascot of red, paisley-patterned silk, a light blue shirt, and tan trousers. His shoes shone with polish. His hair was swept back from his forehead, making his aquiline nose seem all the more impressive. She felt a flutter in her chest. He was certainly one of the most debonair men she'd ever met.

"Mind if I join you?"

"No," Crissy replied. "Not at all."

Mark sat in a chair next to her. "So, you really don't know who I am, do you?"

"I do now," Crissy said. "My friend, Monika, told me after we danced last night, and now I know why you knew so much about the ship."

"Yes," Mark said. "And aren't you a little bit sorry you turned down a chance to visit my stateroom?" He gazed at her with a smile.

Crissy returned his smile. "I'm not so sure about that," she said. "I've just met you, after all."

"Afraid of me?"

"No," she replied, "but I don't know you."

"Maybe you should get to know me better," he replied. "I don't like taking no for an answer, especially from a beautiful and sexy lady like you. I can see that you're a challenge, and I like that. Besides, I don't bite."

"I didn't think you did," Crissy said with a laugh. She was surprised and delighted by his straightforwardness.

"I didn't mean to scare you off," he said in an apologetic voice. "I guess I came on a little too strong considering we'd just met."

"Don't worry about it." She was beginning to feel a little guilty. Besides his looks, Mark had great style and charm, she thought, and perhaps there was substance there as well. There was no doubt that he was appealing to her, and she had to admit that he was very sexy.

"I hope we can get better acquainted," he said. He grinned. "Then I won't be so scary."

"Oh, you're *not* scary," Crissy said, feeling defensive. "I never thought that, Mark. I hope we can get to know each other better, too."

"Good," Mark said. "What are you doing today?"

"I'm going to Pompeii," she said. "I can hardly wait."

"It's fascinating," Mark replied.

"So you've been?"

"Yes. Several times."

"Tell me about it," Crissy said. "Do you mind?"

"Of course not," he replied amiably. His knowledge was vast, and she listened with interest as he shared information about the ancient site, trying to digest as much as she could.

"The eruption of Vesuvius that buried Pompeii was in 79 A.D.," he said. "There were probably about twenty thousand people living there, and around two thousand were killed. I personally think that Herculaneum, which is not far away, is more interesting, but Pompeii is well worth the visit. You won't have time today, but someday you should see the museum in Naples, too. Some of the more interesting artifacts are there."

"Why's that?"

"Because they can be protected better there than at Pompeii. Anyway, you're going to love the mosaics and murals and some of the statues and architecture. Things like that."

As he spoke, Crissy gradually became impressed by his knowledge. Because of his handsomeness and his money, she supposed that it was easy to dismiss him as a nothing more than a playboy, but she discovered that he was very intelligent and had enthusiasm for what he was discussing. She had never met anyone with this combination of looks, money, charms, *and* brains, and she couldn't help but be taken in by him. His interest in her was all the more flattering.

"Wow," she said when he finished. "You really know a lot about it."

He shrugged. "Not that much really," he said modestly. "It's just from having been there a few times and spending time in the area. I think the Bay of Naples and the Amalfi Coast and the islands are really beautiful. I hope you enjoy it."

"I know I will," she said.

"So what are you doing now?"

"I'm going to go change then get some sun."

"I would ask to join you," Mark said, "but I'm afraid you'd think I'm being pushy. You seem a little gun-shy to me, but maybe after you get to know me better you'll see that I'm really not such a bad guy."

"I don't think you're a bad guy," she said.

"Well . . . whatever. I'd better get going," he said with a smile. "I hope I see you tonight at the disco."

Crissy was surprised, and she had to admit that she was somewhat disappointed that he hadn't asked to join her sunning or if she'd go with him to the disco. The more she got to know him, the more attractive she found him. His straightforwardness was refreshing. "That would be nice," she said.

"I'll see you later, Crissy." He rose to his feet. "Have a great time in Pompeii."

"Thanks, Mark."

He turned and left, and Crissy watched his tall, handsome figure disappear inside. *Maybe I was a fool to turn down his invitation last night,* she thought. *I am on vacation, and what's the harm in having a little fun with a sexy guy like Mark?* She sat for a few minutes longer, lost in thought, then pushed her chair back and rose to her feet.

She went through the sliding glass door into the dining room, then on down the staircase to the cabin. She changed into a bathing suit, put her kimono on over it, slipped into sandals, and put her book in her shoulder bag. Towels, she'd noticed, were provided at the pool.

When she reached the pool deck, she found a chaise longue in an area that wasn't yet crowded, dropped her shoulder bag on it, and spread a towel on the chaise.

After ordering a Coke Lite at the bar, she returned to the chaise and put on her sunglasses, then rifled through her shoulder bag for her novel. She began reading, but found herself distracted by the new arrivals and the people passing by on their way elsewhere. Several people were in the pool, and it delighted her to see that some of them were very old, with wrinkled, liver-spotted, sagging, too-skinny or too-fat bodies that some of her friends—Jenny, for example—would either find hilariously ugly or disgustingly repellant. She hoped that when she reached that age she would be as unselfconscious as these people were and could enjoy herself as much as they did.

The pool deck was a never-ending show in several different languages, but its attractions, even the laughter and splashing water, didn't keep her eyes from drooping shut in the heat of the sun. When she awoke, she was momentarily confused, but quickly realized where she was. The book had fallen to the deck, and her glass of Coke Lite sat half empty in a pool of water from condensation. She looked at her watch and was surprised to see that it was almost time for lunch. Gathering up her things, she went back to the cabin, showered, and changed clothes.

Deciding to have lunch in the formal dining room, where she would more likely see Monika, Mina, and the others, she climbed to Deck Five. The maître d' escorted her to their table, where all the others were seated.

"Oh, Crissy, darling," Monika exclaimed. "I'm so happy to see you. How are you feeling today?"

"I'm much better, thanks," Crissy said, taking a seat. She took the menu handed to her by the waiter and glanced down at it.

"Where is your friend?" Dr. Von Meckling asked.

"I'm not sure," Crissy replied. "I think she's probably having lunch with another friend."

"That young officer, no doubt," Monika said.

"She seems to be enjoying his company," Rudy said.

"Yes," Crissy said. "I think they're having a good time together."

"Do you feel up to going on one of the excursions today?" Monika asked.

Crissy nodded. "Yes, I'm going to Pompeii."

"Oh, wonderful," Monika said, clapping her hands together. "We are, too. That will make it all the merrier."

The waiter appeared, and Crissy gave him her lunch order.

"Do you know if your friend is coming along?" Dr. Von Meckling asked.

"I don't," Crissy replied. *Jeez,* she thought. *Is he obsessed with Jen or what?*

"That young man again," Monika said with a nod. "Too bad. She's wasting her time with him."

"Why do you say that?" Crissy asked.

Monika shrugged. "Because, darling, he's only using her for a fling. He probably does this with a different young lady on every voyage. The girl-in-every-port syndrome, you know. Except that they're on the ship."

"I'm not so sure that he's using her any more than she's using him," Crissy said with a laugh. "Jen likes to play around."

Crissy found that she did love Pompeii, as Mark promised, but she'd had no idea the site was so huge. She quickly discovered that it would take many days or many visits to see everything. After more than two hours of constant walking, awed as she was by the beauty of the ruins, she found herself glad to accept Monika's invitation to return to the Sea Gate, by which they'd entered, and have something to drink at a sidewalk café across the street.

"I had no idea that it still smells like the site of a fire," Crissy said as they exited the city. "Did you smell it?"

"Well, it was a vast crematorium," Monika replied, "and I got whiffs of the awful burning odor, too."

"I love the houses with their inner courtyards and fountains," Crissy said. "They must have been beautiful."

"Oh, yes," Monika said. "That's still such a good plan, isn't it? Especially where the weather allows." She paused. "Oh, here we are. Finally. I can rest my feet."

Crissy didn't point out that Monika had worn high heels for sightseeing, walking on large, irregular cobbles and slick marble. She gathered that Monika would have worn the same shoes for mountain climbing, and the same outfit, a dress more suitable for a late-afternoon cocktail party. She gathered that the eccentric woman was so enamored of her glitzy wardrobe that no occasion would warrant her changing into something casual.

They ordered iced coffees and chatted about what they'd seen, and Crissy listened to Monika's running commentary on the terrible dressing standards maintained by most of the tourists that passed by. "Gym clothes," she said disdainfully. "And sneakers. The world is going to the dogs, wearing such apparel to travel. Imagine. And from the looks of most of the people, they've never seen the inside of a gym."

Crissy laughed. "That's true," she agreed. "So many of them are overweight."

"Yes," Monika said. "They are terribly unfit. I hope you never allow yourself to get in such a state. You're far too beautiful to let yourself go. One must keep up one's standards even if the rest of the world is too lazy, too slothful, and too inconsiderate of others to dress appropriately."

The café was situated at the top of a hill up which the access road climbed, and she thought she could see a familiar figure coming their way. As he drew closer, she could see that it was indeed who she thought it was, despite his not being in uniform. Luca Santo was dressed in a sharp-looking sports jacket, sweater, and trousers. Her pulse began to race, and she felt a flutter in her chest as she had when she saw Mark. It was an instinctual response that arose of its own accord, and it frustrated Crissy, because she had no control over it.

When he saw her, he waved, and Crissy returned it. She hoped that Monika didn't notice her sudden excitement at seeing Luca because she didn't want to hear what she might have to say about him, and she certainly didn't want to listen to a lecture about wasting her time with one of the ship's employees.

He drew up to the table and tipped his cap. "Hello, ladies."

Monika was impressed. "How do you do?"

"Hi," Crissy said.

"I hope you're feeling better today," he said to Crissy.

"Yes, Doctor," she replied. She was uncomfortable using his first name in front of Monika, besides which, she didn't want Monika to know to what extent they knew each another. "I'm feeling much better, thank you."

"Oh, so you're the ship's doctor," Monika said, looking at him with more interest. "We are so grateful to you for taking such good care of our darling friend here."

Luca nodded. "It was my duty," he replied, "and my pleasure. She was a very good patient."

Monika's gaze swept him up and down, assessing him as if he were a side of beef. "Would you care to join us, Doctor?" she asked. "We're having a coffee and resting our feet. This is such a large site, you know."

Luca pulled out a chair and sat down, then caught the waiter's attention. "Would you like another coffee?" he asked. "Or something else?"

Crissy nodded. "I think I'll have a refill," she said.

"I will, too," Monika said. "This is quite good coffee for such a touristy spot, isn't it."

Luca gave the waiter their order in Italian.

"You know Crissy, of course," Monika said, "and I am Monika Graf, the novelist."

"Luca Santo," he said smiling. "So you are a writer?"

"Yes," Monika replied, "and my novels are published in Italian."

"I'll have to look for them," Luca said.

"They may not be to your taste," Monika said, although she was pleased with his response. "So you are Italian?" she said, still observing him closely.

"Yes," Luca said.

"And where are you from?" she asked.

"Firenze," he replied. "Florence."

"Lovely," Monika said. "I thought your accent was a bit more northern. The Neapolitan accent is so . . . different." She looked as if she had a bad taste in her mouth.

"Yes," he said. "There are many different accents, of course, as there are in all countries, I guess, but one is hardly superior to the other."

"You don't think so?" Monika said. "Surely you are joking."

"No," Luca said, shaking his head. "I've had extremely intelligent friends at school who spoke with a Palermitan accent that was practically unintelligible until you got used to it. There were a couple from Calabria with that southern dialect, too, but they were top students."

"Of course," Monika said, but it was apparent that she either didn't agree with him or didn't like hearing what he had to say. Crissy remembered how she had made fun of Rudy's and Mina's accents.

The waiter brought their coffees, and Luca thanked him.

"Are you enjoying the trip?" Luca asked, changing the subject.

"Yes," Monika said, "though I prefer larger, more glamorous ships."

Luca laughed. "And you?" He looked at Crissy.

"Oh, yes," she said. "I loved Athens, Taormina, and what I got to see of Catania, and today has been wonderful. I've always wanted to see Pompeii."

"Good," he said. "This trip is a great opportunity to see a lot." He took a sip of his coffee.

"Tell me, Dr. Santo," Monika said, "how do you like working on the ship?"

"It's a good experience," he said. "A good way to start out, I think, but I only plan on doing this for another year or two."

"It seems to me you could do much better for yourself, financially at least, if you were in private practice," Monika observed.

"Certainly," he said, "but this is a way to have a bit of adventure and see a bit of the world before settling down."

"And where do you plan to settle down?" Monika asked.

"I'm not sure yet," Luca said, "but either in Italy or the States."

"The States?" she said, surprised.

"Yes," Luca replied. "My mother is American, and I've been there many times. She grew up near Philadelphia and Florida, but her family lives in Florida year-round now. I like it there very much."

"I see," Monika said. "What part of Florida?"

"Palm Beach," he said. "I love the sea, and I like that it's on the ocean yet a town with a lot to offer. And it's close to Miami, a real city."

"There are a lot of Europeans there now, which helps, I think,"

Monika said. She put the coffee cup down and looked at Luca. "And what brings you here today?" she asked. "To Pompeii?"

"Well . . . " Luca began slowly, as if searching for words. "I—I've been here before, of course, but just wanted an outing, you know. A break from the ship. So I took the train from Naples to see some of the landscape. Get a glimpse of Pompeii." His gaze caught Crissy's, and a little smile formed on her lips.

"I see," Monika said, oblivious to their exchange. "Tell me," she said, looking at him again, "if you practice in Italy, where will it be? Florence?"

"Probably," he said. "My father is a doctor there, and I could go into practice with him. But I think I prefer to start out on my own."

"Ah, an independent streak," Monika said.

Luca shrugged. "I suppose."

"I think that's admirable in a man," she said, looking at him coquettishly.

Crissy was surprised by Monika's flirtatious behavior. She also found that she felt possessive of Luca, irrational though the feeling might be, and thus resentful of Monika's interest in him.

"My father is very controlling," Luca said with a laugh, "so I don't know whether it's so much a matter of my being independent as it is my wanting to get out from under his wing."

Monika put a hand on his arm. "We all have to escape the parental nest to make our own way in the world, don't we? Otherwise, we suffocate."

A momentary look of discomfort clouded Luca's features, but he quickly formed a smile and replied, "I think you must be right."

Crissy saw the tour guide and a number of their party going down the steep road toward where the bus was parked. "I think we must be getting ready to go back to the ship," she said. "I see Rudy and Mina and some of the others leaving."

"Oh, we have time," Monika said, removing her hand from Luca's arm and flapping it breezily in the air. "They will go into that dreadful cameo factory before leaving."

"Don't you want to see the cameos?" Luca asked.

Monika shook her head. "I don't like them. Too old-fashioned for me, and too old-lady, if you know what I mean."

Luca laughed. "Well, I'd better get on my way," he said. "I'm taking the train back, and it leaves soon."

"Oh, no," Monika exclaimed, putting a hand on his arm again. "But you just got here."

"Yes," he replied, "but unfortunately I could only steal a short time away from the ship." He pushed his chair back. "It was a pleasure to have met you," he said to Monika. Then he turned to Crissy. "And you take care of yourself."

"I will," Crissy replied.

He signaled the waiter for the check, carelessly glanced at it, then handed him some euros. "I will see you again," Luca said, then turned and started down the hill.

"He's a promising young man," Monika said, watching him leave. "Very promising, indeed."

"So you approve of him," Crissy said.

"Oh, yes," she said. "He just needs a guiding hand. An experienced hand." She fussed with the pendant that hung from her necklace, adjusting it against her bodice. The rings on her fingers caught the light and reflected it, impressing Crissy as they always did with their dazzling display. "A woman of maturity," Monika went on, "would be ideal for a young man like him."

"But you said yourself that he has an independent streak," Crissy said. "Wouldn't that—"

"My darling," Monika said, giving her that you-poor-ignorant-creature look, "I was humoring him. He is obviously unformed, a malleable and compliant young man who could be shaped and molded into something formidable, distinguished even. Don't you see?"

"I suppose so," Crissy said, not really seeing at all. She thought that Luca knew exactly what he was doing.

"Well," the older woman said, "I guess we'd better start down that infernal road to the bus. If you like, there's still time for you to see the hideous cameos with the others. I'll wait outside at the trinket stands. I'd rather see obscenely decorated tiles and vases than look at those oh-so-precious things." She rose to her feet and picked up the enormous gold leather handbag she carried everywhere. "Are you ready?"

"Yes," Crissy said, "but I think I'll look at the obscene trinkets, too, instead of the cameos."

Monika laughed. "Clever girl."

As they began the descent, Crissy wished that she could have taken the train back to Naples with Luca. She could imagine sitting next to him as he pointed out places of interest along the way. Well, she thought with a sigh, she was lucky to be under the wing of a well-known European author, a lady of sophistication from whom she could learn so much.

Jenny appeared at dinner, which surprised everyone and thrilled Dr. Von Meckling. "I spent the entire afternoon with a friend," she said, smiling secretively, "but he had obligations tonight, so here I am."

She flirted with the old doctor outrageously during the meal, seemingly enjoying his attention enormously, allowing him to brush his leg against hers repeatedly and patting him numerous times on the back or his arm. The table was amused by her behavior, although no one said anything about it directly.

Afterward they went to the show together, tonight's labeled "Around the World." It was very much like the last show, Crissy noted, but with different costumes and music. When it was over, she and Jenny went to the cabin, promising to meet their friends at the disco later, after they had changed clothes and refreshed their makeup.

In the cabin, Jenny changed into a micromini dress with an extremely low-cut top that left little to the imagination. "What do you think?" she asked Crissy.

Crissy looked her up and down. "I think you're asking for trouble," she replied with a laugh.

"I hope I get it," Jenny said, twirling in front of the mirror.

"Is Manolo going to be there?" Crissy asked.

Jenny shrugged. "Who knows? Maybe, maybe not."

Crissy looked at her quizzically, dumbfounded by her attitude. "What's this? You suddenly don't care? What happened?"

"Nothing," Jenny replied. "It's just that, well, I'm ready to move on, you know? Somebody new. Manolo was great for a few good screws, but he's not all that fascinating, you know?" She paused thoughtfully, then added, "Besides, he's getting a little too close. A little too . . . serious."

Uh-oh, Crissy thought. Now we're getting at the heart of the issue. Manolo was actually falling for her, and Jenny wasn't ready for that. At least not with him. Since her divorce, she'd hopscotched from one man to another. Maybe, Crissy thought, Jen was gun-shy. Maybe deep down inside she'd actually suffered more when she left her ex-husband than she'd let on.

"So he's getting serious about you and you don't feel the same way about him. That's it?" Crissy said.

"Honey, I'll miss that big cock, but that's all," Jenny said with a laugh.

Crissy laughed helplessly. "Oh, you really are too much."

Jenny looked at her. "You look terrific," she exclaimed. "Seductive without being in-your-face."

Crissy was pleased with the compliment, and thought Jenny had hit the nail on the head in describing the dress. The top was sheer black chiffon that covered her arms to the wrists and went up to a high neck. Underneath the chiffon was a very low-cut bodice of black satin. It was revealing but demure at the same time. It certainly wasn't as daring as much of Jenny's wardrobe. The skirt was cut above the knee and was great for dancing because it was full, and the layers of chiffon fluttered about her as she moved in a very romantic way, she thought.

"Well, let's get a move on," Jenny said.

At the disco, they took seats at the small round table with the others, Crissy noticing that Jenny was squeezing in next to old Dr. Von Meckling. She'll try to drive the poor old man completely crazy, Crissy thought, taking a seat between Monika and Rudy.

"I ordered a bottle of champagne for the table," Rudy said. "I hope you'll have some."

"I'd love just a tiny bit," Crissy replied.

Rudy began pouring. "No more," she said. "Please."

He quit instantly. "Are you sure?" he asked.

"Unfortunately, if I have much more than that, you'll have to carry me out of here," she said.

"Well, if you change your mind . . ." Rudy said.

When the glasses were filled, Monika raised her glass in a toast. "To Rudy," she said, "for providing us with this delightful treat."

"Here, here," Dr. Von Meckling said, and everyone sipped the champagne.

Crissy had no sooner set her glass down than she saw Valentin descend from his roost at the bar and head her way. "Would you care to dance?" he asked.

"Yes," Crissy said, getting up.

He escorted her to the dance floor and led her in a foxtrot. "Where were you last evening?" he asked, his penetrating gray eyes focused on her. "I missed dancing with you."

"Oh, did you?" Crissy said, tilting her head to one side. "I bet you had plenty of dancing partners, Valentin. I've seen you dancing with lots of the ladies."

"Yes, but it is not the same when you are not here."

"That's sweet of you to say," she replied.

"Your friend was here," he said, "dancing with one of the ship's officers."

"Yes," Crissy said. "She told me."

"You never answered my question. Where were you?" His demeanor was serious, and Crissy didn't quite know what to make of it. "I was feeling a little under the weather," she said, "so I went to bed early."

He looked alarmed. "Nothing serious, I hope?"

"No," she said. "Just a little bug or seasickness or something."

"You must take care of yourself," he said, drawing her closer to him, his eyes boring into her again. "We wouldn't want anything bad happening to you."

What a strange thing to say, she thought. Then she amended the thought: *Maybe not such a strange thing to say, but the way he said it was definitely odd. As was the deadly earnest voice. The steely eyes. Pulling me against him.* She felt an involuntary shiver run up her spine, then told herself as he gracefully swept her around the dance floor that she was being melodramatic. Valentin was simply Bulgarian, and Monika had said he was uncultured and primitive. Maybe she was right and that explained his peculiar nature. In any case, she thought, he dances with many of the women, so he's got to be a stand-up guy. Just a little odd.

When the dance was over, he asked her to dance another, and she did. It was a fast one, and she enjoyed it—especially watching Valentin, because he really was a great dancer, no matter what the music happened to be. When it was over, she told him that she had to take a rest.

"Oh, no. You haven't tired yourself too much, have you?" Valentin asked with concern.

"I'll be fine," Crissy said. "I just need to take a break, Valentin. Don't worry about me."

"But I do," he said, squeezing her hand in his as he took her back to her table. "We want to see you in the best of health, ready for anything, don't we?"

"Yes," Crissy said, now thinking that perhaps language difficulties made Valentin sound odder than he actually was. He spoke with a slight accent, but perhaps his vocabulary and basic understanding of English were not as good as his accent would make one think.

"Thank you very much," he said as they reached her table, then, as he had the night before last, he retreated immediately.

"He's a wonderful dancer," Monika observed, "but it's rather sad about the clothes."

"What do you mean?" Crissy asked. She thought he paid a great deal of attention to his dress and grooming.

"Haven't you noticed?" Monika asked in surprise. She had one of her fans in hand, and it fluttered furiously for a moment.

"No," Crissy said. "What are you talking about?"

"My darling," Monika said in an indulgent voice, "they will soon fall apart at the seams, and they aren't the best fit, either. Look at him on the bar stool, talking to that dreadful Romanian singer with the pitch-black hair. His trousers are a wee bit too short, aren't they? The blazer is certainly too tight. The tie is outdated. The shoes, well! They're simply all wrong."

Crissy looked toward the bar and studied Valentin's clothing briefly. He was so engrossed in conversation with Petronella, the Romanian singer Monika mentioned, that he was oblivious to her staring. His trousers were too short, Crissy decided, and his blazer was indeed very tight. His tie, while outdated, she had thought part of his effort to achieve a certain style, a little wit or irony, maybe. The same with his shoes. But what did she know? she asked herself.

"Oh, look," Crissy said. "Jen and Dr. Von Meckling are dancing."

"Yes," Monika said. "They've danced two or three dances together. Even some of the fast ones. But of course he more or less moves in place, doesn't he?" She laughed. "But at his age I suppose that's a triumph."

"I think it's wonderful," Crissy said.

"See the way he holds her?" Monika said. "So close. I bet the old devil took some Viagra with his champagne, and he's rubbing himself all over Jenny right now."

Crissy thought she would collapse with laughter, and Monika grinned at her with evilly glittering eyes.

"Good evening," a familiar voice said from behind them.

They both turned to look at the source of the greeting, and Crissy quit laughing at once. "Dr. Santo," she said. "How nice to see you."

"It's very nice to see both of you ladies again, too," he said.

Monika batted her eyelashes with great effect, so heavy with mascara were they.

"Would you care to dance?" he asked Crissy.

"I'd be delighted," she said. She saw that Monika's eyes darted from Luca to her and back again, but the older woman didn't say anything.

Luca led her onto the dance floor and took her in his arms for the slow number that was still playing. "I'm glad you're here."

"I'm glad you're here, too," she said, "and that you asked me to dance."

He smiled but was silent, leading her about the floor with an easy grace that surprised her.

"I thought you weren't a dancer," she said.

"I'm not much of one," he replied. "Certainly not like some of these people."

"You're a fine dancer," she said. She caught sight of Jenny, straining to look at her and Luca over Dr. Von Meckling's shoulder. She smiled at her, and Jenny raised her eyebrows questioningly. Luca, however, turned her in another direction, and Jenny and the doctor disappeared from view.

They danced another dance, and then he asked her to join him at his table.

"I came up with the captain and a couple of officers," he said, leading her off the dance floor, "but why don't we get a table to ourselves?"

Crissy nodded. "Oh, but I need to get my purse. I left it at the table."

They stopped at the table, where Monika sat alone, fanning herself. She smiled broadly when they approached. "Are you joining us, Doctor?" she asked.

"How nice of you to offer," he replied graciously. "We're going to another table for awhile, but we'll see you later, I'm sure."

Crissy retrieved her purse. "See you soon," she said to Monika.

Monika watched them weave their way toward the back of the disco until they disappeared in the people milling about tables and finally the darkness. The scowl on her face, however, was quickly replaced with the smile that she perpetually wore in public.

He led her to the darkest corner of the room, where no one was seated on the banquette beneath the windows overlooking the bow. She slid in behind the little table, and Luca slid in next to her rather than taking the chair opposite.

"This is nice," she said. "Away from the lights and the worst of the noise."

"Yes," he said. "Maybe we can actually talk here."

A waitress appeared to take their orders. "What would you like?" Luca asked Crissy.

"Water," she replied. "I've already had some champagne, so I shouldn't have anything else to drink."

Luca told the waitress to bring them a large bottle of mineral water, and she left.

"You could've gotten something," she said.

"I told you I'm not much of a drinker," he replied, "and I had a glass of wine with dinner. Besides, I have to be on my toes, as they say in English, in case there's an emergency."

"Does that happen often?" Crissy asked.

"Not too frequently," he said, "but it does happen. There are a lot of elderly people on the ship, so of course there are inevitably problems."

"Like what?" she asked.

"Heart attacks, strokes, falls, sometimes with broken bones. It runs the gamut, from colds to death."

"I never thought about that," she said. "What do you do if somebody actually dies?"

"We have a morgue on board," he said. "The bodies are usually off-loaded at the next port, then flown home." He looked at her and smiled. "But why don't we change the subject."

"I think it's fascinating," she said. "Grim, but fascinating. Besides, it's part of what you do, and I'm interested in that. In you."

"And I'm very interested in you," he said. "So why don't me tell me about yourself?"

"What would you like to know?"

"Everything."

"I don't think you would find my life very interesting," she said. "Not like yours."

"I think you'd be surprised," he said. "So don't stall. Tell me your story."

The waitress brought the mineral water and two glasses of ice with lemon. After she had poured and left, Luca nudged Crissy gently. "Now," he said, "tell me about yourself."

Crissy told him about her childhood and family, her schooling and work, leaving out a lot of the more painful and, to her, unsavory details. He listened intently, stopping her to ask questions, to goad her on. As she spoke, he slid an arm across the back of the banquette, brushing her shoulders, and she felt safe and protected, as if shielded from the unpleasantness of the world. When she finished, he asked her more questions, probing into the recesses of her life, anxious to know as much as she would tell him. Finally, she told him it was his turn, that she was exhausted with the topic of herself.

He told her about his parents in Florence. His Italian father, a doctor, as she already knew, was an aloof and busy man and also a controlling one when he chose to participate in his son's life. His mother, an American, had met his father when they were both students in England. She worked as a restorer of paintings in Florence, and her son obviously adored her. He had an older sister who was married and lived in the country near Siena. When he had finished telling her about his past, which he embroidered with anecdotes regarding his family and friends, she asked about his plans for the future.

His dark eyes, even in the dim corner in which they sat, seemed to gleam, as if they were liquid. They were, she thought, the epitome of bedroom eyes, making her anxious to please him, to satisfy his every wish. "I want to settle down and get married," he said. "I want to have a family, if possible. One child or ten. It doesn't matter."

She nodded in silence.

"City or country or both," he went on enthusiastically, "but I have to be near the water. I love the water, and I love to swim. And I love the sun. In Italy or the States. And I want a medical practice of my own, or I will go into a small office with others. I want to be an old-fashioned family doctor, not part of some huge institution." He paused and smiled. "And at this very moment I want you."

Crissy felt as if her heart stopped beating for an instant, then started again, racing at breakneck speed. So stunning was his revelation, she was at a loss for words.

"I know it's sudden," he said.

"It's caught me off guard," she replied, realizing that she was afraid of her own feelings, but knowing that she wanted to go to bed with this man. The heat and smoke in the disco abruptly seemed suffocating, and the driving beat of the music with its powerful bass beat was like a hammer at her temples, throbbing through her head, unnerving her. She had to get out of the room.

"I need some air," she said.

"Let's go for a walk on deck," Luca replied. Then he added, "Unless you want to be alone?"

"Oh, no. No. I didn't mean that at all," she quickly replied, shaking her head. "Really. I just need some air."

He offered her his hand, and they went to the exit along the perimeter of the disco, avoiding the dance floor and the tables near it. Neither of them observed the eyes that followed them as they left together. When they reached the hallway outside, Crissy breathed a sigh of relief.

"This way," Luca said, taking her to the port side. "There will be fewer people, and you can get all the air you want." He held the heavy door open for her, and they went out onto the deck.

The cool evening wind was powerful and picked up Crissy's chiffon skirt and tossed it about her. She laughed as she tried to hold it down, and finally gave up, her efforts useless against the gusts. Luca put a protective arm around her, and they went to the railing and stood, looking out at the dark sea. Fine spray misted them from head to toe.

"Do you want to move back against the bulkhead?" Luca asked.

"No," she said. "This feels wonderful, and I don't care if my hair and dress get a little wet."

He hugged her closer, and she relished the warmth of his body next to hers. He kissed the top of her head, and she looked up at him. He smiled and wrapped his arms around her, his lips seeking out hers. They kissed, tentatively at first, but their passion quickly overcame them. They kissed with abandon, his tongue exploring her sweetness as she yielded to him. She felt his hands stroking her back, then cupping her buttocks and pulling them gently toward him. He groaned, and she felt his hardness pressing against her. She shivered slightly in his arms, and he hugged her closer still, then his lips brushed across her cheek to her ear.

"This is wonderful," he whispered. "You are wonderful, and you make me feel like no one ever has."

"I'm so glad, Luca," she breathed. "You make me feel wonderful, too."

His lips trailed down her neck, his tongue flicking at her. Crissy moaned with pleasure, aroused by his masculine scent, which even in the sea air was like an aphrodisiac, and his hardness against her, which made her body come keenly alive. He brought his lips down to her breasts and began kissing and licking them through the sheer chiffon, pushing them up to his lips tenderly with one hand.

Beneath the satin and chiffon, Crissy felt her nipples harden as he thrummed them between finger and thumb, and her hands grasped his tight, rounded buttocks and pulled him harder against her. She wished more than anything that he could strip off his confining uniform and she could dispense with her dress. Luca brought his lips back up to hers and kissed her, and she felt his hand beneath her dress, sliding up her leg. Her knees weakened as he reached the mound between her thighs and began caressing her, his breath coming in gasps as he felt her wetness seeping through.

"Oh, my God," he moaned, gently pulling down on her panty hose.

Crissy mewled with pleasure when she felt his bare hand against her nakedness, and gasped aloud when she felt his finger enter her. "Oh, Luca," she whispered. "You feel so wonderful . . . so wonderful."

He was panting, almost as if in pain. Crissy began to stroke him through the white trousers of his uniform. He jerked at her touch, then with a moan that seemed to come from deep down inside him, he yielded to her touch, grinding himself against her, all the while continuing to delve inside her most secret place.

Suddenly they heard laughter and voices and loud off-key singing behind them, and they quickly silenced their desire, yet remained entwined with each other.

He looked down into her eyes and smiled. "Maybe they'll pass on by," he whispered.

Crissy returned his smile, then let her head fall against his chest. "I hope so," she said.

They stayed immobile, waiting, but the revelers, very drunk by the sound of their laughter and talk and singing, grew in number and volume as the door to the deck swung open again and again. It finally became apparent that they were part of a conga line that had formed in the disco and was now working its way out onto the deck.

Crissy and Luca, frustrated as they were, finally laughed, realizing that they were to have no privacy, at least not for quite some time. They discreetly straightened their clothes and resumed looking out to sea, his arm around her shoulder, holding her close, but the raucous crowd made conversation impossible, so they left the railing and went back inside, smiling at the revelers but refusing their demands to join the conga line.

"We can go to the pool deck," Luca said, gently squeezing her hand. "It's probably deserted at this hour."

When they reached it, they were surprised to find several people in lounges stargazing, chatting, and drinking. "Damn," Luca swore. "This ship never sleeps." He laughed. "I wish we could go to my quarters, but I don't think that's a good idea. All the crew would know tomorrow." They leaned against a railing to talk, away from the other passengers on the deck.

"We could go to mine," Crissy said. "At least I think we could. I'm never sure what Jenny's up to. She could be there with someone or bring somebody in. You never know."

"Maybe it wouldn't be a good idea then," Luca said.

"I heard you're not really supposed to mix quite so closely with passengers," Crissy said.

"It happens, of course," Luca said, "but I don't want you to be the object of gossip and possibly ridicule."

"What do you mean?" she asked.

"The crew will talk," he said, "and some of them will talk to passengers they are familiar with, too. And in the most pejorative terms. Just like they talk about the American I've seen you with who's stayed over with Manolo, one of the officers. It's a tightly knit little community on board."

"Jenny," Crissy said. "That's who I was taking about. She's my friend, and we're cabinmates."

"I didn't mean to disparage your friend," Luca said, "but I don't like the idea of you being the subject of nasty jokes and gossip like she is."

"Oh, so they're talking about Jenny, huh?" she said.

He nodded. "Yes. It's silly, of course, but all the guys are going to be hitting on her now. I don't think that's what you want."

"No," she said. "Definitely not."

"I didn't think so, and I wouldn't want it for you," Luca said, taking her hand in his. "It would make me crazy." He sighed. "Let's go out on the deck just fore of here," he said. "Maybe there won't be anyone out there. There almost never is."

"Yes," Crissy said, getting up. "Let's give it a try."

He led her around the bar area to a door that led out onto a small stretch of deck that was fortunately deserted. Luca took a lounge from a stack and placed it near the bulkhead. "Here," he said, "you can spread out."

Crissy sat down and took off her heels, then spread out on the chaise. When she saw that Luca was joining her, she scooted over as much as possible. He sat down at her side and gazed at her. "You are so beautiful," he said, leaning down for a kiss.

"And so are you," Crissy replied, putting a hand on his head, running her fingers through his thick black hair.

They kissed for a long time, Luca's lips and tongue tracing a path to her ears and neck as before. He began fondling her breasts, and Crissy found herself once again responding to him with complete abandon. She wanted to give herself to him, and she wanted him. When his hand slid under her dress and up her thigh, she parted her legs, anxious to feel him inside her again. She lifted herself off the lounge, and Luca pulled her panty hose down, then his lips pressed against hers as he slipped a finger inside. Crissy moaned and pushed herself against him, and then his one finger was joined by another. She gasped and felt for his crotch. He shifted on the lounge accommodatingly, and Crissy felt the hardness as before.

Maddened by desire, she felt she would gladly pay any price to have him—all of him.

Luca was panting, his desire reaching a point of no return as he probed the recesses of her sweet wetness, but he abruptly withdrew and sat back. "Come with me," he said, standing up and offering her a hand.

Crissy quickly got up and grabbed her shoes. He was already leading her toward a metal staircase that led up to the area around the ship's funnel. There was a chain across the entry, and he unhooked it, let her through, then followed her after he'd hooked the chain back in place.

"Up," he said. At the top of the stairs, he took her hand again and led her around to the back of the funnel to a small, almost flat area. "No one will come up here," he said.

He embraced her, kissing her passionately before slowly unzipping the back of her dress, brushing his lips against her naked back as he did so. When he was finished, he helped her sit, then sat down beside her. He put his arms around her again and gently eased the top of her dress off her shoulders. Staring at her creamy breasts in the moonlight, he sucked in his breath. "You are so perfect," he whispered as he began fondling her, then kissing and licking her nipples.

Crissy felt a shiver of pleasure run up her spine, and she undid his belt,

133

then unbuttoned his trousers. He was fully engorged, and when she touched him he groaned aloud. "Oh, my God," he rasped.

Crissy felt him throbbing for release in her hand as she stroked him, and when he began pulling down her panty hose, she could hardly wait for him to enter her. He buried his face in her breasts, licking and kissing her passionately as she pulled her dress up out of the way and he maneuvered himself next to her. She felt the head of his cock hard against her mound and thought she would have an orgasm before he entered her, and when he did, she let out a cry of ecstasy. "Oh, Luca," she whispered. "Oh, you feel so good. So wonderful."

He moved farther inside her, then gently rolled her onto her back, holding himself above her without putting all of his weight on her, so as not to make her any more uncomfortable against the hard deck. He slowly began pushing himself inside her, then in one thrust, entered as far as he could go.

Crissy felt as if she couldn't possibly accommodate him, but she wanted all of him and nothing less. She pushed against him, her desire overcoming any other concerns, and he began moving slowly in and out, in and out, until she suddenly felt contractions and was engulfed in waves of ecstasy.

Luca, spurred on by her orgasm, let out a lusty growl as he came, his body tensing momentarily as he flooded her with his desire. "Oh, my God," he rasped. "Oh, my God." He rolled her onto her side again and lay against her, panting, his lips brushing against her lips, her nose and eyes, her cheeks, and forehead.

Crissy lay catching her breath, bathing in the afterglow of their intimacy. She felt fulfilled as never before, and knew without a doubt that no one in the past had ever aroused her like this. Her thoughts drifted to Tom Gentry and the way she had felt after their one night of lovemaking, but something deep down inside told her that this was different. Luca's behavior had been anything but calculating or manipulative. He had a purity, an innocence, that seemed to her unspoiled.

"What are you thinking about?" he whispered as he kissed her ear.

"Oh, just how wonderful you make me feel," she replied.

He hugged her to him. "Isn't it a dream come true? It is for me, Crissy."

"Oh, yes, for me, too," she said. "A dream come true."

He smothered her in kisses again, and Crissy returned them, wanting to trust her feelings for him, to believe in the magic of the night.

At last she drew back reluctantly. "We're liable to be found here at dawn if this keeps up."

He grinned. "I know, but I can't help it."

"Maybe we should start getting back to our cabins," she said, running a finger down the side of his face. She didn't want the night to end, but she knew that it must soon. "Will you help me with my dress?"

"Of course. Just a second." He carefully zipped up his pants, buttoned them, and redid his belt. They both got to their knees, and he helped her into the sleeves of her dress, then zipped up the back.

They descended the metal stairs to the empty deck below. She slipped into her heels, and they walked hand in hand back to the pool deck. A few people were still chatting in lounges or stargazing. He led her to her cabin, where he took her into his arms and kissed her with passion.

"Have fun tomorrow," he said, "and I'll see you after you board the ship in Nice."

She nodded. "I can hardly wait," she said.

He reluctantly released her. " 'Night," he said, brushing her lips with his fingertips.

" 'Night, Luca."

He went back down the corridor, then turned toward the stairwell. Crissy got the key card out and let herself into the cabin. Jenny wasn't there, for which she was grateful. She would love to share the excitement she felt about the evening, but had mixed feelings about sharing the experience with Jenny, who would probably dismiss it as nothing more than a sexual tryst. As she undressed and got ready for bed, Crissy realized that she'd never heard Jenny actually talk about being in love with any of the men she'd gone out with. Not even her ex-husband, for that matter. Men were toys for Jenny, she thought, nothing more.

After she got into bed and turned out the light, her head was still spinning. She had never dreamed that one night could change her so completely. She'd always feared that fate had dealt her a hand so humdrum, so ordinary, that she would spend the rest of her days feeling as if she'd never lived. Now she knew that her fears had been groundless. She had a date with destiny, and its name was Luca.

* * *

Georgios Vilos paced the marble floor of his luxurious library in the exclusive Athenian suburb of Kifissia. Stopping for a moment, he dabbed at the sweat that beaded his face and neck. *Goddamn it!* he thought, irritated by his body's response to his extreme state of nervous agitation. The sweat simply wouldn't stop pouring, and he was beginning to feel too exhausted to deal with it.

He went to the chair behind his desk and sat down, fumbling for one of the cell phones that were aligned in a neat row to the right of the desk's leather surface. *Oh, dear God,* he thought with a sense of growing horror. *It's come to this. I've got to get hold of Mark and get him off that damned ship.*

There was a slight tremor in his hand as he picked up the cell phone, irritating him even further. *There's time,* he thought. *Plenty of time. Mark will be okay. Mark will be fine.* He took a deep breath and flipped the cell phone open, then pressed the buttons for the telephone number, his thick fingers hitting the correct buttons, despite their minute size and the tremor in his hand.

The phone rang and rang. Three rings. Four. Five. Six. Seven. Eight. *Goddamn it!* Ten rings. Twelve. *Nothing!*

Nothing! Mark wasn't answering his cell phone as he'd promised he would. Now what? Georgios Vilos waited for his son's voice mail to pick up, and when the disembodied computer-generated voice finally responded, he almost shouted his message.

"Mark. Mark! You promised to answer your cell phone," he cried. "Call me immediately! Immediately!"

He slammed the cell phone shut and banged it against the desktop in a fury. *What is he doing? Why is the little shit doing this to me* now? *Why? Why?*

Georgios Vilos abruptly stood up and began pacing the marble floor again. *Goddamn him,* he thought. *Goddamn him! Why is he doing this to me?* He would give anything to get his hands on his son, to beat some sense into him. He was just like his mother. Unpredictable. Uncontrollable. Ungrateful.

Georgios Vilos quit pacing and went to the drinks table, where he poured himself a glass of ouzo. Dispensing with ice, he tossed back a long swallow of the fiery, anise-flavored drink, then threw the glass to the floor, where it shattered, shards flying across the room.

The plastic explosives were in Mark's suite. Under his very nose. The madman who would be using them had no regard for human life. *Any human life, Mark's included.*

He retraced his steps to his desk and picked up the cell phone again, then dialed the number. It rang and rang, as before. Georgios Vilos felt as if he would explode with fury.

Why? he asked himself again. *Why is he doing this to me? My own son!*

Chapter Ten

"Oh, my God! My feet! I can hardly walk!"

The loud wail awoke Crissy, but she was so groggy that she hardly registered what she'd heard. She only knew that for some reason Jenny must be in great distress. She slowly sat up, propping herself on her elbows, and looked at the other bed. Jenny was sitting on its edge, still dressed in the revealing outfit she'd worn the night before. Her hair was a disheveled mess, and her makeup was badly in need of repair. She sat with one leg propped atop her knee, foot in hand. She was studying the foot as if it were a rare biological specimen. Crissy watched as she carefully touched the bottom of her foot with a finger and saw her jerk.

"Je-sus!" she wailed again.

"What is it, Jen?" Crissy asked sleepily. "What's wrong?"

"Oh, damn!" Jenny cried. "I don't believe this."

"What don't you believe?" Crissy asked, sitting up fully. She glanced at her wristwatch on the bedside cabinet and saw that it was seven o'clock.

"My feet," Jenny moaned. "My goddamn feet." She gingerly placed the one she'd been looking at on the floor and placed the other one on her knee, examining it as she had the other one. "I started a conga line last night," she said. "I danced a lot on the carpeted area in the disco," she replied, "then on some of that fucking Astroturf out on deck." She looked down at her foot again. "The fucking stuff burned my feet! I mean, *burned* them. I can hardly walk."

"They're that bad, huh?" Crissy threw back the covers on her bed and got up and went over to look. Peering down closely, she could see nothing out of the ordinary, except that maybe the bottoms of Jenny's feet were a little more red than pink.

"This hurts like hell," Jenny said.

"I'm sorry, sweetie," Crissy sympathized. "Is there anything I can do to help? Maybe if you soaked them in cold water and put some lotion on them. What do you think?"

Jenny glanced at her as if she were mad. "What is that? Some kind of ancient Vietnamese folk medicine?"

Crissy was miffed by the remark, but in a neutral voice she replied, "I really don't know the first thing about Vietnamese folk medicine. I just thought that since they feel burned, the cold water might help, and a little moisturizing lotion never hurt anything. I don't know if it'll actually help."

"That's ridiculous," Jenny said. "I'm going to have to go to the doctor."

"The hospital opens at eight o'clock," Crissy said. "Do you want me to take you down there?"

"No," Jenny said impatiently. "I'm quite capable of taking care of this myself, thank you very much."

Jenny was always so carefree and happy-go-lucky that her unpleasantness came as a surprise to Crissy, but she told herself that it was because she was in pain. "I know you're capable," she said. "I just wanted to see if I could do anything to help."

Jenny put her foot on the floor and sighed. "I look a mess, and I've got the world's worst hangover," she said, ignoring Crissy's remark. "Plus I didn't get any sleep."

"None at all?"

"No," Jenny replied. "I partied with some people from Montreal and just came in a few minutes ago." She gave Crissy a penetrating look. "Some of us aren't early birds like you."

"I wanted to get some sleep before today's excursion. It's a long one. More than ten hours."

Jenny flapped a hand in the air as if what Crissy had said was of no consequence. "I'm not going," she said. "I'm staying on the boat."

"That's too bad," Crissy said. "I'll miss you, but maybe you should stay off your feet."

For lunch, Crissy loaded a tray at the cafeteria-style dining room and went outside to find a place to eat on deck. Thankfully, she found an empty table next to the port side. No one joined her, but she enjoyed looking out to sea, the cool morning air, the sun, and sky. Birds wheeled about in the air near the ship, and she saw several boats in the distance. Suddenly she realized that the ship was slowing considerably. Seeing land, she got up and stood at the railing.

The hills of the Ligurian coast of Italy were just ahead, and she could see that they were dotted with houses and apartment buildings. Along the shore were large hotels and behind them what looked like the business center of San Remo. The town looked beautiful, tumbling down the hills to the sea, and she took several pictures while they were heading in to the pier. When the ship was finally docked, she followed the crowd toward Deck Two, where they would disembark.

Once she had finally gone through security and was on the dock, she walked to the waiting buses, looking for her friends. Monika's wild silver hair was not visible anywhere, but she soon saw Mina, who was waving to her.

"Rudy has saved seats as usual," Mina said.

"Thanks," Crissy said.

"Did you have a good time last night?" Mina asked, smiling mischievously.

Crissy nodded. "I did," she said, unable to keep her lips from forming a smile.

Mina laughed merrily. "I'm so glad," she said. "He's a terribly handsome man. Sooo sexy."

"He's very nice, too," Crissy said.

"Oh, how convenient," Mina replied. "I often find that very good-looking men aren't necessarily pleasant to be with. Rudy's an exception, of course."

"He certainly is," Crissy said, "and that's convenient for you."

"Touché," Mina said with a laugh, then her attention was drawn to the crowd still getting off the ship. "Good. Here comes Dr. Von Meckling. Everyone else is on the bus. I'll wait for him, and you can go on and take a seat if you want."

She boarded the bus and saw Monika and Rudy. "Here," Monika called from several rows back. "Have a seat next to me, darling."

Crissy joined her, saying hello to Rudy across the aisle.

Monika patted her arm. "We missed you last evening," she said, "going off with that young man the way you did."

"I'm sorry," Crissy said, "but I needed to get away from all the noise and smoke and get some air."

"He's Italian, you know," Monika said unnecessarily. "That could mean a lot of trouble for you."

"Why's that?" Crissy asked, perplexed by her comment.

Mina and Dr. Von Meckling said hello as they took the seats Rudy had saved for them, then Crissy repeated her question. "Why's that?"

"Oh, surely you know about Italian men," she said. "Mistresses. All of them have mistresses, my darling. All of them arrogant and concerned with appearance." She paused, then added in a whisper, "And Roman Catholic, but not like us Austrians. Primitives. The worst sort of primitives as far as the church goes."

Crissy almost laughed aloud. Wasn't this similar to what Monika said about Valentin and Bulgarians? Was there not a man worthy of attention who was not Austrian or German? She wondered whether or not Monika really believed what she said or was simply trying to keep her away from men so she had her all to herself.

"Monika," she finally said, "Luca is a very nice man. A civilized man. He's a doctor, for God's sake."

"Doctor!" Monika practically spat. "That means nothing anymore. And a ship's doctor to boot! I ask you, if you were a decent medical man, would you deign to practice on a ship? I don't think so."

"Well, I enjoyed spending time with him," Crissy said, "and I think he's very intelligent. His father is a doctor in Florence, and his mother is American. An art restorer. And, he's not planning on practicing on the ship forever. This was a place for him to start and to see some of the world before settling down."

"*Gott in Himmel,*" Monika said. "You know an awful lot about him." She grabbed Crissy's arm. "Be careful. I've heard rumors about him."

"What kind of rumors?" Crissy asked.

"Oh, all sorts of things," Monika said. "He's a terrible womanizer." Her voice dropped to a whisper. "And he has very . . . exotic, shall we say . . . tastes."

"What on earth do you mean?" Crissy asked.

"I'm speaking of sexual proclivities," Monika whispered. "Very peculiar."

Crissy couldn't help but wonder what Monika was talking about. Luca had seemed to have anything but exotic tastes, as Monika had put it, but she reminded herself that she really knew very little about him. Perhaps he had restrained himself last night, for their first time together. A wave of despair came over her. Could what Monika was saying really be true?

Jenny was glad she had been to a spa before leaving for the trip. She'd had a pedicure among many other treatments, and she had refreshed the pinkish pearl polish on her toenails only yesterday. She couldn't help but laugh, thinking that she wanted to put her best foot forward for the doctor. When she'd seen him with Crissy, she'd made up her mind, then and there, that she had to have him, despite whatever feelings Crissy might have for him. Crissy could have him back after she was through, so what difference did it make? Manolo had become a bore, actually getting serious about her. And this doctor, from what she'd seen of him at the disco, was one hot stud. Just her type for a few days of sexual acrobatics.

When she reached the reception area, she was disappointed to see that several people were waiting to see the doctor. She picked up one magazine after another, leafing through them for something interesting. The receptionist came in and asked Jenny to fill out a form. Jenny took it from her, thinking what a hideous and unpleasant woman she was.

The wait went on and on. She began to wonder if her mission would ever be accomplished and was about to abandon it when the doctor helped one of the patients to the door. *Oh, no,* she told herself. *I'm sticking this out. He is one hot number, and I'm going to have a shot at him.* He was even better-looking in daylight than he had been in the disco last night.

Finally the monster, whose name was Voula, called her to the back. Jenny noticed that she watched her closely, looking at her as if she were some sort of specimen that she found particularly distasteful. She was slightly unnerving, but Jenny got up and stretched, making certain that her breasts strained against the front of the lightweight T-shirt she'd worn. She wasn't wearing a bra, and knew that the impression her nipples made on the fabric was clearly visible for all to see. At the same time, her T-shirt, which hung just short of her belly button, rose up to fully expose the gold ring with which it was pierced. She hoped the diamond stud on the ring blinked in the light.

Voula watched Jenny's show, then led her to the back, where she introduced her to Dr. Santo.

142

He shook Jenny's hand and asked her what had brought her to the hospital.

"I was dancing last night for a long time," Jenny replied, "and this morning my feet were burning. They still are, and it's all I can do to walk."

"Maybe those stiletto-heeled mules aren't the best shoes to wear under the circumstances," Luca observed. "They put a strain on your feet, besides which, they slap against them every time you take a step."

Jenny shrugged. "What's a girl to do? I didn't come prepared for something like this."

"Well," he said, "have a seat on the examination table and let me have a look."

Jenny slid up onto the paper-covered, padded table and put her hands down on it, thrusting her breasts forward at the same time. If he noticed anything, he didn't let on. She spread her legs as far apart as she could in the micro-miniskirt she was wearing. Since she had no underwear on, he should have a very good view, she thought, if he looked in that direction.

"Take off your shoes for me, please," he said, sliding a chair over toward her and sitting down.

Jenny leaned down and slipped off first one stiletto, then the other. She wiggled her toes. "Oh, they're so sore," she complained. "What am I going to do tonight? I mean, if you can't dance on this ship, what the hell are you supposed to do?"

"I don't want to tickle you," he said, carefully taking one foot in a latex-gloved hand.

"Ooooh," Jenny cooed. "Is that a proposition?"

Luca ignored her comment and examined first one foot, then the other. He kept his eyes averted from the view up her thighs. When he was finished, he announced, "You have a classic case of rug burn, Ms. . . . Ms. . . . ?"

"Jenny," she said. She wriggled her ass on the paper, then stretched her arms, pulling her T-shirt tight again and exposing her belly button ring with its diamond.

"The best thing for you to do," he said, "is soak them in cool or cold water a few times a day, and I'm going to give you some ointment to use on them. They'll just be a source of discomfort for another couple of days, then be good as new."

"Are you sure about that?" Jenny asked.

He nodded. "Yes," he said. "Of course, if they should start bothering you more or become especially painful, don't hesitate to come back, but I don't think you'll have any problems with them. Also, you might try to give them a couple of days of rest." He smiled. "Maybe you shouldn't do too much barefoot dancing on the rugs for awhile."

"That's a tall order," Jenny said, "because I'm a dancing fool." She made a pout. "I guess I'm just going to have to keep my feet up, huh? Maybe in bed. What do you think?" She looked at him provocatively.

Luca was becoming embarrassed by her overt flirting. He had experienced it countless times, both in and out of his office. It was a professional hazard—it went with the territory.

"There's something else," Jenny said. "I didn't mention it before because I thought I'd wait till I got home to see about it, but . . . " She shrugged. "Maybe you could take a look for me?"

"What's that?" Luca asked.

"I think I feel a little lump in my breast," Jenny said. "You know, I check them regularly to see if I feel anything out of the ordinary."

"A lump?" he said. "You're certain?"

"Not completely, no," she replied. "But it's so hard to know. I keep thinking I feel something in my left breast. Maybe you could see if you feel something."

"Of course," Luca responded, wondering if this was simply another sexual ploy. "Would you take off your T-shirt for me, please?"

Jenny immediately began sliding the T-shirt up over her head.

"Wait," Luca said. "Let me give you a gown to cover yourself." He quickly took a hospital gown off a hook on the back of the door. "Here," he said, handing it to her. "Put this on, please. With the opening in the back."

His eyes were averted from her, and Jenny could tell that this was going to be more difficult than she'd imagined. She finished taking off her T-shirt, then sat bare-breasted before slipping the gown on as he'd instructed.

"Are you done?" he asked from a desk where he made himself busy looking through some papers.

"Yes," she said.

He approached her, the latex gloves still on his hands. "You say it's the left breast?"

"Yeah," Jenny said. "Definitely the left one."

"This will only take a moment," he said. "My hand may feel cold at first."

"That's okay," Jenny said. "I'll warm you up."

Ignoring her, he slipped his hand beneath the gown and began examining her breast, moving it this way and that, feeling for any indication that there was a lump within the mass.

Jenny spread her legs, making certain that they brushed against him, but he deftly moved aside. In a matter of moments, he slipped his hand back out and sat down again. "I don't feel anything," he replied, "but you might want to see your doctor as soon as you get home. Just in case I've missed something."

She was a beautiful girl with a spectacular figure, he thought, but he knew it wasn't all natural, because he'd felt an implant. It was a shame that she felt the need to throw herself at men the way she did. If she was friends with Crissy, she must be nice otherwise.

"Okay," Jenny said. "I'll make an appointment as soon as I get back."

"Good," he said.

Before he realized what was happening, Jenny slipped the gown off her shoulders and sat with her breasts exposed before him. Her chin was raised defiantly, and her legs were spread wide. She licked her lips slowly, looking at him with a come-hither expression.

"Please get dressed," Luca said, turning away. "The nurse will give you the ointment."

Jenny felt as if she'd been slapped. She yanked on her T-shirt and slipped into her heels. *The son of a bitch,* she thought. *Who does he think he is?* When she was ready, she went back out into the reception area, heading toward the door.

Voula called to her. "Miss! Miss!"

Jenny turned to face her.

"Your ointment. Wait a moment while I get it, please."

"Keep it," Jenny said. "It's probably snake oil anyway." She opened the door and swept out of the office. *I'll get even with that prick if it's the last thing I do,* she thought. *I'm going to make his fucking life miserable.*

Chapter Eleven

Crissy was surprised by her first glimpse of Monaco. After the beauty of the coastline up to this point, she decided that Monte Carlo was a modern blight on the landscape, its high-rise towers more befitting Manhattan than the Mediterranean shores.

"Isn't it gorgeous?" Monika said enthusiastically. "It's one of my favorite places in the world."

"Is it really?" Crissy replied. "It's so . . . so vertical."

"Well, my darling," Monika said, "they have to build up. There's no room to build out."

"It looks like they've used every square inch of land," Crissy said, "and have left hardly a tree or plant."

"Oh, you'll be surprised," Monika retorted. "There are a couple of lovely gardens and public squares with trees and plants." She leaned over Crissy for a better view. Clapping her hands together, she said, "It's so glamorous. I simply adore it."

Crissy could see beautiful yachts moored in the famous harbor, and some of the older buildings looked quite grand, but she honestly couldn't understand what Monika thought was so glamorous about it. Maybe on closer inspection she would change her mind, she thought.

"You can wear your jewelry here without any worries whatsoever," Monika said. "Imagine. Millions of dollars' worth, if you like, without giving it a thought."

"Why's that?" Crissy asked.

"The police, of course," Monika said. "And cameras. They're absolutely everywhere, watching, watching, watching. Thieves don't dare bother one here. They're simply not tolerated. And it's clean," she said. "It's so clean and tidy. Oh, you're going to love it. I know you are."

The bus took them to an underground parking garage, and when they got off it, they took an escalator up to ground level. An immense *belle epoque* building sprawled before them.

"What is this?" Crissy asked.

"Oh," Monika said dismissively, "that's the Oceanographic Institute. Jacques Cousteau's place. They have these huge fish tanks with all sorts of terrifying creatures in them."

"Oh, I have to see it," Crissy said.

Monika looked at her in alarm. "That's preposterous," she said. "There's the casino and the lovely Hôtel de Paris and the Hermitage. You mustn't waste your time with the fish, my darling."

"But I've read that this place is fabulous."

Rudy, Mina, and Dr. Von Meckling drew up to them. "Well, are you ready to walk to the casino?" Mina asked.

"Quite," Monika said.

"I want to see the Oceanographic Institute," Crissy said. "Could I meet you there?"

"Of course," Rudy said.

"You're making a mistake," Monika said, "but you'll discover that for yourself. We'll watch for you."

They walked off in the direction of the casino, and Crissy went to the ticket booth for the Oceanographic Institute. She wandered among the tanks, some of them giant, others small and built into the walls. She was drawn to the astonishingly beautiful colors of the different sea creatures or in some cases the forms they took. She lost all track of time exploring the exhibit, losing herself in this extraordinary display of nature at its most colorful and bizarre.

Rounding a corner from one room into another, she walked straight into Mark. She laughed in embarrassment, and he smiled in his smug way.

"Sorry about bumping into you, but I was so caught up in the exhibits I wasn't paying attention to where I was going."

"It is a fantastic place, isn't it?" he said.

"Yes, I love it," she agreed. "I'd read about it, but had forgotten it was here. Everybody talks about the casino and the palace and stuff like that. I'm sure they're very nice, but this is out of this world."

"Actually, this is very much in this world," he said, "and that's one of

147

the things I like about it. This is the natural world and its beauty on display. It is not artificial like the beauty you'll see in the casino."

"I'm going to try to see that, too," Crissy said.

"This is your first time in Monte Carlo?" he asked.

She nodded. "Yes."

"Oh, then you should see the casino and that area. The Hôtel de Paris, the Hermitage. They're lovely. And you can't miss the harbor. There are some of the world's most beautiful yachts anchored there."

"I saw it from the bus coming down into the city," Crissy said.

"Why don't you let me walk you to the casino?" Mark said. "I know Monte Carlo well, and since you don't have much time, I can point out the highlights."

"I'm supposed to meet some friends at the casino," Crissy said. She wasn't certain that she wanted to spend time with Mark.

"Then I'll walk with you there, if you don't mind," he said. "Remember? I don't bite."

Crissy laughed. Why not at least walk that way with him? "Okay, I'll walk with you, since you promise not to bite."

"Wonderful."

They took the elevator up and went out through a large room in which ship models were exhibited. Outside, he offered her his arm, and Crissy took it.

"It's not far," he said, "and we can get a closer look at the yachts in the harbor on the way."

"You seem to like boats," Crissy said. "I remember the first day we boarded, you knew a lot about the *Sea Nymph.*"

"You are observant. I am obsessed with boats," Mark said. "I love them."

"Do you have a favorite?" she asked.

"That's an impossible question to answer," he replied, "because there are so many different kinds for so many different purposes. But I love sailing yachts. Those that Camper & Nicholson make are beautiful. And Perini. I love the old Feadship motoryachts. The Wally and Benetti and Baglietto yachts. The Riva speedboats, of course. The old Greek caïques. I love nearly all boats, you see." He turned to her and grinned. "Even canoes and sunfish and rowboats."

His enthusiasm was apparent, and she could see that he really did love boats. They began climbing stairs that would take them up toward the casino, and when they reached a terraced area, he pointed in the direction of the harbor. "Look," he said.

Crissy looked toward the harbor. Many of the yachts were huge and beautifully designed. All of them appeared to be like Monte Carlo itself, immaculately kept. "They're quite impressive," she said.

"This harbor has been home to some of the greatest ever built," Mark said, somewhat wistfully she thought. "It still is, although it's changed some since the days of the famous feuds between Niarchos and Onassis."

"What kind of feuds?" she asked.

"Size," he said, looking at her with a mischievous smile. "Actually, yacht size. You know, who has the biggest toy? There were feuds between others as well. The Americans, Revson and Lefrak. The same sort of games are played today, but the names are different. The costs have multiplied, too, of course. See that white yacht moored at the end across the port?" He pointed toward it.

Crissy nodded. "Yes."

"That would run over forty million dollars, but it doesn't include the special touches. The maintenance alone runs several more million a year."

"I can't even imagine such a thing," Crissy said. She looked back at him. "I'd better get to the casino," she said. "We don't have a long time here."

He offered her his arm again, and they continued up the granite steps toward the casino. When they reached the top, Crissy saw a small street of shops. Gucci and Prada were there, and she thought of Jenny. She would be disappointed to hear that she'd missed an opportunity to pick up merchandise from two of her favorite retailers. There were also antiques dealers with museum-quality pieces in their windows. They passed the lovely Hermitage Hotel and around the corner stood in front of the Hôtel de Paris, where Bentley and Rolls-Royce cars were lined up as if they were waiting taxis. She'd never seen so many in one place before. The casino was katty-corner to the grand hotel, and across from the casino was the Café de Paris, where dozens of tables were set out on the sidewalks around it.

"This really does have a fairy-tale quality," Crissy said, "even if you can see the high-rises all around."

"Yes," Mark agreed. "Some people's idea of a fairy-tale place anyway."

"What do you mean?"

"Oh, you know what they say about Monte Carlo." His lips formed a slight smile. "It's a sunny place for shady people."

Crissy laughed. "I didn't know that." She looked at him. He didn't join in her laughter, and his smile had disappeared., replaced by a strange expression.

"How would you like to go to the casino?" he asked. "There are *salons privées* where we could have a drink together without all the tourist riffraff around. At this time of day, there probably wouldn't be anyone around."

"I don't know . . . " Crissy began. She didn't like the look on his face, nor did she like being referred to as tourist riffraff.

He grabbed her arm. "Come on," he said irritably. "You've played this waiting game long enough."

"I'm *not* playing a game, Mark," she replied.

"Of course you are," he said arrogantly, increasing the pressure on her arm.

"I think I'd better go," she said.

"No. Come with me. Now." His fingers dug into her arm sharply.

"Let go of me," she said, her voice louder than she'd intended.

Mark quickly looked about, then relinquished his hold of her. "Fine," he said. "Go."

Crissy gazed up at him for a moment, and the superior smile she'd seen before appeared on his lips. He didn't say anything, and she turned and walked away. She would try to find Monika and the others, but the joy had gone out of the day, replaced by the distinct sensation that she'd had a brush with something—some*one*—strange and distasteful.

The ship was surprisingly lively when they boarded, and Crissy discovered that most of the passengers for the trans-Atlantic voyage had gotten on board in Nice. There had been less than two hundred, and now there were nearly eight hundred. Promising to see everyone at dinner, Crissy went to the cabin to shower and change. The day had been a very busy one, fascinating but tiring, and she welcomed the opportunity to refresh herself.

Jenny was sprawled on her bed, filing her fingernails.

"Hi," Crissy said, smiling. "How are your feet?"

"Oh, they're okay," Jenny said in a pouty voice.

"Did you get something at the hospital for them?"

"Yeah," Jenny said, absorbed in her nails. "I think that doctor is a first-class pervert, but he gave me something."

Crissy felt herself redden. "What do you mean?" she asked.

"Oh, never mind," Jenny said mysteriously.

"He was perfectly nice to me," Crissy said. "I can't imagine that he seemed like some kind of pervert to you."

"Believe me," Jenny said. "He's a perv. No two ways about it. I wouldn't go near him again."

Crissy found herself extremely perplexed and frustrated. She wished that Jenny would be more forthcoming, but she knew that trying to get specific information out of her would be like pulling teeth. If Jenny didn't want to talk, she might as well forget about it. Her mind was like a whirl-wind. She thought about what Monika had said. That Luca had "exotic" sexual tastes, so the rumor mill had it. Now this. Jenny was calling him a pervert. She didn't know what to think, but asked herself if she could have been wrong about him. She had certainly been wrong before, but no one had ever seemed as genuine as Luca.

"So what are you so quiet about?" Jenny asked. "Didn't you have fun today?"

"It was great," Crissy replied as she undressed. "It was a lot to see in a day, but I'm glad I went." She hung up her clothes and put on her kimono. "What did you do all day?"

"Oh, I hung out around the pool for awhile," Jenny said, "but there were nothing but a bunch of old prunes out there reading books—you know, so old they couldn't get off the boat. I took a long nap because I didn't get any sleep last night. That's about it, except for going to see the pervert that calls himself a doctor."

Oh, damn! Crissy thought. There's that word again. She was begin-ning to get angry. "Why do you say that?" she asked Jenny. "I mean, what did he do to make you call him that?"

Jenny looked at her with a smirk. "I don't think you even want to know," she said.

"But I do," Crissy said.

"Why?" Jenny asked. She was enjoying torturing Crissy.

"Because . . . well, I . . . would like to know, that's all," Crissy sput-tered. She still didn't want to tell Jenny anything about her wonderful ex-perience with Luca the night before.

"Well, you'll just have to find out for yourself," Jenny said, "because I don't even want to talk about it." She threw down her nail file. "So don't ask me about it again. Okay?"

151

Crissy had never seen Jenny in this particular mood before, and she didn't like it. "No, of course not," she said. She went into the bathroom and closed the door. For a minute, she thought she might cry, but she forced the tears back. *She's got to be wrong,* she told herself. *And Monika, too. Luca cannot be like that. I just know it.* But even as the thought came to her, doubts surfaced at the same time, niggling at her mind, worrying her.

After dinner with the usual group, the table left together for the show, where they sat in their customary seats near the back. Afterward, Jenny and Dr. Von Meckling joined the crowd on the small dance floor to dance to a few slow tunes played by the show's three-man ensemble. Mina and Rudy, who hardly missed a dance, joined them.

"Jenny seems to be very interested in Dr. Von Meckling," Monika said to Crissy when they were alone.

"Do you really think so?" Crissy asked.

Monika nodded. "Indeed. She's much more clever than I first gave her credit for."

"How's that?" Crissy asked.

"She's discovered that there is satisfaction to be derived from something other than very good-looking young men who can make love all night."

"And what kind of satisfaction do you think she's getting from the doctor?" Crissy asked.

Monika looked at her and laughed. "Money, of course. Which translates into security, my darling."

"So the doctor is rich?" Crissy asked.

"Very," Monika said. "Everyone in Germany knows of his family and their great wealth. I'm sure that Jenny has heard of it now, too." She laughed again. "She's a heartless little tart, but she'll go far, I expect."

"But she has money of her own," Crissy said. "She got a big divorce settlement and alimony."

"I would doubt that it compares to the wealth of the Von Meckling family," Monika said. "Nor does it assure her the kind of social position marrying him would automatically give her."

"Marrying?" Crissy laughed. "You don't seriously think that Jen would even consider such a thing do you?"

Monika slowly nodded her silvery head, then smiled secretively at

Crissy. "I don't just think it," she said. "I'm quite certain that before the trip is over, Dr. Von Meckling will ask her, and she will accept."

Crissy was speechless for a moment. "I can't believe it," she said. "She's always gone after really good-looking younger men. One after the other. She's never gone after an older man."

"Crissy, my darling," Monika said patiently, "don't you see? Jenny doesn't even care about men. Not really. That's one reason she goes from one to the next. She uses them merely to entertain herself. Rather like some women use a . . . vibrator."

Crissy laughed. "You don't mean that."

"Of course I do," Monika said. "Jenny only cares about Jenny."

Crissy sat in silence, digesting this comment. Monika wasn't the first person to say something along that line about Jenny. Adonis, the man they'd met in Athens, had said something similar. And come to think of it, so had Luca. Her mind immediately turned to thoughts of him. The confusion and seeds of doubt sewn by Monika and now Jenny left her in a quandary. She didn't know what to think, but she could hardly wait to see him again tonight. In fact, she was surprised that there had been no message from him when she boarded the ship in Nice, but so far she'd heard nothing at all. Maybe he was very busy in the hospital, she told herself. With all the new passengers who boarded in Nice, he might have his hands full.

The others returned to the table as the ensemble ended its string of dance numbers, and packed up and got ready to go to the disco. "Well," Rudy asked, "is everybody ready for some real dancing?" He did a corny pelvic thrust and twist and threw his hands into the air, much as one of the showgirls might have done. Everyone laughed. "Mina and I will run on ahead," he offered, "and save a table. With all the new people, it might be very crowded tonight."

Crissy watched with fascination as Dr. Von Meckling led Jenny away on his arm as if she were a decorous trophy he had acquired. Monika turned to her and nodded as if to say "I told you so." They gathered up their purses, Monika her customary enormous gold leather one, and followed along. Monika made a spectacle of herself in the way she dressed and wore her hair and makeup, but Crissy thought that her look was perfectly suited to a sophisticated woman who was the author of numerous novels of romance and glamour.

Rudy waved to them, and they wove their way through the crowded disco to the table and sat down. "You see, it's very crowded tonight," he pointed out.

He had thoughtfully ordered champagne as he always did and immediately poured them glasses. "Jenny and the doctor are dancing," he said, nodding his head toward them on the dance floor.

Crissy looked and saw that Jenny's head was laid on the old doctor's shoulder, her eyes closed. She looked content, happy even, and the doctor held her to him as if she were a piece of priceless Meissen porcelain. "I can't get over it," she said.

Mina laughed raucously, her red lips gleaming in the reflection of the ever-changing lights roving over the dance floor and the area surrounding it. "My dear," she said through her laughter. "It is one of the oldest stories in the world. Jenny is clearly a girl who has made up her mind about what she wants, and it has very little to do with sex."

Crissy glanced toward the back of the room, hoping to see Luca, but there was no sign of him or the captain's party. She wondered why she hadn't heard from him since boarding in Nice. He must have had duties at the hospital that prevented him from contacting her, she thought. Despite the seeds of doubt that Jenny and Monika had sown, she found that she missed him and wanted to see him as soon as possible. She would confront him with the truth, she decided. Or rather, she amended the thought, with what Jenny and Monika had said.

Suddenly Monika took out one of her many fans and started fluttering away madly. "Oh, darling," she said, excited, "here comes the most divine man on the ship. Don't be a fool again." She half stood and lifted a hand into the air and began waving. "Darling, do join us," she called. "Over here."

Crissy tried to see who Monika was summoning, but she couldn't see anything except the people who were standing around in front of the table, moving to the beat of the music and blocking her view. *Monika must have radar*, she thought. Then, twisting this way and that to get through the wall of people, Mark appeared.

He went straight to Monika and gave her air kisses on both cheeks. "Madame Graf," he said, "it's such a pleasure to see you. How are you enjoying the trip?"

"It's lovely, my dear," she said. "And I've discovered the most delightful young lady from the States. But you've already met her. Crissy Fitzgerald—" She gestured to Crissy with her fan. "You know Makelos Vilos. Called simply Mark."

He looked at her with that superior smile, and Crissy smiled back. "Yes, we've met," she said. "Several times in fact."

"You have?" Monika said, surprised. She turned to Crissy. "Why didn't you tell me? Or did I forget?"

"I guess I didn't think of it," Crissy replied. "Besides," she added jokingly, "you might not have approved, and I would never hear the end of it."

"Ach!" Monika said. "Never. Not with Mark." She gestured to him. "Sit down, darling. Join us for a glass of champagne, won't you?"

"I would love to," he replied. He took a seat facing them both at the little round table.

"So you two met on the ship, I presume," Mark said.

"Yes," Monika said, "and I'm so lucky because Crissy is a divine creature. Like you."

Mark smiled. "How fortunate for you both," he said. "Traveling alone can be tiresome," he said. "It's so much more interesting to have a good traveling companion, isn't it?"

"Oh, yes," Monika agreed. "Crissy is traveling with a friend, Jenny, but she's left Crissy adrift, if you'll pardon the expression. She's always off with one man or another. Having quite a time for herself with the men."

"I'm sure Crissy could do the same if she chose," Mark said.

"Our Crissy is much more selective than her friend," Monika said.

One of Mark's eyebrows arched, and he looked at Crissy. "One must be careful not to end up all alone," he said. "Even a beautiful young lady such as yourself."

"I don't think there's too much danger of that," Crissy said.

"I've been hibernating myself," he said. "How would you like to dance?"

"Fine," Crissy replied, although she didn't actually relish the idea after his strange behavior in Monte Carlo.

"You don't mind, do you, Monika?" he asked politely.

"No, my darling," she said gaily. "Of course not."

Mark led Crissy to the dance floor, and as they began a slow dance, Monika observed them closely. They made a very good-looking pair, she thought, and would be a very good match. Crissy was a nobody from nowhere, but that didn't really matter. She was beautiful, well-mannered, decent, and had good instincts. She was also a quick study and would pick up the necessary social skills overnight. She was malleable, Monika thought, and that was a vital consideration. She could help mold her into the perfect wife for a man like Mark. *Oh,* she thought with a thrill, *how his family would embrace me. Welcome me to its bosom for making certain that their precious Makelos was on the right path at last.* There was much to be gained by manipulating these two into each another's arms. Much indeed.

As she watched, she saw them laughing together, enjoying each other's company, and it made her heart soar. *Oh, yes,* she thought. *Crissy and Mark. A couple. And I'll forever be their fairy godmother, the woman who introduced them, brought them together.* She felt a frisson of excitement surge through her body. It was more exciting than sex, she thought. The power and influence that would accrue to her from such a match was infinitesimal. Her work had just started, she realized, but like a warrior, she was prepared to do battle. And her first order of business would be to make certain that Crissy and that Italian doctor didn't see one another again. That was essential. She knew that Crissy, naive that she was, had already developed feelings for the Italian, but she would see that it went no further. To allow feelings to interfere in an affair like this was ridiculous.

When the dance was over, Mark brought Crissy back to the table. "You're going to hate me," he said to Monika.

"That's not remotely possible," she replied.

"I've asked Crissy to have a drink with me in my suite," he said, "and she's agreed. So we'll be leaving."

Monika clapped her hands together, her many rings clanking audibly. "Wonderful," she said. "Absolutely wonderful."

Crissy was surprised by her reaction. She knew that Monika approved of Mark, and she realized that the woman considered him the greatest catch, but her reaction seemed too enthusiastic, Crissy thought.

"We'll be back soon," Crissy said. "I just want to see his fabulous stateroom." Mark had been so charming on the dance floor that she decided his behavior in Monte Carlo had been something out of the ordinary. Perhaps he'd simply been having a bad day. Anyway, she would give him the benefit of the doubt.

"Stay as long as you want, my darling," Monika said. "The night is young, and I'll have plenty of company here."

"Don't misbehave while we're gone," Mark said to her.

Monika laughed girlishly and waved her fan.

As they weaved their way through the tables toward the exit, Crissy didn't see Jenny watching her from the dance floor, where she had a clear view over the old doctor's shoulder. Her eyes narrowed as she watched Crissy leave with yet another handsome young stud, just the sort of man she should be with rather than the old doctor. Wrenching *him* away from Crissy's greedy little claws would be easy, she thought. He didn't look like the type to have scruples like that creepy ship doctor. No, she decided, she could do worse than set her sights on the shipowner's son.

Nor did Crissy see the crestfallen expression on Luca's face. He had just arrived with the captain's party, and as was his custom, taken a table reserved for them toward the back of the room. His heart had leapt when he saw Crissy come off the dance floor and stop at the table where Monika sat alone. Then he had seen the man, and his hopes and excitement had plunged as his face had darkened. *Him,* he thought. *Of all people, Mark Vilos.* For a moment he thought he would chase after them, but he changed his mind. She was a grown-up after all, and she could make her own decisions. He sank down into a chair, grateful that the rest of his party was already heading to the dance floor or had started conversation with people standing about them.

Suddenly he couldn't stand being in this room anymore. He rose to his feet and rushed out, headed for his cabin. He didn't want to wait to find out if she was coming back. If she didn't, that meant she was spending the night with another man.

When they entered his stateroom, Mark's shoe kicked something on the floor. He leaned down and picked up an envelope. Crissy could see his name written on it.

"Damn," he muttered.

"Something wrong?" Crissy asked.

"No," he said. "Nothing." He tossed the envelope on a desk.

"This is spectacular," Crissy said, looking about Mark's suite. They were still on Deck Seven, only a short walk from the disco.

"I'm glad you like it," he replied. "What would you like to drink? I have practically anything you might want, or I can order something sent up."

"I'll just have a mineral water," Crissy said.

"That's all?"

She didn't want to have to explain about her inability to handle alcohol unless it was absolutely necessary. "That's all," she said.

As he busied himself at the minibar, Crissy looked about his huge suite. There was a large entry hall, bathroom, and the living room in which they stood. Through a doorway she could see a large separate bedroom. "This is beautiful," she said, "and so enormous."

"Yes," Mark said distractedly.

"What a huge trunk to travel with," Crissy exclaimed, looking at the steamer trunk she'd seen the first day of the cruise. It was placed against a wall in the sitting room. "Is that a family crest on it?"

"Yes," Mark replied irritably, turning around and gazing in her direction. "It's my father's. I brought it along for him. I don't normally travel with a trunk despite what I told you the other day. I'm just safekeeping it for him."

"Oh, I see," Crissy said, although she didn't understand. "I wonder what's in it?"

"Who knows?" Mark said, shrugging.

Crissy noticed the cross expression on his face. "I didn't mean to be nosy again."

He smiled. "You're not nosy," he replied and turned back to the minibar.

Crissy focused her attention on the living room again. Directly ahead of her were sliding glass doors that led out onto a balcony. *This must cost a fortune,* she thought. *It's five or six times the size of the stateroom Jenny and I have.* On the desk she noticed several unopened envelopes like the one he'd just picked up. They looked as if they'd been casually tossed there. The message light on the telephone, which was on the desk next to them, blinked red.

"You have messages on your telephone," she said.

"Forget it," Mark said dismissively. "I'm not picking up messages on this crossing."

"But what if—"

"I said to forget it," Mark snarled.

"Sorry, I didn't mean to—" Crissy began.

"No," he said, "I'm sorry. I shouldn't have snapped at you like that. It's just that I have a very . . . difficult family, you might say." He handed her a glass of mineral water with ice and a lime and smiled.

"Thank you," Crissy said.

"You're welcome," Mark replied. He poured some ouzo over ice and swirled it around, watching the drink turn cloudy. "Cheers, Crissy." He lifted his glass toward her.

"Cheers," she said.

"I've upset you by being so unpleasant," he said, apologizing again, "but my family really does smother me to death. Or try to, at least. That's why the telephone messages never get answered and those messages sent to the ship never get opened." He smiled again. "I even have my cell phone turned off, and for a Greek, that's a desperate measure."

Crissy laughed. "I believe that," she said. "Everybody in Athens was glued to a cell phone."

"Would you like to sit on the balcony?" he asked.

"I would love that," she said. "I've wondered what they were like."

He opened the sliding glass door and let her precede him out onto the balcony. "Have a seat," he said, but Crissy stood looking out to the darkness of the sea.

"The stars are unbelievable," she said. "It's so beautiful, and I love your balcony."

"There's another one off the bedroom," he said, edging up closely behind her.

"Your suite is drop-dead gorgeous," she said. "And huge. I never imagined there was anything like it on the ship." She abruptly realized that he was directly behind her, breathing down her neck, in fact, and she turned to face him.

"It's the only one," he said, smiling. He placed his hands on the railing, trapping her against it. "When they built the ship, the design called for twelve suites on this deck. Sky suites, they're called. But I had them combine two of them into one. So there are ten suites plus mine."

Crissy shifted against the railing nervously, but continued to make conversation. "You had them change the design of the ship?" she said.

He nodded.

"How on earth?"

"As you know, my family owns the shipping company," Mark said.

"Oh, that's right," she said. She slid to her left, trying to escape the entrapment of his arms, but Mark didn't move his hand.

"As I told you before, I don't advertise the fact," Mark replied. "You discover that you suddenly have lots of 'friends' who want to get to know you better, if you know what I mean."

"I can imagine," she said. She moved his hand and slipped to the side. Mark made no protest, but stayed close to her. "I guess it's like being a celebrity. You wonder whether they are really interested in you as a person or interested in you because of who you are or your money."

"Or both," he added.

"I have to admit that I'm impressed," Crissy said with a laugh. "I've never met a shipowner before or been in a huge suite like this."

"Well, my father is the owner," Mark said, "and believe me, he doesn't let you forget it."

"I think I know what you mean," she said. "I have a mother who's very much like that."

"My mother is smothering, too," he said, "but in a different way. She drinks too much and tries to make up for it by smothering me with love in the form of money and gifts."

"My father is sort of like that," Crissy said. "He drinks too much, then tries to make up for it by suddenly acting like a father. You know, visiting me, wanting to take me out to dinner. Things like that."

"We have a lot in common," Mark said. He moved to the railing next to her, looking out to sea.

Crissy turned and gazed in the same direction. "Well, I'm certainly not from a ship-owning family like yours," she said with a laugh. "My family is a mess."

"Mine is a mess, too. Just a mess with money."

The difference in their backgrounds was quite glaring, and she decided to change the subject. "So you know Monika?"

Mark shook his head. "No," he said. "Her publicity people emailed the company to alert them that she was going to be on this crossing, and I happened to be in reception when she boarded. The captain introduced me to her, and she was all over me. She'd met my parents at some party somewhere. I don't remember where." He shrugged. "Anyway, she's a bit of a monster, I suspect, but I humor her."

"A monster, huh?" Crissy said.

"Oh, maybe that's an exaggeration," he replied, chuckling. "I've known more than my share, and she's a lightweight." He stepped back and stood behind her again. "But she likes attention and a lot of it. You know, she really expects special treatment."

"I can see that," Crissy said. For some reason, she didn't feel comfortable with his close proximity, and she turned to face him again.

"She's the sort who needs to be surrounded by sycophants," he said.

"Laughers and clappers, I call them. I've met a lot of celebrities who are like that."

Crissy smiled. "Laughers and clappers," she repeated. "I like that. I think I could use some myself."

"We all need them from time to time, I guess," he said, and they both smiled.

"Instead of smothering parents?" she ventured. She felt more at ease after seeing him smile what appeared to be a genuine, heartfelt one.

He nodded. "Oh, yes. I'm running away from mine right now. It's ridiculous. I'm thirty-three years old and running away from home, so to speak."

"I don't think it's ridiculous at all," Crissy said. "I have to put a distance between my mother and myself. She would totally run my life if I let her."

Mark seemed to make a decision, and he put a hand on her arm. "Would you join me for dinner tomorrow night?" he abruptly asked. "Not in the dining room, but here in my suite?"

"I-I don't know . . ." Crissy began. She was nonplussed by his invitation.

"The chef will be doing something special," he said in a rush of words. "I don't know what yet, but he buys things along the way to prepare for those of us in the suites up here." He saw that she was hesitant and added, "I've been all alone, quite frankly, and would really appreciate the company."

Crissy slowly nodded. "I would be delighted," she said. How could she say no after he'd been so hospitable?

"Wonderful," he said. "I don't think you'll be disappointed. The chef is really capable of creating superb dishes."

"I'm sure I won't be," she said.

"Eight-thirty?"

"Perfect," she said. "But now I'd better get going."

He was taken aback and placed his hands on the railing again, trapping her against it. "So soon?"

"It was a very long day," she said. "From San Remo to Monte Carlo and Nice. I want to say good night to Monika and the others, then get a good night's sleep."

He stared at her a moment, then drew back. "I will take you back to the disco," he said, though he was clearly disappointed, "and look forward to seeing you tomorrow night."

When they reached the disco, he talked her into dancing one more slow dance with him. Crissy noticed that several people watched them, not only Monika and the others at her table, but several of the officers who were dancing and employees. They knew who Mark was, of course, and she felt as if she had become a kind of celebrity simply by being with him. It wasn't an unpleasant feeling; in fact, it was quite enjoyable, having attention lavished upon you, but she knew that it was ephemeral. She would see Mark for dinner and that would be the end of it. She had searched the back of the room for signs of Luca when they came back into the disco, but hadn't seen him, nor did she see him on the dance floor, although the captain was there, dancing as usual. With a certain degree of guilt, she felt that the events of the day and meeting Mark had made the previous evening seem almost as if it had never happened. But then, even as Mark held her more closely, she remembered Luca's embraces the night before and felt a longing that the mere memory of his tenderness stirred within her.

After the dance, she retrieved her purse, said good-night to Monika, and let Mark take her back to her cabin. She took out her key card and thanked him for an enjoyable evening.

"I look forward to tomorrow," he said.

"So do I," Crissy responded. "I'll see you at eight-thirty."

"Yes," Mark said, then he leaned down and quickly brushed her cheek with his lips. "Ciao." He turned and left.

Crissy touched the spot on her cheek that his lips had brushed. She could hardly believe that the shipowner's son had just kissed her. That he had invited her to dinner tomorrow night in his suite. And that he was a very handsome young man who was interested in her enough to ask her out. Mark could have his pick of women on the ship, she thought, and he had asked her. Still, she couldn't forget his bizarre behavior in Monte Carlo. What would account for someone capable of such charm to behave so inappropriately then revert to the perfect gentleman again? She didn't know, but she couldn't shake the feeling that there was something amiss about him, something she couldn't put her finger on.

After she had turned out the light, her thoughts drifted once again to Luca, and she wondered why he hadn't tried to contact her today. She was disappointed when she saw that the message light on her telephone wasn't blinking as Mark's had been. She told herself that something had happened at the hospital. That would also explain why he hadn't appeared at the disco tonight. She didn't know what to think, but she thought that he surely could have taken the time to call. Perhaps, she thought, there was some truth to what Monika and Jenny had said, but the thought didn't trouble her now, not with Mark's visage swimming before her mind's eye. She finally fell asleep, but not before thinking that whatever tomorrow would bring, her life was suddenly becoming much more exciting.

Chapter Twelve

The blasts from the ship's horn told Crissy that they were close to shore. Barcelona, she thought excitedly. She saw several other crafts in the water, but she was on the starboard side and couldn't see land. She hurried back inside and down to her cabin to get her camera, then rushed back up to the pool deck to take some pictures as they docked. The crowd, much bigger since Nice, had flocked to the railings to watch. From her position she could see the cable car that went from the pier to a mountain in the distance, and she also saw what must be the statue of Christopher Columbus near the harbor that she'd read about. The city looked beautiful from here, and she could hardly wait to go ashore. After discussing it with Monika, who knew the city well, she had decided not to sign up for any of the excursions today, and instead she would walk about on her own.

Before leaving the ship, she thought she might try to reach Luca in the hospital, but then decided that she didn't think that would be wise. He was working, for one thing; for another, she wanted to see how long it would take him to call. She was loath to think that he had taken advantage of her, but she was beginning to wonder. They were supposed to meet after the ship left Nice, and nothing, she decided, could have been so important that he couldn't have at least sent her a message by now.

She tried to forget about it, and when she finally left the ship, she was on foot and alone, with a small map provided by the cruise line and the little guidebook she'd purchased before leaving. Passing the Christopher Columbus statue, she headed for the famous walk known as *Ramblas de Flores*. Walking down the wide pedestrian street, lined on both sides by elegant old buildings, she was struck again and again by the beauty she saw all around her. Beneath huge, ancient trees were many flower vendors with blossoms from the world over; newspaper vendors and booksellers; a bird market offering exotic caged birds. Many of the small hotels, theaters, apartment buildings, and cafés that she passed on the walk were exquisitely beautiful, with baroquely painted exteriors or neoclassical facades complemented by statuary and ironwork. The people who crossed her path were a breed apart, she thought. Full of energy, sophisticated, and fashionably dressed. Barcelona was obviously a very progressive city. At one point she decided to turn off the *Ramblas*. According to her map, the street she took would take her into the city's ancient gothic quarter, and only a block away she stopped at the fifteenth-century cathedral and admired the stained glass and stonework. Once back outside, she walked down narrow, cobbled streets, fascinated by the little shops. Every trade was represented—bakers, butchers, clothiers—and anything you might have wanted you could find here in the tiny shops. Quickly becoming lost, even with her map in hand, she was glad when the narrow lane she was on opened up onto a large, sunlit plaza.

She saw a small group of people gathered around a musician of some sort, and she walked toward them. The musician was a ragtag version of Emmett Kelly, the famous clown, and he played the accordian and hurdy-gurdy as mechanical dolls danced. It was a charming performance, and she tossed a few coins into the hat he'd placed on the cobbles before strolling across the plaza to a major thoroughfare.

There, she hailed a taxi and asked him to take her to Gaudi's famous unfinished cathedral of the *Sagrada Familia*. She paid the driver and got out, already awed by her first sight of the art nouveau monument. After wandering about outside the church, she caught another taxi to Park Güell, which Gaudí also designed as a hillside garden suburb of Barcelona. Her feet began to ache, and she decided to find a sidewalk café and have something to drink while resting. She took a taxi to the Plaza de Catalunya, at the far end of the *Ramblas*.

She'd read that this plaza was the hub of Barcelona life, and she believed it after sitting at a café for awhile, drinking strong coffee and watching the energetic crowds that thronged the streets. As she surveyed the scene, her mind wandered back to Luca, and she worried anew why he hadn't tried to contact her. Their night together had been so special that she thought perhaps something serious might have happened. *Maybe I'll go back to the ship early and see if I can find him,* she decided. She looked at her wristwatch and realized she had plenty of time, so she ordered a simple lunch of arroz con pollo, which turned out to be deliciously spiced and unlike any she'd tasted before. She paid the check, then began the walk back down toward the dock on the *Ramblas.* It was no less beautiful this time than the last. The sun was warmer now, but the huge trees provided shade for her.

Once back in her cabin, she found that Jenny was gone, but she could see that she'd been in to change clothes: The outfit she'd worn last night had been thrown on the bed, and her shoes were on the floor.

She went to the telephone and dialed the number for the hospital. The nurse-receptionist answered the phone and told her the doctor was out.

"Do you know where I can reach him?" Crissy asked.

"Is this a medical emergency?" the nurse asked.

"No," Crissy replied. "I'm a friend of his."

"I see," the nurse said. "Well, you'll have to call back during hospital hours."

"Could I leave a message, please?"

"Of course," the nurse replied.

"Please tell him that Crissy Fitzgerald called." She also gave the nurse her cabin number.

While she was taking a nap, an announcement over the PA system awoke her. She looked at her watch and discovered that she'd slept for a long time. It was time for the second dinner seating, which meant that it was time for her to leave for Mark's stateroom. She quickly applied makeup, brushed her hair, and dressed.

As she approached Mark's stateroom on the top deck, she realized that she was nervous. Her heart was pounding in her chest. She wondered why. It was Mark, of course. While he had behaved as a gentleman, the superiority that seemed an intrinsic part of his character was daunting, and she still hadn't shaken the sense that there was something . . . off . . . about him. As she neared his stateroom, she told herself that she was imagining things. He was the shipowner's son after all, rich, handsome, and interested in her.

She tapped on the door, and it was opened at once. Her anxiety was immediately laid to rest by Mark's friendly smile and demeanor. "Come in," he said. "I'm so glad you're here."

"It's nice to be back," Crissy said, once again impressed by his enormous and beautifully appointed suite. At the balcony doors, a dining table was set with china and silver on a white linen cloth. In its center was a bowl of fresh flowers. Lit candles produced a flattering light.

"Would you like a glass of champagne?" he asked. "I know you don't drink much, but I thought we could at least have that."

"Yes," Crissy said. "That would be lovely."

"It's a little rough out," Mark said as he poured the golden liquid into crystal flutes, "so I think we might want to have our drinks in here. Why don't you have a seat on the couch."

Nervous, Crissy plopped down on the couch, nestling into a corner. Glancing across the room, she saw the large trunk emblazoned with Vs propped against a wall near the entrance hall. "I think it's so funny that you're traveling with that huge trunk," she said with a laugh. She abruptly covered her mouth with a hand. Too late, she remembered Mark's cross expression the last time she'd mentioned the trunk, and she expected him to react negatively to her remark. But surprisingly, he took it in stride. Perhaps he was simply in a better mood, she thought.

"Oh, I guess my father's a bit old-fashioned," Mark said with a shrug. "In fact, he's very old-fashioned." He laughed and smiled as if they shared a harmless family secret.

Encouraged by his response, Crissy asked, "Have you opened it? I mean, what on earth is it for?"

Mark shrugged again. "I'm not really sure. Probably paperwork and such, I guess. It's just stuff that he's sending to our apartment in Miami for safekeeping."

"Oh, so you have an apartment in Miami?"

"Yes, the company does," he replied. "We have an office that does a lot of business there, so it makes sense. But I'm practically the only person in the family who ever uses it. My mother's used it a couple of times." He handed her a flute of champagne. "There are some hors d'oeuvres on the table. Help yourself."

Crissy took the wine. "Thank you, Mark." She looked at the elegantly arranged bowl of caviar on ice, surrounded with toast points, on the coffee table. In the caviar was a spoon made of horn. He was obviously served a menu that wasn't available in the dining rooms.

He sat down on the couch, positioning himself in the other corner. "To a wonderful journey," he said, clinking his glass against hers. "And a wonderful evening."

"Yes," Crissy said, her anxieties reasserting themselves beneath the steady gaze of his dark eyes.

"Did you like Barcelona?" he asked.

"I thought it was beautiful," she replied. "I didn't go on any of the excursions, but I saw quite a bit." She took a sip of her champagne. "Did you go ashore?"

He shook his head. "No. I had a lot to do, so I stayed aboard."

Crissy wondered what could have kept him so busy. She had already noticed that the stack of unopened envelopes was still stacked on his desk. In fact, it looked as if the stack had grown overnight. "Oh, so this is a working trip for you?"

"Something like that," he said vaguely. He slid an arm across the back of the couch and twisted around in his seat to face her. "But let's not discuss work. Or my family."

"Sorry," she said. "I didn't mean to—"

"Forget it," he broke in. "Tell me about your day."

Crissy described her walk in Barcelona in detail, and when she finished, she saw that he was smiling. "What do you find so amusing?" she asked.

"Your excitement," he replied. "It's refreshing. Most of the people I know are so jaded they wouldn't get excited by the walk you described. They've seen it all a dozen times, and nothing excites them anymore."

"Are you like that, too? Jaded?"

He shrugged. "In ways, I suppose. The great cities of the world are all beginning to blend into one for me. Like hot clubs, fast cars, and beautiful women. They seem the same everywhere, even with their differences. It's all become a bore."

Crissy couldn't imagine being as world-weary as Mark was. "Isn't there anything that excites you anymore?"

"I still love ships and the sea," he said. "And I'm obviously excited by you."

As disarmingly as he smiled, Crissy didn't believe him. She felt like a mere distraction for him, nothing more. He'd said she was refreshing. *A shower is refreshing,* she thought, *or maybe a drink.* "That's very nice of you to say," she replied.

"You don't believe me, do you?"

"I . . . I don't know," Crissy confessed.

There was a knock at the door, and Mark got up. "Excuse me. That must be our food."

Two waiters entered, carrying heavily laden trays that they set down on the dining table in front of the balcony doors. They quickly laid out the food, then stood behind the two chairs, waiting to seat them.

"Ready?" Mark asked, holding his arm out for her to take.

"Yes," Crissy said, rising to her feet. He walked her the few feet to the dining table, where one of the waiters drew her chair back. After she was seated, Mark sat as well.

"I think we can serve ourselves," he said to the waiters. "We don't want to be disturbed, so I'll ring when I want you to clean up."

They nodded and bowed obsequiously, then left the suite.

Mark poured white wine into their glasses, apparently forgetting that Crissy couldn't drink more than the glass of champagne she'd had. She took one sip, savoring it on her palate, suspecting that it was a very expensive wine she was not likely to taste again soon. She didn't dare have more. They began eating while talking about the ship, his favorite in their fleet. After appetizers of foie gras in a cognac sauce, which melted in Crissy's mouth, Mark took the lids off the entrée, a sautéed sole, which was the best fish she'd ever eaten. Even the vegetables, white Belgian asparagus with a Hollandaise sauce and tiny new potatoes topped with sour cream and caviar, were sublime. Finally, they had a dessert of crème brûlée in a nest of spun sugar. She had never seen anything like it before, nor had she tasted anything better.

"I think this is the best meal I've ever eaten," she told him when they were finished.

"I'm pleased you liked it," he said. "The chefs are very good, and they don't get to demonstrate their talent for the hordes in the dining rooms."

They talked awhile longer at the table, Mark telling her about the stops that were coming up on the ship's itinerary. He had been to all of them, some of them several times, and Crissy asked him many questions, absorbing as much as she could. He warmed to the subject, she was glad to see, as he had to the discussion of the ship, and the world-weariness that seemed to permeate his every word slipped away, temporarily at least.

"I want to stand out on the balcony," he finally said, pushing back from the table. "Join me?"

"Yes," she said, glad for the invitation. The sea air would be bracing after a good meal, she thought.

The wind was powerful and the spray high, but they leaned back against the glass balcony doors, where they were protected by the panels that separated them from the adjoining balconies. Without being able to help it, she shivered.

"You're cold," he said, slipping an arm around her shoulders.

Crissy almost jerked away but restrained herself, letting him keep his arm around her but hoping he didn't go any further. She didn't want to disappoint him, nor did she want to encourage him. They stood together in silence, content to gaze out at the rough seas and the dark sky. The vast expanse was beautiful to her, even with the less than pleasant weather, and she was reminded of nature's power and beauty as she never was driving the streets of Albany.

"Have you enjoyed yourself?" Mark asked after awhile.

"Yes," Crissy said. "It's been lovely."

"Would you join me in the disco?"

Crissy hesitated.

"Only for a few dances," he added.

"Okay," she said. "I'd like that."

They went back inside and left for the disco after Mark called to have the dining table cleaned up. In the disco, he led her to a small table at the back, away from the dance floor, its ever-changing lights, and the throng of people that surrounded it. *Just like Luca did,* she thought. They were hardly seated before a solicitous waitress appeared, her eyes bright as they focused on Mark.

"What can I get for you?" she asked, her lips, heavily painted in red, spreading in a smile. She shifted her weight, thrusting a long leg toward him.

Mark turned to Crissy. "What would you like?" he asked.

"A mineral water with lime," Crissy replied.

"Make that two," he told the waitress, who smiled and curtseyed, then left.

"I think she likes you," Crissy said.

"She knows who I am," Mark replied with disgust. "It's a nuisance, the way they throw themselves at you like whores."

Crissy was surprised by his vehemence, even if she could imagine the come-ons he had to endure. "She's probably a little starstruck," she said, hoping he would lighten up.

"Let's dance," he said, abruptly getting to his feet.

This was less an invitation than a demand, she thought, but she rose to her feet. "Will my purse be okay?"

"Of course," he said. "The help wouldn't dare touch it, and they wouldn't let anyone else either."

She let him lead her to the dance floor, where he took her into his arms for a slow number. Valentin, who was partnering an attractive middle-aged lady, almost imperceptibly nodded to her, then immediately turned his attention back to the woman he was dancing with.

"So you know Valentin, I see," Mark said, the familiar smirk on his face.

He doesn't miss a thing, Crissy thought. "I've danced with him a few times," she said. "I don't really know him."

"He dances with all the ladies," Mark said. "That's what he's here for."

"What do you mean?" Crissy asked, looking up at him.

"Just what I said," Mark retorted. "He gets a small salary, a free trip, and a drink discount for keeping the women happy. Especially women who are traveling alone or don't have husbands."

"He's *paid* to dance with passengers?" Crissy said in astonishment.

"Of course," Mark replied. "You didn't know that?"

"No," she said. She didn't tell him that she had assumed Valentin was interested in her.

"He's like a gigolo," Mark said with amusement. "There are usually a couple of real ones operating on any trip, preying on older women, lonely women, looking for money in exchange for sex or just attention, but we make certain that there's always someone like Valentin. He poses no risk to the women and is always available to dance."

"How weird," Crissy said. "Dancing your way around the world for a living."

"Oh, no," Mark said. "It's not like that. We hire a different man for every trip, and never use the same one twice."

"Why?"

"We have many repeat customers," he said. "Especially women who travel a lot. Widows, whatever. We don't want them to know that the man asking them to dance is paid to do it. It would insult some of them. So we use a service that provides presentable men for the job."

"So it's not a problem to find men to do it?" she asked.

"Never," he said. "There's a long waiting list, especially of Eastern European men who want to get out of Romania or Bulgaria. Some of them are Albanian, Serbs. You get the picture."

Crissy was still somewhat shocked by this revelation. Valentin was very good at his job, she thought, because he certainly made her feel as if he was more than a little interested in her.

Another slow dance was played, and they didn't leave the floor. Mina and Rudy came into view, and she waved to them. Rudy saw her and gave her a thumbs-up.

Mark observed the interchange, then looked down at Crissy. "Peasants," he said.

"What do you mean?" she asked.

"Those people. One foot still on the farm," he said. "Have you noticed that Monika likes to surround herself with people who are, shall we say, less exposed to the world than she?"

Crissy felt as if she'd been burned, his remark was so insulting, and she blushed with embarrassment.

"I didn't mean you, of course," Mark said. "You're different."

"How?" Crissy asked, not certain she wanted to hear the answer.

"You're beautiful, for one thing," Mark said. "You're also very intelligent. A quick study, as you say in English. You are also very sensitive, I think."

"I don't have one foot still on the farm?" she said tartly.

"No," he replied, "but I don't think you ever did. Not like that Austrian couple."

Crissy had a vision of extricating herself from his arms and walking off the dance floor, leaving him behind, so angry had his remarks made her. Mina and Rudy had been very nice to her since they'd met, and she didn't like hearing them talked about in such a derogatory way. Maybe they were peasants, as he'd put it, but they had become her friends.

The dance ended, and they went back to their table. Their drinks were waiting, and they both sipped the mineral water. Crissy noticed that a large bottle had been brought, without Mark asking for it. One of the privileges of being the owner's son, she thought. She glanced around the disco, wondering if Luca and the captain's party had arrived, but she didn't see him or any of the others.

"You're very quiet," Mark said.

"I was just thinking," she said.

"About what?" he asked.

"It's getting late," she replied, "and I think I should get back to my cabin soon."

"I've upset you, haven't I?" he said, reaching over and placing a hand on her arm.

172

"Actually, you have," Crissy replied. "I-I don't like to hear my friends trashed. They've been really nice to me."

"I'm sorry," Mark said in a voice that sounded sincere. "I didn't mean anything by it, really."

Crissy didn't respond but took another sip of water.

"You're not European," Mark said, "so you couldn't really understand, I suppose. But I wasn't being nasty."

"You could have fooled me," Crissy said flatly.

"Please," he said, almost pleading, "don't be upset. I apologize if I insulted you or your friends. Do you want me to ask them over for a drink?"

"No," Crissy said, shaking her head. "I think I really should get going in a minute." She forced a smile. "I think it's all the wonderful food I had with you tonight. It's made me sleepy."

Mark smiled ruefully. "At least you enjoyed that."

"Oh, I've enjoyed the evening very much," Crissy said. Without thinking, she reached over and put a hand on his arm. "I hope you don't think otherwise."

"I'm glad," he said. "Maybe we can have a nightcap in my cabin."

She shook her head. "I can't have anything else," she said, begging off, "and I really am exhausted."

"That's too bad," Mark said. "I'll walk you back to your cabin. Maybe we can have dinner again soon."

"That would be great," Crissy said.

Mark got up and slid her chair back from the table. Crissy picked up her purse, then took the hand he extended to her. He led her toward the exit, and Crissy noticed Jenny and Dr. Von Meckling on the edge of the dance floor. It was a fast dance, and the elderly doctor was making a valiant effort to appear to be dancing by moving his arms about and shuffling his feet. He was a good sport, Crissy thought, but she still had trouble imagining Jenny, of all people, devoting time to him rather than the younger men who would gladly rush to her side if she gave them the slightest sign of interest.

Once inside, she slumped against the door for a moment. Having dinner with a rich man was exhausting. What did Mark see in her, when he looked down on everyone else? His attraction to her, she decided, was a result of his loneliness on the trip; that and the fact that she was different from the types of women who usually pursued him. They came from such different worlds that she didn't think the gap could ever be bridged. He made her feel as if she were a bonbon, a treat he would indulge in.

She had begun to undress when the telephone bleeped. Answering it, she was thrilled to hear Luca's voice.

"I-I wondered if I could see you," he said haltingly.

Crissy felt her heart soar. "I would love to," she replied. Any fatigue she'd felt evaporated immediately.

"You would?" he asked, surprised.

"Of course I would," she said. "What would make you think anything else? I've tried to get hold of you, and I've really been worried that I didn't hear from you."

"Oh, my God," Luca said. "I see that I've been completely wrong."

"About what?" Crissy asked.

"I saw you in the disco with Mark Vilos," he said, "and I thought . . . Well, I thought that—"

"Oh, Luca!" she exclaimed. "If you only knew. I'd been waiting to hear from you. I looked for you, but didn't see you. I thought maybe you weren't really interested in me."

"Oh, my God," he repeated. "Meet me right now. This minute."

"Where?" she asked without hesitation.

"On the pool deck," he said. "Do you know where we went the last time?"

"Yes," she replied. "I'm on my way." Without giving it any further thought, she rushed out the door and up to the pool deck.

The music in the background was an electronic dance mix on low volume, the perfect accompaniment, she thought. Not too slow, not too fast. Jenny kicked off her heels and slipped out of the glittery, revealing top she was wearing. Her ample breasts sprang free, her darkish nipples already hard. She swung her head, throwing her hair back out of her eyes, then unzipped the top's matching miniskirt, letting it fall to the floor. She wore no underwear, and she heard the moan of pleasure from the bed at the sight of the shaved mound between her thighs. Sliding a finger in her mouth, she laved it with her tongue, then placed it on her mound, thrusting her hips forward lasciviously, rubbing her finger up and down, before inserting it and moving her hips slowly around it, a look of wanton desire etched on her features. She moved closer and closer to the bed, puckering her lips provocatively, gyrating on her finger, watching him watch her, taking delight in his arousal, in teasing him mercilessly.

He rose slowly from the bed, his erection swinging out in front of him, his eyes never leaving the sight of her in her naked glory. When he reached her, he put a hand on each of her shoulders and pushed her to her knees. She was prepared for this, for they had done it last night, and she willingly, gladly took him in her mouth and began licking him with her tongue, letting him slowly push himself farther in, then pull nearly out, before pushing in again. Over and over until he couldn't bear the sensation any longer. Moaning again, he slowly pulled all the way out, and her tongue slid to his balls, flicking them lightly, then licking them in earnest before he helped her to her feet, a hand under each arm.

His mouth closed over hers, and he kissed her with passionate desire, his tongue engulfing her while his hands found her breasts and kneaded them, then thrummed her nipples between his fingers. A lustful sigh escaped Jenny's lips, and she reached down and stroked his engorged shaft. She could hardly wait to have it inside her.

As if reading her mind, he led her to the bed, where she lay back, spreading her legs wide. He got onto the bed, kneeling between her legs. He put a hand on her shaved mound, slipping his thumb inside her, feeling her wet readiness, before removing it and sliding it in his mouth, tasting it, his eyes burning into hers. He lowered his body atop hers, and he entered her, pushing himself in as far as he could.

Jenny almost levitated with ecstasy. "Oh, my God," she cried. Swept up in a tidal wave of desire, she began to move against him, grinding her pelvis against his. He groaned, then began thrusting himself in and out, in and out, his body seemingly possessed by hers. Unable to control his desire, he thrust with abandon, and Jenny, engulfed by his manhood, flung her legs out and clawed his back as she came, flooding him as she contracted over and over, her head twisting from side to side. He let out a loud grunt as he exploded inside her, his body stiffening momentarily before he collapsed atop her, panting from the effort.

"Ahhhh," she rasped, reveling in the feel of his sweaty body against hers, "that . . . that was the best yet. The best . . . ever."

He didn't reply but continued to pant, catching his breath, enjoying the sensation of his cock inside her. He lay motionless for awhile, still silent except for the sound of his labored breathing, in his own world and thinking his own thoughts, Jenny presumed. Finally, as his breathing returned to normal and he began to shrink inside her, he pulled out and rolled off her in one fluid motion.

A gasp escaped her lips when he withdrew, and she frowned in disappointment as he turned his head away. She had hoped for a repeat performance, but he apparently wasn't interested. He didn't like a lot of foreplay, she thought, and he certainly didn't indulge her in sweet nothings afterward like some men did. In fact, he didn't seem to want to touch her when it was over. And he was so silent, as if he were a million miles away. Jenny had no lack of confidence in her appearance, and thought her body was as near perfect as that of any woman she knew. Her face was strikingly beautiful. Hadn't everyone told her so? What's more, she had brains and was decently educated. She wasn't a bimbo. So why did he act like she was a stranger when it was over? The problem, she decided, if there was a problem, had to be with him. Maybe it was because he was filthy rich and came from an important family. *So what?* she thought. She had money, and her family, while not rich and socially prominent like his, was well-off enough.

His silence became unbearable, and she placed a hand on his back and began gently stroking him. "You're one hell of a stud," she said, hoping to get a reaction out of him.

"Get dressed and go," Mark said without turning to face her. "I want to be by myself now."

"What?" she began.

"Just go," he snapped from between clenched teeth.

Jenny wanted to ball up her fist and sock him, but she resisted the impulse, sliding out of bed and quietly getting dressed. When she was finished, she picked up her purse and regarded him on the bed. "I'm leaving," she said.

He rolled over, got out of bed, and went to the door. "See you later," he said, his handsome features in a superior smirk.

"I hope so," she said, raising her hand and waggling fingertips at him. "Bye."

"Ciao." He opened the door, and she went out.

Jenny heard it shut behind her as she went down the corridor in a state of utter confusion. What was with the weirdo anyway? she wondered. After she'd seen him with Crissy, she'd followed them to their cabin last night, then she'd followed him back to his. She'd acted quickly before he opened the door to his cabin, dropping an earring to the carpet and exclaiming that she'd lost one. He'd immediately come to her aid and found the earring at once. He'd also responded with alacrity when she'd brushed her nearly naked breasts against him and told him she would like to buy him a drink as a way of thanking him. He'd invited her into his cabin instead, and although they'd never had the drink, they'd had sex virtually all night, sleeping, then waking and screwing, then sleeping again.

She'd expected the same again tonight, and was not only disappointed but angry. *It's Crissy,* she thought. *Miss Goody Two-shoes probably told him something about me while they were having their damn dinner tonight. The bitch.*

She wasn't ready for bed yet, and didn't want to go back to the cabin. *Maybe there's a live one in the disco,* she thought. *If nothing else, I can count on Manolo for a good lay.* She stopped in a restroom outside the disco, refreshed her makeup and ran her hands through her blond mane to tousle it even more than it already was. *Bed head,* she thought, looking at herself in the mirror. *They can't resist it.*

Spread out as if at a picnic beneath the ship's huge funnel, Luca held a protective arm around Crissy's shoulders, his lips brushing her face tenderly. They had propped themselves against the base of the funnel after making love and had been stargazing, Luca pointing out the constellations that were visible between the clouds in the sky.

"After we head toward Cape Verde," he said, "the skies will probably be a lot clearer, and I can show you more. I'm afraid we're going to have some dicey weather between here and there."

"It's amazing what you know about the stars," Crissy said. "I couldn't point out anything but the Big Dipper and the Little Dipper, and anybody could do that."

"Not anybody," he said, pushing her hair away from her face and kissing her ear. "It's easy when you're at sea, because there aren't any city lights or pollution to interfere."

"But you have to know what you're looking for," she said.

"That's why I always had a celestial map from the time I was a kid," he replied, "and a telescope." He kissed her again. "Are you comfortable enough?"

Crissy nodded. "Hmmm," she murmured, then looked at him. "I feel like I'm in heaven, Luca," she said. "Metal never felt so good."

They both laughed quietly in the darkness. "I would like to take you to my cabin," he said. "You know that. But like I said before, I don't want to expose you to ridicule on the ship. Wilma, the manicurist who runs the spa, well, she keeps an eye on the crew quarters, too."

"She does?" Crissy said. "How odd."

"I think she sleeps with her eyes and ears open," Luca said, "always looking and listening for trouble. She goes straight to the captain with any information that she thinks he should know, and, believe me, if I was entertaining a lady in my quarters he would know right away."

"Would he get upset?" she asked.

"I'm not really sure," Luca replied, "because I've never done it. I know he doesn't pay any attention to the affairs that develop between crew members. There's no way that could be controlled. It's like musical beds down there. But when it's between a crew member and a passenger, that's different. It brings up liability issues for the shipping company."

"I never thought about that," Crissy said.

He nodded. "A lady could claim rape," Luca said. "All kinds of things like that."

"I wonder if he knew about Manolo and Jenny," she said.

"He almost certainly did and put a stop to it," Luca said, "because I know that Wilma knew about it, and everybody was talking about it. Did she say anything to you?"

"No," Crissy said, "but I've hardly seen her. She comes and goes at odd hours to change clothes, so I think she must be seeing somebody. She dances all the time with Dr. Von Meckling, which amazes me."

He debated about telling her what Jenny had done—the way she had thrown herself at him—and decided that he didn't want to do anything to spoil the friendship that Crissy had with Jenny. Jenny had probably all but forgotten the incident anyway, he reasoned, and what she'd done was certainly nothing new for him.

He ran a finger down the side of her face, then brushed his lips across the spot. "Let's not waste our time talking about that," he said, giving her a hug. "I feel so . . . so relieved about you and Mark Vilos. It really had me worried—and angry."

She touched his lips with her fingertips. "You don't have anything to worry about," she said. "I told you that. He was a perfect gentleman, and I think the only reason he danced with me or asked me to dinner was because he's so lonely."

"Ha," Luca grunted. "Don't count on it. I hear he's trouble. Big trouble."

"What does that mean?" she asked with a little laugh. She thought he was simply jealous and overreacting.

"Trouble with women," he said. "There've been rumors in the past, but it's hard to know what's true. Everybody tiptoes around. The captain is adamant about leaving Mark Vilos alone and won't even hear a complaint about him."

"I guess he could get away with murder," Crissy said, "being the owner's son."

Luca nodded. "Exactly." He hugged her again. "I'm so glad you're here with me. I was really getting desperate. He's so rich, and the women think he's so good-looking. I thought maybe you'd fallen for him."

She touched his lips with her fingertips again. "Shh," she said. "Let's not waste our time talking about him either. He's not an issue anymore. It's just us." She paused. "And the stars."

"I can't believe my luck. I must be the luckiest man alive." His lips closed over hers, and he kissed her with passion.

"And I'm the luckiest woman alive," Crissy said.

They began kissing again, unable to restrain their hunger for each other. They had already dressed after making love, but one of his hands fondled her breasts through her dress. Crissy felt herself becoming aroused again, and Luca began moaning with lust.

Finally, neither of them could bear it any longer, and he quickly freed himself from his trousers and entered her, slowly and gently. Clutching each other as if they never wanted to part, they began to move together rhythmically, quietly whispering and gasping, until they climaxed together, their excitement heightened by the necessity to restrain their joy. When it was over, they clung to each other, breathing heavily, Luca brushing his lips across her face and neck with tenderness, gently licking her.

Crissy sighed ecstatically. "We don't need a bed, Luca. We have the perfect place under the stars. I can't imagine anything more perfect."

"Maybe you'll be able to soon," he whispered.

"How's that?" she asked.

"Tomorrow we have all day at sea. Two days later, the same," he replied, still brushing her face with his lips. "I think you'll have to make appointments with the doctor."

Crissy laughed quietly. "Do you mean that?"

He nodded. "Absolutely. I don't know why I didn't think of it before, but I've never done it. Even if I have to work overtime so that nothing interferes with my seeing other patients, you can call to schedule appointments on those days. Starting tomorrow."

"That's brilliant," she said, "but what will I tell the nurse?"

"Tell her it's your stomach," he said. "You don't have to be more specific."

"Will it be safe in the office?"

"Yes," he said. "We'll have to be quiet as usual, unless there's nobody else around. Maybe you'll have to be scheduled at the end of the day."

"I can hardly wait," she said.

"Neither can I, but until then we have our special place here."

She hugged him. "And it is very special, Luca."

"The most special place in all the world," he replied.

Crissy slid her key card in the slot on the door and opened it when the green light appeared. Jenny wasn't in the cabin, and she took her time getting ready for bed, showering, moisturizing, and putting on her big T-shirt, planning to sleep in. She was still excited but felt sated, fulfilled, and at peace. Nothing in the world could separate Luca and her, she thought. Nothing in the world. What they had together was indestructible. True and beautiful. She felt invincible.

The telephone bleeped, and she stood for a moment, staring at it. *Who on earth?* she wondered. Then she smiled. *It's Luca, calling to tell me good night.*

She picked up the receiver. "Hello."

No one spoke, but she could clearly hear breathing.

"Hello?" she repeated.

There was still no response but the unmistakable sound of breathing.

"Hello?" she said again, angrily.

The breathing continued, and Crissy slammed the receiver down. "Who the hell?"

She sat down on the edge of the bed, staring at the telephone as if it held the answer. Maybe it was an accident, she thought. The wrong number. Or somebody playing a joke. Well, it sure wasn't funny. Not one little bit. Or, she told herself, it could be . . . Mark. Maybe he was upset that she hadn't come back for a nightcap with him. The more she thought about it, the more certain she was that the telephone call had been from Mark. But a long time had elapsed since she'd left the disco, she reminded herself. If it was Mark, why did he wait until now to call?

She felt a chill run up her spine and wrapped her arms around herself. The call had come soon after she came back to the cabin. As if someone knew when she would be there. But, she reminded herself, she had showered off, so whoever it was had given her a few minutes. The message light hadn't been blinking when she came in, but then no one making a call like that would leave a message, would he?

"Oh, damn," she cursed. *I'm working myself up into a frenzy over . . . over . . . nothing. It's probably some kid playing a joke.* Her mind began to whirl with questions but no answers. She stood up and paced the cabin, wondering about the wisdom of reporting the call. *But to whom? And what should I say?* They would probably laugh and think she was just a hysterical woman. Or worse, that she was a big tease and had come on to some man in the disco and was getting what she deserved.

She sat back down on the bed, trying to quiet her mind. *It's no big deal*, she told herself, *and certainly nothing to worry about. I'm on a ship with more than seven hundred other people, including security men and Luca. Nothing will happen to me as long as he's nearby.*

The man flipped his cell phone closed and smiled with satisfaction. Old Man Vilos was shaking in his boots. As bad a case of the jitters as he'd seen in a long time. He blurted a laugh. Seeing the rich and powerful down on their knees gave him great pleasure. Especially when it was an egomaniac like Georgios Vilos. He'd thought he had the world by the balls, but he'd found out it was the other way around, hadn't he?

Suddenly the old fool was worried about Sonny Boy. What a joke! Why didn't he think about the arrogant bastard beforehand? The kid wasn't answering his cell phone. Tough shit! Serves him right.

His lips spread in a thin, evil smile. When he told Vilos about the sluts coming and going from his son's fancy suite, the old man was practically apoplectic. Worried about the plastic explosives being safe with tramps going in to service Sonny Boy. Worried they might be taking drugs and get it into their stupid, fucked-up heads to see what was in the trunk.

Jesus! The old man was really getting paranoid. Why would some bimbo give a damn what the kid had packed? Might try to rip off the stud boy, Daddy said. Or even take a look for sexual aids, the old goat thought. The man blurted another laugh. What century was Vilos living in, anyway?

He leaned back against the bulkhead and slipped the cell phone into a pocket. He'd had to slip into the kid's suite to take another look at the trunk, just to reassure Georgios Vilos that the explosives were still where they were supposed to be. Nothing less would do. And of course they were there, as he knew they would be. But when he told Vilos, do you think that calmed the old man down? No. Not for a minute.

Now he was still obsessing about the explosives being safe until it was time to use them and, more irritating, consumed with the welfare of his son. The man spit on the deck. He didn't give a damn about the son. He was hired to do a job, and he was going to do it and do it right. If Sonny Boy got blown to Kingdom Come with the rest of the people on the ship, it was no skin off his back.

Fuck him. And fuck the old man, too, he thought. *I'm getting paid to blow up the ship, not be a nursemaid.*

Even in the darkness of the deserted deck, his eyes glittered. The man was enjoying this job more than he thought he would.

Chapter Thirteen

She awoke later than usual and hurriedly dressed for breakfast. The telephone call almost immediately came to mind, but she decided to dismiss it as a prank. If it happened again, she would know it was directed at her. Then her late-evening rendezvous with Luca replaced everything else in her thoughts. She could hardly wait to call for an appointment to see him. She left for breakfast humming a happy tune.

She had breakfast, as had become her habit, on the deck outside the cafeteria-style dining room, preferring the out-of-doors in the morning and saving the more formal dining room for lunch and dinner. The sky was a uniform gray this morning, and there was rain in the air. She found an empty seat near the railing. From there she could follow their progress along the coast of Spain, visible in the distance.

Around ten o'clock, passengers began to flock to the deck railings because the ship was about to pass Gibraltar. Crissy fetched her camera out of her shoulder bag and took several photographs of the giant rock, then turned her attention to the coasts of both Spain and Africa. *I can't say I've been to Africa*, she thought, *but I can say that I've seen it*. The ship soon passed the famous rock and churned on through the choppy sea, headed for their next destination, Tenerife, in the Canary Islands. They wouldn't arrive there until tomorrow afternoon, and she couldn't help but smile, thinking that today she was supposed to call the hospital for an appointment.

She decided that no time was better than the present, so she returned to the cabin to place the call. Luca had told her to try to make it as late in the day as possible, so that she would be his last patient. When the gorgon of a nurse, Voula, answered the phone, Crissy told her that she had to see Dr. Santo.

"What seems to be the problem?" she asked.

"It's my stomach," Crissy replied.

"Your stomach," Voula said.

Crissy could visualize the woman's eyes, magnified by her glasses, and her terribly bleached hair, which was streaked with brassy gold and orange. "Yes," she said, "my stomach."

"This is not an emergency," Voula said. It wasn't a question, Crissy noted. She supposed that if your problem was stomach-related, then Voula wouldn't under any circumstances consider it imperative that you see the doctor as soon as possible.

Crissy replied anyway. "No, it's not an emergency. I saw him once before, and I'm taking antibiotics. But something's still wrong."

"I see. . . ." Voula's voice trailed off for a moment, then she said, "You can come tonight. At nine-thirty or nine forty-five." In a triumphant voice, she added, "No sooner, so if your stomach bothers you, it will have to bother you. The doctor is booked."

"Nine forty-five," Crissy replied, thinking: *Perfect!*

"Your name again?"

"Crissy Fitzgerald," she said.

"Nine forty-five," Voula said, slamming the receiver down.

I should tell Luca to give her some lessons in customer relations, she thought.

She heard the cabin door open, and turned to see Jenny come into the room. "Hi," she said gaily. "What've you been up to?"

Jenny shrugged and kicked off her heels, the same stilettos she'd been wearing last night, Crissy observed. "Not much," she said in a flat voice. "Not anything that would interest you anyway."

That's a good answer, Crissy thought. Good and hostile. This from the young divorcée who had shared all of her sexual exploits with Crissy since she'd left her ex-husband. She obviously didn't want Crissy to know what she'd been up to, so, Crissy decided, Jenny wasn't going to hear anything about her activities either. The thought was not a happy one, for Crissy really wanted to share the joy she had found with Luca, and she and Jenny had always shared information about the men in their lives. Well, no more, she supposed. She didn't understand what had happened, why Jenny had cut her out of her life, but she didn't think that she should push for answers because Jenny wasn't in a talking mood.

She watched as Jenny silently slipped out of her glittery top and matching miniskirt, dropping them to the floor in a pile, then saw her go into the bathroom and close the door without another word. What was the silence all about? she wondered.

Who cares? She's not going to take the shine off my day, Crissy thought. Nothing, not even the gray skies and threatening rain, was going to do that. She retrieved her shoulder bag, deciding she would take a stroll about the ship.

She took the stairs up two decks, where the shops, casino, library, card room, and piano bar were located. Seeing a duty-free shop that looked interesting, she decided to browse for presents she could take back home. A very pretty young German woman—GUDRUN, the tag read—ran the shop, and in her perfect, unaccented English she asked Crissy if she would like to volunteer to be a guinea pig.

"For what?" Crissy asked.

"See the rollers with the diamonds by the yard?" Gudrun pointed to a display table on which several large metal rollers were wound with yards of gold chains set with sparkling stones every six inches or so.

Crissy nodded. "What are those anyway?"

"First, they're not actually diamonds," Gudrun said with a rueful smile. "The chains aren't gold, either. They are rhinestones set on different gold-tone chains. See?" She regarded Crissy questioningly.

"Yes," Crissy said, "but what are they for?"

"Oh," Gudrun replied. "They have many uses. I can cut lengths to make bracelets or necklaces, one strand or several, depending on what you want. Also, they're great to weave in your hair if you wear it up. Remember"— she raised a finger in the air in a gesture reminiscent of a schoolteacher— "tonight is a formal night, so you want to be extra-beautiful." She smiled brightly, and her pale blue eyes glittered impishly behind her glasses.

Crissy laughed. "I think I can pass," she said. "I don't really have the money to spend on them."

"You don't even know how much they are," Gudrun replied.

"How much are they," Crissy retorted.

"For you, free," Gudrun said conspiratorially.

"Free? But why?"

"Because you will be my advertisement," Gudrun said. "You are one

185

of the most attractive women on the ship, so everyone will see these on you and want them. They will think that if they buy them, they will look more like you." Her flow of words ceased, and she stood as if at attention, her hands folded in front of her, daring Crissy to challenge her logic, but smiling all the same.

"You're serious," Crissy said.

Gudrun nodded. "I will cut bracelets for you, a necklace, and even wind them in your hair." She approached Crissy with a serious expression. "May I?" she asked, her hands rising to Crissy's hair, but not touching it.

"Yes," Crissy said.

Gudrun ran her hands through Crissy's shoulder-length hair, then let it drop back into place. "You have just enough to put in a French twist or a chignon, either of which I can wrap in our world-famous diamonds by the yard."

They both giggled.

"Well, are you interested? All you have to do is wear my precious phony gems, look beautiful, and tell everyone that you got them here. How's that?"

"I-I guess it's all right," Crissy said.

"I promise to make you look beautiful—enhance your beauty I should say—but restrain myself from making you look like a walking advertisement. I get a commission on these, so I want you to look your best."

"I'll do it," she said.

"Oh, you're a sport," Gudrun said. "I'll cut the bracelets and necklace now. Then if you don't mind, come by tonight before dinner, and I'll do your hair."

"I can have it put up," Crissy said, "so it shouldn't take long."

"You are wonderful," Gudrun said. "Give me a few minutes, and I'll have the bracelet and necklace. I'll have to fit them on you."

Crissy watched as Gudrun selected a length of gold-tone and rhinestone chain from one of the rollers then snapped it off. She draped it around Crissy's wrist, where, surprisingly, it looked much better than on the roller.

"This will wrap around three times," Gudrun said. She unrolled another length of the same golden chain set with rhinestones, this one much longer, and cut it off. She draped it around Crissy's neck, then stood back. "I think it's perfect," she pronounced, "but look at it in the mirror on the counter."

Crissy did as she was told and agreed with Gudrun. It would be a glamorous touch with her simple formal gown tonight. "It is perfect," she said. "I don't know how you do it."

Gudrun laughed. "From doing it so many times," she confessed. "A lot of women don't like to travel with valuable jewelry nowadays, then they see this and want it to dress up their outfits. It's a relatively inexpensive way to do it, and if somebody should rob you, God forbid, you haven't lost something valuable or of sentimental value."

"That's what I'll tell everyone," Crissy said with a laugh. "That I left all of my real jewelry at home and had to get these."

Gudrun laughed. "Very good," she said. She busied herself with small metal cutters and a pair of pincers, first cutting a link, then securing it to another one to create the bracelet and necklace. "Maybe with your hair we can try a different style chain and a rhinestone of a different cut." She looked up from her work at Crissy. "What do you think?"

"I think so," Crissy said. "Why not?"

"You're my perfect model," Gudrun replied. "Is there anything else you want?"

"No, I don't think so," Crissy replied. "I'd thought about buying a small bottle of the *Femme* perfume, but even here it's expensive, so I'll pass on that."

Gudrun went to the shelf where the various size bottles of *Femme* were displayed and took a small one. She brought it back and slipped it into Crissy's shoulder bag. "There," she said. "A thank-you."

"Well, thanks," Crissy said. "I feel sort of like Cinderella now."

They both laughed again. "I'll see you around eight," Gudrun said.

In the hospital, Monika sat down on the examination table, wrinkling her nose at the crinkling paper that was spread down it. She knew it was for hygienic purposes, but the noise it made was unpleasant nevertheless. Crossing her long, shapely legs—her best feature, she thought—she hiked up her skirt just a bit to give the doctor a better view while not appearing to be unladylike. When he came in and introduced himself, she could see that he was even better-looking than she remembered.

She held his extended hand longer than necessary. "I'm Monika Graf," she said, "the writer."

"Yes, of course. We met in Pompeii," Luca said, removing his hand from hers. Was she flirting with him? he wondered. He thought it best not to say that he wasn't familiar with her books. He looked down at the form she'd filled out for Voula. "I'm sorry it's under the present circumstances," he went on. "I see you have a stomach problem."

"Yes," she said, patting it lightly with one hand, her rings flashing in the light. "*Mal de mer?* A wee seasickness? Something I ate? I don't know." She fluttered her eyelids coquettishly.

Luca looked back down at the form, as if searching for vital clues to her sickness. Who was she kidding? he wondered. She could almost be his mother. "Could you describe the symptoms?"

"It's been upset," Monika replied vaguely, shifting on the examination table, uncrossing and crossing her legs.

"Have you been running a fever?" Luca asked. "Or had any other symptoms?"

"No," Monika said. "It's just my tum-tum."

"I can give you something to help settle your stomach," Luca said, "and if you don't feel better tomorrow, then I want you to give me a call. Okay?"

Monika could see that he wasn't interested in her and was neither surprised nor disappointed. She wasn't to many young men's taste—few of them liked mature women such as herself, regardless of their superior knowledge and abilities—although there were those who would gladly worship at her feet. "That's so sweet of you," Monika gushed. Then she added, "I can see why Crissy likes you."

He was surprised by her reference to Crissy and a little embarrassed by this personal intrusion into his professional life. He couldn't ignore the woman's remark, however. "Ah, you can?" he said. He pulled a pad from the pocket of his lab coat and began scribbling on it.

"But I must warn you," Monika went on, "she's not the innocent abroad she seems. No, indeed." Her eyes lit up malevolently, and she held a finger in the air to make her point. "She's a vixen, wanton and dangerous, and you'll be sorry you ever met her. Mark my word, if you continue to see her, you'll regret it, Doctor."

Luca stiffened at the torrent of words.

"She's caused no end of trouble," Monika continued, "and she'll—"

"Frau Graf," he said, "you'll forgive me, but I have patients waiting. Please give this to the nurse." He handed her a slip of paper. "And call me tomorrow if you don't feel better."

He turned to leave the room.

"You'll thank me for this," Monika said to his back.

Luca ignored her and kept going.

There, Monika thought with satisfaction, not in the least disturbed by his reaction. *I've planted the seeds of doubt.* She picked up her big gold leather handbag and slipped off the examination table. *Crissy's a useful girl, malleable and moldable, and he'll not steal her away from Mark. Or me.*

Crissy waved good-bye to Gudrun through the window of the duty-free shop, then patted her hair and blew her a kiss. Gudrun laughed, and Crissy went on her way, happy to have made a new friend, even if only for the duration of the trip. She also felt especially glamorous and could hardly wait for Luca to see her. Her hair was gathered in a French twist, and Gudrun had expertly woven a length of the golden chain set with rhinestones through it, then encircled it to great effect. So what if the gold and gems were fake? Crissy thought. Her dress wasn't by a well-known designer either, but it looked great on her. A creamy white, it was made of a crinkled and loosely pleated silklike fabric and was cut much like a Grecian toga with an empire waist trimmed in gold and cream braiding. Floor-length, the back was cut a little longer, giving a hint of a train. When she moved, the pleated fabric swirled out behind her, and she appeared to float.

On the way to the shop, she hadn't failed to notice the many admiring glances she received, and she wondered if she was overdressed. She wasn't used to the attention that was being directed toward her, and she felt self-conscious.

When she entered the large, elegant room, the maître d' crooned. "You look beautiful tonight," he said. "The most beautiful woman here."

"Thank you," Crissy replied as he led her to the table.

Heads turned in the dining room, watching her progress from the entrance to the table. When she reached it, the maître d' pulled her chair back, and she sat down, using a hand to gather excess fabric and pull it to the side.

"You look like an angel from heaven," Rudy declared.

"Divine," Monika crooned, kissing her cheek.

"Sexy, too," Mina said with a laugh.

Dr. Von Meckling nodded in her direction and mouthed something indecipherable, but it sounded appreciative.

"Thank you," Crissy said, glancing about the table. "Everyone looks

189

fabulous." Monika, unsurprisingly, was in floor-length sequins that were nearly blinding in the light, casting reflections with her every move, and Mina was in red ruffles again, only a different dress, this one of taffeta with the largest ruffles Crissy thought she'd ever seen. Rudy and Dr. Von Meckling were in black tie, the doctor's jacket emblazoned with several medallions. Crissy wondered what they were.

"I love your hair," Monika said.

"I got the 'jewels' in the duty-free shop," Crissy replied.

Monika looked momentarily alarmed. "Don't tell a soul," she said. "They look like a million dollars."

"I'm going there tomorrow," Mina said. "I must have some."

"Where's Jenny?" Monika asked.

"I have no idea," Crissy replied. She was beginning to feel peculiar, constantly being asked the whereabouts of her friend and never knowing the answer.

"I'm sure she'll be here," Rudy replied. "Just late as usual."

"Now," Monika said, "you must tell us what you've been doing."

"Oh," Crissy said, as if she'd forgotten something trivial. "I was invited out to dinner last evening."

Eyebrows raised expectantly, but Crissy took a well-timed sip of water.

"You are being terribly mysterious," Monika said. "You force me to ask with whom you dined."

"Mark Vilos," Crissy replied in a matter-of-fact voice.

"Indeed," Monika said, her interest piqued. "In his cabin?"

"Yes, in his cabin," Crissy said.

"How was your dinner?" Monika asked.

"Nice," Crissy replied.

Monika looked at her crossly. " 'Nice,' " Monika parroted, "is an almost meaningless word. You are being extremely difficult, my darling. Twice now you've seen the most ravishing and richest young man on the ship—the owner's son and only heir!—and even been to his cabin. You must be more forthcoming, my darling. Don't you see that we're all dying to know if there is romance in the air?"

"Romance?" Crissy paused dramatically, took a bite of her salad, then shook her head. "No," she finally said.

Monika's face fell, and she fingered the rings on one hand nervously, turning them this way and that. "How disappointing," she said. "Are you certain? I don't think he would have asked you to dinner unless he was extremely interested in you." She looked around the table as if seeking confirmation of what she'd said.

"Maybe Crissy is not so interested in him," Mina said.

Monika looked at her. "Can that be true? That you aren't interested in one of the most eligible bachelors in all of Europe?"

"No," Crissy said. "I mean, no, I'm not particularly interested in him."

"You are being very stupid," Monika pronounced. "I thought you were a much more sensible young lady than that."

"I can't simply manufacture feelings," Crissy retorted. "Certainly not romantic ones. You should know that, Monika, being a romance novelist."

"True enough," Monika said, "but I should think you would give him some consideration. It's that young Italian doctor, isn't it? He's caught your eye, hasn't he?"

Crissy wanted to confide in someone about her involvement with Luca. She wanted to shout it from the rooftops, in fact, but this was neither the time nor place. Nor, she thought, was Monika the person.

"I like him," she finally said to Monika. "The doctor, I mean. But he has nothing to do with Mark Vilos. I just don't click with Mark, and I'm not going to force it."

"You don't 'click' with him," Monika mimicked. "How extraordinary. And you 'click', as you say, with the doctor?"

"I guess you could say that," she said, "but I don't really want to talk about it."

Monika glanced about the table again, this time as if to confirm that Crissy was being a difficult young woman. "Well," she finally said in a disappointed voice, "I'm surprised by you." Then she abruptly brightened and reached over and gently squeezed Crissy's arm. "But I love you nevertheless." She smiled charmingly.

"Oh, Monika," Crissy said. "You are . . . some lady." She kissed her cheek impulsively. "And I'm so glad I met you." She looked around the table. "I'm glad I met all of you."

"And we're glad to have met you," Rudy said. Mina nodded, and old Dr. Von Meckling stared at her appreciatively.

They had finished the salad course when Jenny arrived, drawing a great deal of attention. In one of her signature animal prints with a plunging neckline, a back cut just below the top of her buttocks, and slits up both sides, she was once again barely, if very expensively, dressed. Dangling from her ears and hanging around her neck was a small fortune in precious and semiprecious gemstones set in gold. "Hi, everybody," she said enthusiastically. "Sorry I'm late, but I took my clothes and everything and went up to the spa for a massage. Got dressed there."

Dr. Von Meckling's eyes lit up, Crissy noticed, as he drank in Jenny's striking beauty. "There's still some champagne, my dear," he said.

"Wonderful," Jenny said dramatically. "I see my timing is superb as usual." She sat next to the doctor, where the maître d' had pulled out her chair and waited for her.

"You look ravishing as always," Mina said.

"Oh, yes," Rudy agreed, pouring her a glass of champagne.

"Quite something," Monika muttered in a noncommittal way.

"I love your necklace and earrings," Crissy said. "I haven't seen them before."

"I don't show you everything," Jenny said teasingly. "I love your hair, by the way. It looks great."

Crissy was gratified that Jenny seemed to be her fun-loving self, that whatever had been bothering her wasn't an issue anymore. They talked and laughed while eating, and Crissy noticed that Jenny often patted or put an arm around Dr. Von Meckling. He obviously enjoyed the attention, participating in the conversation more than usual and beaming at Jenny's every touch.

They were having dessert when Monika turned to Crissy and asked, "Do you think your young Mark Vilos will come to the disco tonight?"

"I haven't the faintest idea," Crissy said. "I haven't seen him or talked to him today, and I'd just as soon not see him tonight."

"Why not, my darling?" Monika asked.

Crissy hadn't planned on saying anything to Monika or anyone else about the telephone call the previous evening, but she felt compelled to do so now. "Well, after I had dinner with him, we went to the disco for awhile," she said, "then he wanted me to come back to his stateroom for a nightcap." Everyone at the table turned to listen to her. "I didn't go, but later the telephone rang. Somebody was breathing on the other end of the line."

"Oh, my God. How frightening," Mina said, her eyes widening in alarm.

"I know," Crissy said. "It was. I kept asking who it was, and whoever it was just kept breathing."

192

Monika patted her arm with a hand. "That's horrible, my darling," she said. "Horrible. I think you should tell the captain at once."

Crissy took a sip of water. "I'm suspicious that it might have been Mark," she said.

Monika's hand jerked away from Crissy. "That's absurd," she said.

"It's not absurd," Crissy said in self-defense. "He seemed really upset that I wouldn't go back to his stateroom with him."

"You've got it all wrong," Jenny said.

Everyone at the table turned to look at her.

"Why?" Crissy asked.

"Because Mark's not interested in you," Jenny said. "Not at all. And I know that for a fact."

Crissy looked at her in puzzlement. "But how, Jenny?" she asked. "He—"

"Mark is after *me*," Jenny said. "He couldn't have called you because we were in the sack together." She smiled triumphantly as Monika gasped.

Crissy blushed with embarrassment. "You mean that you were there after I was?" she said in a soft voice.

Jenny nodded, her smile still in place. "Yeah," she said. Crissy noted the resemblance between Jenny's smug expression and that habitually worn by Mark.

She suddenly felt her stomach twist into a knot. *Why am I such a fool?* she wondered anew. Mark had been lying to her, and her friend had seen him but hadn't mentioned it. Until now.

"Well, that changes everything, doesn't it, my darling," Monika said, apparently relieved that Mark Vilos was in the clear and not particularly concerned that Crissy might be distressed by Jenny's treachery. Jenny should have told her she had seen Mark, and she should have told her in private, not at the dinner table, where she knew it would embarrass Crissy.

"Yes, it does change things," Crissy said. She glanced around the table. "I was all wrong," she said with a valiant effort. "I should have been certain before I made any accusations."

"You didn't mean harm," Mina said. "Anyone could have made a mistake like that. You shouldn't feel badly about it. But the mystery is still unsolved, isn't it? Who might have made that awful call?"

"Not Mark Vilos," Monika said firmly. "An absurd notion to begin with." She looked at Jenny. "So you're seeing him, my dear," she said in an ingratiating voice. "I hope you're having a wonderful time with him. Such a handsome young man, so well-bred, and such a good family."

Crissy watched in fascination as Monika changed allegiance before her eyes, stroking Jenny's ego with her words, as it were. She had certainly never fought for Monika's attention, nor had she sought it out to begin with. But seeing how easily her affections shifted from her to Jenny was sickening—and yet another reminder that she couldn't trust anyone. She suddenly felt like crying or laughing hysterically. The situation was ridiculous, she told herself, and she wished she could rush into Luca's arms at this moment. It wouldn't be long, and she took comfort in that thought.

Still, in the back of her mind was the matter of the telephone call. If Mark hadn't made it, who had? Maybe it was a fluke, she thought, and it would never happen again. She would have to wait and see, but of one thing she was certain: The next time she would go straight to one of the officers on the ship without advice from any of her acquaintances.

Crissy stole a glance at her wristwatch, and was surprised to see that it was nearly nine-thirty. Good. She would have just enough time to go by the cabin and refresh her makeup before going to the hospital.

During dinner Crissy had been aware of the ship's movement, but as she walked back to the cabin she realized that the vessel had begun to pitch to and fro in the water, making walking treacherous. When she reached the cabin, the phone was ringing. She hurriedly flicked on the light and rushed to answer it.

She was thrilled to hear Luca's voice, but wondered if something was wrong. "Something's come up, hasn't it?" she said.

"We've hit a bad patch of weather, and that means I'm going to be very busy," he replied.

Crissy could hear the disappointment in his voice. "Seasickness?"

"That and a lot of cuts and bruises," he replied. "Maybe even some broken bones and concussions."

"Oh, my God," she said. "Walking back from dinner was tricky, but it's that bad?"

"Yes," Luca replied. "Especially with a lot of the older people. If this lasts for a few hours, people get antsy and want to get out and move around. They end up being thrown off their feet, take some bad falls."

"So the hospital's going to be busier than usual," she said.

"That's an understatement," he said. "A lot of people panic, too, especially unseasoned travelers. This place is going to have people hanging from the rafters. It happens a lot in this area."

"What do you mean?"

"More or less where the Mediterranean and the Atlantic meet," he replied. "It can get really rough. Add bad weather to that, and you've got the perfect recipe for a lot of sick and wounded passengers." He paused, then added, "I'm so sorry, Crissy. There's no way I'll be able to meet you tonight."

"I'm sorry, too," she said. She tried to conceal her frustration and disappointment. "But it won't be long."

"No," he agreed. "I'll call when I get a chance. Just remember that I'll be thinking of you."

"I'll be thinking of you, too," she said.

She hung up the receiver and sighed. *Damn.*

Turning around, she glanced about the cabin. *Jenny is such a sloppy pig,* she thought, seeing underwear strewn all over her bed. *She could have thrown her dirty underwear on her own bed.* She went to the bed and started to pick up the underwear and toss it on Jenny's bed, but after picking up a pair of panties, she let out a shriek and dropped them as if they had scorched her hand.

"Oh, my God!" she wailed. "Oh, my God!" She backed away, her hand over her mouth, her eyes riveted to the ghastly sight on her bed. Her stomach twisted into a knot, and for a moment she thought she would throw up. The acrid taste of bile rose in her throat, but she managed to control the urge to expel it. She felt sweat bead her brow and the back of her neck, and she began to tremble.

The underwear—*her* underwear—had been slashed into tatters. Bras, panties, panty hose, and slips lay strewn across her bed in coils, as if they were poisonous snakes. Crissy felt as though she herself had been slashed, her body cut up haphazardly by a knife-wielding maniac and left in obscene, bloody pieces in some sick, twisted ritual.

The telephone bleeted, and she jerked as if bitten. *Oh, God, no!* she thought, putting her hands over her ears. *Not again. It can't be. Please, God. No.* Then, as before, it occurred to her that it might be Luca. She looked at the telephone, and it bleeted again. Her breath caught in her throat. How could something inanimate, a simple piece of plastic and metal and wire, have such power over her? She decided that she wouldn't allow it to. She slowly advanced toward the telephone, one hand on the vanity/desk surface for support, and picked up the receiver.

195

"Hello," she said, her voice as calm as she could manage.

The sound of breathing assaulted her senses, threatening to make her spin out of control.

"Damn you!" she cried, slamming the receiver down.

She stood, her body trembling, gazing at the floor. There were tears in her eyes, but she didn't want to cry. *That's the last thing I'm going to do,* she told herself. *I'm not going to cry. I'm going to get the bastard who's doing this.*

She grabbed her shoulder bag and went to the cabin door, prepared to get help, but thought better of it. First, she thought, she would take pictures of her bed so she would have a record of the perverse crime that had been perpetrated against her. She retrieved her camera from her shoulder bag, then took several photographs of her bed from various angles. That done, she put the camera back in her shoulder bag and went back to the door. She had to grasp the handle and hold on as the ship rolled to port. When her feet felt more secure on the floor, she opened the door and went out into the corridor, determined to find help.

Chapter Fourteen

She left the cabin in furious haste, heading for the Information Desk one deck below. She didn't know who to talk to, but she would find someone out there.

At the semicircular Information Desk, a young man looked up at her quizzically. "How may I help you?" he asked.

"I want to talk to someone in Security," Crissy replied. "At least that's who I think I should talk to."

A plump young woman with a halo of frizzy black hair who was busy at a computer keyboard next to him—MARIA, her name tag read—looked up when she heard Crissy's request.

"What seems to be the problem?" the young man asked.

"I've been getting obscene telephone calls," Crissy said, "and tonight I returned to my cabin to find my underwear torn up and thrown on my bed. Is there anyone here with authority whom I can speak with?"

The young man didn't reply immediately, but the woman sitting near him spoke up. "I think she should talk to the captain. Wait just a minute," Maria said, holding up a finger. She lifted her considerable heft out of the chair and disappeared into an office behind the Information Desk.

Crissy didn't have to wait long before the woman reappeared. "Follow me," she said, nodding toward the office door. Going around the semicircular desk, Crissy went into the office. "Have a seat," Maria said. "He'll be down here in just a minute." She went back out to the Information Desk, closing the door behind her.

Crissy had hardly sat down before an inner office door opened, and the captain strode in, the smile he perpetually wore replaced by a look of concern that seemed sincere. "What's the problem?" he asked.

"I've gotten a couple of phones calls from a 'breather,' " Crissy said. "Then this evening I came in, and somebody had torn up my underwear and thrown it all over the bed."

The captain looked appalled. "Let's go," he said, already heading toward the door. "I want to see this myself."

Crissy followed the captain out of the office. He was fast on his feet, seeming to move with the ship, which was no easy task, since the seas had become increasingly rough in the last couple of hours and the boat was pitching and rolling.

He saw Crissy grasp a rail along the corridor wall. "The trick," he said, "is to walk sort of sideways." He looked at her and grinned. "Each step is a forward one, but just slightly to the side. Practice and see how you do."

Crissy discovered that he knew what he was talking about. Aping his walk helped her keep her balance and keep up with him. He moved swiftly, and then she remembered the beautiful way he danced. When they reached her cabin, he stood back for her to swipe her key card.

Inside, she showed him to her bed. "This is exactly the way I found it," she said. "Except that I picked up a pair of panties and threw them back down when I realized what had happened."

The captain was visibly shaken. "This is deplorable," he said. "Very sick." He looked at her. "What was it about telephone calls?"

She told him about the calls and her suspicions.

The captain sighed, looked down at the floor, then back up at her. "I'm sorry you've had to go through something like this," he said. "It's disgusting. You say you suspected Mark Vilos?"

Crissy nodded. "I did, but probably unfairly." She explained the situation to him.

"I see," he said, looking thoughtful. "And these calls and this"—he gestured toward the shredded underwear on the bed—"happened just after you came in?"

"Yes."

"So you were out on dates at dinner?"

"Yes," she replied.

"Then your friend obviously couldn't have done this because you were with him," he said, thinking aloud. He looked at her. "I'm sorry. I don't mean to insult you or your friend, but in cases like this it sometimes is someone close, I believe. You're traveling with Ms. . . . her name eludes me. . . ."

"Jenny Blakemore," Crissy said.

"Yes, I've met her in the disco," he replied. "I think we'll have to get a list of the people you know on the ship. Your friends, acquaintances, anyone you've dated."

"I-I have to list . . . everyone?" she asked.

He nodded. "We've got to find out who's doing this," the captain said. "I don't think it's a laughing matter."

"Neither do I," Crissy replied. "It's just that . . . Well, I'm dating someone . . . someone who is employed by the shipping lines."

The captain's eyes lit up momentarily, then he waved a hand dismissively. "Don't worry about it," he said. "I know it happens, even if it's not supposed to."

"I just don't want to involve him any more than I have to," she said.

"Okay," he said, rubbing his hands together. "I'm going to go stir up Mikelos Christopolous and get him on this. He's the head of security on the ship and very good at his job. In the meantime, if you will, please sit down and make a list of all the people you know on the ship. Give that to him when he gets here."

"Fine," Crissy said.

"He'll take it from there, and if you need anything, don't hesitate to come to me." He took a wallet out of his trouser pocket and extracted a card from it. "My private telephone number is here. Don't hesitate to call me at any time, day or night. I'll be in touch with Mikelos, so he'll keep me abreast of things."

"Thank you so much," Crissy said.

"Do you feel a little more secure?" the captain asked.

Crissy nodded. "Yes." She looked toward the bed. "Should I leave this mess for him to see or can I clean it up? I took some photos."

"Very smart thinking," the captain said, "but I would leave things the way they are until he comes." He headed to the door crisply. On his way out he said, "Remember. Call me if you need to. Christopolous is good at what he does, like I said, and I'll be speaking with him immediately."

"Thanks again," Crissy said, bolstered by the thought that help was on the way. She looked around at the violence spread over her bed and shuddered. The pervert who did this had to be stopped.

Jenny awoke after a short doze, and he was sitting up in bed, wearing a bathrobe, staring down at her. She smiled at him and stretched, then threw off the bedcovers and slid out of bed, standing before him naked.

"I'll be right back," she said, and went to the bathroom.

When she came back into the bedroom, she stopped and stared at him. He had taken off the bathrobe and was spread out on the bed, his head propped up on pillows. His hand was between his thighs, and he was stroking himself. He was fully aroused, and there was a look of grim determination on his face.

"Come here," he said.

She stepped toward the bed hesitantly. *Oh, God,* she thought. *Not now. Not again.* Her mouth was dry, and she had a headache, the result of a copious amount of champagne.

"Come on," he said, continuing to stroke himself.

Jenny complied, going to the bed, where she sat down facing him. She smiled and licked her lips, hoping to give the appearance of a lascivious appetite, although she was in fact merely trying to lubricate them.

He nodded and looked down at his aroused state, and Jenny got the message. Sliding closer to him, she reached over, brushing her hand across his thighs then between them as if she truly wanted him. Tentatively at first, she took him in her hand and held him gingerly before she began stroking slowly, looking up into his eyes, then back down at his engorged manhood.

He groaned with pleasure, removing his hand and letting her do the work, but only moments passed until he grasped her head between both of his hands. Pushing her hair back away from her face with his fingers, he shoved her head down with surprising strength, intent on her taking him in her mouth.

Jenny wanted to recoil in revulsion, but told herself it was what she had to do, must do. Besides, she thought, she'd done it countless times before, hadn't she? His was just another cock in a long line of them, smaller than some, larger than others. The big difference was that his was the key to unlocking a huge fortune that came with a powerful family of international repute and all the trappings that implied. What could be sexier? With that thought, she overcame her disgust and flicked at him with her tongue, teasing him, enjoying his whimpers of desire, making certain that her breasts brushed against his legs tauntingly. She began licking him as if she was desperate for him, and finally took him into her mouth as if his was the most desirable cock in the world.

He emitted a long, low moan as she laved him with her tongue, moving her head from side to side and up and down, his hands pushing down on it relentlessly, forcing as much of himself inside her as possible. He came quickly, letting out a little grunt, then relaxed his hold on her.

Jenny went into the bathroom without saying anything, then came back out. His eyes were closed, and he looked like a dead man, she thought, except that she could see the rise and fall of his chest. She slid onto the bed again, cuddling next to him. "That was wonderful," she cooed into his ear, playing her role to the hilt.

He opened his eyes and smiled. "You are wonderful," he replied. "You make me feel like a new man."

Yeah, me and all that Viagra you take, Jenny thought. "It makes me feel so . . . so . . . well, fabulous that I make you happy," she said. "You know how I've played around. It's no secret. But I've been so desperate, and no one has shown me any real love. With you, it's different. I know you don't want me just for my body, and it doesn't really matter to me so much about the sex. It's you. All of you. Your goodness and integrity. Your wisdom and fairness."

When he didn't reply, she struggled for more words. Words that would bolster his ego, words that would make her look good in his eyes. "You know I don't need your money: I've got enough of my own. No, it's not that. It's who you are, deep down inside that matters to me."

He turned to her and smiled. "Well said," he replied. "I think you are quite the diplomat, Jenny." He patted her bare thigh.

You bet I am, she thought. She smiled sweetly. "Thank you, Ludwig," she replied, fluttering her eyelashes. "Coming from a Von Meckling, I will accept that as a great compliment."

The old doctor nodded slightly. "Yes, my dear," he said. "Indeed, it is one of the highest compliments I could give you."

Jenny smiled as if thrilled. *I'll get you, you old goat,* she thought. *You and your ancient name and all your beautiful money and estates and the prestige and social standing that go with them. And when you're gone— only a matter of a few short years at the most—I can have any man in the world I want.*

"Oh, Ludwig," she cooed, "you make me so happy."

* * *

The door opened, and a tall behemoth of a man filled the doorway. He was big-boned and muscular-looking, but his smile was friendly. "Ms. Fitzgerald," he said, offering his hand, "Mikelos Christopolous." Crissy took it to shake, and her hand was engulfed by his huge, meaty paw of a hand. "Mind if I look around?" he asked.

"Of course not," she replied.

Mikelos Christopolous stepped into the cabin, his eyes scanning the room. He stopped at the bed, staring down at the torn underwear. "Does all of this belong to you?" he asked.

Crissy nodded. "Yes."

"None of it belongs to your travel companion?"

"No, it's all mine," she said. "None of it belongs to Jenny."

He stared down at the bed again. "Odd," he said after a few moments.

"What's that?"

"There doesn't appear to be any evidence of seminal fluid," he replied. He looked at her with intelligent eyes. "That's often the case," he added.

"I see," Crissy said.

"Did you move anything here?" he asked.

"I picked up a pair of panties," Crissy said. She walked to the side of the bed and pointed to them. "Those black ones. Then I threw them back down."

"Don't touch anything else," he said. "I'm going to have our forensics man come up and take pictures then bag everything. You never know what he might find."

"I took some pictures with my digital camera," Crissy said.

"Very good," Christopolous said. "If you don't mind, I'll take your camera with me and download your pictures. We'll have yours to supplement his. I'll get your camera back to you right away."

"That's fine," she said.

Christopolous took a small notepad and pen from a pocket. "Now, Ms. Fitzgerald," he said. "If you—"

"Crissy, please."

"And I'm Mikelos," he replied with a smile. "If you don't mind answering some questions?"

"Not at all."

"Okay," he said, looking over at her. "Let's have a seat, then I want you to tell me exactly what happened."

Crissy repeated what she'd told the captain, adding that Mark was upset by her not wanting to return to his cabin for a nightcap, but also telling him what Jenny had said about being with Mark.

"What time did you come back from the dining room?"

Crissy answered his questions as best she could for the next fifteen minutes or so, and he jotted down her responses. "I've talked to the captain," Christopolous said at last. "He told me you were going to make a list of the people you know on the ship?"

"Yes," Crissy replied. She handed him the sheet of ship's stationery with the names. "I think I've listed everyone."

"Very good," he said, looking down at it. Crissy noticed that he gave no outward sign of recognition when he saw Luca's name on it. He folded it and tucked it inside his notepad.

"We have a record of every single call made on this ship. We know from which telephone they're placed and to what telephone number they are made."

"That's incredible," Crissy replied, her eyes brightening with hope.

He nodded. "Someone could've used a cell phone, of course, but we'll get to the bottom of this, Ms. Fitzgerald, I promise you that. If a public telephone was used, we can also install a minicam near the telephone where the calls were made to see if we can eventually get the caller on video. I think if we catch the caller, we're going to be catching whoever got in here."

"I wonder who could've gotten in here?" Crissy asked, suddenly more worried than ever. She had felt violated by the calls, but this was so perverse, she didn't know what to think.

"We're certainly taking that into consideration," Christopolous replied.

"Thanks, Mikelos," she replied. "I feel a lot better now. The telephone calls were scary, but this—" she gestured to the bed—"this really frightens me."

"We'll do everything we can," he reassured her. "We're going to be putting a plainclothes security person on you the rest of the trip, or until we catch whoever is doing this."

"You think that's necessary?"

"I think we have to do anything we can to make certain you're safe and that we catch this sicko," he said. "Sorry about your underwear, by the way, but it looks like it's all ruined."

"Yes," Crissy nodded. "I don't think I could touch it even if it wasn't."

"I can understand that," Christopolous replied. "Do you think you need to see the ship's doctor? Maybe he could give you a tranquilizer or something."

"No," Crissy said, shaking her head. "I'll be okay."

There was a knock at the door. "That'll be my forensics man," Christopolous said. "Stefanos Sitara. I'll get it." He rose to his feet, his large frame towering over her.

He opened the door, then introduced Crissy to Sitara. "I won't be long," he told her.

"I'll be off," Christopolous said. "Let me get your camera, and I'll have someone bring it right back to you after downloading."

Crissy fetched it from the vanity and handed it to him.

"Why don't you try to get some rest after Stefanos is out of here," he said, "and tomorrow, say after breakfast, check with the Information Desk. I may know something by then, and I'll leave a message for you."

"I will, and thanks, Mikelos."

He left, and Crissy watched as Stefanos Sitara, a short, wiry man who wore wire-rimmed glasses, photographed the bed from various angles. Afterward, he slipped on latex gloves, then gathered up her torn underwear and put it in a plastic bag.

"We'll have it checked for prints and any fluids," he said. "See if we come up with anything."

"You can do that on the ship?" she asked.

He nodded. "You'd be surprised at the resources we have available to us," he replied.

"But if you don't have fingerprints from the passengers, what good would it do if you found any?" she asked.

"Who said it was a passenger?" Sitara asked, looking at her. "We don't know that. Besides, if we have a suspect, then we can get prints from him to see if they match any we find on the underwear, if there are any."

Crissy opened and held the door for him. After he was gone, she slumped into a chair. Christopolous and Sitara had taken the incident very seriously, and Crissy felt more secure now, knowing that an undercover security person would be in close proximity to her for the rest of the trip.

After he left, she went through her drawers and the closet to see what, if any, underwear she had left. The cabin door opened, and Jenny stepped in.

"What are you doing?" Jenny asked, "and who were those men that I saw leaving here?"

"I'm looking for underwear," Crissy said, "and the men who just left here are from Security."

"Security?" Jenny parroted. "What's Security doing here?"

Crissy told her what had happened.

Jenny's eyes grew large with alarm. "What the hell have you been up to?"

"What do you mean?" Crissy responded, sitting down on the bed and looking up at her.

"Well, these things don't just happen, Crissy," Jenny said. "You've brought it on yourself somehow or other. Some creep you've been sneaking around with might have done it, or that creepy doctor you've been seeing. He's seems like just the kind of pervert who would do something like this." She wondered if Mark had anything to do with this as Crissy had originally thought. Despite her having been there the night when Crissy had a call, she knew that he'd already told her to leave before Crissy actually got the call. She also thought that Mark Vilos was weird—he kicked her out, didn't he?—but she didn't want to share any of this information with Crissy.

"That is not true," Crissy cried, "and I won't sit here and listen to you say things like that about Luca. And I really don't appreciate your saying that I brought it on myself. I haven't been 'sneaking around' seeing anybody, as you put it."

"Well, you don't have to get so damn heated up about it," Jenny replied, shrugging her shoulders. "That's usually the way it works, isn't it? A woman teases some guy, then something like this happens."

Crissy felt like screaming at her, but she restrained herself. "I haven't been asking for anything, Jenny," she replied angrily. "How dare you say such a thing. You know I'm not that kind of person." She paused, ascertaining that the man who'd broken in had taken out all of her good underwear. "You know, I would have expected sympathy from you. I thought you were my friend. This has been really scary. How would you like it if somebody was calling you? Huh? How would you like it if somebody came in here and tore up *your* underwear? I don't think you'd like it very much, would you?"

"Oh, I don't know," Jenny said with a laugh. "He might be pretty hot, right? Anyway, he must think you are."

"That's disgusting," Crissy said.

"Oh, get off your fucking high horse," Jenny said. "You've always got to be Miss Goody Two-shoes, don't you? Here you have an opportunity to meet some really cool guys. Really rich guys, and I mean *rich*. Not Albany rich, but European rich. And what do you do? Get all crazy over some weirdo making phone calls and date the ship's doctor, some Italian lowlife who probably got his medical degree in Guatemala or someplace."

Crissy glared at her for a moment, then asked, "Why have you turned on me? Why aren't you my friend anymore, Jenny? Did I do something to change things? Or is it because I've always been the wallflower when we've gone out and suddenly there are men actually paying attention to *me*, not just you? Is that it?"

Jenny laughed. "Think whatever you want to," she said, "because I don't really give a damn. I don't have a problem getting men, that's for sure, and as far as I know, you don't have any prospects. That so-called doctor's probably screwing any chick that'll have him."

Crissy wanted nothing more than to get up off the bed and smack Jenny's face. Hard. But she remained sitting, trying to calm down her overwrought feelings. "I don't want to discuss this anymore," she finally said.

"Fine," Jenny said. "It's really a bore, so let's forget about it. Besides, I've got to go to bed. All this fucking is wearing me out."

Chapter Fifteen

Crissy slept very late after being up so long dealing with Christopolous about the slashing incident, and when she finally got out of bed, it was nearly time to disembark for the shore excursions in Tenerife. As much as she wanted to see the island, she simply wasn't in the mood after what had occurred last night. After showering, she dressed and went up to the cafeteria. Even though breakfast was soon over, she knew that the coffee urns were replenished throughout the day, and coffee was all that she really wanted. She didn't have the stomach for food, and it wasn't because of the increasingly rough sea. The events of last night had left a bad taste in her mouth.

Keeping her feet spread wide to help keep her balance, she found an empty seat where she could see out both port and starboard windows. It was useless to try to go outside. The wind was fierce, and the ship's pitching and rolling, even while docked, was severe. Periodic showers doused the decks. Looking toward shore, she could see how the wind lashed at the palm-studded island, and looking toward the sea, she saw that the waves were much bigger than usual, forming whitecaps as far as the eye could see.

She ate to the accompaniment of little shrieks from all around the dining room as trays slid from tables, glasses overturned, and other minor disasters occurred. No one fell, however, at least not while she was there, but there were very few passengers in the dining room. She supposed that a lot of people were forgoing breakfast from fear of falling or because of seasickness, and others were lining up to go ashore.

After she had some coffee, the rain stopped. She ventured out on deck, carefully grasping at chairs and tables until she reached the staircase that would take her up to the pool deck. She wanted to look out to sea from there and get a better view of the storm. By the time she reached the top deck, her clothes were nearly soaked through from the spray. But Crissy didn't mind: it felt cleansing after the scene in her cabin. Several other intrepid souls such as herself had already commandeered positions at the railing. Some of them were taking photographs; others stared out as if mesmerized by the raging sea and stormy skies. For awhile, she surveyed the choppy swells and dark skies with them, her spirits paradoxically calmed by the tempest, but when it began raining again, the wind whipping the raindrops against her in stinging blows, she decided it was time to go back belowdecks.

She decided that she would have to call the hospital and tell Luca what had happened. She would also have to tell him that she put his name on the list. She didn't want to interrupt him while he was working, but she certainly didn't want him to receive a surprise visit from Christopolous or one of his men.

Back inside, protected from the elements, Crissy cautiously made her way back down to her deck, taking her time and holding onto the numerous railings along the walls and on the stairs when she could. She considered using the elevators for the first time, but they weren't operating due to the ship's rolling and heaving. Carefully descending the stairs, she saw a tiny elderly woman she'd seen many times before, only now she had a sling on her left arm. An attendant was helping her down the stairs.

"Hello, there," the woman said in English.

"Hi," Crissy said. "I see you've had an accident. I hope it's not too serious."

"Oh, dear," the woman said in a birdlike voice. "I fell down the steps, so it could have been a lot worse, but it's just a sprained shoulder. Watch your step, because this is a dangerous storm. I've been on many, many cruises, and this is the first time I've been injured."

"I will," Crissy said, "and I hope you feel better soon."

"Oh, that wonderful young doctor tells me I'll have to wear this thing for the rest of the trip. Imagine! Well, I guess I'm lucky—after all, at my age, I could have been killed."

"Feel better," Crissy said, starting back down the stairs.

Once she reached her cabin, she dialed the hospital, and when Voula answered, she asked to speak to Dr. Santo.

"Who may I say is calling?"

"This is Crissy Fitzgerald," she replied, "and I—"

Without letting her finish, Voula said, "One moment, Ms. Fitzgerald. I'll put you through."

Crissy was surprised but pleased. She had expected the woman to take a message at best. Why was she suddenly being nice to her? she wondered.

"Hello," Luca said.

"Hello," Crissy said, her heart leaping at the sound of his voice. "I hate to bother you at work, but I have a good reason to call." Then she told him what had happened and why she was calling.

Luca was extremely disturbed. "But you're okay?" he asked, alarmed by her news.

"Yes," she said quickly.

"No, I mean, how are you, *really*, Crissy," he said. "Tell me the truth."

"I'm . . . I'm upset, of course . . . but I'm really okay."

"Thank God," he said. "Now listen to me. Don't you worry about putting my name on the list. Don't even give it a thought. I'm going to call Mikelos as soon as we hang up. We're good friends, you know."

She felt relieved with his response. "I was so worried," she said, "because I know how you feel about not breaking the rules and not having to listen to nasty gossip about us."

"Crissy," he said, "that was to protect you. I can take care of myself, so don't worry about me. I just didn't want you to be an object of ridicule among the crew like Jenny is."

"Thank you, Luca," she replied.

"Just promise me you'll take care of yourself. Damn, if I hadn't been so busy last night at least you might not have been alone when you discovered this."

"It's not your fault, Luca," she replied. "You have to do your job."

"I'll meet you tonight. How's that?"

"That would be wonderful."

"Then take care until tonight when we're together," he said. "I'm going to call Mikelos now and get his take on this." Then he added, "Check for messages after dinner, or better yet, call me."

She hung up the receiver, looking at it affectionately. In a time of feeling violated, as if the pervert had invaded her very being, she was grateful for a strong man like Luca. Of all the people she had met on the ship, he was the only one she could truly trust.

She looked at her watch, remembering what Christopolous had said. If he knew anything, he'd said, he would call her or leave a message for her at the Information Desk. She might as well go down there now, she decided, but before she got to the door, the telephone rang.

She picked up the receiver. "Hello?"

"Ms. Fitzgerald?"

"Yes?"

"This is Mikelos Christopolous. I'm afraid I have bad news for you."

Crissy's heart sank.

"The telephone calls were made from a public telephone outside a men's room on the Venus Deck, so we don't have an answer."

"That is bad news," Crissy responded.

"But as I promised you," Mikelos said, "we will install a Minicam near the telephone where the calls were made to see if we can eventually get the caller on video."

"Thank you," Crissy said. "I really would appreciate anything that you can do."

"We'll get the creep," Christopolous said. "It may take awhile, but rest assured, we'll do it."

"Thanks again," Crissy said. She hung up the telephone and sat down on the bed, dejected. She didn't know any more than she did before. Anybody could've dialed her cabin from that telephone.

Crissy spent the afternoon engrossed in her book. At one point she fell asleep, and when she awoke, it was time to get ready for dinner. On her way to the bathroom, there was a knock at the door. She answered it and was surprised to see an unfamiliar steward with a huge bouquet of flowers for her.

Crissy took the bouquet from him. *Luca is so thoughtful,* she told herself, putting her nose to the bouquet and inhaling its sweet aroma. *To take the time out from his schedule to do something like this for me.*

"Also this," the steward said, holding a creamy vellum envelope out to her.

Crissy took the envelope and saw her name written in script on it. "Hold on just a minute," she told the steward. She put the bouquet and envelope on the table in the sitting area and retrieved her wallet from her shoulder bag. Taking out two euros, she handed them to the steward. "Thanks," she said.

"That isn't necessary."

"I insist," she replied.

"Thank you very much," he said, taking the euros. He smiled, then turned and went down the corridor.

Crissy picked up the envelope and tore it open. She could hardly wait to see what he had written.

Dear Crissy,

These flowers are a small token of my gratitude for your having dinner with me. I realize that I behaved inexcusably when you wouldn't return to my cabin for a nightcap, and I apologize. I hope that I can make it up to you by asking you for lunch tomorrow. Since we will be at sea all day today and tomorrow, I thought it was the ideal opportunity to repay you and get to know each another better. If you will, let me know by this evening so the chef can prepare something special. I'll look forward to your call.

Sincerely,

Mark Vilos

Crissy wanted to wad the invitation up and throw it in the wastebasket, but it suddenly occurred to her that she might be making a mistake. She wondered if Mark had somehow gotten word of the investigation into her harassment and was consequently trying to make himself look good in her eyes and to the men in Security. If that's what he was doing, she reasoned, it was a good move. A guilty man surely wouldn't ask her to lunch, would he?

If she accepted his invitation, she wouldn't be taking a risk, she thought. Someone from the security detail was going to be posted near her at all times, so she wouldn't be in any danger, would she? Besides, she would alert Christopolous and Luca as to her whereabouts beforehand. Lunch with Mark Vilos might offer the perfect opportunity to find out if he was the person who'd been making the calls and then gotten into her cabin to destroy her underwear. She thought his reclusive behavior very odd. He hardly left his cabin—he'd told her so himself. That seemed to fit the profile of a man who would slash a woman's underwear.

Having lunch with him would answer some of the questions she had about him. She went to the telephone and dialed his cabin.

He picked up on the third ring. "Hello."

"Hi, it's Crissy."

"I'm so glad to hear from you," he replied. "Will you come to lunch?"

"I'd be delighted to," Crissy said. "What time?"

"About one," he said, "if that's convenient for you."

"I'll be there," Crissy said.

"Great," Mark said. "I'll look forward to it. I hope you're enduring the storm okay."

"Yes," she said. "The scopolamine patches seem to be working for me."

"I use them, too," he said. "Even growing up on ships, I can get seasick in these conditions."

"Oh, I almost forgot," she said. "Thanks for the flowers, Mark. They're really beautiful."

"You're welcome."

"Till tomorrow then," Crissy said.

She replaced the receiver in its cradle. *I'll call Christopolous and tell Luca later,* she thought. Then they would be in place.

Mina, Rudy, and Monika were seated when the maître d' took her to the table, but Jenny's and Dr. Von Meckling's chairs were empty.

"Hi," Crissy said.

"Hallo," Mina and Rudy said in unison.

Monika nodded and looked at her appraisingly.

"We're saving champagne until the storm is over," Rudy said. "Too much of it is ending up lost, if you know what I mean."

Crissy laughed. "Have any of you been seasick?"

"I was just a little," Mina said, "but I think it's passed. Rudy hasn't felt a thing. How about you, Monika?"

She shook her head. "Oh, no," she said. "I wear the patches, and I've been through much worse than this. I never get sick."

"Have you been okay?" Mina asked Crissy.

"I've been fine," Crissy said, "at least as far as the storm goes."

Monika looked at her quizzically. "What do you mean? Has something else happened? Another one of your telephone calls?"

"That and more," Crissy said.

Jenny and Dr. Von Meckling arrived together and took their seats.

After greetings all around, Monika looked at Jenny. "Your friend was just about to tell us the latest distasteful episode with the caller."

"Oh, that," Jenny said, tossing her head, her hair swinging back.

When Crissy didn't continue, Monika prodded her. "Please finish, Crissy," she said. "Now you've begun, we must hear the rest."

"I got back to my cabin last evening, and someone had been in and slashed my underwear to pieces and left it on the bed," she said.

Mina threw her hand over her mouth and gasped, while Monika's eyes opened wide with alarm.

Rudy's face curdled into an expression of disgust. "That's horrible."

"Then the telephone rang," Crissy continued, "and it was the breather again."

Mina gasped and banged her hand on the table, rattling china and crystal. "You must get Security on this."

"I have," Crissy replied.

"What do they say?" Rudy asked.

"They're working on it," Crissy said, "but they've asked me not to discuss their plans with anyone."

The waiter appeared and took their orders, during which time there was no talk of what had happened.

"You must've been scared to death," Mina said when the waiter left.

"I was," Crissy admitted, "but I think they'll take care of it."

"I still say you've been teasing some guy and made him crazy enough to do it," Jenny said.

"That's absurd, and you know it," Crissy said.

"Don't you think that women so often ask for trouble of that sort?" Monika said to no one in particular.

"If you're talking about me," Crissy said angrily, "the answer is no."

The waiter appeared again and began serving dinner. With Mina's help, Rudy steered the dinner conversation over less serious topics.

Later, Crissy excused herself and left without any further explanation. They would assume that she was going to see Luca, but she wasn't going to offer them any information she didn't have to.

She went down to the cabin and called the hospital.

"Hello," Voula answered.

"It's Crissy Fitzgerald," she said. "Could I speak to Luca, please?"

"Of course," Voula said. "Just one minute."

Crissy was put on hold for quite some time, but Luca finally picked up. "Hi," he said. "Sorry to take so long, but it couldn't be helped."

"How's it going?" she asked.

"Okay," he said. "It could be worse. It looks like I'll be free with scheduled appointments somewhere around midnight. Something could come up after that. You never know, but why don't you come down here around then? Or why not meet in the disco? You won't have to sit around in the cabin waiting, and maybe we can have a couple of dances. Is that all right with you?"

"All right? I can hardly wait," she said.

Luca laughed. "Neither can I," he said. "Now I have to run."

Crissy hung up the telephone and sat smiling at her reflection in the mirror above the desk area. *I am the luckiest woman in the world,* she thought. She decided to change into a dressier outfit for the disco, but she took her time. If she got there early, she could sit with her dinner partners. The music and dancing would make conversation difficult, with much less argument, and besides, Mina and Rudy would be there to help diffuse matters. When she was finally ready, she carefully climbed the stairs to the top deck, wondering what it would be like on the dance floor tonight, considering the terrible pitching and rolling of the ship.

Going into the disco, Mina spotted her and waved from the table they usually occupied. There wasn't a crowd to worm her way through, because of the storm, she supposed. She took a seat next to Mina, who was alone at the table.

Mina gave her an air kiss. "I'm so glad you made it," she said. "Rudy is dancing with Monika, and Jenny and Dr. Von Meckling are dancing, too." She laughed. "So here we are, like two old maids."

There was a light tap on Crissy's shoulder. "May I have this dance?"

It was Valentin.

"Sure," Crissy said. She turned to Mina and winked. "One old maid now."

Valentin led her the short distance to the dance floor and took her into his arms for a slow number. "I'm so glad to see you, Crissy."

"It's nice to see you, too, Valentin."

"You haven't been here for awhile," he said. "What have you been doing?"

"Oh, this and that," she said, smiling up at him.

"We've missed you," he said. "*I've* missed you."

"That's sweet of you to say, Valentin," she said, "but you're always busy dancing with someone, so I don't see how you could have missed me." She didn't want to tell him that she knew he was paid by the cruise

214

line to dance with the ladies. Why not let him play his little game of being interested in her?

"Yes, I'm always dancing," he replied, "but the others aren't like you."

Crissy laughed lightly. "How's that, Valentin?"

"You are beautiful," he said, "and you have nice manners."

"Thank you," Crissy said, "but I think you've told me this before." She couldn't take anything he said seriously, but she had to admit that it was nice to hear such compliments.

"That's because I mean what I say," he replied, "but you still don't take me seriously." He pulled her closer to him, and Crissy felt uncomfortable. His strength was formidable, and she was much more aware of the contours of his body and the heat that emanated from him.

The music changed to a fast number. "I'd better sit this one out," Crissy said. "I have to talk to my friends."

Valentin looked momentarily disappointed, but he led her back to her seat, then immediately disappeared as usual.

Mina was still sitting alone, smoking a cigarette and taking tiny sips of her wine. "How was it?" she asked.

"He's a very good dancer, but I wish he would quit acting like he's interested in me," Crissy said.

"He seems very interested in you," Mina said.

"And nearly every other woman in the place," Crissy said with a laugh.

"How are things going with your doctor, if you don't mind me asking?"

"I don't mind *you* asking," Crissy said. "It's the others I'd rather not discuss it with."

"Listen, darling," Mina said, "they're just jealous. That's all there is to it. You mustn't pay any attention to them."

"I try not to, but it's not easy. Especially when they say nasty things about Luca."

Monika and Rudy returned to the table, so they quickly changed the subject. "Valentin seems like a harmless sort," Mina said.

"Oh, I think so," Crissy agreed.

"Don't tell me that you two are discussing that wretched Bulgarian," Monika said.

"Yes," Mina said. "He's already asked Crissy to dance with him. She thinks he's pretending to be interested in her."

215

"No doubt," Monika said. She looked around. "Jenny and Dr. Von Meckling haven't returned?"

"No," Mina said. "They'll be along soon, I think. They've danced nearly every dance—a miracle, considering the way the dance floor moves under your feet."

"Such a happy pair," Monika said, "and so appropriate, don't you think?" She focused her shrewd eyes on Crissy.

"Appropriate?" Crissy repeated. "I really don't know, Monika," she said. "I don't see anything wrong with it, but I didn't picture Jenny marrying a man old enough to be her grandfather. She always seemed to like them young and . . . energetic."

"How naive of you," Monika said. "But I shouldn't have expected more from you. Appropriateness has nothing to do with age, Crissy. Besides, youth and energy, as you put it, are soon gone. Wasted, usually."

Jenny and Dr. Von Meckling reached the table at that moment. "Hi," Jenny said, waving a hand in a circle. "We've danced every dance so far. Between trying to stay on my feet and Ludwig, I'm exhausted."

Ludwig? So they were on a first-name basis? Something Crissy gathered took a very long time to achieve among Europeans as opposed to Americans.

"She is a wonderful dancer," the old doctor said as he took a seat.

"You looked perfect together," Monika enthused.

Jenny gazed across the table at Crissy. "So you're here alone?"

Crissy nodded.

"Where's that quack that calls himself a doctor?" Jenny asked.

Crissy felt her blood boil, and before she could think, she spat back, "Why must you demean him? Did he refuse your advances or something?"

Jenny turned crimson.

"That's it, isn't it?" Crissy went on. "You tried to get him into bed, and when he wasn't interested, you turned on him."

Jenny picked up her wineglass and threw its contents across the table at Crissy. "You bitch," she snarled.

Wine hit Crissy's face with a splash and rolled down onto the bodice of her dress. She grabbed cocktail napkins and started slowly wiping the wine away, as Mina and Rudy quickly gathered up more and handed them to her.

Mina dipped a napkin into a glass of water and began wiping at the

216

bodice of Crissy's dress. "There," she said after a few moments. "It's going to be all right."

Monika wore a tight, smug smile when she turned to Crissy. "My dear," she said, "I think I would watch my tongue if I were you. One doesn't make such outrageous accusations in public and expect to suffer no consequences."

"I don't need your advice, Monika," Crissy said. She knew she had already gone too far to return to that place where she had been a dutiful, uncomplaining, submissive companion who would put up with anything, no matter how demoralizing. "You're the same kind of backstabbing 'friend' that Jenny is, and I think I'd be a lot better off without knowing either one of you."

"What an ungrateful little hellion you are," Monika said. "Spiteful, willful, and *common*."

"Maybe I am," Crissy said, "but if you're an example of what's highborn, then spare me. You both make me sick."

Jenny stood up abruptly. "I'm going down to our cabin," she said, "and I'm getting an attendant to help me move my things right now."

"You're welcome to use my cabin," Monika said. "I have a suite, and there are two beds, my darling, as well as the sofa bed."

"Thank you, Monika," Jenny said. "That's what I'll do if you mean it, otherwise . . . I think Ludwig would let me camp out there."

"It might be much more appropriate if you camped out with me for the time being," Monika said, giving Jenny a significant glance. She knew that Dr. Von Meckling would want to keep up appearances, and having Jenny there for meals or sleepovers was one thing, but moving her in was another.

"Good," Jenny said. "Could I have your key card?"

"Certainly, my darling," Monika said. She fished in her enormous gold leather handbag and extracted the card. "Here it is. Let yourself in and use whatever space you need."

"Thank you," Jenny said. She leaned down and whispered into Dr. Von Meckling's ear, gave him a pat, then stood up, glared at Crissy, and swept out of the disco, grasping at chairs, tables, and support beams to maintain her balance.

"Would you like to dance, Crissy?" Rudy asked.

God bless him, she thought. "I'd love to, Rudy," she said.

He took her to the dance floor, and began moving to the slow tempo

217

of the music. "You mustn't let them upset you," he said. "They're both well-heeled, smart, attractive, sophisticated women." Then he added, "And monsters who will chew you up and spit you out."

He and Crissy both laughed. "I just wish I hadn't lost my temper," she said, "and especially here in a public place."

"If I were you, I wouldn't give it a second thought," Rudy said. "They've been taunting you for days because they're jealous that the handsome doctor is after you."

"It's so hard to escape it," Crissy said. "I can't just jump overboard."

"A definite disadvantage to a cruise," Rudy agreed.

After the dance, they returned to the table, and Crissy looked at her wristwatch. It was almost midnight, so Luca should be here soon. She sat down next to Mina, avoiding Monika's glances, trying to appear as if all was normal. She glimpsed the captain and his party arriving, but she couldn't tell if Luca was with them or not. They had gone toward the back—a swath of white moving across the disco—and she didn't get a good look.

She felt a tap on her shoulder, and there stood Luca, smiling. "Hello," he said.

"Hello," Crissy said, barely able to keep from rising into his arms.

"Care to dance?" Luca asked with feigned formality.

"Why, thank you, Doctor," she replied.

They danced for a long time, slow and fast dances, unable to contain the joy they felt at being together. Finally, he led her by her table to pick up her purse.

Monika looked up at them, her fan moving rapidly at her bosom. "Are you off?"

"Maybe," Crissy said noncommitally. "Good night, if I don't see you later."

Monika nodded slightly.

As they headed out, Luca said to her, "So, I think it must be time for your appointment."

She clutched his arm a little harder. "I think you'll find I'm a very compliant patient."

The man entered Mark's cabin as easily as always, closing the door quietly behind him. Mark had left lights on as usual, and he saw the trunk where it always was. As he approached it, he heard the distinct sound of a key card being slipped in the door behind him.

Jesus Christ! he thought. He practically flew across the room to the balcony door, slid it open, and slipped out onto the balcony, hunching down to the side of the door to make himself as invisible as possible.

As he watched, Mark tossed his key card onto a table, shrugged out of a sports jacket that he tossed on a chair, then made himself a drink.

Fuck! the man thought. *I could be here all night at this rate, waiting for him to go back out or go to bed. That crazy old man of his. It's his fault, wanting another check on the goddamn explosives.* He'd told him that he would get them out of the trunk tonight and take them down to his own cabin. It would soon be time to use them anyway. He had wanted to wait until the last minute because he was subject to searches, should there be any reason to conduct one. Not only that, but he had less privacy in his cabin and little in the way of a secure hiding place.

Now Mark, the son of a bitch, was screwing up his plans. He watched as he sipped his drink slowly, turned on a CD player, then set his drink down on a coffee table. Mark crossed to the trunk and opened it.

Suddenly the man's eyes widened with alarm. *Jesus! Is he actually going to go through the damn thing?*

He watched as Mark idly picked up an old quilt at the top of the trunk, then dropped it to the floor. He picked up several more, letting them slip to the floor with the first one. Then he began rummaging through the quilts more quickly, grabbing one and holding it up to the light and looking at it before tossing it back down.

I may end up having to kill the bastard, the man thought.

Finally Mark scooped up the quilts on the floor and threw them back into the trunk, crossed back to the coffee table, picked up his drink, and went into his bedroom. He didn't bother closing the trunk, leaving the lid yawning open.

What do you know? the man thought. *He didn't even see the Semtex.*

He scooted over to try to get a better view of the bedroom door. It was open, and light poured out of the room. *Shit! I could be here all night waiting for him to go to bed.* One thing for sure, he promised himself. When he came back the next time it would be to get the Semtex out of there and take his chances storing it in his own cabin.

He sat on his haunches, waiting and watching. In less than fifteen minutes, all of the lights in the suite went out at once. *He's got a master switch at his bedside,* the man thought. He could tell that Mark hadn't closed the bedroom door, or he might try to take the Semtex with him now. But he decided against it. He could slide the balcony door open and shoot across the room and out, fast and unseen. He was certain of that. But he didn't want to chance going to the trunk and taking out the Semtex with Mark's bedroom door open. For all he knew, the bastard had a gun.

He waited for another fifteen minutes or so, then slowly slid the balcony door open. Slipping inside the suite, he closed the door behind him as quietly as possible, then stood stock-still, listening. Nothing. He couldn't hear anything except the ticking of a clock somewhere.

Taking a deep breath, he shot toward the hallway door, unlocked it, and was out in the passageway in an instant. He walked hurriedly, but not *too* hurriedly, toward the nearest turn off the hallway. Once around the corner, he stopped, peered around it, saw that no one was coming, and took another deep breath.

Close call, he thought. *Too damn close. I've got to get the explosives out of there soon. Very soon.*

Once down in the hospital, he quickly closed the door behind them. "My God," he said, taking her into his arms. "You must be the most beautiful woman in the world."

Crissy held onto him as if he were a life preserver in a storm-tossed sea. "Oh, I'm so glad to be alone with you," she said. "So glad."

He kissed her passionately, then drew back, looking at her worriedly. "Are you all right about what happened?" he asked.

"We don't need to talk about it now," she said.

"Yes," he said, "we do. Here, sit down." He indicated the bed in the hospital room. Fortunately, there were no patients required to stay overnight. He had turned off the overhead lights but left on the more subdued light under a wall-mounted cabinet.

Crissy did as she was told, sitting on the edge of the bed. Luca stood in front of her, looking down at her. He put a hand under her chin and lifted her face to meet his gaze. "Tell me how you feel," he said. "Please. I love you, Crissy, and I want to comfort you."

She felt tears well up in her eyes, and she fought them back. She didn't know until that moment that his caring for her—and his words—were exactly what she needed to hear. "I-I . . . Oh, I feel so humiliated, Luca," she stuttered. "I-I just feel so . . . used."

He put his arms around her and hugged her to him. "Tell me, Crissy. Please," he said.

She let the tears come then, crying silently against his chest. When she could finally speak, she told him what had happened, then let out a laugh. "I-I'm sorry, Luca. This is so silly. So . . . stupid."

"No," he whispered. "You're not silly or stupid. Not at all. Crissy, I'm so sorry you've been hurt," Luca said, stroking her back tenderly, "but you've got to remember who did it. Those people are unhappy and uncaring. They're only out for themselves. Monika Graf and Jenny are both manipulative bitches."

"I think you may be right," she said.

"I know I am," he said. "I wasn't going to tell you because I didn't want to interfere with your friendship with Jenny, but when she came to see me about her feet, she threw herself all over me. Really acted sleazy."

"Oh, my God," Crissy said. "Why am I not surprised?"

"It gets worse," Luca said. "Monika made an appointment about a stomachache, which I'm sure was just an excuse to see if I might be interested in her. When I didn't show any interest, she warned me that you were trouble."

"What!" Crissy exclaimed.

Luca nodded. "I didn't want to tell you that either, because I know she doesn't really mean it. She just wants to come between the two of us."

"I can't believe it," Crissy said. "She's been so nice to me, or she *was*. On excursions and everything, she's been . . . Well, it's like she's . . . she's taken me under her wing like I'm her . . . her daughter or something."

"Crissy," he said, "a woman like her would never simply be nice to you without expecting something in return."

"But what?" she asked, looking up at him.

He shrugged. "Who knows? Maybe just your company. I think she's a very lonely, unhappy woman."

"But she's famous and has everything," Crissy said.

"Believe me, she's unhappy," he said. "She doesn't have a husband or boyfriend, does she? She's traveling alone, and there's nothing wrong with that. But I think she probably doesn't have many friends, and I think she was using you to keep her company."

"I thought she really liked me," Crissy said.

"I think she does like you in her way," Luca said, "but I also think she would use you." He paused. "As for Mark Vilos, I wouldn't put anything past him. He's a spoiled, arrogant brat who's used to getting his way no matter what. I don't know whether he made the telephone calls or tore up your underwear, but something tells me he's the type."

He hugged her, then sat down next to her and put an arm around her shoulder. "Just remember, you've got me, and you're safe with me." He kissed her cheek. "I love you, Crissy."

"Oh, Luca," she whispered. "You do make me feel safe, and I-I love you, too. And that's what's important."

They kissed passionately, their desire for each other overcoming any other considerations. He finally drew back and looked into her eyes. "Let's get undressed," he said. "Now that we can."

"Yes," she replied.

He stood up and offered her a hand. Crissy slid off the bed, and Luca took her into his arms, kissing her again before reluctantly parting. He turned her around and unzipped the back of her dress slowly, caressing her all the while. As he slipped it off her shoulders, he kissed each one in turn, then brushed his lips across the nape of her neck, nuzzling her tenderly. Letting her dress slide to the floor, Crissy turned to him, and he stared at her, standing before him in a white lacy bra and panty hose, the beautiful dress gathered around her ankles in a heap.

"Ah," he said in a whisper, "you're so beautiful. So beautiful. Even more beautiful than in the moonlight." He took her into his arms again, kissing her while unhooking her brassiere, then tossing it onto a chair. When her breasts leapt free, he brought his hands to them, cupping each one and leaning down to kiss them, his tongue licking her rosy nipples. He moaned in pleasure before going down on his knees, and, lifting one leg at a time, he slipped her gown from around her ankles, then removed her high heels. He left them on the floor while he reached up with his hands and gently pulled her panty hose all the way down to her feet, reverently lifting each foot and pulling the panty hose off. She was naked now, her body fully exposed for him to see, and he sat back on his haunches, his gaze traversing the landscape of her body as if she were a goddess and he her supplicant.

"Magnificent," he breathed.

Crissy smiled shyly. She didn't think she'd ever felt so vulnerable, for she had never opened her heart and soul to a man before, not like this. She was afraid, she realized, but her desire for him and to give herself to him overcame her fear.

Luca moved forward to his knees again, placing a hand on each of her rounded cheeks. Burying his head in her stomach, he kissed her, his tongue swirling around and around her navel, then tracing a path down to the mound between her thighs. Crissy put her hands on his head, her fingers splayed in his black hair, caressing him as he began to kiss her, shivering with desire as his tongue found her most private place. Luca moaned as he was enveloped in her heat, and his hands pushed her to him as he delved deeper, her juices attesting to her lusty readiness. Crissy was overcome with passion for him, and grasped his head forcefully and ground herself against him, then cried out when he stopped and withdrew.

Luca stood up and embraced her, kissing her, his breath coming in pants that were like those of an animal. "I've got to undress," he rasped.

He drew back and led her to the bed, where Crissy sat watching him. Leaning down, he picked up her dress and panty hose, draping them across a chair. He turned and stood before her, then slowly began removing his uniform. First, he shrugged out of his white jacket, underneath which he wore an undershirt. He slid it over his head, and Crissy let her eyes linger on his broad shoulders and muscular arms, the patch of black hair between his pectorals, and the trail that led to his navel. He looked so strong, so fit and able, and his masculine hardness in the light increased her desire for him. He untied his shoes and took them off. When he'd unbuckled his belt and unbuttoned and unzipped his white pants, he slid them down his legs and stepped out of them. His manhood, fully aroused, was trapped by the white jockey shorts he wore. Sliding those down, he took them off. Standing back up, his aroused cock sprang out in front of him, and for the first time, Crissy saw him fully exposed to her. She drank him in, her eyes hungrily studying his chiseled body, its defined musculature, at last coming to rest on his face.

Luca smiled. "See what you do to me?" he said, approaching her.

"You're more handsome, more . . . everything than I ever imagined," she breathed.

He got onto the bed with her, and they spread out next to each other, Luca taking her into his arms. "It's so wonderful to be with you," he said. "Naked and in bed." He began kissing her passionately, his tongue exploring her mouth, his hands caressing her breasts, then trailing down to the mound between her thighs. His lips found her nipples, and he licked them in circles until they were distended with desire.

Crissy swept her hands down his long back to his buttocks, massaging their astonishing hardness before finding his engorged manhood and balls, brushing them lightly with her fingers before stroking him slowly and gently. She took pleasure in his lustful moans, and when his fingers slid inside her, she emitted a sigh of ecstacy.

Their explorations continued, their joy in each other seemingly endless, but Luca finally could wait no longer before mounting her and entering her tenderly. They moved rhythmically, slowly at first, Luca engulfing her with his manhood, and Crissy responding by taking him with abandon, opening herself wide for him, glorying in their craving for each other. Their desire was ravenous, and Luca soon began to move faster, the urge for consummation overcoming all else.

"Oh, my God," Crissy cried. "Luca, Luca . . . " Crissy suddenly felt her body contract, and in a spasm of ecstacy, she cried out and flooded him with her orgasm.

Silent but for his panting, Luca bucked wildly, her orgasm engendering his own, and his muscles stiffened as he burst inside her, a tidal wave of pent-up desire sweeping before him. He moaned. "Ahhh, Crissy, I love you. I love you."

He clutched her to him and peppered her face and neck with kisses as he caught his breath. Crissy wrapped her arms around him, savoring the feel of him still inside her, of the touch of his lips against her sated flesh. They lay together for a long time, basking in the afterglow of their love for each other, their sweat-sheened bodies as one.

His breath had returned to normal when Luca gently rolled to his side, bringing her with him, still inside her. Embracing her again, he kissed her lips, then drew back, propping his head on a hand and looking into her eyes. "I love you so much," he said.

"I love you, too," Crissy said, in a state of wonderment that anything on earth could be this heavenly. "I still can hardly believe it's true."

He nodded. "I know," he replied. "It seems impossible—like a miracle—that we've found each other." He embraced her again, holding her tightly. "It's like a dream come true, Crissy. Like a whole new world, and I never want it to end."

"It won't," she said. "Our love will never end. Never."

She felt him growing inside her, and he began to slowly move, taking her in his arms, kissing her with renewed passion. They made love again, more slowly this time, their eyes on each other, expressing every moment in silent but watchful desire, their lust piqued by their love. When they lay exhausted at last, they talked and talked, discovering more about the other's history, their wants and needs, their goals and ambitions—past, present, and future—until late into the night.

"We would have to leave around six in the morning," Luca said, "but we can sleep here if you want."

"I want," Crissy said. She squeezed him. "Oh, yes. I definitely want."

He kissed her. "Good. I've never wanted anything more in my life." He reached down and pulled a sheet up over them.

"How will we wake up?" she asked.

"I'm a doctor, remember?" he said. "I have an internal alarm clock, so don't worry. I'll get us up."

He put an arm around her shoulders, and Crissy nestled her head against him. He kissed her hair, and they slept at last.

Luca awoke her with a kiss, and Crissy, disoriented at first, quickly realized where she was. She returned his kiss. "Hmm," she whispered, "I wish we didn't have to get up. Ever."

"We have a few minutes," he said, taking her into this arms. They made love again, the realization that they had to part compelling them to enjoy each other once more before separating.

"Everybody's going to know I've been somewhere all night," Crissy said, "but I don't care."

"Nor do I," he said. "If I have to break the rules from now on, then that's what I'm going to do." He took her into his arms again. "I can't do without you. It's impossible." He kissed her, then reluctantly drew back and relinquished his hold on her. "Go, my beauty," he said.

Chapter Sixteen

Getting a sweater out of the closet and grabbing her shoulder bag, Crissy let herself out of the cabin. As she walked up the corridor, she idly wondered about Jenny and Monika, and how they were getting along. They were probably having a wonderful time dishing her, she thought. The idea didn't really bother her as much as it might have, she realized, because of her relationship with Luca. Still, she smarted from Jenny's betrayal. She thought she had known her, and she had appreciated their friendship. Jenny had always been fun and generous, but when she thought about it, she decided that she hadn't really known her all that well. Before and after her marriage, they had gone out together, Crissy always serving as a kind of tag-along. While she was married, Crissy had hardly heard from Jenny. Now she felt that she had been used as a kind of colorless sidekick, someone to help fill the gap between men, someone who served as a kind of backdrop against which Jenny could play out her dramas.

Going to the stairwell, she climbed up to the top deck and went down the corridor that led to Mark's cabin. Knocking on his door, she glanced up and down the corridor. She didn't see anyone about, but she guessed she wasn't supposed to.

Mark opened the door himself. "Welcome to my humble abode," he said, bowing his head and sweeping a hand toward the entrance hall.

"Thank you," Crissy said with a laugh as she entered. She stepped in and walked toward the living room. She saw the steamer trunk with its large, emblazoned Vs. Its top was open, propped against a wall.

"Oh, you've opened that beautiful trunk," she said.

"Yes," Mark replied. "You've been so curious about it, I decided to open Pandora's box and let you see what's inside."

Crissy laughed. "I can't believe you did that."

"It's pretty dull," Mark said. "Just a bunch of old quilts. I didn't even bother going through the whole thing."

Crissy stepped toward the trunk. "They look handmade," she said. "They're really beautiful."

Mark smirked. "Worthless, if you ask me."

"Maybe your father treasures them," she replied. "Somebody in his family might have made them a long time ago."

"Who cares?" Mark said. "Anyway, I hope you're surviving the storm unscathed," he said, turning to her.

"I'm fine. How about you?"

"No problems here," he said. "Have a seat." He indicated a couch. On the coffee table in front of it was a silver tray on which sat two champagne flutes and a silver cooler. Inside the cooler a bottle of champagne was perched on ice. "I'll be back in a flash. I wasn't quite ready, as you can see." He was standing in his bare feet, and his hair was still wet from the shower.

"That's okay," Crissy said. "Take your time."

He dashed off through the living room toward the bedroom and closed the door behind him. When he was gone, Crissy looked over at the pile of messages on the desk. She hadn't planned on pilfering any of his messages, but she had to take advantage of the opportunity: They might indicate his involvement in harassing her. Forcing herself to her feet, shoulder bag in hand, she casually walked over to the desk. Looking toward the bedroom door, then back at the messy pile of messages, she felt her heart thumping in her chest. She quickly slipped out a couple from the bottom and shoved them in her shoulder bag. She repeated the process, taking two or three from the middle of the pile, then finally took a couple from near the top.

She felt sweat bead on her forehead as she rushed back to the couch and sat down, her heart beating wildly. Propping her shoulder bag next to her, she reached down into it, rearranging its contents to make certain that the envelopes were out of sight. That done, she searched until she found the small packet of Kleenex that she always had with her, pulled several out, and dabbed her forehead. When he came back into the room, she was still recovering and hoped that her nervousness didn't show on her face.

"Are you too warm?" Mark asked.

"Oh, no, I'm fine," Crissy said. "I was just out on deck. I guess the change in temperature got to me for a minute."

"Why did you go out on deck?" he asked, sitting at the end of the couch.

"I just like to go out and look at the sky and sea. Even in this weather, I love the salt air and the wind."

"You're like me," he said, smiling. "A primitive at heart. I love the feeling of being close to nature, its wildness, its power and strength. Nothing man has done can compare. Not even close." He poured two glasses of champagne. "I know you can't drink much, so I thought we'd have a glass of champagne before lunch. How's that?"

"Fine," she said. "I'll have a tiny bit."

He handed her a glass, then clinked his against it. "To Mother Nature," he said, "whose power and strength and beauty know no bounds."

"Aren't we poetic today," she said teasingly.

"Well," he admitted, "I do get carried away sometimes. I guess it's the storm: It excites me."

"It is exciting," Crissy said, "but I think it would get old fast, don't you?"

"Like the mistral or the meltemi," he said, "the winds. In France, the mistral will blow for days, weeks even, and drive people nearly crazy. In Greece, it's the meltemi, roaring down from the north. A lot of people enjoy the first day or two, but then it really makes them crazy. They try to stay indoors to avoid it. It kicks up sand and soil, stings you all over, and it makes sailing a fierce proposition or brings it to a halt. Once I was sailing from Mykonos to Seriphos and got caught in it. It was treacherous, waves crashing over the boat. You get the picture. But I made it."

"It sounds as though you like to take risks," Crissy said, "that you enjoy danger."

"I don't know," he said. "I didn't deliberately set out to get caught in the meltemi that day, but I'm not afraid, either."

He slid an arm across the back of the couch and drew nearer her. "What about you? Are you a risk-taker? Do you like danger?"

"Oh, my life has been so mundane, so ordinary," Crissy said. She laughed nervously. "There haven't been many risks or dangers. I guess you could say that I've sort of let things happen. Do you know what I mean?"

"Instead of *making* them happen?" he said, his eyes flashing.

She nodded. "Exactly." She looked down at her drink thoughtfully. "There have been times when I've had to make decisions, and I did. Like

228

when I dropped out of school and studied to be a hairdresser and colorist." She laughed again. "I think I made the wrong decision, but I didn't know it at the time. It seemed like the best and quickest way for me to start earning money to support myself so I wouldn't have to depend on my mother or anyone else."

"It sounds to me as if you made something happen," Mark said. "You didn't let the world swallow you up."

"No," Crissy said, thinking his choice of words a bit melodramatic, "I didn't let the world swallow me up. I'm not quite that passive."

"I didn't think so," he said, looking into her eyes. "I think you're a fighter." He took a swallow of his champagne, finishing the glass. "Ready?" He looked at her glass. "Here, I'll top it off." He filled Crissy's and poured another one for himself.

"I hope you don't mind the informality," he said, "but I didn't want stewards hovering about today."

"Not at all," Crissy said.

"I wanted to be alone with you," Mark said, looking into her eyes again.

Crissy smiled wanly.

He set his glass down on the coffee table and scooted next to her on the couch. "I wanted us to enjoy each other as we should." He leaned over and kissed her lips.

Crissy drew back. "No, Mark," she said. "This isn't why I came here. It's—"

He took her glass of champagne and set it on the table, then grabbed her wrists in his hands. "Come on," he said in a whisper. "You know you want me. I know that's why you came today." He forced her arms back, then began kissing her face and neck, shoving his body against her roughly.

"No!" Crissy cried. "Stop it, Mark. Stop it now."

But he didn't stop. Holding both of her wrists in one hand, he shoved up the top she was wearing and started licking and kissing her exposed cleavage. Crissy struggled against him, but his strength was too much for her. He was about 6'2" and must weigh 200 pounds, she thought, and there was no way she could force him off her.

For a moment she went limp, hoping that by doing so he would relinquish his hold on her wrists. The tactic worked, and with a grunt he began jerking her bra down and licking her exposed breasts. Crissy quickly slid off the couch before he could grab hold of her. She landed on the floor, but scrambled to her feet. She ran toward the door, but Mark grabbed her from behind, almost pulling her to the floor. One of his hands went across her mouth, and he began pulling her toward the bedroom.

At first Crissy felt like a rag doll in his grip, but when she realized where he was taking her, anger and fear propelled her into action. She tried to kick, but her feet didn't connect with anything but air. Biting his hand, she was rewarded with a heavy smack on her lips.

"Ahhhh, Mar—!" she began to scream.

His hand landed on her mouth again, harder this time, and the blow sent a bolt of pain through Crissy's head. She tasted blood and felt it running down her chin. She began kicking again, but as before, her feet connected with nothing. At the bedroom door, she saw an opportunity out of the corner of her eye. Using every ounce of strength in her body, she heaved herself sideways. Mark was in the bedroom, still holding onto her, but she'd hooked her legs around the door jamb, preventing him from dragging her inside.

"You bitch," he grunted, pulling on her torso, one hand still over her mouth.

Crissy held onto the doorway with her legs, willing her knees not to give out against his immense strength.

Suddenly, using both hands, he slammed her to the floor, and she went against it hard. She nearly had the breath knocked out of her, but she scrambled across the living room floor away from him. Trying to get to her feet, she felt his hands grab her from behind again, and she began screaming.

"Hel—!" A hand clamped forcefully over her mouth, and she bit it and kicked her legs furiously at the same time, making contact with his shins.

She heard him grunt, then felt his grip loosen. She struggled free and dashed toward the coffee table, Mark close behind her. Grabbing the bottle of champagne out of its bucket, she turned and took a wild swing in his direction. She heard the impact and felt it in her arm. When she looked, she saw that she had grazed the side of his head. He'd thrown a hand up to block the full impact. He came toward her, his eyes wild and his face contorted with fury. Crissy backed away, then ran toward the entrance. She felt his hands at her back again, clawing at her blouse. She gripped the trunk, but Mark continued to grab her blouse ferociously.

Her blouse ripped, and Mark jerked backward, almost thrown off his feet. Crissy fell, pulling the trunk over with her. Its contents spilled out over the living room floor and into the entrance hall. Among the quilts, a package in a plastic bag rolled onto the carpet, but neither of them noticed it.

Mark grabbed her under her arms and started pulling her across the floor, and Crissy began to scream.

The door to the cabin swung open and slammed against the wall with a loud thwack. A woman, revolver drawn, rushed inside.

"Down!" she barked in a deep voice, her hand indicating the floor.

Crissy was momentarily confused, but without thinking, she sank to her knees, then went all the way to the floor. The woman stepped around her.

"Put your hands up!" she said to Mark. "I said *up,* fucker," she snarled.

Crissy turned on the floor and looked behind her. She could see Mark with his hands up, backing away from the woman. Oddly, she thought, the woman, though tall and big-boned, was dressed as any passenger might be in a striped, long-sleeved tee and slacks and sneakers.

"This is all a misunderstanding," he said smoothly. "All a mistake."

The woman slapped a handcuff around one of his wrists. "Turn around and put your hands together behind you," she said. When Mark didn't move, she roared in his face. "Turn the fuck around, or I'll shoot your pretty face off."

Mark turned around and brought his wrists together at the small of his back. "You're going to be sorry for this," he said. "You're not going to be able to get a fucking job anywhere in the world if you live long enough to look for one."

Unperturbed, she snapped the other cuff in place, then pushed him toward a chair. "There," she snapped. "Sit down and shut up."

She turned to Crissy and helped her to her feet. "You okay, sweetheart?" she asked, looking her over.

Crissy nodded, licking the blood that still trickled from her lips into her mouth and down her chin.

"Don't worry about that," the woman said. "I'm getting the doctor now." She'd flipped a phone open and was dialing, but before she could finish, Luca rushed through the open door with Christopolous on his heels.

Luca took Crissy in his arms solicitously, looking over at Mark with rage in his eyes. "Are you okay?" he asked her.

She nodded. "My lip is cut. That's all."

Luca began examining it, and whispering to her at the same time, his eyes filled with tears.

"Good job, Anasthasia," Christopolous said to the woman. He looked over at Mark, who sat upright on the chair, his hands cuffed behind him, a smug smile on his face. "Looks like the little lady did a job on him, too." He strode over to Mark. "Clipped you on the side of the head, didn't she?"

Mark was silent.

"Less than you deserve, you son of a bitch," Christopolous said, roughly pulling Mark's hair back to look at the wound, then letting go.

Mark flinched but still remained silent.

"Get the captain down here," Christopolous said to Anasthasia.

She flipped her phone open again.

"Would you take a look at him, Luca? See if you can take care of them both down in Security," Christopolous said. "If we can avoid taking them to the hospital, let's do it. No need to upset passengers in the waiting room."

Luca examined Mark's wound. "This is going to take some sutures," he said, "but I can do it in Security."

"What about her?"

"I just need to wash her wound," Luca said. "I'll go down and get what I need, then meet you in Security." He went to Crissy and hugged her to him. "Will you be okay here?"

"Sure," she said, although she didn't want to stay in this room another minute.

"We're going to have to take a statement from her," Anasthasia said. "I'll take her down to the office myself." She looked at Crissy. "Okay? We'll make it quick, sweetheart."

Crissy nodded, and Anasthasia put a strong arm around her. "Hurry, Luca," she said. "Let's get this over with for her."

The captain marched into the cabin, closing the door behind him. His perpetual smile was missing, a look of concern in its place. Crissy could imagine the dilemma he found himself in. The shipowner's son caught trying to rape a passenger. It wouldn't look good for him or anyone else involved.

The captain asked her if she was okay. "Yes," she said.

"Can you briefly tell me what happened?" he asked. "We'll get a complete statement later."

232

"He tried to rape me," Crissy said, "and I hit him with a champagne bottle."

The captain walked over to Mark, examined his wound, then looked him in the eye. "Is this true?" he asked. "Did you try to rape her?"

"It's all lies," Mark said. "She was after me. Has been ever since the trip started."

"How do you explain her lip?" the captain asked.

"She likes it rough," Mark said. "She's a real sicko. Kept begging me to bite her."

Crissy's shoulders slumped, and Anasthasia held onto her firmly, giving her a few pats.

"I want them both brought down to Security for complete statements," the captain said. "Anasthasia, you take Ms. Fitzgerald down now."

Anasthasia nodded. "Yes, sir," she said.

"And Mikelos, get Garefi in here to take Mark down, but get him out of those handcuffs first." He gazed at Mark. "You'll behave, won't you?"

"Of course," Mark snarled. "I've done nothing wrong."

The captain nodded and glanced around the suite. "Mikelos, you stay here with me.

Anasthasia left with Crissy, and Garefi soon appeared and took instructions from Mikelos Christopolous. He left the suite at once, with Mark walking along beside him.

The captain turned to Christopolous. "You'd better get Sitara up here with his camera to document the scene," he said.

Mikelos Christopolous nodded idly. "I've already called down for him," he said. His gaze was focused on the quilts that spilled out over the floor in the living room and entrance hall. Bending down on a knee, he took a pair of thin latex gloves from a pocket and put them on.

"What is it?" Captain Papadapolis asked.

"Look at this," Christopolous said, indicating the Hondos Center shopping bag. The package that it held was partially exposed, and even though he was wearing the gloves, Mikelos gingerly slipped the parcel out into full view, then carefully pulled back the common butcher paper that hid its contents.

"What is it?" Captain Papadapolis asked, kneeling beside him.

Mikelos held the butcher paper aside with a pen. "Semtex," he said, directing his gaze at the captain. "Plastic explosives."

"Explosives?" the captain said, eyeing the package suspiciously.

233

"Enough to blow a gigantic hole in the ship and sink her," Mikelos said.

"Jesus," Captain Papadapolis said, his voice almost a whisper.

"What the hell would Makelos Vilos be doing with Semtex?" Christopolous asked.

"I don't know," the captain said, rising to his feet, "but we're going to find out."

Christopolous stood up, snapping off the latex gloves at the same time. He couldn't take his eyes off the small package that lay among the quilts. "I sure don't have a good feeling about this," he said. "Makelos Vilos has a lot of explaining to do."

In a small room in Security, Mark, the captain, and Mikelos Christopolous sat around a metal table. Christopolous had placed a tiny but very powerful tape recorder on the table, and it was picking up every word they said.

"What were these explosives doing in the trunk, Mark?" Christopolous asked.

"I don't have any idea," Mark replied with an astonished expression.

The captain had noted what he thought was genuine surprise when they'd told Mark that they had found the Semtex, but he couldn't be certain. Mark might be a very good actor.

"Come on," Christopolous said. "You had the trunk brought aboard, but you didn't know what was in it? You expect us to believe that?"

"I did *not* know what was in that trunk," Mark said, emphatically shaking his head. "Do you think I'm crazy? I would never have knowingly brought anything like that aboard the *Sea Nymph*."

"Then how do you explain it?" Christopolous asked, shifting in his chair.

"The trunk belongs to my father," Mark said. "I brought it aboard for him."

Christopolous stared at him intently. "For your father? That makes no sense."

"He said it was family stuff he wanted taken to the apartment in Miami," Mark replied. "That's all I knew."

"And you didn't even look inside it?" Christopolous asked incredulously. "You didn't have any idea what was in it?"

"No," Mark persisted. "I didn't even open it until today. Crissy had

234

asked about it, and I took a look for myself. Only I didn't see any explosives." He glared at Christopolous, and his voice rose angrily. "All I saw was a bunch of old quilts. Probably something that my father's old *yaya* made a hundred years ago."

The captain sighed in exasperation. He didn't know if Mark was telling the truth or not, but he knew that something very fishy was going on. Clearing his voice, he looked at Christopolous. "I'm going to make a phone call," he said, scooting back from the table. "You can continue questioning him, and I'll be back in a few minutes."

Christopolous nodded.

In one of Security's offices, Captain Papadapolis sat down at a desk and removed his cell phone from its holder on his belt. He flipped it open and dialed Georgios Vilos' telephone number, hoping that he would be able to reach him.

The telephone was picked up on the fourth ring. "*Nea?*"

"Mr. Vilos, this is Captain Demetrios Papadapolis."

"Hello, Captain," Georgios Vilos replied in a friendly manner that belied the suspicions he felt the moment he realized who was calling. It was highly unusual for Demetrios Papadapolis to be phoning him during a trip. "How are you?"

"We have a problem, Mr. Vilos," the captain said, "or I wouldn't be calling you."

Vilos chortled amicably. "What seems to be the matter, Captain?"

"We've found a package of Semtex, a plastic explosive, on the ship, Mr. Vilos," he said.

"You what?" Vilos cried. Sweat began to bead his forehead.

"Yes, sir," the captain said. "It was in your son's stateroom."

"No!" Vilos practically shouted. "That's impossible."

"I'm sorry, sir," the captain said, "but that's a fact. It was in a trunk he says that you gave him for safekeeping. He said he was taking the trunk to Miami for you."

Georgios Vilos' hand shook on the cell phone. He was trying to think of what to say, but his mind was racing in a dozen different directions at once. Finally, he cleared his voice and said, "Captain Papadapolis, what my son says is true. I asked him to take the trunk to Miami, but I can assure you that there were no explosives in it when I gave it to him. Someone must have tampered with it."

"Of course, sir. Sitara, our forensics man is still in the stateroom," the captain said. "If it's been tampered with, he ought to be able to tell us."

"I'm sure that's the case," Georgios Vilos said. He paused, then continued.

"How did you discover this, Captain?"

"That's the other problem, sir."

"What? Explosives on my ship is not enough of a problem?"

"A young lady, a passenger," the captain said, "claims that Mark tried to rape her."

"What are you saying, Captain?" Georgios Vilos roared.

The man was nearly apoplectic as Demetrios Papadapolis suspected he would be. "Yes, sir. I'm sorry, but it looks like she's telling the truth. Mark invited her to his stateroom for lunch, then attacked her. The trunk was knocked over during the attack. Mark claims that he's innocent, but—"

"This is . . . this is . . . outrageous!" Georgios Vilos said angrily. "Lock him up in the brig overnight! Maybe he'll come to his senses."

"We're still taking statements, sir," the captain went on, trying to ease the shock for Georgios Vilos, "and I'll keep you posted."

"Thank you, Captain," Georgios Vilos said. "And the explosives?"

"Mikelos Christopolous is taking care of the Semtex. He's an expert on such matters, so you don't have to worry about that."

Georgios Vilos heaved a sigh. "Thank God you found them, Captain," he said.

"I only regret that it happened the way it did," Captain Papadapolis said.

"Yes, well . . . " Georgios Vilos momentarily seemed to be lost in thought. "Do whatever you have to do, Captain."

"Yes, sir." The cell phone went dead in his hand. Georgios Vilos had hung up.

When all the statements had been taken, Mark was put in the ship's brig. Anasthasia, stating what she had heard before she entered the cabin and seen after, was the deciding factor as far as the captain was concerned. Crissy's statement was convincing, but he couldn't rely on her word alone. He knew that he had to give Makelos Vilos every benefit of doubt, but there was no debate in the matter after Anasthasia made her statement. He felt that he had no choice but to put Mark in the brig. Besides which, Georgios Vilos had told him to do so.

Whether he was guilty of anything else was an unanswered question. Christopolous repeatedly asked Mark if had been placing calls to Crissy, but Mark flatly denied it. When asked if he'd slashed her underwear, Mark denied that, too. Watching the questioning, it was hard for the captain or anyone else to decide whether or not he was lying. He still appeared to be completely convinced that he hadn't tried to rape Crissy, and repeatedly stated that she had begged him for sex, haunting him the entire trip.

Luca wanted Crissy to come to the hospital after he had washed her wound with antiseptic and she had given her statement, but she refused. "Luca, I'm okay," she insisted. "The tranquilizer you gave me is already working, and besides, you've got your hands full. I would just be in the way."

"You would never be in the way," he said. "You can spread out on one of the beds where I can keep watch over you."

"Luca," she said, "I can spread out in my cabin. Anasthasia said she would take me up and stay awhile."

"Then why don't you come down later and have dinner with me and Voula?" he said. "We'll eat off trays there, and you can join us. I know it's not much fun, but—"

"I'd love to do that," she replied.

He hugged her to him as if he never wanted to let her go. "I'll miss you," he whispered.

"I'll miss you, too," she said.

He reluctantly released her. "See you tonight." He turned and left the Security office.

Anasthasia, who had been waiting discreetly in an adjoining room, came into the office. "You ready to go upstairs, sweetheart?"

Crissy nodded. "I'm ready, but you really don't have to do this, Anasthasia," she said.

"Oh, yes, I do," the tall, big-boned woman replied. "I'm going to see that you get back to your cabin safely at least. Come on."

She led Crissy upstairs to her cabin. "Got this all to yourself?" Anasthasia asked.

"I do now," Crissy replied, "but it didn't start out that way. A friend came with me, but we had a spat. She moved in with someone else."

"Jeez," Anasthasia said. "This hasn't exactly been a dream trip for you, has it, honey?" She crossed to the desk area and turned the ringer on the telephone off. *No need for anybody to bother her now,* she thought.

"Yes and no," Crissy said, taking things out of her shoulder bag and putting them away.

"I bet I know what the yes part is," Anasthasia said with a laugh. "Couldn't help noticing you and Luca making nice-nice."

Crissy smiled. "That's definitely a dream part," she replied. "Do you want something to drink, Anasthasia? Luca said I shouldn't with the tranquilizer, but there's plenty in the minibar if you'd like something."

"Thanks," she said. "I'm still on duty, but what the hell? My duty is to watch over you right now. If you'll kindly spread out on the bed and look like you're resting, then I'll sit down here and have a little drink and watch you."

They both laughed. Anasthasia, rather fearsome-looking amazon that she was, also had a sharp sense of humor, Crissy thought.

Crissy stretched out on the bed, propped up on pillows, and watched as Anasthasia went through the minbar, looking for what she wanted. "Aha," she said at last. "Just what I was looking for." She rose to her feet with a bottle of Mythos beer, a popular Greek brand. She popped the top and took a long swig. "Ahhh, that tastes good." She looked at Crissy. "Sure you don't want something?"

"No," Crissy said. "I'm fine."

"How's your lip feel," Anasthasia asked.

"Sore, that's all," Crissy said. "It could've been a lot worse. My nose feels sore, too, but Luca said it'll probably be okay tomorrow."

"You're lucky," Anasthasia said, "because if you hadn't alerted Security the way you did, he might have gotten away with this. Bastard. I hope they lock him up and throw away the key."

"Have you had things like this happen before?" Crissy asked.

"You bet," Anasthasia replied, "but of course I'm not supposed to talk about it. The cruise line likes to pretend that every cruise is paradise on earth, you know."

"How did you get into this work?" Crissy asked out of curiosity.

"It's a long story," she said, "but I did time in the Israeli army, then came back home to Greece. Looked around for work, then ended up doing this because I had a couple of friends who were doing it. Sort of an accident, but I like it. And I'm good at it. They need women to handle some things, you know. Like today. Some of the men tiptoe around situa-

238

tions like this. Sometimes they also band together against the victim, especially a female victim. That little shit Vilos might have convinced Christopolous and the others that you really had been after him. But he couldn't deny what one of his own heard and saw. That's *me*." She pointed at her chest. "Now we've got the bastard by the short and curlies."

"Thank God," Crissy said. "I still wonder about the telephone calls he said he didn't make. They know that the last one came from a public telephone, so they don't know who made it. Christopolous said they'll put a videocam there and try to catch whoever it is on film." Crissy sighed. "So we don't know anything more than we did, except for one thing."

"What's that?" Anasthasia asked.

"That Mark Vilos is a rapist, or a potential one."

Anasthasia looked pleased. "The fucker. And maybe we can keep him and his sick dick off the streets for awhile at least." She sipped her beer.

Crissy could feel her body relaxing and her mind slow down. The tranquilizer had started to work earlier, but now she felt that it was overpowering her, rendering her thinking processes slow, her body limp. "Wow," she said. "I don't know what Luca gave me, but it must have been strong."

"You just go with it," Anasthasia said. "This has been a shock to your system, and you need rest."

"But what about you?" Crissy said.

"Sweetheart, pretend I'm not here," Anasthasia said. "Just drift off. I'm going to rest my feet awhile, so don't you worry. I'll be here."

After all she'd done for her, Crissy felt that she should stay awake and entertain Anasthasia, but sleep overwhelmed her. She fell into a deep and peaceful slumber before she could say another word.

The big woman slipped off her sneakers and socks, wiggled her toes, and massaged her feet, then propped them up on the bed next to Crissy's. She was wearing a pager in case anyone wanted her, in addition to the cell phone she carried at all times, but she doubted that Christopolous would try to get hold of her unless it was to check up on Crissy. The young woman was a material witness in an attempted rape case now, and she was the doctor's girlfriend. Not only that, Anasthasia thought, but she had a case against Mark Vilos. Whoa! She didn't even want to think about the implications of that. She knew her job was on the line because she had given a statement that sent the shipowner's son to the brig. Georgios Vilos was going to know about it, if he didn't already. *Well,* she thought, *I didn't have a choice, did I? Not if I wanted to see justice served.*

With somebody like Mark Vilos, it would be a miracle if he ever spent a day behind bars after leaving the ship's brig. Money coming out his ears and a very powerful family added up to the kind of "justice" that often meant a slap on the wrist, at best.

Crissy slept for a long time, and after she got up, she insisted that Anasthasia leave. "I'm going down to the hospital to have a late dinner with Luca," she said, "so I'll be fine."

"Okay, sweetheart," Anasthasia said. "Just remember that if you need anything—anything at all—give us a call."

Later, when Crissy reached the hospital, Voula took her to the back office, where the three of them had dinner together. Voula's behavior toward Crissy had radically changed when she discovered that Luca was serious about her and that Crissy wasn't simply another passenger chasing after him. They didn't discuss the earlier events, but laughed at Voula's stream of jokes and excellent mimicry. It was a wonderful respite from her worries, and Crissy left feeling buoyed up by their company.

"I'll see you in the disco," Luca said, showing her to the door. "It shouldn't be long."

"I'll be there," she told him. "Bye."

"Bye." His lips formed a kiss, and Crissy returned it, then stepped out into the corridor. She went up to her cabin, freshened her hair and makeup, and decided to change into a cocktail dress.

When she finally reached the disco, she knew Luca wouldn't be there yet, but she looked toward the back of the room where the captain and his party usually sat. The captain and several other officers were there, but Luca hadn't yet arrived. Her gaze shifted to the dance floor, where she saw Rudy and Mina dancing. They were as elegant as ever, Rudy sweeping Mina about as if she were a weightless feather. Then she caught sight of Jenny and Dr. Von Meckling. Jenny was clasped firmly against him, her head on his shoulder, and they were moving very slowly together to their own time, which had little to do with the music.

She walked to the back of the large room to sit at a table along the curving banquette under the windows. She turned to the window behind her. Rain was lashing against it, but nothing beyond that was visible. Turning back around, she was surprised to see a man looming over her in the darkness. It was Luca, and he was staring down at her, smiling.

"Oh, you scared me!" she said with a nervous laugh.

"I'm sorry," he said. "I wanted to surprise you." He leaned down and kissed her, then sat down on the banquette next to her, sliding an arm around her shoulders, hugging her to him. "I should've realized that you might be . . . jumpy."

"No," Crissy said. "I'm not really. I'm just thrilled to see you."

He kissed her again. "I find it very difficult to keep my hands off you," he said.

"Would you like to go someplace where we can be alone?" Crissy asked.

"Let's dance first," he said. He led her to the dance floor, took her into his arms, and they danced slowly, so absorbed in each other that they didn't notice the eyes that were observing them with interest. When the dance was over, they remained on the floor for another, then another, in their own world, enjoying being together to the extent that the rest of the world hardly existed. They returned to their table at last and sat down.

"When you're ready to leave, let me know," he said.

"I'm ready," she replied, "unless you want to stay for one more."

He shook his head and grinned. "I think we'll have a better time elsewhere, don't you agree?"

"You'll get no argument from me," she replied.

They got up and left the disco. "Do you mind if we step out on the deck?" Crissy asked. "I'd like to see the wild, raging sea. It's like a scene out of Melville."

"I should say no," Luca replied, "but for you, anything."

He pushed the nearest exit door open, and they stepped outside. The wind was powerful, and spray lashed the deck. They remained next to the bulkhead, Luca's arm around her shoulder.

Down the deck, she thought she saw movement. "What was that?" she asked Luca.

Following her gaze, he shrugged. "I didn't see anything," he said.

"I could have sworn I saw somebody between the lifeboats," she said.

"It could have been one of the crew," he said. "They're constantly checking to make sure everything's secure in this kind of weather. Besides, you don't have anything to fear, Crissy. I'm here with you." He hugged her to him.

She gazed out to sea, but in the next moment a huge wave crashed against the ship, sending a veritable wall of water up toward them. It came within mere feet of drenching them. "This is a little too wild," she said with a laugh. "Spray's one thing, but this is something else. Let's go back inside."

"I think that's a great idea," Luca said, gazing at her mischievously. "We can get warm and cozy, and we don't have to get wet."

Georgios Vilos was sitting alone in his Kifissia study, where he had been pondering his next move for hours. He thought that he had memorized every vein of gray in every piece of white marble that lined the walls and floors of the palatial room. He had to come up with a new plan fast. His creditors were preparing to descend on him like so many vultures, eager to pick at the flesh and bones of his empire. He was almost certain he knew what he had to do. It was very risky, but it would work.

His cell phone rang, and its sound jerked him out of his reverie with a start. "*Nea?*" he said, flipping it open.

"The package that you sent will not arrive as planned," the voice said.

"I know that," Georgios Vilos said, heaving a sigh. "I've had a call about it. Unfortunately the package and its contents will never get there."

"So what do you suggest?" the voice asked. "There is no way I can recover the package now."

"I realize that," Georgios Vilos said impatiently. "I have another plan, and it will do the trick just as well. It will require your help, of course."

"What do you have in mind?"

"Listen carefully," Georgios Vilos said, "because I don't want to repeat myself."

After he finished detailing his new plan, the caller didn't respond for a moment, then finally said, "It's . . . doable."

"Yes," Georgios Vilos said. "I want to make certain that my son is off the ship. He must disembark with you. When you have everything set up, then you will get Mark and take him with you, so that he won't be aboard later."

"Sensible," the voice replied. Then he added in a tone that sounded gleefully sarcastic to Georgios Vilos's ears, "If you want to spare him."

Georgios Vilos swallowed, making a valiant effort not to yell at the animal on the other end of the line. What kind of man did he think he was? That he would kill his own son? He had sent him repeated messages to get

242

off the ship, but to no avail. "That is a necessity," he murmured. "An absolute necessity. And you'll see to it that he is off the ship with you."

"And if he's in lockup?"

"It only takes one phone call from me to free him," Georgios Vilos snapped. "You'll not leave that ship without him."

"That's easy in any case," the voice said. "I know all the ship's officers and security detail. I can get around them."

"Very good," Vilos said.

Very good for you, but a nuisance for me. I'm not going to fool around trying to free Mark Vilos. Something could go wrong, and I wouldn't be able to get off the ship. The hell with Mark Vilos.

Monika heard a strange sound in her suite and sat bolt upright in bed. The room was in darkness, but she didn't reach over and switch on the light. She didn't want to disturb Jenny, not unless she had to. She listened, straining to hear what it was that had awoken her. For a few moments, there was silence, except for the white noise of the air-conditioning, then she heard it again. Coming from the sitting room of her suite. *Yes!* she thought with alarm. *There is definitely someone in the sitting room.* Her jewelry was locked in the built-in safe in the closet, here in the bedroom, so she wasn't concerned about that, but whoever it was might decide to come in after it.

She eased out from under the bedcovers and slipped off the bed. Tiptoeing on bare feet to the door to the sitting room as quietly as possible, she stood there listening. There! There it was again. Rustling noises. Then the quiet but unmistakable cadence of grunts and groans. After another moment of listening at the door, she slid her hand toward the switch on the wall, the one that she knew would light every lamp and overhead spot, illuminating the entire room. In one swift movement, she pressed the large switch, and the sitting room came to life.

Monika threw her hand to her mouth to stifle a shriek of disgusted surprise. She gasped instead, then drew herself up to her full height, her chin out, head thrown back imperiously. Her face gleamed in the light from the various moisturizing creams she slathered on before going to bed, and the finger she flung toward them was encased in the white cotton of the gloves she slipped on to cover the heavy application of cream to her hands at bedtime.

"You *schwein*!" she said in a low-pitched rumble. "*Schwein!*"

There was a whoop of release as a young man hammered himself into Jenny. On the floor in the center of the sitting room, Jenny was on all fours, completely naked, her hair tumbling down over her face, hiding it from Monika's insults, and mounted atop her, doggy fashion, was a young man whom Monika recognized as one of the stewards, also naked. One of the Ukrainians, if she wasn't mistaken. Short flaxen hair framed his sweaty, flushed face, and his thick lips were curled in a rictus of release. His ecstacy was such that his expression resembled nothing so much as agony. After a final thrust of his hips, he turned and looked at Monika, panting. His lips spread in a wide smile when he saw her.

When Monika didn't move but continued to stare in disbelief at the scene, the young man dismounted, stood up, spread his muscular thighs wide, and held his cock in a hand, waving it at Monika.

"You?" he said in heavily accented English. "Want?" His grin exposed even white teeth.

"Get out of here!" she said in a low, rumbling voice of authority. "Get out at once."

The young man smiled and shrugged, then gathered up his clothing from the couch. He dressed slowly, enjoying the sight of Monika watching him, but she soon shifted her gaze to Jenny, who had lifted herself up off the carpeting and now sat on the couch, making no effort to conceal her nakedness.

"We didn't mean to disturb you," Jenny said to her in an unapologetic voice. She put her hand to her mouth, covering a yawn. "I guess we got a little carried away."

Monika's eyes blazed with a fiery intensity, and her thin brows lifted skyward as she trained a glare of repulsion and anger at Jenny. Her fury was short-lived, however, as the young man finished dressing and went to the cabin door.

"Have a nice day," he called to them with the same thick accent. He waved and strutted out the door, letting it slam behind him.

Jenny giggled and slapped the couch with a hand. "Is he a riot?"

Monika sat down on a chair facing her. Truth be told, she found the young man's shameless naïveté and the incident itself somewhat amusing, but she didn't like surprises. "You gave me a quite a fright," she said calmly.

"I'm sorry, Monika," Jenny said. "Really, I swear. I didn't mean to wake you up." She tossed her blond tresses out of her eyes, and licked her lips, then looked at Monika with Bambi eyes. "I-I was just so desperate," she said in a little-girl voice. "You can imagine what it's like with Ludwig."

"I'd rather not," Monika responded succinctly.

Jenny laughed. "No," she said. "You don't even want to think about it." She retrieved a bathrobe, draped it about her naked body, and sat back down.

Monika fell into a thoughtful silence, her gaze trained on Jenny, gloved fingers silently tapping the chair arms, her mental gears turning swiftly and efficiently as she considered how best to use this incident to her advantage.

Jenny's robe fell open, exposing her body. It was beautiful, if not entirely the work of nature, and she knew it.

When Monika finally spoke, it was in an even, low voice. "You are a very reckless young woman."

"I suppose so," Jenny replied in a bored tone.

"And if you go through with this marriage to Ludwig," Monika went on, "you are going to have to be very careful, especially regarding these sorts of indiscretions."

"I know," Jenny said, "and I can be, believe it or not."

Monika nodded. "Oh, I have no doubts as to your abilities to deceive, Jenny. Your acting talents are exceptional, I think, but you must be very careful about who you take into your confidence."

Jenny looked at her with curiosity. Something in the tone of Monika's voice alerted her to the importance of what was coming.

"Tonight, for example, it makes no difference that I was a witness to your little romp with the help," Monika said, "because we are the best of friends, aren't we? And you can trust me not to tell Ludwig about this."

Jenny nodded, but she wasn't feeling quite as confident as she had a few moments ago.

"On the other hand," Monika continued, "were I not your dear, trusted friend and mentor, or were something to come between us, Jenny, I could destroy your chances of marriage to Ludwig like that." Her eyes brightened, and she made the motion of snapping her fingers together, but there was no sound because of the gloves.

Jenny nodded again. "I know," she said, "but I know you wouldn't do that, Monika."

"We both know that Ludwig trusts me implicitly, as he would a sister. We have a history together, Ludwig and I. We are both from old European

245

families, mine not as rich as his, but my accomplishments and fame have secured our mutual respect and devotion. So, believe me when I say that no matter what solace you might bring to him in his old age, if I should betray our trust—yours and mine, Jenny—Ludwig will see you chased out of Europe." She sat back, her eyes glittering with intensity.

"I understand perfectly," Jenny responded, and she did, too. She realized that Monika was throwing down her gauntlet, and she'd better be on her guard.

"I'm glad you do," Monika said with a smile. "I think we will get along magnificently, you and I. You're going to need a guiding hand—someone who knows the ins and outs—dealing with his estates, all the relatives, the many burdensome social occasions. They can be a bit daunting for one as young and inexperienced as yourself, and believe me, Jenny, they are very important to Ludwig."

"I know that," Jenny replied. "He's made it very clear that I'll have a lot of duties."

Monika nodded. "And I'll be there for you, helping you every step of the way. I wouldn't want to interfere, of course, but I think you'll discover that I make a great ally." She paused for a moment, then added, "I can even be helpful when you feel the need to . . . express yourself in ways that Ludwig would not approve of. Tonight, for example."

"I understand, Monika," she said, "and I appreciate it."

"*Wunderbar*," Monika said. "In the meantime, our lips are sealed, and Ludwig will know nothing of little escapades like tonight."

No, Jenny thought. *Not as long as I do whatever you want me to do.* She had known that her campaign to win Ludwig Von Meckling was going to be challenging, but she'd had no idea that she was going to have to please not only him but this monster sitting across from her. She told herself that it was worth it, that his hundreds of millions were worth it, that she wouldn't have to sacrifice her own, real desires for too long a time. In the meantime, she would have to make certain that Monika was always on her side.

Georgios Vilos picked up his cell phone again and pressed in the number for Captain Papadapolis, who picked up almost immediately.

"Demetrios," Georgios Vilos said. "I need a favor from you right away."

"Of course, Mr. Vilos," the captain replied. "What can I do for you?"

"I want you to put Mark ashore in São Vicente."

"You what?" Captain Papadapolis exclaimed. "But—"

"But nothing," Georgios Vilos replied. "I'm ordering you to put him ashore the moment you dock in São Vicente, Captain."

"Mark has committed a crime, Mr. Vilos," Captain Papadapolis replied. "A very serious crime."

Georgios Vilos restrained himself from shouting. "I don't give a goddamn what he's done, Captain Papadapolis," he said between clenched teeth. "I order you to put him ashore in São Vicente. I will fire you otherwise and see to it that you never get another job in shipping anywhere in the world."

"There could be a lawsuit, Mr. Vilos," the captain pointed out. "Against the shipping line, Mark, you, and myself personally. This could get very nasty."

"I'm aware of that," Georgios Vilos said, "but I want my son out of lockup. Do you understand?"

Captain Papadapolis' mind raced. He was in a quandary: There was no justification for letting Mark Vilos go free, but he didn't want to lose his job, either. He knew Vilos well enough to know that he was as good as his word. *I'll never be able to get another job in the shipping industry,* he thought. *Never.*

"Mr. Vilos," he said, "what if I put Mark under house arrest? That way, he could return to his stateroom. He would be confined there with a security detail posted at the door 24/7."

"An excellent suggestion, Captain," Georgios Vilos replied. *And it would make getting Mark off the ship very easy,* he thought.

"I'll go talk to him right away," Captain Papadapolis said. "I think this would work out for all parties concerned."

"Yes," Vilos agreed. "Very good, Captain. Get back to me later."

"I will, Mr. Vilos. Good-bye," Captain Papadapolis said. He flipped his cell phone closed and sighed. He didn't like this, but it was the only way he could see to save his job and do the right thing. As long as Mark Vilos was under house arrest, he told himself, the plan would work. He decided to go down to the brig and speak to him immediately.

The guard opened the door to Mark's cell, and the captain stepped inside. "I want to talk to you," he said as the guard closed the door behind him.

Mark was propped against a pillow and spread out lengthwise on the cell's built-in metal bed. He stared up at the captain with a smug smile. "I guess I don't have any choice but to listen, do I, Captain?"

"I've spoken to your father," the captain said.

"And?"

"We've decided that you can be put under house arrest, Mark. That way, you can return to your stateroom." The captain cleared his throat. "I'll have to put guards from Security at your door, of course," he added.

Mark sat straight up in bed, glaring at the captain. "I've been arrested, Captain Papadapolis," he snarled. "You yourself had me put in the brig. So I'll stay in jail, thank you."

Demetrios Papadapolis sighed. *The smug son of a bitch,* he thought. *His sense of dignity has been wounded, so he's going to be pigheaded about this.* "I think this would be an excellent compromise, Mark," he went on. "It would satisfy your father and wouldn't upset Ms. Fitzgerald, since you'd be under guard. I think it's a fair solution for everyone, myself included."

"I don't give a damn about satisfying you, that slut, Crissy Fitzgerald, or my father," Mark spat back. "You put me here, and I'm staying here. I refuse to leave. Now get out of my cell, Captain."

Captain Papadapolis realized that nothing he could do or say would change the arrogant, recalcitrant young man's mind. "Have it your way," he said at last.

"I will." Mark laid back against the pillow, his smug smile in place again.

The captain tapped on the cell door, and the guard opened it immediately. "Think about what I've said, Mark."

"Get out."

Chapter Seventeen

The ship approached São Vicente, in the Cape Verde Islands, about eight o'clock in the morning. The weather had cleared, and the skies were sunny. The sea was once again calm, without a whitecap in sight. Crissy had just finished breakfast and found a place at the railing to watch their arrival. The name for the islands, she thought, was a misnomer. There was hardly any green in sight. The island appeared to have been stripped of every tree, bush, and blade of grass that had ever been there. Other than a few weathered tankers and fishing boats, the docks were empty. It looked as if the *Sea Nymph* would be the only cruise ship in port. As they neared the dock, she rushed down to the debarkation deck, where she was supposed to meet Luca.

He spied her first and led her to the exit, where they were hurried through before anyone else. On the dock, they watched as men in small fishing boats approached the aft deck of the ship, calling up to crew who were gathered there as if waiting for them.

"What's going on?" Crissy asked.

"They're selling fish," Luca explained. "The kitchen staff will buy some to cook for the passengers in first-class cabins, and they'll buy some for themselves and other crew, too."

As they walked along the pier toward the shore, young men hawked jewelry that they either carried or had spread out on blankets. They were primarily very simple necklaces and bracelets carved of wood, some with wooden beads, others on cords or leather thongs.

"You need my good-luck necklace," one of the men told Crissy.

The young man looked so poor and ill-fed that she had to stop. "How much is that one?" she asked, pointing to a necklace of wooden beads with a small wooden disc hanging from it.

"One dollar," the young man replied.

"Let me get it for you," Luca said.

"But I've got a dollar bill," Crissy said, taking it out of her wallet. "I bet you don't have anything but euros." She paid the young man, and he thanked her profusely.

They went on their way down the pier. "I'm not so sure that's going to bring you good luck," Luca said, watching her put the necklace in her shoulder bag.

"I'm not, either," she replied. "It doesn't seem to have done much for him."

Luca led her through the down-at-the-heels town. Every building seemed to be on the verge of collapse, but they were very colorfully painted. The streets were filled with litter, and graffiti was on walls everywhere. Broken glass was embedded into the tops of walls, and windows were covered with iron bars. They walked up and down the blighted streets. Some of the buildings had once been beautiful, their architecture imposing. Peeking into a pharmacy, Crissy saw that it had once been magnificent, with heavily carved paneling and mosaic tile work.

"It's a pity to see all of this crumbling to pieces," Crissy said, "and there seems to be a problem with crime."

Luca nodded. "It's a very poor place. It used to be a Portuguese possession, and it was pretty much stripped bare of everything of value a long time ago. It was also used as a slave-trading center. That's why nearly everyone is African. A handful of Portuguese own virtually everything."

"It's so sad," Crissy said, "because the island looks like it could be really beautiful."

"There are some nice beaches," Luca said, "but it's a pretty desolate place otherwise."

They reached a small, run-down town square. In the center was a concrete kiosk, outside which were two or three plastic tables with umbrellas. A sign advertised Coca-Cola. "Want a Coke before we go on?" Luca said. "We can have a seat and people-watch for a bit."

"Yes," Crissy said, fascinated by the poor but colorful spectacle around her.

Their Cokes were served in old-fashioned glass bottles, which she hadn't seen in years, and they cost a nickel each. "I think I'll move here," she joked. As they drank their soda, they watched tall black women, carrying heavy baskets on their heads, walk in and around the square. Many of the baskets held vegetables and fruit.

"They're going to the market," Luca said, "to sell what they can."

They finished their sodas and walked around the small square, looking into the shop windows. Almost without exception, they were owned and tended by Chinese immigrants who sold merchandise from China. Clothing, housewares, sports goods, toys—almost anything one could ask for was available, nearly all of it shoddy in quality.

"This is amazing," Crissy said. "Here on the other side of the world the Chinese own nearly all the stores and sell Chinese merchandise."

"It is amazing," Luca agreed, "especially when you think that the Portuguese owned the place and its closest neighbor is Senegal."

They walked on for a long time, passing a church, where beggars sat on the steps, then on past a derelict-looking school. Eventually, they strolled into an entirely different neighborhood that was mere yards away but light-years in appearance. There was a large square filled with trees and flowers. Benches were arrayed around a fountain that was empty of water, and an ornate but empty kiosk sat at one end. The square was surrounded by beautifully maintained homes, apartment buildings, and a few office buildings with shops on the ground floor. There were a couple of art galleries and craft shops that sold goods made by islanders and small clothing and sporting goods stores.

The day was heating up, and the humidity was stifling. "You want to stop for a glass of wine?" Luca asked. "Maybe something to eat?"

"Yes," Crissy replied. She hadn't realized how far they'd walked, so interested had she been in the sights, depressing though many of them were.

They went into a café along the square. It was very modern, thankfully air-conditioned, and paintings by local artists were hung on the walls. The owners were a very friendly Portuguese couple, who served wine that was made on their estate and simple chicken sandwiches on delicious homemade bread.

Crissy broached the subject first. "What do you think will happen to Mark?" she asked Luca.

Luca shook his head. "It's hard to say. He's committed a crime, of that there's no doubt. But he's also the son of a rich and powerful shipping line owner. I'm a little surprised that the captain is even keeping him in the brig."

251

"No!" Crissy exclaimed. "But . . . but—"

"Crissy," Luca said, "you shouldn't be surprised. You know how most of the world works. If Mark was impoverished and couldn't afford good lawyers, it might be easy to throw him behind bars for a long time. But Mark is filthy rich, his father has legions of lawyers working for him, and the captain's livelihood depends on Georgios Vilos."

"I understand," she replied. "It's going to be very difficult to beat Mark in court."

"You bet it is," Luca said. "They'll try to crucify you. Knowing the way they work, they'd dig up 'witnesses' who are willing to testify that you will have sex with anybody. That sort of thing."

Crissy saw the truth in what he said. "But the captain? Do you really think he would side with the Viloses in a matter like this?"

"I don't know," Luca replied. "But I do know that he loves his job, and that he would think long and hard before he put himself in a position to be fired from it. No only that, but he would be persona non gratia in the entire shipping industry. The Vilos family would see to that. He wouldn't be able to get a job anywhere."

"I hadn't thought about that," Crissy said. "We'll have to wait and see how it plays out."

When they had finished eating, they left the café. Hand in hand, the lovers walked back toward the dock. It was soon time to board the ship, so they went on ahead in order to beat the crowds who would be coming back from the excursion buses. Luca looked at his watch. "We depart in about thirty minutes," he said. "Let me check with Voula and see what's going on. If she's not swamped, what about a quick . . . drink or something in my cabin?"

Crissy saw the mischief in his eyes. "I'd love a drink . . . or something."

Luca called Voula, who told him that everything in the hospital was under control, so he and Crissy went directly to his cabin.

"Welcome to my humble home," he said, swinging the door wide.

Crissy stepped in to see a cabin much like her own, except that on the desk there were framed photographs. She stepped over to look at them, and Luca joined her. "They're on double-sided tape," he said, "so they won't get thrown off."

"That's clever," Crissy said.

"It's necessary," he replied, "unless you want to have broken glass all over the place. That's my parents," he said, pointing to an elegant couple who appeared to be in their sixties. They were both tall and well-dressed, his mother fair and blond, his father a shade darker, with black hair. "And that's me with Bocco, my old golden retriever. He died while I was in college. Isn't he beautiful?"

"You look so happy," Crissy said. "And he looks like he's smiling."

"He always smiled," Luca said.

"What does his name mean?"

"Good for nothing," Luca said with a laugh. "I called him that because when he was a puppy he was always jumping in the shower with me. Or the bathtub. He loved water."

"And those are my aunt and uncle and cousins at a wedding. She's my father's sister. Me, when I got my medical degree."

"I think you're even better looking now," Crissy said, turning to him.

He wrapped his arms around her and kissed her passionately. "Love does that," he said.

He quickly stripped off his uniform, then helped Crissy undress.

"It's the heat," he said. "I think it makes me horny."

"Then maybe we should live in the tropics," Crissy said.

"I think so," he said, taking her into his arms and kissing her deeply.

They made love, quickly but passionately, their desire fed by their close proximity for the last few hours. When it was over, they were both covered with the sheen of sweat. "I would like to lick you clean," Luca said.

Crissy laughed. "I don't think you have time."

"Maybe we should take time," he replied.

He was still inside her, and Crissy felt him becoming engorged again. She gasped and clung to him as he began slowly moving in and out of her, kissing her tenderly and gently stroking her. When they came, it was sudden and powerful and as one. She didn't think she'd ever known such ecstacy before. Luca moaned as he flooded her with his seed, then held onto her tightly, as if he would never let her go.

They heard the ship's deep horn announcing its departure, and that was the signal that Luca needed to get back to the hospital. Although they couldn't enjoy the afterglow of the lovemaking for long, they made plans to meet at the disco later.

As Crissy walked back to her cabin to change clothes, she looked up at the funnel, discharging its dark smoke, which the wind immediately picked up and carried in an almost horizontal line behind them.

She remembered that Luca had told her the trip from the Cape Verde Islands to Brazil would only take two days aboard the *Sea Nymph,* whereas it was often up to five days on most ships. She could hardly believe that she was on her way across the Atlantic to South America and the Amazon River. Glad she'd already eaten something, she decided to bypass lunch and go up to the pool deck and enjoy the sunshine. After two days of gray skies and rain, it would be a welcome change.

In her cabin, she quickly showered and changed into a bathing suit, over which she wrapped and tied a long, colorful sarong. She was reaching for her handbag when she remembered the envelopes she'd taken from Mark's cabin.

Oh, my God! she thought. *I can't believe I forgot all about them.* The near rape experience had been so frightening, the envelopes had been wiped from her thought. She dug deeper then, making certain that she retrieved all of them from the bottom of the bag where she had put them. They were most likely of no consequence now, she reasoned, but she decided to have a look. She looked at the plain white envelopes with Mark's name in black ink on the front of each one, along with a date in the upper right-hand corner. His name and the date were written in block letters that looked almost childish.

She opened the envelope with the earliest date and unfolded the note that it held. Suddenly she felt as if she were invading someone's privacy. *That's exactly what I'm doing,* she told herself. *These notes are addressed to Mark.* Yet there might be information that would be useful to the authorities.

She opened the first one and began to read, noting that the notes were written in the same childish block letters that was used on the envelopes.

> Makelos,
> You must get off the ship at the next port of call. Don't ask any questions, just do as I say. It is imperative that you get off as soon as possible. This is a situation beyond my control.
> Your Father

Crissy read it again, then folded it back up and slipped it inside the envelope. Why disembark? she wondered. Was the message just a demand that Mark return home? Was his father simply being the suffocating parent that Mark had said he was? She didn't know, of course, but she picked up the next envelope and opened it.

Makelos,

    Get off that ship now. Disembark immediately. The port does not matter. This is a matter of life or death. Please, I beg you. Get off now.

    Your Father

The man was nearly hysterical, Crissy thought, or he certainly gave that appearance. It didn't make sense to her that his language would be as dramatic as it was if he was simply trying to lure his son back home. Was it really a matter of life or death, or was that just a ploy on his father's part?

Sighing with frustration, she opened the next envelope.

My Son,

    I beg and plead with you to disembark. You can have anything you want after you do. I cannot emphasize enough that this is a matter of life or death. I am not playing games with you, Makelos. You must disembark at once. Your mother and I beseech you. Please.

    Your Father and Mother

How odd, she thought. Makelos is suddenly "My Son," and he'd also included Mark's mother in his plea, while she'd been left out before. Well, maybe it wasn't so odd. Was this a ploy to strengthen his argument? Maybe Mark had some affection for his mother that he didn't have for his father. His initial demand had become a plea, his tone softer. Crissy put the message back in its envelope and opened the next one.

Makelos, My Precious Son,

    Please believe me and your mother. You must get off the ship in São Vicente. This is your last chance. I beg you, your mother begs you. Anything is yours if you disembark in São Vicente. Please. It is your last chance to save yourself.

    Your Father and Mother

Crissy knew, of course, that São Vicente was the town where they had just docked in the Cape Verde Islands, the *Sea Nymph*'s last stop. Why was that the last chance to save himself? she wondered. From what? Or whom? If Georgios Vilos wanted Mark to get off the ship so desperately, why didn't he spell out the danger to him? She wondered if Vilos knew that his son couldn't get off the ship now. He obviously hadn't when he'd sent this message, but she was fairly certain that the captain had informed Vilos by now that Mark was locked in the brig.

Crissy tapped the note against her chin, wondering what course of action she should take. *I'll have to go to the captain. No one else will do. And unfortunately, I'll have to confess to him that I stole these notes from Mark's cabin.* He shouldn't be too upset about that, she thought. After all, Mark did try to rape her, and she was trying to find out if he was the caller and if he'd torn up her underwear. She'd thought the notes might be helpful in discovering if he was the culprit.

She placed all of the envelopes in her shoulder bag, carefully positioning them in the bottom again.

She found the captain's card and dialed his number. When a machine picked up, she left a message indicating that she had information about a possible emergency situation aboard the *Sea Nymph* and that she would be in her cabin waiting to hear from him.

That done, she sat down on her bed, waiting for the telephone to ring. After nearly an hour during which she tried to read, she began to lose patience. She tried his number again, and again got his machine.

At a knock on the cabin door, she went to answer it. Captain Papadapolis stood in the hallway, his perpetual smile in place. "Hello," he said. "I've been trying to reach you for the longest time, but got no response. So I decided to come to your cabin and see what's going on."

"But my telephone didn't ring," Crissy said.

"May I come in?" he asked.

"Oh, sorry," she said, "of course." She opened the door wide and stepped back out of his way.

"Mind if I have a look at your telephone?" he asked.

"No, of course not," Crissy said.

He went to the telephone, then let out a laugh. "The ringer is turned off," he said.

"But I didn't turn it off," Crissy replied.

"Well, someone did," the captain said. "No matter. It's working now." He turned to her. "Care to tell me what the emergency is, if there is one?"

"First I have to tell you how I came by the information," Crissy said in a serious voice. "When I suspected that Mark Vilos was making the telephone calls to me, I went to his stateroom for lunch. The day that he tried to rape me. When I got to Mark's, he wasn't quite ready. He went back into the bedroom to finish dressing, and when he did, I took some messages from his desk. I'd seen them the first time I went there for dinner, and he said they were messages from his father. He wasn't opening them, so I don't know how he knew. But anyway, I thought maybe they might have information in them that would be useful as far as finding out whether or not he was making the calls. Do you know what I mean? I didn't know whether they were really from his father or what. I thought he might be lying." She paused and looked at the captain.

The captain nodded. "Go on."

"Anyway, when he was out of the room, I took a few of them. There were a lot of them, and I picked a few from different parts of the stack. Then with everything that happened, I forgot all about them until this afternoon. I had them in my shoulder bag, so I got them out and read them."

Crissy extricated the messages from the bottom of her shoulder bag and handed them to the captain. "I think it's best if you read them for yourself," she said. "When I read these, I thought you should see them at once."

He took the envelopes from her and looked them over carefully.

"They're all dated," she said, "and I read them from the earliest date to the latest. I felt like I was invading someone's privacy, but I'm glad now that I did it."

"Well, I'll do what you did, if you'll bear with me," he said. He took the earliest message out of its envelope and read it, then went through the others with increasing speed. By the time he had read the last one, the expression on his face had turned to one of concern.

He looked up at Crissy. "I don't know what to make of all this," he said. "The question is, of course, whether or not there is any validity in what Georgios Vilos says at all. I know him quite well, and wouldn't put anything past him. Georgios Vilos is obviously desperate to have Mark back home for whatever reason."

He smoothed his hair back at one side, lost in thought for a moment. "On the other hand," he continued, "this is a bit extreme even for Georgios Vilos. I can tell you this much. After Mark attacked you, we found plastic explosives in his stateroom."

"What?" Crissy exclaimed.

The captain nodded. "Yes. In a steamer trunk that Mark had brought aboard, there was a package of Semtex. Enough to blow a hole in the ship and sink her."

"Oh, my God," Crissy said. "I wouldn't have thought that he was capable of such a thing. He seems to really love the ship. He told me he'd brought the trunk aboard as a favor to his father."

"Yes," the captain said. "He claims not to know anything about it, and his father denies any knowledge of it, too. We're working under the assumption that the Semtex was planted by terrorists. I must say they were very clever to hide them the way they did."

"This is unbelievable," Crissy said.

"Unfortunately, it's not," he responded. "In any case, you said that there were more of these messages?"

"Yes," she replied. "Quite a few more."

"We'll have to get those," he said, "and see what they have to say."

"What can be done about it?" she asked. "Don't you think some kind of immediate action is required?"

"The first thing I'm going to do is get the rest of the messages in his suite, then I'll get hold of Georgios Vilos again," the captain said. "See what he has to say about this."

He paused and looked her in the eye. "I trust you haven't told anyone else about this?"

Crissy shook her head. "I just read the letters a little over an hour ago, and I wouldn't tell anybody anyway."

"Then please do me a favor and don't say a word about this or the explosives. If any passengers found out there were explosives aboard, they would get hysterical."

"I understand," Crissy said. "I won't breathe a word of it to anyone."

"Good," he said. "I know it makes it hard on you, but please keep it to yourself. I'll start trying to chase down Vilos and see what this is about."

"Will you let me know?" she asked.

He looked thoughtful for a moment, then nodded. "You deserve that much," he said, "for coming up with this information, however valuable it may or may not be. There is something very mysterious about this business, and frankly," he said with a scowl, "very disturbing."

Chapter Eighteen

The remainder of the day at sea was uneventful as the ship progressed through calm waters toward Brazil. The weather was perfect—sunny with clear skies and warm breezes. In the evening, Crissy went to the disco to meet up with Luca. She was a little early, but Valentin appeared at her shoulder within minutes.

"Care to dance?" he asked.

"Why, yes, Valentin," she replied.

On the dance floor, he held her closely. "I hardly see you at all, Crissy," he said.

"I've been around," she replied, deliberately being vague. "How have you been? Did you get seasick or anything during the storm?"

He shook his head. "Oh, no," he said. "Iron stomach, I guess." He smiled. "And you?"

"I was fine," she said. "I—"

There was a tap on Valentin's shoulder, and he jerked. The captain, all gleaming teeth, said, "Hello. Could I break in, please?"

Crissy saw a momentary flash of anger in Valentin's eyes, but he smiled and nodded to the captain graciously, then looked at Crissy. "I will see you later," he said, and walked toward the bar, his bearing stiff, his hands balled into fists at his sides.

"I hope you don't mind, Crissy," the captain said.

"No, not at all," she replied. "It's a pleasure."

The captain took her into his arms, holding her at an appropriate distance, and began leading her about the floor in his graceful manner. "I have to confess that I have an ulterior motive," he said, still wearing his public smile.

"Oh?"

"Do you mind sitting with me for a few minutes after this dance?" he asked. "I would like to talk to you privately."

"No, of course not," Crissy replied, wondering what Captain Papadapolis wanted to talk to her about.

The dance soon ended, and he led her to an unoccupied table at the back of the room where the tables close by were unoccupied as well.

He leaned in close. "We went into Mark Vilos' cabin," he said, "to get the rest of the messages you said you had seen there."

"Yes? And did they tell you something useful?" she asked.

The captain shook his head. "No. The messages weren't there."

"What?" she exclaimed. She immediately realized that she'd spoken too loudly and quieted her voice. "But I saw them there," she insisted. "On his desk."

He gazed into her eyes. "Oh, I believe you," he said. "I don't doubt your word at all. But that's not what I wanted to talk to you about."

Crissy gazed at him with curiosity. "What is it?" she asked. "Have you found something else?"

"No, but I've talked to Georgios Vilos about the messages."

"And?"

"He says that he wrote the notes to Mark because he had received a threat that someone might place a bomb on the ship."

"Did he mention that to you before?" Crissy asked.

The captain shook his head. "No, and I think that's odd. He told me that he didn't think the threats were important enough to cancel the cruise. He thought that they might be coming from a business competitor. He explained the messages by saying that he decided to take extra precautions and get Mark off the ship just in case."

"I think that's outrageous," Crissy said.

The captain nodded. "Well, I didn't appreciate not knowing about the threats myself, but if we cancelled a cruise every time someone calls in a threat, we'd seldom leave the dock." His expression turned thoughtful. "Still, I find it very strange that Vilos has been trying to get Mark to leave the ship if he doesn't think there's any real danger."

"Yes," Crissy agreed, "and the notes really sounded desperate."

The captain looked at her thoughtfully. "You're right about that."

"If there's anything I can do," Crissy said, "I'll be glad to."

"You've been a great help already. I just wish I could shake this feeling that something is terribly wrong."

Luca still hadn't shown up at the disco by midnight. She spent the evening chatting with a Canadian couple, then went back to her cabin to give Luca a call at the hospital. Even if he was busy with an emergency, she could find out from Voula if and when he was going to be able to get away. That was one of the drawbacks to dating a doctor, Luca had told her—a part of your life was sacrificed to the emergencies that arose regularly, and his frequent and unpredictable unavailability. Crissy smiled at the thought. She didn't feel as if she was sacrificing anything being with Luca.

She opened the door to her cabin and went straight to the telephone, but just before she picked up the receiver, it rang. It startled her initially, but then she smiled. *Luca.* There hadn't been a call since Mark had been in the brig, so she had nothing to fear.

She picked up the receiver. "Hi, sweetheart," she said.

The sound of breathing assailed her as never before.

She jerked and almost dropped the receiver, but recovered herself, although the hand she held the receiver with was shaking. "Who is this?" she demanded.

The breathing continued, an intake of breath followed by an exhalation, even, rhythmic, and mortifying in its noisy silence.

"Who is this?" she demanded again. She felt her heart begin to race and cold sweat bead on her forehead.

The breathing continued, in and out, in and out, in and out.

Crissy wanted to scream, but she didn't want the caller to get the satisfaction of hearing the fear in her voice. She slammed down the receiver, then turned off the ringer in case he called back. She stood staring at herself for a moment in the mirror that ran the length of the wall above the desk, angry that she could see herself trembling. She turned around to face the opposite wall and took a few deep breaths. She had to call the captain and Luca, but she could hardly bring herself to touch the telephone again. The captain, she remembered, was in the disco, and Luca was still at work in the hospital.

Forcing herself to pick up the telephone receiver, she dialed the number for the hospital.

Voula answered immediately. "Hospital," she said.

"Voula, it's Crissy," she said. "Is it possible to speak to Luca for just a second?"

"Hold on, Crissy," she replied.

Luca picked up at once. "Hi," he said. "How are you?"

"Luca," she said. "I've had another one of those telephone calls."

"What?" he exclaimed. "Oh, God, no, Crissy. I can't believe this."

"I can't, either," she replied. "You can guess what really puzzles me now."

"Yes," he said. "Mark Vilos is in the brig without a telephone."

"Exactly," she said. "So who's doing this? I feel more confused than ever."

"I'll be finished here in a few minutes," Luca said. "Why don't you come down here and wait for me. You won't have to be there alone."

"Okay," she replied.

"Have you talked to Mikelos or anyone yet?" he asked.

"No," Crissy replied. "I called you first thing."

"I'm going to call Mikelos as soon as we hang up," Luca said. "This may be a break for us. To find out who the real culprit is."

"How's that?" Crissy asked.

"Well, we know for certain that it's not Mark," Luca said. "And depending on where Mikelos has minicams set up, he may have the caller on tape."

"I hope so," Crissy said. "I thought it was all over."

"Crissy," Luca said, "it's going to end soon. I'm sure of it. Just get yourself down here. I'm calling Mikelos now." He made kissing noises. "Love you."

"I love you, too," she said.

She hung up the telephone and fetched her purse, then went to the door. She could hardly wait to get out of the cabin and down to the hospital and Luca.

Luca was waiting for her, and the two went to his cabin. Once there, he told her what Mikelos had said.

"First, they're checking to see where the call originated," Luca said.

"Like the last time," Crissy said with a sigh.

"Then they'll see if they've got anything on tape," he went on. "It's going to take awhile."

"If they've got a videocam on the telephone where the call was made," Crissy said. "And that's a big 'if.' "

Luca nodded, massaging her shoulders. "I know," he said. "But don't worry. Mikelos is going to catch the bastard who's doing this. I'm sure of it, Crissy." He kissed her neck tenderly.

"I wish I felt so certain," she murmured. She felt his lips brushing against her and shivered. "You feel so wonderful. Let's forget about this tonight." He put his arms around her, and his mouth sought hers.

As wondrous as their lovemaking was, Crissy still couldn't shake a single question that persisted in occupying her thoughts: If Mark hadn't made the calls and torn up her underwear, then who did?

Chapter Nineteen

Crissy returned to her cabin early to change clothes for breakfast, then went back to put on a swimsuit. The day at sea was beautiful, and she decided to spend most of it sunning on the pool deck. But before she had the chance, there was a knock on the door, and it startled her. Who on earth? she wondered. Crossing to it, she opened the cabin door slightly and saw Mikelos.

"Hi," she said, swinging the door back. "Come in."

Mikelos stepped just inside the door. "Would you come with me down to Security?"

"Sure," Crissy replied. "Let me get my shoulder bag." She fetched it from the chair where she'd dropped it earlier. "What is it, Mikelos?" she asked, rejoining him at the door.

"You'll see," he said, going back out into the hallway.

She followed him to the stairwell, and they walked down to Security, Crissy rushing to keep up with the big man's gait. At the Deck Two landing, still curious, Crissy asked, "Mikelos, has something happened? Please, tell me."

He kept walking. "You'll see," he repeated.

They reached Security, and he opened the door and held it for her. Crissy stepped into the office. "We're going in there," Mikelos said, indicating another door. He swung it open, and Crissy went into the adjoining office. She was surprised to see Monika sitting at a desk, her big gold pocketbook in her lap.

"Hello, Monika," she said. "What are you doing here?"

Monika's lips were fixed in a tight slash of red, and she didn't respond to Crissy.

"Here," Mikelos said, waving a hand at a chair. "Have a seat, Crissy."

"Thank you," she replied, sitting down, her curiosity more aroused than ever.

She watched as Mikelos went to a wall switch and dimmed the lights. The room was almost dark, but as her eyes adjusted, Crissy could see what he was doing. "I have something I want you to look at," he said, nodding toward an array of monitors on a long, narrow built-in desk. "Both of you."

He picked up a small videocassette from where it lay on the desk and slipped it into a player. One of the monitors came to life, casting off a pale, flickering light in the room. In the upper right-hand corner of the screen, Crissy saw that the time was noted, the seconds ticking off one by one. Her attention was momentarily averted from the screen when she saw Mikelos reach for the dimmer switch again, turning the light all the way down.

Refocusing on the monitor, Crissy immediately recognized one of the ship's public telephones. The picture, although it was black and white, was of excellent quality. She almost gasped, suddenly realizing why Mikelos had brought her here. He had succeeded in capturing her mysterious caller on video.

The monitor was static for several seconds, as the time continued to tick by in the upper right-hand corner. Abruptly there was movement, and Monika's unmistakable figure appeared, her big gold pocketbook in hand. Crissy watched as the woman placed the pocketbook on the carpeting. With one hand she picked up the receiver, then she pressed in a number, using the long, lacquered nails of the other.

Fascinated but simultaneously repulsed, Crissy saw Monika turn slightly, her profile captured by the camera. The woman began breathing in and out, her mouth almost touching the telephone receiver, her every intake and expulsion of breath visible on the monitor. After several seconds, she replaced the receiver in its cradle, then turned around. She stood facing the camera. Crissy watched as Monika began to laugh. For a moment, she held one of her bejeweled hands at her stomach, as if to calm its heaving, then she moved it up to her mouth, covering her lips, the rings on her fingers reflecting light. Finally, her merriment contained, she reached down and picked up her gold pocketbook by its handles and strode out of the camera's range.

Mikelos turned the dimmer switch, and the room was bathed in light again. "So you can see who's been harassing you, Crissy," Mikelos said.

Crissy gazed over at Monika, who sat mutely staring into the distance, her lips still fixed in a scarlet line. She looked, Crissy thought, as if she was in another world, refusing to accept the reality of this one. Crissy wanted to slap her face, yet at the same time, she felt pity for the woman. *Why?* she wondered. *What would drive her to do such a thing?*

Clearing her throat, Crissy asked her. "Monika," she said, "why did you do this?"

Monika continued to stare into the distance, refusing to acknowledge Crissy's question.

"I used to think that you were my friend," Crissy said. She felt on the verge of tears, but was determined not to shed any. "I don't understand why you would do such a thing."

Mikelos stood near the wall watching, but didn't interfere. He wanted Crissy to have her chance to get some answers before he began his own questioning.

Monika took a deep breath. "I—I was just playing a little joke," she murmured. She flicked a glance at Crissy out of the corner of her eye.

"A joke!" Crissy exclaimed. "You had me scared half to death. I can imagine how you would react if somebody did something like that to you."

"I—I didn't mean any harm," Monika said. "I really didn't."

Crissy felt compelled to slap her again, she was so enraged, but she restrained herself. She wondered if Monika's words had a grain of truth in them. Was she jealous, as Luca had suggested? Was she sick? She didn't know, but whatever the reason, she found Monika's behavior reprehensible.

The room was silent, Monika now staring at the floor, one hand at her brow, agitated fingers hiding her eyes, as if she didn't want anyone to see tears that might well up in them.

"The telephone calls may have been like a mean, childish joke," Crissy said, "but tearing up my underwear was . . . was sick, Monika. Really sick." She paused, waiting for a reaction, but none was forthcoming. "How did you get in my cabin, anyway?"

"I . . . I had Jenny's key card," Monika replied in a barely audible voice. "I'd borrowed it from her earlier because I had to go to the ladies' room, and your cabin was close by."

"Do you still have it?" Crissy asked.

Monika shook her head. "Oh, no. Of course not." She voice choked. "I-I don't know what possessed me." She gazed at Crissy with pleading eyes. "I-I didn't mean any real harm."

Crissy glared at the older woman. Monika looked like an old, broken doll slumped in the chair. Worse, she looked pathetic.

"Do you want to press charges?" Mikelos asked quietly.

Crissy shifted nervously in her chair, wondering what to do. Monika deserved nothing better, she thought. She could really cause trouble for the woman. She was a minor celebrity in Europe, and if word got out of her misadventures aboard the *Sea Nymph,* it would be very embarrassing for her, if nothing else. Word would probably leak out anyway. Mikelos would inevitably tell his pals in Security, and the tale would spread, no doubt reaching Vienna in a matter of weeks, if not hours.

Crissy gazed at Monika, the hand at her brow shaking slightly. "Will this be the end of it, Monika?" she asked.

The head, topped by its wild Medusa-like hair, nodded. "Oh, yes, Crissy," she said softly. She rummaged in her gold back and extracted a Kleenex. "I-I will never . . . play a joke like this again."

"Do you promise me that?" Crissy asked.

"Yes, darling," Monika said, finally peering over at her with a pitiable expression. "I'm so very sorry. It was a silly trick to play."

Silly doesn't even begin to describe it, Crissy thought. "Okay," she said. "If you promise, then I won't press charges." She looked up at Mikelos, who stood with his arms across his chest. He nodded.

"Thank you, Crissy, darling," Monika said. "I-I just hope you won't say anything to anyone. I see that I've done a very foolish thing, and I'm very sorry for it." She dabbed her eyes with the Kleenex, as if wiping away tears, but Crissy didn't see any. "I hope you forgive me, darling," she added. "Please."

"I-I forgive you, Monika," Crissy said, although she knew in her heart that she hadn't. Not yet. The wound that Monika had inflicted on her was still too fresh in her mind for that.

"Well, I guess that wraps it up," Mikelos said. "That is, if you're absolutely certain, Crissy." He gazed at her with a questioning look.

Crissy nodded. "I'm certain," she said. "I don't see any point."

Monika quickly rose to her feet. "Thank you, darling," she murmured. Lifting the Kleenex to her eyes, she dabbed them again.

Maybe she imagines tears, Crissy thought.

Monika hurried out of the room, her high heels click-clacking on the tile, letting the door slam behind her.

"I have to say that I was surprised," Mikelos said.

"Me, too," Crissy agreed. "I still can't believe she did it, and she claims it was just a joke!"

Mikelos shook his head. "It was no joke. She's got a twisted mind, that one."

"I wonder why she did it," Crissy asked him.

"Who knows? She probably envies you, Crissy," Mikelos said. "She's not young and good-looking like you are, and she resents you."

"Well, whatever it was," Crissy said, rising to her feet, "this should put a stop to it. Thank God."

Mikelos nodded.

"Thank you very much for the trouble you've gone to, Mikelos," she said.

"It's my job," he replied. "I'm glad we finally caught her at it." He paused. "Would you like me to take you back up to your cabin?"

"No," Crissy replied. "I'm . . . fine, but thanks. You've been great."

He opened the door for her and held it, then walked her to the outer door. "Call if you need anything," he said.

"I will."

Crissy dropped her shoulder bag and heaved a sigh. She was relieved that her tormentor had been caught, but she had expected to feel joyous. The sight of Monika in Security had only been depressing. She remembered how she had been in awe of Monika at the start of the cruise. She'd thought the woman had everything: She was sophisticated, and she had both money and fame. She could hardly believe that such a rare creature had taken her under her wing. Now, she saw that Monika was a sad, lonely, desperate woman, her mind twisted by envy and jealousy and greed.

The telephone rang, and Crissy gazed over at it, then went to pick it up. "Hello," she said, realizing that she no longer feared answering it.

"Crissy, it's Gudrun from the duty-free shop. How are you?"

"I'm fine," Crissy said. "And you?"

"Oh, I'm always okay," Gudrun said with a laugh, "but I wondered if you might be interested in a proposition that Anna, the Russian girl who runs the shop opposite me, has for you."

"Oh, no," Crissy said, laughing. "What is it this time? Hairpieces? Jewel-studded combs?"

"No, no," Gudrun said. "She has some beautiful formal gowns. Absolutely beautiful. She saw you when you were all ready for the last formal night and thought you were beautiful. Anyway, she asked me to see if you would wear one of the fabulous gowns that she has. If anybody asks, you tell them where you got it. Simple. And you can keep the gown."

"Really?" Crissy said.

"Really," Gudrun echoed. "And it's probably a very expensive one. Why don't you come up and try some on, and we'll decide? You can wear it tonight and in the future. Think, when you and Luca get married, you are going to need lots of formal gowns."

"When Luca and I—?" Crissy was momentarily nonplussed by Gudrun's statement.

"Oh, the whole crew knows about you and Luca, Crissy," Gudrun said. "Didn't you realize that? They're all talking about the two of you and what a wonderful couple you make."

"No, I didn't realize," she responded.

"Well, so you see," Gudrun said. "You are the talk of the ship, so you have to look especially beautiful, don't you? So I'll see you in thirty minutes or less." With that, Gudrun hung up the phone.

Crissy replaced the receiver in its cradle and sighed, but it was a happy sigh. The telephone call took her mind off Monika. It also excited her, because the word of her relationship with Luca was out, and everyone considered it serious. She picked up her shoulder bag and headed to the door, thankful for a diversion.

She created a sensation when she walked into the dining room on the arm of the maître d'. As she proceeded to the table, heads turned, and Crissy heard gasps of delight and murmured conversation. The dress that she, Gudrun, and Anna had decided on was a full-length silk chiffon. The low-cut bodice was a dark purple entirely covered with beaded flowers that reflected the light, and the flowing skirt, layered chiffon of varying lengths in the very palest purple, was beaded in flowerlike patterns that formed bouquets at the waist, descending to sprinkled flowers and tendrils toward the hem. She wore her hair in a simple chignon at her neck with no adornment. Small amethyst studs—Gudrun's— decorated her ears, and a tiny diamond and amethyst bangle—Anna's—

was at her wrist. She carried a small golden minaudière from Anna's shop.

When they reached the table, everyone looked at her with expressions she could only describe as awe. Rudy rose to his feet and bowed, and Dr. Von Meckling half rose and ogled her admiringly. "My God!" Mina declared. "You look ravishing! That is one of the most beautiful dresses I've ever seen."

Monika gazed at her with a tight smile. "Lovely," she murmured.

Jenny smiled at her. "I think you get the message," she said. "You're a killer."

"Well, thank you, everyone," Crissy said, enthused by their reception, although she expected Monika to be nice—after all, Monika was worried that she would tell the others about their visit with Mikelos. "All of you look wonderful. Oh, and Rudy, I love your striped bow tie and cummerbund."

Rudy nodded his thanks.

Crissy noticed that Jenny was in one of her less outrageous gowns with a silk throw wrapped about her shoulders. It concealed her décolletage to some extent, and Crissy wondered if she was making an effort to be more modest to suit Dr. Von Meckling.

"I got this from Anna in one of the duty-free shops," Crissy said. "She has some really beautiful things."

"I'll have to have a look," Mina said. "I've passed it dozens of times, but haven't bothered to go in. It's so small, I wouldn't have thought it had such treasures. You look a dream."

The waiter appeared with menus, and they perused them, discussing the options. It was, Crissy thought, as if there had never been any trouble among them at all. After they ordered, the conversation turned to the Amazon and Belém, the port in northern Brazil where they would be stopping early in the morning. No one aside from Monika and Dr. Von Meckling had been to Brazil before, and even they had yet to see Belém.

"Are-are you taking an excursion?" Monika asked Crissy sweetly but haltingly, as if she were treading on dangerous ground and must be careful.

"Yes," she said. "They sounded very interesting, so I'm taking the all-day one."

"That's wonderful," Monika replied. "You'll learn so much. And what about you, Jenny, dear? Are you taking an excursion?"

"Ludwig and I may go ashore," Jenny said, "but if we do, we'll just go to a restaurant close by. He doesn't want to go on any excursions. The heat and humidity are too much, he says."

"I'm sure it will be terribly hot and humid," Monika said.

"I hear we have to disembark on tenders," Mina said. "That can be very tricky."

"Yes," Rudy remarked. "The place we're going to dock can't handle the ship, so we anchor offshore and take the tenders in. It shouldn't be difficult if the weather is nice."

"I think it sounds very exciting," Crissy said. "Everything from the opera house and cathedral to a zoo and a walk through the jungle."

"It is a place to be on your guard," Monika said.

"There are lots of places like that, aren't there?" Crissy replied, gazing at Monika.

"Well, yes," Monika said sheepishly. She cleared her throat. "It's like many places in Brazil, unfortunately. Pickpockets, children begging, that sort of thing. And remember that the animals can have fleas when people offer to take your picture with a pet monkey or sloth."

"Oh, that's disgusting," Jenny said.

"It's true," Monika replied.

"The area got rich from rubber," Dr. Von Meckling said. "Or rather a few families did, but the wealth was spread about a bit. That's how they built the Teatro da Paz. It's a lovely rococo building. Nowadays, it's mostly timber and jute and nuts and cacao that bring in the money, but there's still dire poverty and lack of education. There are schools, but many of them don't have teachers. A sad state of affairs."

Crissy had never heard him contribute this much to the conversation, and wondered if Jenny was having a salubrious effect on the man. Perhaps she was good for him. Her youth and vitality, let alone her attractiveness, were probably just what the doctor needed.

"We have banker friends in São Paulo," the old doctor continued, "and they have a virtual army of bodyguards to protect them. They helicopter from their *finca* in the countryside where they live to the roof of their banking headquarters in São Paulo where they work. This is not merely a convenience, you understand. It is practically a necessity because of the danger of kidnapping or robbery. I've visited them a few times over the years, and their *finca* is somewhere in the neighborhood of two hundred thousand acres. There, they have a small army to protect them. I

271

remember one time going with them to visit friends of theirs several miles away, and we went in armored Mercedes limousines, surrounded by jeeps with machine guns mounted on them. Back and front of us and on both sides."

"You must have felt very safe then," Jenny said.

Dr. Von Meckling shook his head. "On the contrary, my dear, it had the reverse effect. One felt extremely threatened. All those guns and soldiers or bodyguards were intimidating, even if they were supposed to be protecting you. One wondered why they were necessary. I knew, of course, but still it gave me an uneasy feeling. What if they turned on their employers? It happens all the time, you know."

"Is it still like that, Dr. Von Meckling?" Crissy asked.

He nodded. "Oh, yes, my dear," he replied. "I'm not talking about my youth, but visits made in the last few years."

"I guess that's why our excursions will have armed guards," Mina said.

"Really?" Crissy said.

"Yes," Mina said. "They don't emphasize it, but the cruise director told me that armed guards will be on all the buses."

"Well, it really does sound exciting," Crissy said. "Even more exciting than I'd thought."

There was laughter.

"I'm sure we'll be perfectly safe," Monika said. "They won't take us into dangerous areas."

"Is everyone going to the show tonight?" Rudy asked.

There were assents around the table.

"Wonderful," he said. "Mina and I will go ahead and reserve our usual table, and I'll order champagne."

"We'll see you there," Crissy said.

Later, the disco was very crowded, a sea of black ties and gowns swirling about the dance floor, gathered around the tables, and standing three deep at the bar, the stools at which were all filled. Crissy had danced several times with Rudy and once with Dr. Von Meckling. One of the ship's young officers asked her to dance to a number of fast tunes, and she enjoyed it, the time passing in a blur. From time to time, she searched the back of the room for signs of Luca, but he had yet to show up. The captain and his party had arrived very late, but he hadn't been with them. She assumed that he was taking care of a medical emergency. The heat and smoke in the crowded disco began to close in on her, and she didn't want to dance anymore, at least not for awhile. She saw the captain and his party leave.

Crissy picked up her minaudière and headed for the door, intending to cool off out on deck. She left the disco by the port exit and went to the restroom, then walked down one flight of stairs and out the nearest exit to the deck. There was no one else on this stretch of deck, but at this hour she didn't expect there would be unless strollers leaving the disco passed by.

The breezy night air, humid though it was, felt wonderful after the smoke-filled disco, and it smelled fresh and reviving, and surprisingly, a bit earthy. Brazil, she thought. It had to be. How strange it was, this aroma of land in her nostrils. It was powerful and unmistakable, and something she had never experienced before. They must be nearing the coast. She knew that the ship would enter the Amazon River around four o'clock, but they wouldn't reach the little port near Belém until about nine o'clock.

She stood at the railing, leaning against a support beam, looking up at the sky. It was another night for stargazing, with hardly a cloud visible. Looking out at the sea, she couldn't see another ship's lights in the distance or any other light; only the reflection of the *Sea Nymph*'s lights on the surface of the water winked up at her. She leaned over the railing, the chiffon of her skirt blowing out behind her. The quiet was soothing after the din of the music and laughter inside, and the steady hum of the engines and the perpetual splash of hull against water were almost hypnotic.

Her peaceful silence was interrupted by a distant grunt, followed by the rustling of what seemed to be canvas and nylon. There were several dull snaps, then a thump. Crissy felt the hairs at the nape of her neck stand up, and a shiver ran down her spine. She leaned back to peer around the beam she was standing next to. In the shadows she could see movement near one of the tenders. As her eyes adjusted to dimmer light, she could clearly see that someone had removed a portion of the canvas that covered one of the small motorboats. These boats were secured directly on the deck below the much larger tenders that were suspended from davits. As she stared at the motorboat, she saw a man come into view. He was working his way around the boat, unsnapping the heavy canvas covering, then stopping to unknot and unlash rope that secured it to the deck.

A shaft of moonlight abruptly lit that area of the deck, and Crissy saw what looked like a medium-size gym bag stowed inside the motorboat. Then she saw the face of the man when he suddenly looked up. *Oh, my God!* Her body stiffened momentarily, then she quickly jerked back in behind the protection of the steel beam. *Oh, God, I hope he didn't see me.* Her heart began to race, and a tremor of fear ran up her spine.

It was Valentin Petrov. She listened for any sound from him, but heard nothing except what she'd heard before: the unsnapping of the canvas, canvas brushing against canvas. She willed herself to disappear into the steel beam, plastering herself against it as narrowly as possible, praying that he hadn't seen her. She had no idea of exactly what he was doing, but he seemed to be preparing the motorboat for a getaway, that much was obvious. But why?

She had to check her impulse to peer around the beam again and see what he was doing. Some instinct told her to remain concealed, and she dared not risk exposing herself. Looking toward the door that led to the safety of the ship's interior, she wondered if she could make it.

There was nothing she could do here. She would rush back upstairs to the disco to safety, then alert the captain or someone in Security that Valentin Petrov was apparently about to abandon ship. She took a deep breath, her eyes trained on the door, and—

A gloved hand clamped across her mouth, and the scream that rose in her throat could not escape.

Crissy instinctively started to struggle against the powerful grip across her mouth, her hands flying up to claw it. She arched her back against the beam and placed one of her heels against it, trying to push herself away from it, but her actions were useless against his muscular grip.

Suddenly there was hot breath in her face, and Crissy's eyes widened in terror. His face was next to hers, his terrible gray eyes focusing intensely on hers. For a moment he didn't say anything, but continued to breathe, exhaling his hot breath against her flesh, staring into her eyes, a smile on his lips.

"Don't you recognize me, Crissy?" he whispered. His smile widened.

Crissy tried to kick him, but he had rammed his powerful body against hers, pinning her to the steel beam, forcing all of his considerable might on her. She tried to scream, but it was impossible. She could hardly breathe. She thought she would suffocate if he didn't remove his hand from across her mouth.

"It was your beautiful dress that gave you away, Crissy," he whispered. "Your beautiful dress fluttered around the beam. You should be more careful."

His face was next to her, his nose practically touching hers, and she was sickened by the smell of his breath, by his terrifying eyes, and more than anything else, by his eerie smile.

"Now I have to take you with me, Crissy," he whispered. "You're going on a little boat ride with me before the ship explodes."

Ship explodes? she thought miserably. *God help me. What am I going to do?* She tried to kick him again, but she was completely pinned against the beam and couldn't move.

Luca strode into the disco and scanned the busy room. There was always a bigger crowd on formal nights, and the guests always stayed up drinking and dancing much later than usual. Tonight was no exception. Walking toward the back of the big room, he looked from table to table, but saw no sign of Crissy. Nor did he see the captain and his party—an odd circumstance, since he or some of the officers should be at a table in this area. *The dance floor,* he thought, reassuring himself that all was well.

He walked toward the packed dance floor, scanning its perimeter, but seeing neither Crissy nor any of the ship's officers. The constantly moving lights made seeing difficult, and their constantly changing colors didn't help either. Moving closer to the dance floor, he kept searching, but to no avail. Finally, he walked onto the floor itself and began weaving his way through the throng of writhing bodies, but Crissy was nowhere in sight. He walked toward the port side of the room, his eyes constantly on the lookout, but he was rewarded with nothing.

From a table nearby, Monika Graf called to him. He focused on her. *The breather,* he thought. *The miserable bitch who harassed Crissy.* Monika was fanning herself with an old-fashioned hand fan, and a smile wreathed her heavily made-up face. "Doctor Santo," she called, waving him toward her.

Luca went to the table at once. "Have you seen Crissy?" he asked, making an effort to be polite. He would like nothing more than to give the woman a good tongue-lashing, but restrained himself.

"I saw the darling child leave only a few moments ago," Monika said. "She went out alone after the captain and his party left."

"The captain left?" he said.

Monika nodded. "Odd, isn't it? He always closes the place." She laughed lightly. "But I imagine Crissy was only going to the loo. Why don't you sit with me and wait for her? We have some wonderful champagne. A Taittinger, I believe. Quite good."

Luca's eyes continued to search the room. "Thank you," he said, "but I don't think so. I'll have a quick look for Crissy."

"Oh, you mustn't worry, darling boy," Monika said. "She'll be back any minute. I know she was waiting for you. No doubt with bated breath." She laughed lightly again and patted the seat next to hers. "Do have a seat and some champagne, won't you?"

"No, thanks," Luca replied. "I must go find her." He left the table, rushing toward the starboard exit.

Captain Papadapolis, followed by five officers, reached the Security office. Rather than wait for one of his underlings to open the locked door to the area, he took out his keys and searched for the correct one.

"Who made the call, sir?" Thrassos asked.

"Christopolous," the captain replied. "Said he needed every hand here. I don't get it. There's no one in lockup but Vilos, but we'll soon see what the problem is." He finally found the right key, a short, thick, round-barreled steel one that was virtually impossible for an outsider to duplicate, and the lock it fit would present a time-consuming difficulty to even the most accomplished criminal. The small brig was inside the Security office, and although it was seldom needed, it was built to hold the most hardened of criminals.

Captain Papadapolis inserted the key in the lock and turned it to the right. The door lock sprang loose at once, and he entered the office, his officers in their dress whites close behind. "Close and lock that behind you, Thrassos," he said.

"What the hell—?" the captain stood, arms akimbo, surveying the sight before him, his officers gathered around him.

"Jesus, sir," Thrassos swore as he turned around after locking the door.

Christopolous, Anasthasia, and five other security personnel lay immobile on the floor, their hands and feet bound securely with duct tape. Across their mouths and wrapped around their heads, duct tape made certain they would make no sound, if indeed they could breathe.

Captain Papadapolis looked for signs of life, but he only had an instant to witness the scene. Before he could detect anything, the air in the room suddenly filled with fumes, their powerful stench stinging their nostrils and burning their eyes. The gas seemed to come from every direction, and the captain swiveled his head, trying to ascertain where a gas canister might be, but his eyes shut before he could see the source of the gas. The first to enter the room, the captain was the first to collapse, falling to his knees, then head and torso over onto Christopolous' legs. The other five men fell almost as a unit, collapsing in a heap just inside the door, hardly aware of what had caused their falls.

"We're on a collision course, Crissy," he whispered, still smiling. "With a tanker loaded with propane." He slammed against her even harder, and could hear rather than feel the slight expulsion of air from her mouth on his glove. "The *Sea Nymph* will be blown out of the water. There will only be bits and pieces of anything or anyone left, and that includes your boyfriend, Crissy."

She tried to kick him again, but she couldn't move her legs at all. She could feel tears rolling down her cheeks, and it infuriated her that this monster could see her anguish and fear.

"Now you're going to be a good little girl, aren't you, Crissy? I'm going to put you in the boat where you'll be safe and sound. Aren't you happy? I'm saving your life so we can have some fun when we reach land." His intense gray eyes held an evil glint that was more frightening than ever, and his lips formed a kiss. "Yes, Crissy, we'll have a lot of fun together, you and I."

Suddenly he jerked her away from the beam, so quickly she didn't know what was happening at first. One hand was still across her mouth, the other arm was wrapped around her back, and he was taking her toward the boat, still pressed hard against his body. Her heels barely touched the deck.

They reached the boat in what seemed an instant, and she felt the back of her thighs hit it hard. The impact sent a sharp bolt of pain up her spine, and she tried to struggle against him again. It was then that she realized she had one arm free. She had been so frozen with terror that it hadn't dawned on her that he couldn't keep her mouth covered and restrain both of her arms at once.

As Valentin started to drag her over the top of the boat's side, she brought her free arm back as far as possible, then swung up with it, aiming at his head, golden minaudière in hand. She felt the blow in her arm

277

as metal met skull, and pain shot up the length of her arm. Valentin jerked, and the hand that had been clamped over her mouth automatically flew up to his head. Then, without warning, he slammed the hand across her cheek with such force that she thought every bone in her cheek must be broken.

Crissy began to scream like she'd never screamed before. At first almost no sound came out. He had almost suffocated her, and that, combined with the blow to her face, had left her winded. But before he could clamp his hand across her mouth again, she let out a bloodcurdling scream. His hand clamped across her mouth quickly, this time with such force that it knocked her backward over the side of the motorboat and down into it. He went with her, forcing her head to the floor with his hand. Her legs pedaled in the air, and she tried to kick at him. Valentin knew what he was doing, however, and he already had a length of rope in his free hand and expertly looped it around her legs. He pulled them tight together, then shoved them down inside the boat.

Crissy furiously kicked the boat with her legs, bound together though they were. Even in her state of panic, she realized she was hardly making any noise and that she was hardly deterring him from his mission at all. Then her eyes caught the glint of silver as a roll of duct tape appeared in his hand.

Oh, God, no! she thought. *No, no, no.*

Luca darted into the ladies' restroom outside the disco and shouted Crissy's name. When there was no response, he banged on closed stall doors, but only got little shrieks in answer. Rushing out onto the deck nearest the disco, he looked fore and aft, but didn't see anyone. He shouted her name as he ran down the deck a few feet, but there was no response. He decided there was no one about, and went back inside and ran down the stairs to the deck below. It occurred to him that Crissy liked this deck because it was less trafficked by people from the disco.

Shoving the door open, he burst out onto the deck and looked fore and aft as he had on the deck above. At first he saw no one, nor did he see anything out of the ordinary. He began going aft, his eyes scanning the deck. Suddenly he saw movement in one of the motorboats.

Moving closer, he saw that the canvas covering it had been unsnapped, and the ropes that should be lashing it down were nowhere to be seen. Then, to his horror, he saw the boat begin to swing on its davits, up and out.

Oh, jeez, no! he thought, rushing to the motorboat. He reached it and, with both arms, lifted himself over the side. The boat hadn't yet cleared the railing, but it would in another minute, then begin its descent to the sea. He jerked apart the canvas, pulling it back so that he could see inside the boat, and when he saw her bound and gagged on its floor, he thought for an instant that he would be sick.

"Crissy!" he shouted. "Jesus! Crissy!" With both arms, he pulled himself up and over the boat's side, jumping down into it. Without hesitation, he pulled her up off the floor, gathering her in his arms. There wasn't a moment to spare, and he stood up, pulling her up with him. He took her under her arms, which were taped behind her back, lifted her into the air, then slowly, carefully let her down toward the deck.

Her feet didn't meet it, but Luca had no choice. He had to drop her. He slid his hands out from under her arms and let go. Crissy fell to the deck and rolled onto her side. He jumped after her, landing right beside her. Grasping the duct tape wrapped around her head, he pulled fiercely and quickly, knowing that it was going to be painful but having no choice.

The instant the tape was off her mouth, she cried out to him. "Luca! Oh, Luca! Watch! Watch! He's . . . he's—"

Luca felt mighty hands clamp his shoulders and his body being dragged backward, away from Crissy. When he tried to turn and face his opponent, Valentin let go of one of his shoulders and slammed a fist into the side of his head. Luca was momentarily senseless, but when he saw Crissy, still bound at feet and hands in front of him, a furious rage filled his body with a strength he didn't know he had. With a roar, he leapt to his feet, and both elbows out and raised, turned on Valentin like a whirlwind.

Valentin was caught off guard, and when Luca's elbow caught his head, the impact sent him reeling backward. He fell to the deck with a loud thud, but quickly found his feet and jumped into a low squat. Luca cocked a leg and kicked the side of Valentin's head with all his might.

Valentin was knocked off his feet again and sprawled on the deck, one hand going up to his head. Before he could regain his feet, Luca let go with his leg again, this time kicking him in the gut. Once. Twice. Three times. He then reached down and grabbed his head between his hands and slammed it down onto the deck. Once. Twice. Three times.

Valentin lay motionless.

Luca scanned the deck around the motorboat and found what he needed. It wasn't a lot of rope, but he didn't need much. He tied Valentin's hands together, then ran a length of the rope down to his ankles and tied them, pulling them up toward his hands in a hog tie.

That done, he rushed over to Crissy and removed the duct tape from her hands and ankles, then took her into his arms. Hot tears ran down her cheeks, and she shook from fear and relief at once. Luca hugged her tightly, whispering to her constantly. "It's going to be all right, Crissy," he promised. "I'm here now, and it's going to be all right."

"Luca," she said. "Luca, the boat's going to explode."

"What?" he asked. "What do you mean?" He thought for a minute that her words were a result of shock. Obviously, she had undergone an ordeal: There was no telling what she might say.

"He told me," she said. "Valentin. He said the ship's on a collision course. It's going to hit a propane tanker."

"You're sure about this?" he said.

"Yes, I'm positive," Crissy said. "We have to do something right away. He was leaving the ship to escape the explosion."

Luca helped her to her feet. "We've got to inform the captain right away."

"He went down to Security," she said. "I heard that he and all the officers in the disco were called down there just before I came out here."

"What? All of them? What the hell's going on?" He took out his cell phone and put in the captain's number, but he only got his voice mail. "I'll try Christopolous," he said. "He'll know what's going on." He got his voice mail, too. "This is weird," he said.

"We'd better go down there, hadn't we?" Crissy asked. "Or to the control room on the bridge?"

"The bridge? Why go there?"

"Luca, the ship's on automatic pilot, and we're headed toward a tanker. This ship won't automatically alter course, even with that tanker on its radar. Sheila and Tommy, these people I met, told me about it. They took a tour of the control room on the bridge."

"I know that, Crissy," he said, "but there are officers in the control room, so we don't have to worry about that." He looked at her thoughtfully. "Or are there? Demetrios and the others were called down to Security. . . ."

280

"Maybe we should run down to Security first," she said.

"I think we have to check it out, but the bridge is our first concern. If we are on a collision course, that's the only place to change it." He looked toward Valentin. He was still out, but Luca feared he might come to at any moment.

"Give me two seconds," he said to Crissy. He went to the motorboat and lowered it back down onto the deck. Searching inside, he found the duct tape. Hunching over Valentin, he wrapped several lengths around his ankles, then his hands.

"Just to make certain he doesn't come to and get away," he said, looking at Crissy.

Then, dragging him by his feet, he pulled him over to the motorboat. Picking him up under the arms, Luca lifted his torso and, with a grunt of exertion, heaved his body into the boat. As Valentin landed on the bottom there was a loud thud. Luca grabbed the loose canvas cover and draped it across him so that a passerby wouldn't notice him.

"We don't want to unnecessarily alarm anyone, do we?" he said. Taking Crissy's arm, he started for the door. "Let's head up to the bridge."

"Maybe we should split up, Luca," she said as they went through the door into the corridor. "I could check out Security while you go up to the bridge."

He stopped in his tracks and turned her to face him. "Absolutely not," he said. "I'm not letting you out of my sight," he said. "I almost lost you just a few minutes ago, and I don't want to risk that again. Not now, not ever."

Crissy couldn't argue with that. "Okay. To the bridge."

Rather than wait for the elevator, they rushed up the stairs and through the ship. They passed a couple walking drunkenly down a corridor, but they only smiled and nodded, paying little attention to the two of them, hurrying though they were. When they reached the top deck, Luca led the way to the bridge. Crissy had been there, but she didn't think she could ever have found the way back again. When they reached the door, she paused to catch her breath.

Luca slipped a card out of the inside breast pocket of his dress white uniform jacket.

"Will that work?" Crissy asked, looking up at him.

"It works like a pass key," Luca said. "I have to have it so that I can enter any room on the ship in case something happens to a passenger or one of the crew."

He started to swipe the card, but the door, heavy though it was, shifted slightly ajar. "Jesus, it's not locked," he said. Opening the door all the way, he stepped into the bridge, Crissy's hand firmly held in his.

The huge room, which ran the width of the ship, appeared to be empty. There was no one stationed at any of the control consoles, but when they reached midway across the width of the bridge, they saw that it wasn't deserted. Inside the offices, through the huge windows that looked out to the bridge, they saw three officers. One of them was slumped over his desk, a second one lay on the floor, and the third was in his desk chair, sitting up, his head thrown back over the top of the chair.

The door was open, and they stepped inside the office. Crissy saw blood pooling on the industrial blue and green carpeting. It came from the young officer who lay on the floor, facedown. When she focused on his head, it looked as if a huge bite had been taken out of his skull.

Crissy's stomach lurched, but she took a few deep breaths and looked away. Luca bent down and turned the young man over. There was a single bullet hole in his forehead, small and round and almost bloodless. It was pointless to feel for a pulse. At the desks, the two other officers had been killed the same way: a single shot to the forehead, a small point of entry in each of them, with their brains blown out the back of their heads.

Crissy's mind reeled, and suddenly the stench of coppery blood made her stomach lurch again, and she was certain that she would be sick. She could taste the bile that rose up in her throat, but she fought it down, turning her head away from the sight.

"Is there anything you can do, Luca?" she asked, knowing what the answer was but feeling the need to ask the question nevertheless.

"No, nothing," he said. "Come on, let's get out of here. We've got to get down to Security and find an officer, somebody who knows how to manually run this ship. I know a lot about this ship, but that's one thing I don't know a damn thing about."

Crissy's eyes glanced at the control consoles with their computer screens, joysticks, and seemingly countless controls of various sorts. It was hopeless, she thought. Absolutely hopeless. She focused on one screen in the central console, then pointed at it. "Luca, look."

He followed her gaze to the computer screen. "Jesus," he said. "We're headed straight for it, whatever it is."

"A tanker ship," Crissy said. "Loaded with propane. That's what Valentin said."

On the radar screen, the position of the *Sea Nymph* was clearly indicated by a moving circle, and directly in front of its path was an unmoving circle, representing another vessel.

"Let's go," he said, grabbing her hand.

They rushed across the bridge and out the door, then practically ran down the stairs, six decks in all, one deck after another, until they reached the deck where Security was located. Down a long corridor, a left, then a right, down another corridor, then finally the door to Security loomed before them.

Luca shoved on it, but it didn't move. "Damn," he said. "Locked."

Crissy didn't see a card-swipe. "What do we do?" she asked. "There's no card-swipe."

"I've got keys," Luca said. "I have to be able to get in anywhere, remember?" He smiled, his hand already pulling a key chain out of his trouser pocket. He quickly found the small, thick, round one, the only one of its kind on his key chain. He inserted it in the lock, turned it, then pushed on the heavy door. Something on the other side was blocking it, and Luca put his shoulder against it and pushed hard. It moved another few inches, and he looked in.

"Damn," he said.

"What is it?" Crissy asked.

"More bodies," he said. "It looks like the captain and most of the officers." He put his shoulder to the door again and shoved harder, making a gap wide enough for them to get through.

He stepped inside, and Crissy followed him.

"Oh, my God," she whispered.

"Wait!" Luca exclaimed. "I smell some kind of gas. Get back out in the corridor."

Crissy did as she was told without questioning him. In the corridor, she could detect the lingering odor of the gas but could see nothing in the air. She watched as Luca took a handkerchief out of his pocket and held it to his nose. He stepped over one of the officers and flipped a switch on the wall that turned on a ventilator fan built into the ceiling, then going down on a knee, felt for the captain's pulse. He went from one body to another, repeating the process.

"Are they alive?" Crissy asked.

Luca nodded. "They're all alive," he said, "but they may be out for awhile, depending on what kind of gas it was. I'm going to pull them away from the door so we can open it all the way and let some air in here."

"Luca," she asked, "who else knows about running the ship?"

"I don't know of anyone," he replied, struggling with Anasthasia's heft. His eyes were tearing and his face was flushed. "I'm going to have to go down to the engine room and hope that somebody there knows something about it. The problem is, most of those guys don't know anything about any job other than their own. They know engines, but they don't know computers."

He cleared the entrance enough that Crissy could push the door all the way open. The high-speed ventilator was already doing its job, pulling fresh air into the room while sucking out the air that was there. "Okay," he said. "I can't do much more for them now." His eyes searched the office for something to use to keep the door from swinging closed, and he grabbed an office chair and propped it under the door handle, making certain it would stay in place.

He looked at Crissy. "He must've used something like Mace. They'll be all right, but it's going to take time. Now, if we just *had* the time. . . ." He stepped out into the corridor and took Crissy's hand. "Let's go," he said. "Our best chance is the engine room now. Maybe one of the Philippine men has some kind of bridge experience."

They started down the corridor at a run when Crissy abruptly stopped. "What're you doing?" he asked, pulling on her hand.

"Luca, where's the brig?" she asked.

"In Security," he replied impatiently. "Come on, Crissy. We don't have time—"

"Wait!" she exclaimed. "Mark is locked up there, and he knows everything about the ship. He told me he could run it."

"Are you sure about that?"

"Yes," she said. "He said he could sail everything from a tiny sailboat to this ship."

"It's worth a try," he said.

He turned, already fishing in his trouser pocket for his key chain with his free hand. They went through the office to another door, and Luca inserted the same short, barrel-shaped key into its lock. When he heard the lock click, he pushed on the door, and they hurried down another short corridor. To their right was yet another door, this one with a bulletproof-glass panel set in it.

On the other side of the glass, Crissy saw Mark look up at them with a surprised expression from the narrow bunk where he lay reading, dressed in an orange jumpsuit that Crissy knew must be issued by the ship. Looking at him through the glass, she felt a knot form in her stomach, and the memory of his attack rushed back, sweeping through her mind in vivid detail. She tried to push it aside, but as hard as she tried, it wouldn't go away.

Luca inserted his key in the door and swung it open.

"What the hell do you want?" Mark asked, looking at them defiantly.

"We need your help," Luca said.

Mark's haughty smiled replaced the look of defiance. "My help? You must be joking."

"Look," Luca said, "we're on a collision course with a tanker loaded with propane. The ship's on automatic pilot, and there's nobody to operate it manually."

Mark's expression immediately changed. "But the captain," he said. "All the officers—"

"They're all either dead or have been gassed," Crissy cried. "You've got to help us."

Mark shot to his feet. "What the hell's going on?"

"We'll tell you on the way," Luca said. "Let's go."

The three of them ran down the corridor and into the office, where Mark stumbled on one of the officers. "Jesus," he exclaimed, stopping.

"We don't have time," Luca said, dashing out the office door with Crissy.

Mark hurried to catch up.

When they reached the stairwell, they started up the steps, taking them two at a time, not stopping to catch their breath. On the top deck, a group of people leaving the disco for their cabins shrank back from the sight of them running, and one of the women screamed, whether at Mark's jumpsuit or their wild faces, Crissy didn't know. Ignoring the passengers, they ran down the corridor, Mark ahead of them now, running in his bare feet to the bridge. Tripping as they turned a corner, he went sprawling onto the carpet, but heaved himself up by his hands and kept going.

They reached the door to the bridge, and Luca pushed through it without stopping, Crissy right behind him and Mark behind her. Mark passed them then and dashed to the center console, gasping for air.

"Oh, my God!" he exclaimed. "We're nearly on top of them, whoever they are." He started tapping the keyboard furiously. "Goddamn it," he swore as his fingers missed keys.

Looking over his shoulder at the radar computer screen, Crissy and Luca could see the circle representing the *Sea Nymph* closing in on the tanker's circle. In a matter of minutes, the vessels would collide. And then what? If what Valentin said was true, then the *Sea Nymph* and everyone on it would be blown up. Crissy ran to the huge wraparound windows that looked out on the foredeck and the sea in front of it.

"I can't see anything out there," she said. "No lights. Nothing."

"It's there all right," Mark said, "and it's dead ahead."

Just as he said the words, Crissy could suddenly make out the ghostly outline of a tanker. "Oh, my God," she whispered.

Luca went to her side and slipped an arm across around her back. "Mark, it can't be much more than three hundred feet away," he said.

Mark tapped a last key, waited a moment, then grabbed the joystick directly in front of him on the console. "Hang on," he cried.

Chapter Twenty

In the motorboat, Valentin fought against the rope and duct tape that bound his hands and feet. As strong as he was, Luca had knotted in the rope in such a way that made it virtually impossible to escape. The duct tape made it even worse. But he had managed to loosen the length of rope that hog-tied his feet to his hands, frantically running it up and down against one of the metal struts in the motorboat. He didn't know whether he'd sawed through it or if Luca had failed to knot it properly. It didn't matter. Now at least he could stretch out lengthwise and sit up, though his hands and feet were still bound. Sitting up, the canvas cover that Luca had draped over the boat lay on top of his head and added to the sense of suffocation he already felt. He found the strut behind him again, and began rubbing his hands against it as rapidly as possible in small up and down movements, but he quickly realized that he wasn't having as much luck as he'd had with the rope. His eyes had grown accustomed to the darkness, and he searched under the canvas for his gym bag, finally realizing that it was near his bound feet. In the darkness, he managed to shove it toward his hands, using both of his feet, then using both hands, since he had no alternative. He scrabbled around inside the bag, forcing himself to slow down and use his fingers to feel for what he was looking for.

There. He touched it. Unmistakably. Its smooth plastic was cool to the touch. It looked like any normal cell phone, in fact it was a near replica of the one he used to communicate with Vilos in London and Athens and the men he'd hired to position the *Lucky Dragon* at the correct coordinates. They would be off the tanker by now, and were probably already drinking in Belém or somewhere along an Amazonian tributary close by, their

Zodiac inflatable tied up at one of the rickety docks that dotted the waterways like the palm trees ashore.

He managed to get his hands around the cell phone, an easy enough task even if he couldn't see it behind his back. Now all he had to do was depress one button. One little button, he thought, and the tanker and its thousands of gallons of propane gas would blow sky-high. He hadn't planned on using the transmitter—it was part of Plan B—because when the *Sea Nymph* hit the *Lucky Dragon,* the impact would set off an explosion that would destroy both vessels.

Now, however, because of the interfering Crissy Fitzgerald and her doctor boyfriend, he had no choice. They might conceivably rouse the captain or one of the officers in time to avert the collision. *I should have murdered all of them,* he thought with chagrin, *instead of relying on the gas. When I had the guy in Security call the captain to come down and bring the officers with him, I should have killed them all then. I shouldn't have listened to old Vilos. He was a fool.* The old man had been unnecessarily cautious, uneasy about maritime inspectors possibly finding the bodies of the captain or other officers with bullet holes or other wounds. *As if there would have been anything left in the wreckage to inspect,* Valentin thought.

He didn't know precisely how much time had passed since the doctor had knocked him out, but the ship was still going full speed ahead. If he felt the ship slow, he would know to depress the button, because that would be a signal that somebody had taken manual control of the *Sea Nymph.* That was easy. He could feel all of the buttons with his fingers, so no matter what had happened since he'd been out, he could still set off the explosion. Old man Vilos could still collect a fortune in insurance on the loss of the *Lucky Dragon* and its propane, and there would probably be enough collateral damage to the *Sea Nymph* to collect another few million on it. Hopefully, whoever was in the bridge would be engulfed in a fireball that would leave nothing but ashes. As for himself? He was certain that in the confusion after the blast he would somehow manage to loosen his hands and feet, then get overboard and away from the ship. It was a chance that he was willing to take, because if he wasn't killed in the explosion, he was sure to face multiple murder charges and life in prison.

The ship suddenly heaved in the water, first throwing him fore then aft, against the metal strut, and he lost his grip on the cell phone.

Damn, he thought. *Now's the time to press the button.* His fingers scrabbled around the bottom of the motorboat, and he felt it. *Yes,* he thought, his lips parting in an evil smile. *I can still do it.*

The ship suddenly slowed, throwing Crissy and Luca to the floor. Luca reached over toward her. "Are you okay?" he asked.

"Yes," she said, already struggling to her feet. Grabbing the railing running along under the window frame, she pulled herself up, and Luca scrambled up beside her, grasping at the rail for support. Out the window, they could see the tanker looming just ahead in the lights from the *Sea Nymph*. Mark had turned on a foredeck searchlight, aiming it directly at the behemoth. On the rust-riddled black hull they could clearly see LUCKY DRAGON spelled out in white lettering.

"Jesus," Luca breathed. "It looks like we're going to hit it any second now." The ship abruptly heaved sharply to the right, and Crissy was thrown against Luca, knocking him down to the floor again, with her atop him. He struggled out from under her and sat up on his haunches, holding onto the rail for support. "Okay?"

She nodded. "You?"

"All right." Extending a hand to her, he helped her up, and they looked through the window. In the searchlight, they could see the tanker on the port side, pitching and rolling in the huge waves created by the *Sea Nymph*'s sudden drop in speed and dramatic turn.

"We've still got about a hundred feet aft to clear," Luca said, watching wide-eyed as the *Sea Nymph* escaped crashing into the foredeck hull of the huge tanker by a matter of feet. "The wash could shove us into her."

No sooner had he said the words than Mark turned the *Sea Nymph* again, this time sharply to the left. Crissy and Luca held on tightly to keep from being thrown again, and saw the tanker begin pitching and rolling wildly again from the tempest the *Sea Nymph* had created.

Mark slowly righted the ship, adjusting the searchlight as he did so. Now, on the port side, they watched as they sailed slowly by the tanker, which was still tossing ominously, waves crashing over its deck, looking as if its entire superstructure—bridge, davits, *everything*—was going to collapse under the pressure of the heaving sea at any moment.

"We're almost clear," Mark called to them.

As the *Sea Nymph* sailed on, Mark gradually increased her speed, steering her slightly to the right, manually carrying her farther away from the *Lucky Dragon*. Crissy and Luca let go of the railing and crossed to the central console, where Mark sat in the big captain's chair, the joystick in his hand, his focus on the computer screens in front of him.

"You've done something heroic tonight," Luca said.

"I did what anyone who could run the ship would have done under the circumstances," Mark replied. "Now I'm wondering who set this up."

"I know that Valentin Petrov had something to do with it," Crissy said. "I saw him trying to get off the ship earlier, but Luca stopped him."

"Maybe we can get it out of him," Luca said.

"Where is he?" Mark asked.

"Tied up in one of the motorboats on the deck where the tenders are," Crissy said.

"I'm going to have to readjust the coordinates," Mark said, "and put us back on course, then an automatic pilot again."

"Let's go see about the captain and the other officers," Luca said. "They should be coming around soon."

Luca took her hand, and they hurried toward the door. In the corridor just outside it, Captain Papadapolis and two officers were coming toward them in a rush.

"Are you all right?" Luca asked.

"Yes, I think so," the captain said. "Who's running the ship, and what the hell is going on?"

Luca briefed him as quickly as possible.

When he was finished, Captain Papadapolis turned to one of the officers, "Thrassos, you and Malinakis get Petrov and take him to the brig at once. There will still be people leaving the disco, so do it as discreetly as possible. When you're finished there, come back up to the bridge immediately. You'll have to escort Mark Vilos back down. After that, bring three body bags up from the hospital. I want our mates taken down to the morgue as soon as possible, so there's little chance of passengers seeing anything."

"Then I'd better get down to the hospital," Luca said. "We're going to have injuries from the maneuvering he had to do back there, and I'll get the morgue ready for the bodies." He took Crissy's hand. "Why don't you come with me."

Captain Papadapolis looked at Crissy. "You're the hero, or the heroine, tonight," he said, "and I don't know how we're ever going to thank you for this."

290

"Oh, I've already been rewarded, Captain," she said, squeezing Luca's hand. They went on down the corridor to the stairwell, but stopped when they heard a terrific explosion. They looked at each other, then immediately turned and ran back to the bridge.

Mark and Captain Papadapolis were on the port side of the ship, their faces glued to the windows. Crissy and Luca rushed over. In the distance, a roaring fireball reached into the sky, and even from their perspective, they could see pieces of the *Lucky Dragon* blown up into the darkness above the light of the huge fire like bits of shrapnel.

"I wonder what triggered it," Luca said. "Whether it was some kind of timing device or if we did it. We got so close, it was pitching and rolling like it actually might get swamped and go down."

"We'll soon find out," the captain said.

Crissy and Luca headed to the hospital. "Think you could maybe help Voula out for awhile?" Luca asked. "I have a feeling she's going to need it."

"I don't see why not," she said.

"You'll look very good in a lab coat over your gown," Luca laughed. He was making an effort to take her mind off what she had just been through. He knew the events of the past hour might have unhinged a normal woman, or man, for that matter.

Crissy had demonstrated an extraordinary degree of fortitude during the entire nightmare, he thought, overcoming any fears and doubts she might have to help see to it that disaster was averted. He also knew that she might suffer from delayed shock. Now that the ship was safe, the dawning realization of what had happened and the potential consequences might very well overwhelm her. He wanted to keep her close by and preoccupied, the best medicine, he thought.

"Do you think I ought to change quickly?" she asked. "I could meet you in the hospital."

"You're fine," he said. "You can answer the telephone, book patients in, things like that. Believe me, there's going to be plenty you can help do, even in your evening dress."

Valentin heard the explosion and even felt heat from the fireball waft past. He had miscalculated, but he couldn't be faulted for that. He didn't care anymore. What was important was to get out of there. He rubbed the duct tape securing his hands behind his back up and down, up and down against the metal strut on the side of the motorboat, but he knew that he only had minutes and would never break through the tape before someone came for him.

Squatting on his feet, he managed to stand upright by supporting himself with his bound hands against the top rim of the motorboat. Once on his feet, he pulled himself over the side, just far enough to reach the deck-mounted motor that controlled the davits. He hit the button to start the engine, then pushed himself back inside the motor boat. There was a small, fiberglass box in the motorboat that contained a remote. He found it dangling on the small operator's chair, situated aft in the boat, next to the motor. With the press of one button, he raised the boat up off the deck. With the press of another, he swung the motorboat out over the side of the ship, where he dangled on the davits, five whole decks above the sea. The ship was moving at close to normal speed now, and the wind rocked the motorboat on its davits. Pressing a third button, the boat began descending to the water.

He looked down. The sea had yet to settle from the manual maneuvers someone had performed to avoid the collision, much less the explosion moments before. Plus, there was the wake thrown up by the speed of the *Sea Nymph,* but he was certain that if he could get the motorboat on the water, he would easily be able to make it to land, regardless of the duct tape and ropes securing his hands and feet.

Lower, lower, lower, the boat descended, until it hit the water with a loud thud that shook the motorboat from bow to stern. For a moment Valentin thought the boat would split to pieces from the impact. When that didn't happen, he waited for it to be swamped in the sea, but that didn't happen either, although he was taking on water swiftly as it surged over the sides of the boat. He pressed the fourth button, which would release the boat from the davits. He ducked down, knowing that the cables that had held the boat would be whipped about by the wind. One strike to his head could end everything. The cables were made of thickly wound steel and could be lethal.

The motorboat, on the sea now, free of its restraints, pitched and heaved wildly, and Valentin held onto the small, deck-mounted operator's chair with all his might. Pushing with his legs, he managed to shove himself between the chair and the motor, his entire body soaked through with water. Reaching up with both hands, he felt for the manual starter for the boat's engine, but the constant tossing to and fro prevented him from getting a grip on it with his bound hands.

Then suddenly the pitching and heaving all but ceased. The motorboat had cleared the *Sea Nymph* and apparently was in the center of the big ship's wake, where the water was relatively smooth. Using the chair, he pulled himself to a squat. Looking forward, he could see the lights of the *Sea Nymph* disappearing directly ahead of him, bound for Belém. Valentin allowed himself a smile, then pulled himself up into the operator's chair. With both hands, he pulled on the manual start.

The boat's motor roared to life, and he immediately took hold of the control and began steering to the port side of the big ship. He knew that there would be some big waves from its wake coming up, but he was prepared to handle them. Once across, he was virtually home free. Within minutes he would reach Brazil, and he knew that along this coast and the tributaries that ran in and out of it, there were literally thousands of fishing shacks that served as homes, nearly all of them with homemade docks where he would have no trouble pulling the motorboat in. Nor would he have trouble with the local fishermen: He had plenty of euros secured in the Teflon belt he wore beneath his jumpsuit. He cast a final glance at the *Sea Nymph.*

All I have to do now is get in touch with Vilos, he thought. *The old man may not want to give me the rest of the money, but he's not going to have a choice. He pays, or I talk.*

Crissy and Luca reached the hospital, and he unlocked the door. Voula was already seated at the desk, just hanging up the telephone. "What the hell happened?" she asked. "I was almost thrown out of bed, so I knew I'd better get in here fast."

"We hit one of those little tropical storms," Luca said. "One of those squalls that come and go in a matter of minutes, but it played hell with the ship."

Voula's eyes did a quick inventory of them both, noting Crissy's beaded chiffon gown and Luca's dress white uniform. "I see," she said, unconvinced that what he'd said was true.

"That's what you tell the passengers," Luca said, seeing the expression on her face. "We'll tell you all about it later. Anyway, we're going to have three bodies brought in shortly. They'll be coming in the back way so no one can see them here in reception. We'll have to get the morgue ready right away."

"Three bodies?" Voula exclaimed. "What's going on?"

"Later, Voula. There's no time now. What's the story on the telephone?"

"We've got eight people on their way down now," she said, a slight pout in her attitude, "and another ten or twelve have called to make appointments. So far nothing sounds too serious." She shrugged. "But you never know. Thank God it was the middle of the night. Most of the people left in the disco were drunk and didn't notice or laughed it off."

"And nearly everybody else was sound asleep," Luca said. "Some of them were probably thrown out of bed, so injuries shouldn't be too bad."

There was a knock on the door. "Time to roll up our sleeves," Luca said. He turned to Crissy. "Ready?"

"Where're the lab coats?" she asked.

Chapter Twenty-One

Georgios Vilos slumped in his chair. *I've lost everything*, he thought. *Everything*. He felt as if the lifeblood were running out of him, that every ounce of vitality, every reason he'd had for living, was draining away. He glanced at the painting of the *Sea Nymph* that hung over the mantelpiece, a painting that he'd only recently commissioned of the two-year-old ship. It never failed to remind him of the heights to which he'd brought his family's company, the company that he'd worked so hard to grow and leave as a legacy for his son. Now there would be no son, no heir.

Leaning down, he pulled open the bottom drawer on the right-hand side of the desk, his hand feeling for the plastic and steel object he knew was there under a small pile of folders. When he had a grip on it, he slid the Glock 9-mm Parabellum pistol out of the drawer. He removed its form-fitting synthetic holster and placed it on the desk next to the cell phone. Georgios knew it was a draw-and-fire gun; the mechanical safety on the smooth Austrian Glock was built into the trigger. He also knew that the semiautomatic was fully loaded, with seventeen rounds of ammunition in the magazine and one in the chamber, but such considerations were not of any importance now. A single shot would suffice.

He placed the steel barrel against his temple. It felt cold, but only for an instant. He pulled the trigger. The blast of the bullet was the last thing he heard before he slumped over on his desk, the gun falling out of his hand onto the floor. Outside, rain beat steadily against the windowpanes. But Georgios Vilos didn't hear it.

Chapter Twenty-Two

The *Sea Nymph* pulled into the port near Belém around nine a.m., and passengers lined the deck railings, snapping photographs or taking videos of the arrival. The ship couldn't moor here because there wasn't a deep-water dock, and had to drop anchor offshore. Tenders would take the passengers ashore who were going on excursions. There was a great deal of chatter about the squall they'd run through the night before, although many of them were completely unaware of it. The injured, most of them elderly, quickly spread the word, displaying their cuts and bruises, their bandages and canes as if they were medals for surviving heroic action in a war zone. Fortunately, there were no serious injuries. Those who heard the explosion were told that a tanker had caught on fire but had presented no danger to the *Sea Nymph* at all.

When they disembarked onto the tenders for excursions to Belém and a jungle tour, the rickety pier was a mass of color. They were greeted by vendors of all kinds, selling local wood carvings, paintings, jewelry, even tropical fruit, and their numbers were supplemented by beggars and pickpockets. Loud music accompanied dancers on the beaches next to the pier, who shouted and waved to the new arrivals, along with sunbathers and swimmers who braved the sewage-filled waters. The street lining the beach was filled with colorful bars and shops that sold tourist trinkets, but the tour buses were waiting to take the passengers into Belém, so there was little time to browse.

Crissy watched from the pool deck, snapping pictures of the colorful scene. After staying at the hospital late, she got very little sleep, but Luca wanted to show Crissy a bit of Belém if she was up to it.

The passengers who were disembarking had all left, the tenders making several trips ashore to accommodate all of them, and the ship was relatively quiet. She went down one deck to the cafeteria-style dining room to have some breakfast. After filling her tray, she took it out onto the deck, where she had no problem finding an empty table at the railing to eat. There were very few people about, and the crew, she noticed, were taking advantage of the time to do a lot of sprucing up and organizing. The sun was bright, the air hot and humidity-laden, but she quickly became enamored of the colorful scene ashore and the view on the opposite side of the ship. She could see jungle growth on the other side of the tributary in which they were docked, with wooden houses—rundown shacks most of them—set amid the towering palm trees and other vegetation. They all had wooden docks with small boats jutting out into the water.

As she studied the tropical scene, she suddenly heard an uproar on the shore opposite, where the *Sea Nymph*'s passengers had landed. Sirens rent the morning air, and the rumble of a long procession of military or police vehicles almost drowned out the music blasting from the beaches. Turning her head, she saw that the crowds on the beaches, those on the thronged dock, and the people milling about the street lining the shore had all turned to look at the arrival of government vehicles. Jeeps, Humvees, trucks, and cars came to an abrupt stop near the dock, and dozens of soldiers—or police?—jumped from the transports and converged on the dock. They carried weapons that ranged from drawn handguns to what looked like submachine guns.

What now? she wondered, sipping her second cup of coffee.

As she got up to get a better view, speeding boats, sirens wailing, began converging on the *Sea Nymph* from every side. Some of the boats had submachine guns mounted on their decks, and even on the smaller vessels, she could clearly see that men in uniform had weapons of different kinds drawn and aimed at the ship. She set down her coffee cup and rushed inside, heading back down to the hospital to look for Luca. On her way, she saw officers rushing up the stairwell, apparently on their way to the bridge.

When she reached the hospital, the door was unlocked, and she went on in. Voula was at the reception desk and smiled at her. "Back already? You just can't stay away, can you?"

"Is Luca still here?" she asked.

Voula nodded toward the back. "He's with the last patient. At least I hope it's the last one. It's been one hell of a long night, but you know that." She paused and look at Crissy with curiosity. "What's up?" she asked. "You look like you've seen a ghost."

"I don't know what's going on," Crissy said, "but a flotilla of boats are surrounding the *Sea Nymph,* and an army of men just pulled up on shore. They're coming down to the dock. It looks very scary."

"Jesus," Voula said. "I wonder what's going on. Probably something to do with that tanker last night." Luca and Crissy had finally managed to tell her of the events during the night in between patients. "I'm going to call Anasthasia in Security and see what she knows." She picked up the telephone receiver and started dialing.

Crissy nervously sat down and flipped through a magazine, but she didn't really see anything. Her ears were attuned to Voula's end of the conversation, and she could hear Luca's voice in the back as he ministered to a patient.

"Are you shitting me?" Voula said, her magnified eyes growing even larger behind her thick spectacles. "So what do we do?"

Crissy looked over at her, and saw that Voula was tapping orange-painted nails on the desk very anxiously.

When she hung up the telephone, she looked over at Crissy. "You're not going to believe this," she said.

"What?"

"The ship is being impounded," Voula said.

"Impounded?" Crissy repeated. "What does that mean, Voula?"

"It means, sweetheart, that this is where we get off."

"Get off?"

Luca came through the door with an elderly man, leading him out of the examination area into reception. "It's going to be fine, Herr Schroeder," he said. "Just do as I said, and call me tomorrow if you have any problems."

The man nodded. "*Danke,*" he said. "*Danke.*"

Luca opened the door for him, and after the man was gone, he closed and locked the door behind him. Then he smiled at Crissy. "Couldn't stay away, you liked it so much down here, huh?"

Crissy returned his smile. "That's it," she replied. "But there was something else, too."

"Luca," Voula said, "the ship is being impounded."

"What?"

She nodded. "I just talked to Anasthasia in Security, and she told me. Crissy saw a bunch of boats coming in and a lot of police or army on-shore, headed this way, so I called her."

"But why?" he asked.

Voula shook her head. "She didn't know."

Luca sat down beside Crissy and slid an arm around her shoulders, then flipped his cell phone open. He pressed in the captain's number.

"Demetrios," he said. "Luca here. What the hell's going on? We heard the ship's being impounded."

Crissy watched him as he listened to the captain.

"This is unbelievable," he said. "What about all the passengers? The crew?"

He listened for awhile longer, then said, "Okay, Demetrios. I'll remain aboard until it's all taken care of in case there's a medical emergency of any kind." Then, "Okay, I'll talk to you later." He flipped the cell phone closed.

"So?" Voula said, her eyebrows raised questioningly.

"You're right. The ship's being impounded by the authorities in Belém," he said, stroking his chin thoughtfully. "The banks have fore-closed on Georgios Vilos. Vilos didn't come up with the money due, so they're having all Vilos' ships that they've financed impounded. Oddly enough, they haven't been able to get hold of Vilos and haven't heard a word from him about it."

"Je-*sus*!" Voula exclaimed. "If I were the man, I'd go into hiding, too. So what do we do, Luca?"

"We disembark," he said. "Everybody has to disembark. When the passengers on excursions get back, they'll be allowed to board to get their possessions. Crew will be allowed to remain aboard until all passengers have been disembarked, then they'll have to leave."

"But where will everybody go?" Crissy asked.

Luca looked at her. "The passengers will have to make their own arrangements," he said. "Demetrios says that the Information Office is trying to arrange to use the tour buses that they're on now to remain ashore after they bring them back, so they can turn around and take them back into Belém to hotels or the airport. In other words, passengers are pretty much on their own from that point on."

"What about us?" Voula asked. "The crew?"

"The Information Office is working on transport for the crew to the

299

airport. He says that all the crew will be flown back to Athens on a charter flight. At least that's what they're trying to set up."

"I don't believe this," Voula said. "What about our pay?"

Luca looked at her and shook his head. "Demetrios says there won't be any pay. Not for anybody, including him."

Voula slapmmed a fist down on the desk. "That's outrageous!" she exclaimed.

"It certainly is," Crissy agreed. "What if some of the passengers or the crew don't have the money to stay over or wait for planes?"

"Then they're going to have to make do somehow," Luca said. "Most of the passengers have credit cards or enough cash to get home, or they've got relatives they can call. But for the crew it's different. Apparently the Vilos empire is crumbling, and the captain says we'll be lucky if we can even get a charter flight to take the crew back to Athens. There are more than three hundred and fifty men and women who are going to be stuck here otherwise, and most of them don't have the money for a flight back, especially since they're not getting paid. And most of them don't have relatives with the money to wire to them."

"I don't believe this," Voula said again.

"You better start believing it," Luca said. "I suggest we all start gathering up our personal belongs, so that when the time comes we're ready for disembarkation. I'm going to have to be one of the last people off the ship in case of any kind of medical emergency, and I'd really appreciate it if you two would be on hand to help out. There are going to be people with medical issues for certain after they get back and find out they have to pack and disembark." He paused and looked at Voula. "I can understand if you don't want to. You're not getting paid, Voula," he said. He turned and looked at Crissy. "And your trip is ending several days early. So you've both got good reason to disembark without helping out."

"Of course I'll stay," Crissy said.

"Thank you," Luca said.

"I will, too," Voula said. "I don't like it, but I'll do it."

"Thanks, Voula," he said. "I'll make it up to you somehow."

"Maybe you're going to need a nurse when you start your practice," she said. "Looks like it might be sooner than you thought."

Luca laughed. "You're right," he said. "Do you think you could take living somewhere on the Italian coast? Or maybe Miami?"

Voula's orange-painted lips spread in a smile. "I think I could stand it," she said.

"Good. We'll talk about it later," Luca said. "In the meantime, we should all get our baggage ready."

After Voula left, he took Crissy into his arms. "Do you want me to go up and help you with yours before I start?"

She shook her head. "No, I can do it. It won't take me very long, then I can come back down here and help with whatever there is to do."

Captain Papadapolis came in. "Well, it's another eventful day," he said.

The three of them sat down in the reception area. "I'm glad you're here," Luca said to Crissy, because what Demetrios was talking about concerns you."

"What's that?" she asked.

"It's like this," the captain began. "Last night when my men went down to get Valentin Petrov and take him to the brig, he wasn't there."

"What?" she exclaimed. "But that's impossible. Luca had him tied up. And taped up, too."

Luca shook his head. "The guy must be some kind of Houdini, because he definitely got away. The motorboat was gone, with him in it."

"I don't believe it," Crissy said.

"I don't think he represents a danger to you in the future," the captain said. "He's on the run, after all. I also wanted you to know that we believe he was the go-between from Georgios Vilos to his son."

"But he was trying to blow up the ship," Crissy said in amazement.

"That's one reason we think he delivered the messages," the captain said. "We have reason to believe that Georgios Vilos plotted the entire thing to collect on the insurance."

"That's unbelievable," Crissy said. "Surely he wouldn't blow up his own ship and all the people on it?"

"The insurance companies have already got men on the scene," the captain said. "It turns out that the *Lucky Dragon* was owned by Vilos through a string of offshore corporations." He paused, looking at her, then went on. "Which brings me to the other reason I'm here. What do we do with Mark Vilos? Do you still want to press charges?"

Crissy was stunned by the question, and for a moment didn't know what to say.

"He tried to rape her, for God's sake," Luca said, putting an arm around her shoulders.

The captain nodded. "I'm aware of that," he said. "He also saved all of our lives last night by maneuvering the ship out of harm's way."

"Only because Crissy knew the ship was going to be blown up and only because Crissy knew that Mark was the one person left who knew how to run the ship," Luca said.

"That's true, too," the captain said, "but I want to hear what Crissy has to say. Understand, we'll have to take him back to Athens, where the ship originated and was registered."

Crissy looked at the captain thoughtfully. "I'm tempted to say let him go," she said, "and drop the charges." She cleared her throat. "But what concerns me is that other women out there might end up being raped by him. I don't know if a court in Greece or anywhere else will find him guilty, but I'll do my best to see that he's prosecuted."

Luca hugged her to him.

"I understand," the captain said. "You realize that you may have to come to Athens."

She nodded. "I'll cross that bridge when I get to it."

The captain stood up. "Very well. I'll be going now. I wish the two of you the best of luck." He turned and left.

"I'm so proud of you," Luca said.

"Thanks," she replied, "but I'm doing what comes naturally. I don't care who he is, how good-looking he is, or how much he knows about ships. Mark Vilos is potentially dangerous."

"Yes," Luca agreed. "There was something else I wanted to talk to you about before Voula gets here."

"What's that?" she asked.

"You're going to be losing an entire week of your trip," he said. "What do you plan to do with that time now?"

Crissy smiled. "I don't have any idea," she said. "I could always go back to work early."

"Work?" he said. "After losing a week of your vacation? I don't think so."

"Well . . . did you have something in mind?"

He nodded. "I certainly do. I was thinking that since you're missing the Caribbean portion of the trip, I might take you on a trip to one of the islands. "Maybe St. Bart's. I have a friend who has a house there and would gladly let us use it. There'll be sun and water and . . . us. How does that sound?"

"It sounds wonderful," Crissy said.

"It could be a prehoneymoon honeymoon, I was thinking," he said. "What do you think?"

Crissy felt a frisson of excitement rush through her body. "Are . . . are you joking, Luca?"

He shook his head. "Absolutely not. I want you to marry me."

Crissy felt herself blush, but she didn't care. "You really mean it?"

"I've never meant anything more in my life. I love you Crissy, and I want you to be my wife."

"Yes," she said. "Yes, yes, yes!"

He put his arms around her and kissed her deeply.

The door opened, and Voula walked in. "Oh, Jesus," she said. "I'm sorry. I'll come back later."

"No," Luca said. "You don't have to leave. You can have a congratulatory lunch with us."

"For what?" she said, her orange lips already spreading in a smile.

"We're going to get married," Luca said.

About ten feet from shore, he'd killed the engine and let the boat drift in, ignoring the loud scraping of the bottom of the boat against the sand and rock. Even before the boat had hit shore, he saw two men running from a house along the shore.

"Friend," he'd called to them. "Amigo." He didn't know any Portuguese, but had hoped they would get the message. As they neared the boat, they looked at him with curiosity. Valentin held out his hands, showing them he was roped and duct-taped.

The men laughed uproariously, then waded into the water toward him. One of them pulled a knife from a sheath on his belt and in quick, expert strokes, freed Valentin's hands and feet.

"Thank you," he said. "*Gracias.*"

"You're welcome," they told him in good but accented English. They'd pulled the boat farther up on the beach and tied it to a palm tree, then escorted him, gym bag in hand, up to the house, laughing and punching him playfully.

In the house, a wooden shack on stilts, were two women, one spread out on a makeshift couch smoking, the other on a mattress on the floor. They both appeared to be very drunk, as were the men. One of the men offered him a cigarette, which he took, although he wasn't a smoker. He didn't want to appear ungrateful. When they poured him a drink, he looked at it in the light.

"What's this?" he asked.

"Rum, my friend," one of the men said. "Very fresh. Very good. We make it."

Valentin took a sip and discovered that, although it was fiery, it felt good burning its way down to his stomach. He'd asked them if they could take him to Belém to the airport in the next couple of days. He would pay them generously. He took his wallet out of the gym bag and let them get a glance of the money in it, but he didn't show them the stash he had in the Teflon belt he wore inside his jumpsuit.

They assured him that they could get him to the airport, with much slapping of his back and another round of drinks. One of the women got up, adjusting the halter top she wore as she went to the radio, and turned up the Latin dance music. He could kill them all now, he thought, and take his chances on reaching Belém another way. But his boat might be recognized, so it would be better to travel with the locals.

One of the couples began to dance, the woman obscenely writhing all over the short, paunchy man, pulling down her halter to expose her breasts and jerking up her sarong to give him glimpses of her naked pubis. The other couple laughed raucously, clapping, egging them on, and Valentin laughed with them, clapping when they did, pretending to enjoy the show.

They plied him with drink after drink of the homemade rum, and both couples were soon dancing, switching partners, back and forth. Then one of the women grabbed Valentin's hand with hers. He almost drew back from her touch, so repulsed was he, but he let her pull him up to his feet to dance with her. Now the others gathered around Valentin and the short, dark woman as they danced, clapping, singing, and laughing. Drinking more rum, he gave them a show, letting loose and dancing like a madman to please them. They were filthy peasants, he thought, but they were his ticket out, too.

Later in the morning, he realized suddenly that he was very drunk. He couldn't pass out. That was unthinkable. So he kept dancing, letting the woman slither all over him, teasing him mercilessly—or so she thought. Then, without warning, the room and everything in it began to spin like nothing he'd known before, and he lost his footing. He fell helplessly to the floor, and before he passed out, he could see the dark faces gathered above him, still laughing and clapping, their teeth very white against their skin.

He didn't know how long he'd been out, but when he came to he could feel the sun on his naked body. And he could feel movement. But he wasn't in a boat. No. Then he realized with horror that his hands and feet were tied around a length of palm trunk, and he was swinging back and forth on the palm as the two men carried him somewhere, one at each end of the trunk.

He found his voice to ask them what they were doing, but when he tried to speak, he became aware of the tape across his mouth. He couldn't utter a sound. Sweat—the sweat of fear—began to pour down his face, and he tried to kick loose the rope that bound his feet.

But the men abruptly stopped and lowered him to the ground, laying the palm on top of him. He looked up at the one who'd been on the end to which his feet were bound, and saw him smiling. He couldn't see the other man, who stood behind him. He looked to his right and could see nothing but thick vegetation. He swung his head to the left and saw a pond or something like one.

Without warning, the men picked up the palm trunk again and began to swing it slowly back and forth, coordinating their movements. Valentin felt his body swinging out to the left, then to the right, then he suddenly felt the great heave the men gave the palm. He went swinging out to the left, to what had looked like a pond. The moment his body hit the water, he felt a great thrashing around him, then the terrifying hard scales of alligators as they brushed under him, against him, all over him.

The first bite took his feet. The second bite took most of his stomach. Valentin didn't feel the third bite.

Luca had booked a room at the Belém Palace for the night, and made airline reservations for the morning that would take them to St. Bart's via St. Vincent. In the elegant dining room that night, Monika, Dr. Von Meckling, and Jenny had arrived shortly after they did and came by their table.

"Oh, such a pity you're at a table for two," Monika declared. "Would you care to move? We could have a lovely dinner party togther."

"We've already begun eating," Luca said with a slight edge. "Otherwise we would have been glad to."

"So where are you two off to?" Jenny asked.

"We're going to St. Bart's tomorrow," Crissy said.

"St. Bart's!" Jenny exclaimed. "I've always wanted to go there. It's the hottest party island—" Her voice trailed off as Crissy saw Monika squeeze Jenny's arm. Perhaps, Crissy thought, Jenny wasn't permitted to express such desires in the presence of Dr. Von Meckling.

"It's to celebrate," Luca said.

"Oh, and what are you celebrating?" Monika asked.

"We're going to be married," Crissy said. She saw Jenny's face fall, and an expression of hatred come into her eyes. Monika, however, seemed genuinely delighted by the prospect.

"My darling Crissy," she gushed. "You must come to see me in Vienna or have me come to you. You have my card and I have yours, so I'm sure we'll be seeing each another in Florence or wherever it is you settle down."

"That would be lovely," Crissy said.

"Yes," Luca agreed tightly.

"Do keep in touch," Monika said, air-kissing Crissy on both cheeks. "I'll be thinking of you, my sweet."

"Thank you, Monika."

When they'd finally left the table, Crissy and Luca restrained the laughter that they felt. "She's really a dragon, that Monika Graf," he said.

"Yes," Crissy replied, "but she was nice to me in the beginning for whatever reasons, and she taught me a few things."

"Your friend doesn't seem too happy," Luca said.

"No. She told me she's marrying him for his money and can't wait for him to die," Crissy said.

Luca nodded. "She'll be unhappy to discover that he has very good genes for longevity."

"What?"

"It's true," Luca said. "The Von Meckling family all live into their nineties; some of them past a hundred."

"Oh, she will be unhappy to hear that."

"And Monika's going to drive her crazy," Luca said, "putting her nose in everywhere."

"I can only imagine," Crissy agreed.

"But let's change the subject and talk about us," he said, smiling.

"I think that's an excellent suggestion," Crissy agreed.

"Then let's go straight upstairs after we eat."

"I think that's just what the doctor ordered."

For more information on Judith Gould contact:
judithgould001@yahoo.com
www.judithgould.com